I0885592

THE WICKED KING

HOLLY BLACK

LB

LITTLE, BROWN AND COMPANY
NEW YORK BOSTON

Little, Brown and Company
Hachette Book Group
1290 Avenue of the Americas, New York, NY 10104
Visit us at LBYR.com

Originally published in hardcover and ebook by Little, Brown and Company in January 2019
First Trade Paperback Edition: February 2020

Little, Brown and Company is a division of Hachette Book Group, Inc.
The Little, Brown name and logo are trademarks of Hachette Book Group, Inc.

The publisher is not responsible for websites (or their content) that are not owned by the publisher.

"Nymphidia" by Michael Drayton, first published in 1627
"The Fairies" by William Allingham, first published in 1850

The Library of Congress has cataloged the hardcover edition as follows:
Names: Black, Holly, author. | Jennings, Kathleen, illustrator.
Title: The wicked king / Holly Black ; illustrations by Kathleen Jennings.
Description: First edition. | New York ; Boston : Little, Brown and Company, 2019. | Series: [The Folk of the Air ; 2] | Summary: As seneschal to High King Cardan, Jude must fight to keep control of the Faerie throne while her younger brother, Oak, enjoys the childhood she never knew.
Identifiers: LCCN 2017056642| ISBN 9780316310352 (hardcover) |
ISBN 9780316310338 (ebook) | ISBN 9780316310345 (library edition ebook)
Subjects: | CYAC: Kings, queens, rulers, etc.—Fiction. | Power (Philosophy)—Fiction. | Courts and courtiers—Fiction. | Fairies—Fiction. | Sisters—Fiction. | Fantasy.
Classification: LCC PZ7.B52878 Wic 2019 | DDC [Fic]—dc23
LC record available at https://lccn.loc.gov/2017056642

ISBNs: 978-0-316-31032-1 (pbk.), 978-0-316-31033-8 (ebook)

Printed in Indiana, USA

LSC-C

Printing 18, 2025

For Kelly Link, one of the merfolk

Crooked Forest
Palace of Elfhame
Milkwood
INSMIRE
Lake of Masks
Madoc's Stronghold

PRAISE FOR

THE FOLK OF THE AIR SERIES

"An **epic saga** of palace intrigue and deception."
—*Entertainment Weekly*

★ "*The Wicked King* is **intense and entertaining** storytelling at its finest." —*BookPage*, starred review

"*The Wicked King* is so **fast-paced and intense** you won't be able to put it down." —*The Missourian*

"Black is a master at world-building, conveying integral details without that information ever seeming tedious or encyclopedic, whether you're well versed in faerie or a newcomer to the genre.... **The experience of reading a novel like this is something like being surrounded by magic.**"
—*The New York Times Book Review*

"**Lush, dangerous, a dark jewel of a book.** Black's world is intoxicating, imbued with a relentless sense of peril that kept me riveted through every chapter of Jude's journey. And Jude! She is a heroine to love—brave but pragmatic, utterly human. **This delicious story will seduce you** and leave you desperate for just one more page." —Leigh Bardugo, #1 *New York Times* bestselling author of *Six of Crows* and *Crooked Kingdom*

"I require book two immediately. **Holly is the Faerie Queen.**"
—Victoria Aveyard, #1 *New York Times* bestselling author of the Red Queen series

★ "**Spellbinding**. . . . Breathtaking set pieces, fully developed supporting characters, and a beguiling, tough-as-nails heroine enhance an intricate, intelligent plot that crescendos to a jaw-dropping third-act twist." —*Publishers Weekly*, starred review

★ "Another **fantastic, deeply engaging, and all-consuming** work from Black that belongs on all YA shelves."
—*SLJ*, starred review

★ "Jude, who struggles with a world she both loves and hates and would rather be powerful and safe than good, is a compelling narrator. Whatever a reader is looking for—heart-in-throat action, deadly romance, double-crossing, moral complexity—**this is one heck of a ride**." —*Booklist*, starred review

"This is a heady blend of Faerie lore, high fantasy, and high school drama, dripping with description that brings the dangerous but tempting world of Faerie to life. **Black is building a complex mythology; now is a great time to tune in.**" —*Kirkus Reviews*

★ "Black, quite rightly, is the acknowledged queen of faerie lit, and **her latest shows her to be at the top of her game**, unveiling twists and secrets and bringing her characters vividly to life." —*VOYA*, starred review

"With complicated characters, a suspenseful plot, and a successful return to the Faerie setting of many of her popular books, **Black's latest is sure to enchant fans**."
—*The Horn Book*

"**Another enthralling story** in Black's fantasy catalog." —Paste

Map of the Shifting Isles of
ELFHAME
Locke's Estate
INSMOOR
Tower of Forgetting
Mandrake Market
INSWEAL
Hollow Hall
THE UNDERSEA

BY HOLLY BLACK

The Folk of the Air

The Cruel Prince

The Wicked King

The Queen of Nothing

How the King of Elfhame Learned to Hate Stories

The Stolen Heir Duology

The Stolen Heir

The Prisoner's Throne

Other

The Darkest Part of the Forest

The Coldest Girl in Coldtown

Book One

"Say to him thus, 'That I defy
His slanders and his infamy,
And as a mortal enemy
Do publicly proclaim him:
Withal, that if I had mine own,
He should not wear the Fairy crown,
But with a vengeance should come down;
Nor we a king should name him.'"

—Michael Drayton,
"Nymphidia"

PROLOGUE

Jude lifted the heavy practice sword, moving into the first stance—readiness.

Get used to the weight, Madoc had told her. *You must be strong enough to strike and strike and strike again without tiring. The first lesson is to make yourself that strong.*

It will hurt. Pain makes you strong.

She planted her feet in the grass. Wind ruffled her hair as she moved through the stances. One: the sword before her, canted to one side, protecting her body. Two: the pommel high, as though the blade were a horn coming from her head. Three: down to her hip, then in a deceptively casual droop in front of her. Then four: up again, to her shoulder. Each position could move easily into a strike or a defense. Fighting was chess, anticipating the move of one's opponent and countering it before one got hit.

But it was chess played with the whole body. Chess that left her bruised and tired and frustrated with the whole world and with herself, too.

Or maybe it was more like riding a bike. When she'd been learning to do that, back in the real world, she'd fallen lots of times. Her knees had been scabby enough that Mom thought she might have scars. But Jude had taken off her training wheels herself and disdained riding carefully on the sidewalk, as Taryn did. Jude wanted to ride in the street, fast, like Vivi, and if she got gravel embedded in her skin for it, well, then she'd let Dad pick it out with tweezers at night.

Sometimes Jude longed for her bike, but there were none in Faerie. Instead, she had giant toads and thin greenish ponies and wild-eyed horses slim as shadows.

And she had weapons.

And her parents' murderer, now her foster father. The High King's general, Madoc, who wanted to teach her how to ride too fast and how to fight to the death. No matter how hard she swung at him, it just made him laugh. He liked her anger. *Fire*, he called it.

She liked it when she was angry, too. Angry was better than scared. Better than remembering she was a mortal among monsters. No one was offering her the option of training wheels anymore.

On the other side of the field, Madoc was guiding Taryn through a series of stances. Taryn was learning the sword, too, although she had different problems than Jude. Her stances were more perfect, but she hated sparring. She paired the obvious defenses with the obvious attacks, so it was easy to lure her into a series of moves and then score a hit by breaking the pattern. Each time it happened, Taryn got mad, as though Jude were flubbing the steps of a dance rather than winning.

"Come here," Madoc called to Jude across the silvery expanse of grass.

She walked to him, sword slung over her shoulders. The sun was just setting, but faeries are twilight creatures, and their day was not even half done. The sky was streaked with copper and gold. She inhaled a deep breath of pine needles. For a moment, she felt as though she were just a kid learning a new sport.

"Come spar," he said when Jude got closer. "Both of you girls against this old redcap." Taryn leaned against her sword, the tip of it sinking into the ground. She wasn't supposed to hold it that way—it wasn't good for the blade—but Madoc didn't reprimand her.

"Power," he said. "Power is the ability to get what you want. Power is the ability to be the one making the decisions. And how do we get power?"

Jude stepped beside her twin. It was obvious that Madoc expected a response, but also that he expected the wrong one. "We learn how to fight well?" she said to say *something*.

When Madoc smiled at her, she could see the points of his bottom cuspids, longer than the rest of his teeth. He tousled her hair, and she felt the sharp edges of his clawlike nails against her scalp, too light to hurt, but a reminder of what he was nonetheless. "We get power by taking it."

He pointed toward a low hill with a thorn tree growing on it. "Let's make a game of the next lesson. That's my hill. Go ahead and take it."

Taryn dutifully trooped toward it, Jude behind her. Madoc kept pace, his smile all teeth.

"Now what?" Taryn asked, without any particular excitement.

Madoc looked into the distance, as though he was contemplating and discarding various rules. "Now hold it against attack."

"Wait, what?" Jude asked. "From you?"

"Is this a strategy game or a sparring practice?" Taryn asked, frowning.

Madoc brought one finger under her chin, raising her head until she was looking into his golden cat eyes. "What is sparring but a game of strategy, played at speed?" he told her with a great seriousness. "Talk with your sister. When the sun reaches the trunk of that tree, I will come for my hill. Knock me down but once and you both win."

Then he departed for a copse of trees some ways away. Taryn sat down on the grass.

"I don't want to do this," she said.

"It's just a game," Jude reminded her nervously.

Taryn gave her a long look—the one that they gave each other when one of them was pretending things were normal. "Okay, so what do *you* think we should do?"

Jude looked up into the branches of the thorn tree. "What if one of us threw rocks while the other did the sparring?"

"Okay," Taryn said, pushing herself up and beginning to gather stones into the folds of her skirts. "You don't think he'll get mad, do you?"

Jude shook her head, but she understood Taryn's question. What if he killed them by accident?

You've got to choose which hill to die on, Mom used to tell Dad. It had been one of those weird sayings adults expected her to understand, even though they made no sense—like "one in the hand is worth two in the bush" or "every stick has two ends" or the totally mysterious "a cat may look at a king." Now, standing on an actual hill with a sword in her hand, she understood it a lot better.

"Get into position," Jude said, and Taryn wasted no time in climbing the thorn tree. Jude checked the sunmark, wondering what sort of tricks Madoc might use. The longer he waited, the darker it would get, and while he could see in the dark, Jude and Taryn could not.

But, in the end, he didn't use any tricks. He came out of the woods and in their direction, howling as though he were leading an army of a hundred. Jude's knees went weak with terror.

This is just a game, she reminded herself frantically. The closer he got, though, the less her body believed her. Every animal instinct strained to run.

Their strategy seemed silly now in the face of his hugeness and their smallness, in the face of her fear. She thought of her mother bleeding on the ground, recalled the smell of her insides as they leaked out. The memory felt like thunder in her head. She was going to die.

Run, her whole body urged. *RUN!*

No, her mother had run. Jude planted her feet.

She made herself move into the first position, even though her legs felt wobbly. He had the advantage, even coming up that hill, because he had momentum on his side. The stones raining down on him from Taryn barely checked his pace.

Jude spun out of the way, not even bothering to try to block the first blow. Putting the tree between them, she dodged his second and third. When the fourth one came, it knocked her to the grass.

She closed her eyes against the killing strike.

"You can take a thing when no one's looking. But defending it, even with all the advantage on your side, is no easy task," Madoc told her with a laugh. She looked up to find him offering her a hand. "Power is much easier to acquire than it is to hold on to."

Relief broke over her. It was just a game, after all. Just another lesson.

"That wasn't fair," Taryn complained.

Jude didn't say anything. Nothing was fair in Faerie. She had learned to stop expecting it to be.

Madoc hauled Jude to her feet and threw a heavy arm over her shoulders. He drew her and her twin in for an embrace. He smelled like smoke and dried blood, and Jude let herself sag against him. It was good to be hugged. Even by a monster.

CHAPTER 1

The new High King of Faerie lounges on his throne, his crown resting at an insouciant angle, his long, villainously scarlet cloak pinned at his shoulders and sweeping the floor. An earring shines from the peak of one pointed ear. Heavy rings glitter along his knuckles. His most ostentatious decoration, however, is his soft, sullen mouth.

It makes him look every bit the jerk that he is.

I stand to one side of him, in the honored position of seneschal. I am supposed to be High King Cardan's most trusted advisor, and so I play that part, rather than my real role—the hand behind the throne, with the power to compel him to obey should he try to cross me.

Scanning the crowd, I look for a spy from the Court of Shadows. They intercepted a communication from the Tower of Forgetting, where Cardan's brother is jailed, and are bringing it to me instead of to its intended recipient.

And that's only the latest crisis.

It's been five months since I forced Cardan onto the throne of Elfhame as my puppet king, five months since I betrayed my family, since my sister carried my little brother to the mortal realm and away from the crown that he might have worn, since I crossed swords with Madoc.

Five months since I've slept for more than a few hours at a stretch.

It seemed like a good trade—a very *faerie* trade, even: put someone who despised me on the throne so that Oak would be out of danger. It was thrilling to trick Cardan into promising to serve me for a year and a day, exhilarating when my plan came together. Then, a year and a day seemed like forever. But now I must figure out how to keep him in my power—and out of trouble—for longer than that. Long enough to give Oak a chance to have what I didn't: a childhood.

Now a year and a day seems like no time at all.

And despite having put Cardan on the throne through my own machinations, despite scheming to keep him there, I cannot help being unnerved by how comfortable he looks.

Faerie rulers are tied to the land. They are the lifeblood and the beating heart of their realm in some mystical way that I don't fully understand. But surely Cardan isn't that, not with his commitment to being a layabout who does none of the real work of governance.

Mostly, his obligations appear to be allowing his ring-covered hands to be kissed and accepting the blandishments of the Folk. I'm sure he enjoys that part of it—the kisses, the bowing and scraping. He's certainly enjoying the wine. He calls again and again for his cabochon-encrusted goblet to be refilled with a pale green liquor. The very smell of it makes my head spin.

During a lull, he glances up at me, raising one black brow. "Enjoying yourself?"

"Not as much as you are," I tell him.

No matter how much he disliked me when we were in school, that was a guttering candle to the steady flame of his hatred now. His mouth curls into a smile. His eyes shine with wicked intent. "Look at them all, your subjects. A shame not a one knows who their true ruler is."

My face heats a little at his words. His gift is to take a compliment and turn it into an insult, a jab that hurts more for the temptation to take it at face value.

I spent so many revels avoiding notice. Now everyone sees me, bathed in candlelight, in one of the three nearly identical black doublets I wear each evening, my sword Nightfell at my hip. They twirl in their circle dances and play their songs, they drink their golden wine and compose their riddles and their curses while I look down on them from the royal dais. They are beautiful and terrible, and they might despise my mortality, might mock it, but I am up here and they are not.

Of course, perhaps that isn't so different from hiding. Perhaps it is just hiding in plain sight. But I cannot deny that the power I hold gives me a kick, a jolt of pleasure whenever I think on it. I just wish Cardan couldn't tell.

If I look carefully, I can spot my twin sister, Taryn, dancing with Locke, her betrothed. Locke, who I once thought might love me. Locke, whom I once thought I could love. It's Taryn I miss, though. Nights like tonight, I imagine hopping down from the dais and going to her, trying to explain my choices.

Her marriage is only three weeks away, and still we haven't spoken.

I keep telling myself I need her to come to me first. She played me for a fool with Locke. I still feel stupid when I look at them. If she won't apologize, then at least she should be the one to pretend there's nothing to apologize for. I might accept that, even. But I will not be the one to go to Taryn, to beg.

My eyes follow her as she dances.

I don't bother to look for Madoc. His love is part of the price I paid for this position.

A short, wizened faerie with a cloud of silver hair and a coat of scarlet kneels below the dais, waiting to be recognized. His cuffs are jeweled, and the moth pin that holds his cloak in place has wings that move on their own. Despite his posture of subservience, his gaze is greedy.

Beside him stand two pale hill Folk with long limbs and hair that blows behind them, though there is no breeze.

Drunk or sober, now that Cardan is the High King, he must listen to those subjects who would have him rule on a problem, no matter how small, or grant a boon. I cannot imagine why anyone would put their fate in his hands, but Faerie is full of caprice.

Luckily, I'm there to whisper my counsel in his ear, as any seneschal might. The difference is that he must listen to me. And if he whispers back a few horrific insults, well, at least he's forced to whisper.

Of course, then the question becomes whether I deserve to have all this power. *I won't be horrible for the sake of my own amusement*, I tell myself. *That's got to be worth something.*

"Ah," Cardan says, leaning forward on the throne, causing his crown to tip lower on his brow. He takes a deep swallow of the wine and smiles down at the trio. "This must be a grave concern, to bring it before the High King."

"You may already have heard tales of me," says the small faerie. "I made the crown that sits upon your head. I am called Grimsen the

Smith, long in exile with the Alderking. His bones are now at rest, and there is a new Alderking in Fairfold, as there is a new High King here."

"Severin," I say.

The smith looks at me, obviously surprised that I have spoken. Then his gaze returns to the High King. "I beg you to allow me to return to the High Court."

Cardan blinks a few times, as though trying to focus on the petitioner in front of him. "So you were yourself exiled? Or you chose to leave?"

I recall Cardan's telling me a little about Severin, but he hadn't mentioned Grimsen. I've heard of him, of course. He's the blacksmith who made the Blood Crown for Mab and wove enchantments into it. It's said he can make anything from metal, even living things—metal birds that fly, metal snakes that slither and strike. He made the twin swords, Heartseeker and Heartsworn, one that never misses and the other that can cut through anything. Unfortunately, he made them for the Alderking.

"I was sworn to him, as his servant," says Grimsen. "When he went into exile, I was forced to follow—and in so doing, fell into disfavor myself. Although I made only trinkets for him in Fairfold, I was still considered to be his creature by your father.

"Now, with both of them dead, I crave permission to carve out a place for myself here at your Court. Punish me no further, and my loyalty to you will be as great as your wisdom."

I look at the little smith more closely, suddenly sure he's playing with words. But to what end? The request seems genuine, and if Grimsen's humility is not, well, his fame makes that no surprise.

"Very well," Cardan says, looking pleased to be asked for something easy to give. "Your exile is over. Give me your oath, and the High Court will welcome you."

Grimsen bows low, his expression theatrically troubled. "Noble king, you ask for the smallest and most reasonable thing from your servant, but I, who have suffered for such vows, am loath to make them again. Allow me this—grant that I may show you my loyalty in my deeds, rather than binding myself with my words."

I put my hand on Cardan's arm, but he shrugs off my cautioning squeeze. I could say something, and he would be forced—by prior command—to at least not contradict me, but I don't know what to say. Having the smith here, forging for Elfhame, is no small thing. It is worth, perhaps, the lack of an oath.

And yet, something in Grimsen's gaze looks a little too self-satisfied, a little too sure of himself. I suspect a trick.

Cardan speaks before I can puzzle anything more out. "I accept your condition. Indeed, I will give you a boon. An old building with a forge sits on the edge of the palace grounds. You shall have it for your own and as much metal as you require. I look forward to seeing what you will make for us."

Grimsen bows low. "Your kindness shall not be forgotten."

I mislike this, but perhaps I'm being overcautious. Perhaps it's only that I don't like the smith himself. There's little time to consider it before another petitioner steps forward.

A hag—old and powerful enough that the air around her seems to crackle with the force of her magic. Her fingers are twiggy, her hair the color of smoke, and her nose like the blade of a scythe. Around her throat, she wears a necklace of rocks, each bead carved with whorls that seem to catch and puzzle the eye. When she moves, the heavy robes around her ripple, and I spy clawed feet, like those of a bird of prey.

"Kingling," the hag says. "Mother Marrow brings you gifts."

"Your fealty is all I require." Cardan's voice is light. "For now."

"Oh, I'm sworn to the crown, sure enough," she says, reaching into one of her pockets and drawing out a cloth that looks blacker than the night sky, so black that it seems to drink the light around it. The fabric slithers over her hand. "But I have come all this way to present you with a rare prize."

The Folk do not like debt, which is why they will not repay a favor with mere thanks. Give them an oatcake, and they will fill one of the rooms of your house with grain, overpaying to push debt back onto you. And yet, tribute is given to High Kings all the time—gold, service, swords with names. But we don't usually call those things *gifts*. Nor *prizes*.

I do not know what to make of her little speech.

Her voice is a purr. "My daughter and I wove this of spider silk and nightmares. A garment cut from it can turn a sharp blade, yet be as soft as a shadow against your skin."

Cardan frowns, but his gaze is drawn again and again to the marvelous cloth. "I admit I don't think I've seen its equal."

"Then you accept what I would bestow upon you?" she asks, a sly gleam in her eye. "I am older than your father and your mother. Older than the stones of this palace. As old as the bones of the earth. Though you are the High King, Mother Marrow will have your word."

Cardan's eyes narrow. She's annoyed him, I can see that.

There's a trick here, and this time I know what it is. Before he can, I start speaking. "You said *gifts*, but you have only shown us your marvelous cloth. I am sure the crown would be pleased to have it, were it freely given."

Her gaze comes to rest on me, her eyes hard and cold as night itself. "And who are you to speak for the High King?"

"I am his seneschal, Mother Marrow."

"And will you let this mortal girl answer for you?" she asks Cardan.

He gives me a look of such condescension that it makes my cheeks heat. The look lingers. His mouth twists, curving. "I suppose I shall," he says finally. "It amuses her to keep me out of trouble."

I bite my tongue as he turns a placid expression on Mother Marrow.

"She's clever enough," the hag says, spitting out the words like a curse. "Very well, the cloth is yours, Your Majesty. I give it freely. I give you only that and nothing more."

Cardan leans forward as though they are sharing a jest. "Oh, tell me the rest. I like tricks and snares. Even ones I was nearly caught in."

Mother Marrow shifts from one clawed foot to the other, the first sign of nerves she's displayed. Even for a hag with bones as old as she claimed, a High King's wrath is dangerous. "Very well. An' had you accepted all I would bestow upon you, you would have found yourself under a geas, allowing you to marry only a weaver of the cloth in my hands. Myself—or my daughter."

A cold shudder goes through me at the thought of what might have happened then. Could the High King of Faerie have been compelled into such a marriage? Surely there would have been a way around it. I thought of the last High King, who never wed.

Marriage is unusual among the rulers of Faerie because once a ruler, one remains a ruler until death or abdication. Among commoners and the gentry, faerie marriages are arranged to be gotten out of—unlike the mortal "until death do us part," they contain conditions like "until you shall both renounce each other" or "unless one strikes the other in anger" or the cleverly worded "for the duration of a life" without specifying whose. But a uniting of kings and/or queens can never be dissolved.

Should Cardan marry, I wouldn't just have to get him off the throne to get Oak on it. I'd have to remove his bride as well.

Cardan's eyebrows rise, but he has all the appearance of blissful unconcern. "My lady, you flatter me. I had no idea you were interested."

Her gaze is unflinching as she passes her gift to one of Cardan's personal guard. "May you grow into the wisdom of your counselors."

"The fervent prayer of many," he says. "Tell me. Has your daughter made the journey with you?"

"She is here," the hag says. A girl steps from the crowd to bow low before Cardan. She is young, with a mass of unbound hair. Like her mother, her limbs are oddly long and twiglike, but where her mother is unsettlingly bony, she has a kind of grace. Maybe it helps that her feet resemble human ones.

Although, to be fair, they are turned backward.

"I would make a poor husband," Cardan says, turning his attention to the girl, who appears to shrink down into herself at the force of his regard. "But grant me a dance, and I will show you my other talents."

I give him a suspicious look.

"Come," Mother Marrow says to the girl, and grabs her, not particularly gently, by the arm, dragging her into the crowd. Then she looks back at Cardan. "We three will meet again."

"They're all going to want to marry you, you know," Locke drawls. I know his voice even before I look to find that he has taken the position that Mother Marrow vacated.

He grins up at Cardan, looking delighted with himself and the world. "Better to take consorts," Locke says. "Lots and lots of consorts."

"Spoken like a man about to enter wedlock," Cardan reminds him.

"Oh, leave off. Like Mother Marrow, I have brought you a gift." Locke takes a step toward the dais. "One with fewer barbs." He doesn't look in my direction. It's as though he doesn't see me or that I am as uninteresting as a piece of furniture.

I wish it didn't bother me. I wish I didn't remember standing at the very top of the highest tower on his estate, his body warm against mine. I wish he hadn't used me to test my sister's love for him. I wish she hadn't let him.

If wishes were horses, my mortal father used to say, *beggars would ride*. Another one of those phrases that makes no sense until it does.

"Oh?" Cardan looks more puzzled than intrigued.

"I wish to give you *me*—as your Master of Revels," Locke announces. "Grant me the position, and I will make it my duty and pleasure to keep the High King of Elfhame from being bored."

There are so many jobs in a palace—servants and ministers, ambassadors and generals, advisors and tailors, jesters and makers of riddles, grooms for horses and keepers of spiders, and a dozen other positions I've forgotten. I didn't even know there *was* a Master of Revels. Maybe there wasn't, until now.

"I will serve up delights you've never imagined." Locke's smile is infectious. He will serve up trouble, that's for sure. Trouble I have no time for.

"Have a care," I say, drawing Locke's attention to me for the first time. "I am sure you would not wish to insult the High King's imagination."

"Indeed, I'm sure not," Cardan says in a way that's difficult to interpret.

Locke's smile doesn't waver. Instead, he hops onto the dais, causing the knights on either side to move immediately to stop him. Cardan waves them away.

"If you make him Master of Revels—" I begin, quickly, desperately.

"Are you commanding me?" Cardan interrupts, eyebrow arched.

He knows I can't say yes, not with the possibility of Locke's overhearing. "Of course not," I grind out.

"Good," Cardan says, turning his gaze from me. "I'm of a mind to grant your request, Locke. Things have been so very dull of late."

I see Locke's smirk and bite the inside of my cheek to keep back the words of command. It would have been so satisfying to see his expression, to flaunt my power in front of him.

Satisfying, but stupid.

"Before, Grackles and Larks and Falcons vied for the heart of the Court," Locke says, referring to the factions that preferred revelry, artistry, or war. Factions that fell in and out of favor with Eldred. "But now the Court's heart is yours and yours alone. Let's break it."

Cardan looks at Locke oddly, as though considering, seemingly for the first time, that being High King might be *fun*. As though he's imagining what it would be like to rule without straining against my leash.

Then, on the other side of the dais, I finally spot the Bomb, a spy in the Court of Shadows, her white hair a halo around her brown face. She signals to me.

I don't like Locke and Cardan together—don't like their idea of entertainments—but I try to put that aside as I leave the dais and make my way to her. After all, there is no way to scheme against Locke when he is drawn to whatever amuses him most in the moment....

Halfway to where the Bomb's standing, I hear Locke's voice ring out over the crowd. "We will celebrate the Hunter's Moon in the Milkwood, and there the High King will give you a debauch such that bards will sing of, this I promise you."

Dread coils in my belly.

Locke is pulling a few pixies from the crowd up onto the dais, their iridescent wings shining in the candlelight. A girl laughs uproariously and reaches for Cardan's goblet, drinking it to the dregs. I expect him to lash out, to humiliate her or shred her wings, but he only smiles and calls for more wine.

Whatever Locke has in store, Cardan seems all too ready to play along. All Faerie coronations are followed by a month of revelry—feasting, boozing, riddling, dueling, and more. The Folk are expected to dance through the soles of their shoes from sundown to sunup. But five months after Cardan's becoming High King, the great hall remains always full, the drinking horns overflowing with mead and clover wine. The revelry has barely slowed.

It has been a long time since Elfhame had such a young High King, and a wild, reckless air infects the courtiers. The Hunter's Moon is soon, sooner even than Taryn's wedding. If Locke intends to stoke the flames of revelry higher and higher still, how long before that becomes a danger?

With some difficulty, I turn my back on Cardan. After all, what would be the purpose in catching his eye? His hatred is such that he will do what he can, inside of my commands, to defy me. And he is very good at defiance.

I would like to say that he always hated me, but for a brief, strange time it felt as though we understood each other, maybe even liked each other. Altogether an unlikely alliance, begun with my blade to his throat, it resulted in his trusting me enough to put himself in my power.

A trust that I betrayed.

Once, he tormented me because he was young and bored and angry and cruel. Now he has better reasons for the torments he will inflict on me after a year and a day is gone. It will be very hard to keep him always under my thumb.

I reach the Bomb and she shoves a piece of paper into my hand. "Another note for Cardan from Balekin," she says. "This one made it all the way to the palace before we intercepted it."

"Is it the same as the first two?"

She nods. "Much like. Balekin tries to flatter our High King into coming to his prison cell. He wants to propose some kind of bargain."

"I'm sure he does," I say, glad once again to have been brought into the Court of Shadows and to have them still watching my back.

"What will you do?" she asks me.

"I'll go see Prince Balekin. If he wants to make the High King an offer, he'll have to convince the High King's seneschal first."

A corner of her mouth lifts. "I'll come with you."

I glance back at the throne again, making a vague gesture. "No. Stay here. Try to keep Cardan from getting into trouble."

"He *is* trouble," she reminds me, but doesn't seem particularly worried by her own worrying pronouncement.

As I head toward the passageways into the palace, I spot Madoc across the room, half in shadow, watching me with his cat eyes. He isn't close enough to speak, but if he were, I have no doubt what he would say.

Power is much easier to acquire than it is to hold on to.

CHAPTER 2

Balekin is imprisoned in the Tower of Forgetting on the northernmost part of Insweal, Isle of Woe. Insweal is one of the three islands of Elfhame, connected to Insmire and Insmoor by large rocks and patches of land, populated with only a few fir trees, silvery stags, and the occasional treefolk. It's possible to cross between Insmire and Insweal entirely on foot, if you don't mind leaping stone to stone, walking through the Milkwood by yourself, and probably getting at least somewhat wet.

I mind all those things and decide to ride.

As the High King's seneschal, I have the pick of his stables. Never much of a rider, I choose a horse that seems docile enough, her coat a soft black color, her mane in complicated and probably magical knots.

I lead her out while a goblin groom brings me a bit and bridle.

Then I swing onto her back and direct her toward the Tower of Forgetting. Waves crashing against the rocks beneath me. Salt spray misting the air. Insweal is a forbidding island, large stretches of its landscape bare of greenery, just black rocks and tide pools and a tower threaded through with cold iron.

I tie the horse to one of the black metal rings driven into the stone wall of the tower. She whickers nervously, her tail tucked hard against her body. I touch her muzzle in what I hope is a reassuring way.

"I won't be long, and then we can get out of here," I tell her, wishing I'd asked the groom for her name.

I don't feel so differently from the horse as I knock on the heavy wooden door.

A large, hairy creature opens it. He's wearing beautifully wrought plate armor, blond fur sticking out from any gaps. He's obviously a soldier, which used to mean he would treat me well, for Madoc's sake, but now might mean just the opposite.

"I am Jude Duarte, seneschal to the High King," I tell him. "Here on the crown's business. Let me in."

He steps aside, pulling the door open, and I enter the dim antechamber of the Tower of Forgetting. My mortal eyes adjust slowly and poorly to the lack of light. I do not have the faerie ability to see in near darkness. At least three other guards are there, but I perceive them more as shapes than anything else.

"You're here to see Prince Balekin, one supposes," comes a voice from the back.

It is eerie not to be able to see the speaker clearly, but I pretend the discomfort away and nod. "Take me to him."

"Vulciber," the voice says. "You take her."

The Tower of Forgetting is so named because it exists as a place to put Folk when a monarch wants them struck from the Court's memory.

Most criminals are punished with clever curses, quests, or some other form of capricious faerie judgment. To wind up here, one has to have really pissed off someone important.

The guards are mostly soldiers for whom such a bleak and lonely location suits their temperament—or those whose commanders intend them to learn humility from the position. As I look over at the shadowy figures, it's hard to guess which sort they are.

Vulciber comes toward me, and I recognize the hairy soldier who opened the door. He looks to be at least part troll, heavy-browed and long-limbed.

"Lead on," I say.

He gives me a hard look in return. I am not sure what he dislikes about me—my mortality, my position, my intruding on his evening. I don't ask. I just follow him down stone stairs into the wet, mineral-scented darkness. The bloom of soil is heavy in the air, and there is a rotten, mushroomy odor I cannot place.

I stop when the dark grows too deep and I fear I am going to stumble. "Light the lamps," I say.

Vulciber moves in close, his breath on my face, carrying with it the scent of wet leaves. "And if I will not?"

A thin knife comes easily into my hand, slipping down out of a sleeve holster. I press the point against his side, just under the ribs. "Best you don't find out."

"But you can't see," he insists, as though I have played some kind of dirty trick on him by not being as intimidated as he'd hoped.

"Maybe I just prefer a little more light," I say, trying to keep my voice even, though my heart is beating wildly, my palms starting to sweat. If we have to fight on the stairs, I better strike fast and true, because I'll probably have only that one shot.

Vulciber moves away from me and my knife. I hear his heavy footfalls on the steps and start counting in case I have to follow blind. But then a torch flares to life, emitting green fire.

"Well?" he demands. "Are you coming?"

The stairs pass several cells, some empty and some whose occupants sit far enough from the bars that the torchlight does not illuminate them. None do I recognize until the last.

Prince Balekin's black hair is held by a circlet, a reminder of his royalty. Despite being imprisoned, he barely looks discomfited. Three rugs cover the damp stone of the floor. He sits in a carved armchair, watching me with hooded, owl-bright eyes. A golden samovar rests on a small, elegant table. Balekin turns a handle, and steaming, fragrant tea spills into fragile porcelain. The scent of it makes me think of seaweed.

But no matter how elegant he appears, he is still in the Tower of Forgetting, a few ruddy moths alighting on the wall above him. When he spilled the old High King's blood, the droplets turned into moths, which fluttered through the air for a few stunning moments before seeming to die. I thought they were all gone, but it seems that a few follow him still, a reminder of his sins.

"Our Lady Jude of the Court of Shadows," he says, as though he believes that will charm me. "May I offer you a cup?"

There is a movement in one of the other cells. I consider what his tea parties are like when I'm not around.

I'm not pleased he's aware of the Court of Shadows or my association with them, but I can't be entirely surprised, either—Prince Dain, our spymaster and employer, was Balekin's brother. And if Balekin knew about the Court of Shadows, he probably recognized one of them as they stole the Blood Crown and got it into my brother's hands so he could place it on Cardan's head.

Balekin has good reason to not be entirely pleased to see me.

"I must regretfully refuse tea," I say. "I won't be here long. You sent the High King some correspondence. Something about a deal? A bargain? I am here on his behalf to hear whatever it is you wish to say to him."

His smile seems to twist in on itself, to grow ugly. "You think me diminished," Balekin says. "But I am still a prince of Faerie, even here. Vulciber, won't you take my brother's seneschal and give her a smack in her pretty little face?"

The strike comes openhanded, faster than I would have guessed, the sound of the slap shockingly loud as his palm connects with my skin. It leaves my cheek stinging and me furious.

My knife is back in my right hand, its twin in my left.

Vulciber wears an eager expression.

My pride urges me to fight, but he's bigger than me and in a space familiar to him. This would be no mere sparring contest. Still, the urge to best him, the urge to wipe the expression from his smug face, is overwhelming.

Almost overwhelming. *Pride is for knights*, I remind myself, *not for spies.*

"My *pretty face*," I murmur to Balekin, putting away my knives slowly. I stretch my fingers to touch my cheek. Vulciber hit me hard enough for my own teeth to have cut the inside of my mouth. I spit blood onto the stone floor. "Such flattery. I cheated you out of a crown, so I guess I can allow for some hard feelings. Especially when they come with a compliment. Just don't try me again."

Vulciber looks abruptly unsure of himself.

Balekin takes a sip of his tea. "You speak very freely, mortal girl."

"And why shouldn't I?" I say. "I speak with the High King's voice. Do you think he's interested in coming all the way down here, away from the palace and its pleasures, to treat with the elder brother at whose hands he suffered?"

Prince Balekin leans forward in his chair. "I wonder what you think you mean."

"And I wonder what message you'd like me to give the High King."

Balekin regards me—no doubt one of my cheeks must be flushed. He takes another careful sip of tea. "I have heard that for mortals, the feeling of falling in love is very like the feeling of fear. Your heart beats fast. Your senses are heightened. You grow light-headed, maybe even dizzy." He looks at me. "Is that right? It would explain much about your kind if it's possible to mistake the two."

"I've never been in love," I tell him, refusing to be rattled.

"And of course, you can lie," he says. "I can see why Cardan would find that helpful. Why Dain would have, too. It was clever of him to have brought you into his little gang of misfits. Clever to see that Madoc would spare you. Whatever else you could say about my brother, he was marvelously unsentimental.

"For my part, I barely thought of you at all, and when I did, it was only to goad Cardan with your accomplishments. But you have what Cardan never did: *ambition*. Had I only seen that, I would have a crown now. But I think you've misjudged me, too."

"Oh?" I know I am not going to like this.

"I won't give you the message I meant for Cardan. It will come to him another way, and it will come to him soon."

"Then you waste both our time," I say, annoyed. I have come all the way here, been hit, and frightened for nothing.

"Ah, time," he says. "You're the only one short on that, mortal." He nods at Vulciber. "You may escort her out."

"Let's go," the guard says, giving me a none-too-gentle shove toward the steps. As I ascend, I glance back at Balekin's face, severe in the green torchlight. He resembles Cardan too much for my comfort.

I am partway up when a long-fingered hand reaches out from between the bars and grips my ankle. Startled, I slip, scraping my palms and banging my knees as I go sprawling on the stairs. The old stab wound at the center of my left hand throbs suddenly. I barely catch myself before I tumble all the way down the steps.

Beside me is the thin face of a faerie woman. Her tail curls around one of the bars. Short horns sweep back from her brow. "I knew your Eva," she says to me, eyes glittering in the gloom. "I knew your mother. Knew so many of her little secrets."

I push myself to my feet and climb the steps as quickly as I can, my heart racing faster than when I thought I was going to have to fight Vulciber in the dark. My breath comes in short, rapid gasps that make my lungs hurt.

At the top of the stairs, I pause to wipe my stinging palms against my doublet and try to get myself under control.

"Ah," I say to Vulciber when my breathing has calmed a little. "I nearly forgot. The High King gave me a scroll of commands. There are a few changes in how he wishes his brother to be treated. They're outside in my saddlebags. If you could just follow me—"

Vulciber looks a question at the guard who sent him to guide me to Balekin.

"Go quickly," the shadowy figure says.

And so Vulciber accompanies me through the great door of the Tower of Forgetting. Illuminated by the moon, the black rocks shine with salt spray, a glittering coating, like that on sugared fruit. I try to focus on the guard and not the sound of my mother's name, which I haven't heard in so many years that, for a moment, I didn't know why it was important to me.

Eva.

"That horse has only a bit and bridle," Vulciber says, frowning at the black steed tied to the wall. "But you said—"

I stab him in the arm with a little pin I keep hidden in the lining of my doublet. "I lied."

It takes some doing to haul him up and sling him over the back of the horse. She is trained with familiar military commands, including kneeling, which helps. I move as quickly as I can, for fear that one of the guards will come to check on us, but I am lucky. No one comes before we are up and moving.

Another reason to ride to Insweal, rather than walk—you never know what you might be bringing back with you.

CHAPTER 3

You're styling yourself as a spymaster," the Roach says, looking over me and then my prisoner. "That ought to include being shrewd. Relying only on yourself is a good way to get got. Next time, take a member of the royal guard. Take one of us. Take a cloud of sprites or a drunken spriggan. Just take someone."

"Watching my back is the perfect opportunity to stick a knife in it," I remind him.

"Spoken like Madoc himself," says the Roach with an irritated sniff of his long, twisted nose. He sits at the wooden table in the Court of Shadows, the lair of spies deep in the tunnels under the Palace of Elfhame. He is burning the tips of crossbow bolts in a flame, then liberally coating them with a sticky tar. "If you don't trust us, just say so. We came to one arrangement, we can come to another."

"That's not what I mean," I say, putting my head down on my hands for a long moment. I do trust them. I wouldn't have spoken so freely if I didn't, but I am letting my irritation show.

I am sitting across from the Roach, eating cheese and buttered bread with apples. It's the first food I've had that day, and my belly is making hungry noises, another reminder of the way my body is unlike theirs. Faerie stomachs don't gurgle.

Perhaps hunger is why I am being snappish. My cheek is stinging, and though I turned the situation on its head, it was a nearer thing than I'd like to admit. Plus, I still don't know what Balekin wanted to tell Cardan.

The more exhausted I let myself get, the more I'll slip up. Human bodies betray us. They get starved and sick and run-down. I know it, and yet there is always so much more to do.

Beside us, Vulciber sits, tied to a chair and blindfolded.

"Do you want some cheese?" I ask him.

The guard grunts noncommittally but pulls against his bindings at the attention. He's been awake for several minutes and grown visibly more worried the longer we haven't spoken to him.

"What am I doing here?" he finally shouts, rocking his chair back and forth. "Let me go!" The chair goes over, slamming him against the ground, where he lies on his side. He begins to struggle against the ropes in earnest.

The Roach shrugs, gets up, and pulls off Vulciber's blindfold. "Greetings," he says.

On the other side of the room, the Bomb is cleaning beneath her fingernails with a long, half-moon knife. The Ghost is sitting in a corner so quietly that occasionally he seems not to be there at all. A few more of the new recruits look on, interested in the proceedings—a boy with sparrow wings, three spriggans, a sluagh girl. I am not used to an audience.

Vulciber stares at the Roach, at his goblin-green skin and eyes that reflect orange, his long nose and the single tuft of hair on his head. He takes in the room.

"The High King won't allow this," Vulciber says.

I give him a sad smile. "The High King doesn't know, and you're unlikely to tell him once I cut out your tongue."

Watching his fear ripen fills me with an almost voluptuous satisfaction. I, who have had little power in my life, must be on guard against that feeling. Power goes to my head too quickly, like faerie wine.

"Let me guess," I say, turning backward in my chair to face him, calculated coolness in my gaze. "You thought you could strike me, and there would be no consequences."

He shrinks a bit at my words. "What do you want?"

"Who says I want anything particular?" I counter. "Maybe just a little payback..."

As if we rehearsed it, the Roach pulls out a particularly nasty blade from his belt and holds it over Vulciber. He grins down at the guard.

The Bomb looks up from her nails, a small smile on her lips as she watches the Roach. "I guess the show is about to start."

Vulciber fights against his bonds, head lashing back and forth. I hear the wood of the chair crack, but he doesn't get free. After several heavy breaths, he slumps.

"Please," he whispers.

I touch my chin as though a thought has just occurred to me. "Or you could help us. Balekin wanted to make a bargain with Cardan. You could tell me about that."

"I know nothing of it," he says desperately.

"Too bad." I shrug and pick up another piece of cheese, shoving it into my mouth.

He takes a look at the Roach and the ugly knife. "But I know a secret. It's worth more than my life, more than whatever Balekin wanted with Cardan. If I tell it, will you give me your oath that I will leave here tonight unharmed?"

The Roach looks at me, and I shrug. "Well enough," the Roach says. "If the secret is all you claim, and if you'll swear never to reveal you had a visit to the Court of Shadows, then tell us and we'll send you on your way."

"The Queen of the Undersea," Vulciber says, eager to speak now. "Her people crawl up the rocks at night and whisper to Balekin. They slip into the Tower, although we don't know how, and leave him shells and shark teeth. Messages are being exchanged, but we can't decipher them. There are whispers Orlagh intends to break her treaty with the land and use the information Balekin is giving her to ruin Cardan."

Of all the threats to Cardan's reign, the Undersea wasn't one I was expecting. The Queen of the Undersea has a single daughter—Nicasia, fostered on land and one of Cardan's awful friends. Like Locke, Nicasia and I have a history. Also like Locke, it isn't a good one.

But I thought that Cardan's friendship with Nicasia meant Orlagh was happy he was on the throne.

"Next time one of these exchanges happen," I say, "come straight to me. And if you hear anything else you think I'd be interested in, you come and tell me that, too."

"That's not what we agreed," Vulciber protests.

"True enough," I tell him. "You've told us a tale, and it is a good one. We'll let you go tonight. But I can reward you better than some murderous prince who does not and will never have the High King's favor. There are better positions than guarding the Tower of Forgetting—yours for the taking. There's gold. There're all the rewards that Balekin can promise but is unlikely to deliver."

He gives me a strange look, probably trying to judge whether, given that he hit me and I poisoned him, it is still possible for us to be allies. "You can lie," he says finally.

"I'll guarantee the rewards," the Roach says. He reaches over and cuts Vulciber's bindings with his scary knife.

"Promise me a post other than in the Tower," says Vulciber, rubbing his wrists and pushing himself to his feet, "and I shall obey you as though you were the High King himself."

The Bomb laughs at that, with a wink in my direction. They do not explicitly know that I have the power to command Cardan, but they know we have a bargain that involves my doing most of the work and the Court of Shadows acting directly for the crown and getting paid directly, too.

I'm playing the High King in her little pageant, Cardan said once in my hearing. The Roach and the Bomb laughed; the Ghost didn't.

Once Vulciber exchanges promises with us, and the Roach leads him, blindfolded, into the passageways out of the Nest, the Ghost comes to sit beside me.

"Come spar," he says, taking a piece of apple off my plate. "Burn off some of that simmering rage."

I give a little laugh. "Don't disparage. It's not easy to keep the temperature so consistent," I tell him.

"Nor so high," he returns, watching me carefully with hazel eyes. I know there's human in his lineage—I can see it in the shape of his ears and his sandy hair, unusual in Faerie. But he hasn't told me his story, and here, in this place of secrets, I feel uncomfortable asking.

Although the Court of Shadows does not follow me, the four of us have made a vow together. We have promised to protect the person and office of the High King, to ensure the safety and prosperity of Elfhame for the hope of less bloodshed and more gold. So we've sworn. So they let me swear, even though my words don't bind me the way theirs do, by magic. I am bound by honor and by their faith in my having some.

"The king himself has had audience with the Roach thrice in this last fortnight. He's learning to pick pockets. If you're not careful, he'll make a better slyfoot than you." The Ghost has been added to the High King's personal guard, which allows him to keep Cardan safe but also to know his habits.

I sigh. It's full dark, and I have much I ought to do before dawn. And yet it is hard to ignore this invitation, which pricks at my pride.

Especially now, with the new spies overhearing my answer. We recruited more members, displaced after the royal murders. Every prince and princess employed a few, and now we employ them all. The spriggans are as cagey as cats but excellent at ferreting out scandal. The sparrow boy is as green as I once was. I would like the expanding Court of Shadows to believe I don't back down from a challenge.

"The real difficulty will come when someone tries to teach our king his way around a blade," I say, thinking of Balekin's frustrations on that front, of Cardan's declaration that his one virtue was that he was no murderer.

Not a virtue I share.

"Oh?" says the Ghost. "Maybe you'll have to teach it to him."

"Come," I say, getting up. "Let's see if I can teach *you*."

At that, the Ghost laughs outright. Madoc raised me to the sword, but until I joined the Court of Shadows, I knew only one way of fighting. The Ghost has studied longer and knows far more.

I follow him into the Milkwood, where black-thorned bees hum in their hives high in the white-barked trees. The root men are asleep. The sea laps at the rocky edges of the isle. The world feels hushed as we face each other. As tired as I am, my muscles remember better than I do.

I draw Nightfell. The Ghost comes at me fast, sword point diving toward my heart, and I knock it away, sweeping my blade down his side.

"Not so out of practice as I feared," he says as we trade blows, each of us testing the other.

I do not tell him of the drills I do before the mirror, just as I do not tell him of all the other ways I attempt to correct my defects.

As the High King's seneschal and the de facto ruler, I have much to study. Military commitments, messages from vassals, demands from every corner of Elfhame written in as many languages. Only a few months ago, I was still attending lessons, still doing homework for scholars to correct. The idea that I can untangle everything seems as impossible as spinning straw into gold, but each night I stay awake until the sun is high in the sky, trying my hardest to do just that.

That's the problem with a puppet government: It's not going to run itself.

Adrenaline may turn out not to be a replacement for experience.

Done with testing me on the basics, the Ghost begins the real fight. He dances over the grass lightly, so that there is barely a sound from his footfalls. He strikes and strikes again, posing a dizzying offensive.

I parry desperately, my every thought given over to this, the fight. My worries fade into the background as my attention sharpens. Even my exhaustion blows off me like fluff from the head of a dandelion.

It's glorious.

We trade blows, back and forth, advancing and retreating.

"Do you miss the mortal world?" he asks. I am relieved to discover his breath isn't coming entirely easily.

"No," I say. "I hardly knew it."

He attacks again, his sword a silvery fish darting through the sea of the night.

Watch the blade, not the soldier, Madoc told me many times. *Steel never deceives.*

Our weapons slam together again and again as we circle each other. "You must remember something."

I think of my mother's name whispered through the bars in the Tower.

He feigns to one side, and, distracted, I realize too late what he's doing. The flat of his blade hits my shoulder. He could have cut open my skin if he hadn't turned his blow at the last moment, and as it is, it's going to bruise.

"Nothing important," I say, trying to ignore the pain. Two can play at the game of distraction. "Perhaps your memories are better than mine. What do you recall?"

He shrugs. "Like you, I was born there." He stabs, and I block the blade. "But things were different a hundred years ago, I suppose."

I raise my eyebrows and parry another strike, dancing out of his range. "Were you a happy child?"

"I was magic. How could I fail to be?"

"*Magic*," I say, and with a twist of my blade—a move of Madoc's—I knock the sword out of the Ghost's hand.

He blinks at me. Hazel eyes. Crooked mouth opening in astonishment. "You..."

"Got better?" I supply, pleased enough not to mind my aching shoulder. It feels like a win, but if we were really fighting, that shoulder wound would have probably made my final move impossible. Still, his surprise thrills me nearly as much as my victory.

"It's good Oak will grow up as we didn't," I say after a moment. "Away from the Court. Away from all this."

The last time I saw my little brother, he was sitting at the table in Vivi's apartment, learning multiplication as though it were a riddle game. He was eating string cheese. He was laughing.

"*When the king returns*," the Ghost says, quoting from a ballad, "*rose petals will scatter across his path, and his footfalls will bring an end to wrath.* But how will your Oak rule if he has as few memories of Faerie as we have of the mortal world?"

The elation of the win ebbs. The Ghost gives me a small smile, as though to draw the sting of his words.

I go to a nearby stream and plunge my hands in, glad of the cold water. I cup it to my lips and gulp gratefully, tasting pine needles and silt.

I think of Oak. An utterly normal faerie child, neither particularly called to cruelty nor free of it. Used to being coddled, used to being whisked away from distress by a fussing Oriana. Now growing used to sugary cereal and cartoons and a life without treachery. I consider the rush of pleasure that I felt at my temporary triumph over the Ghost, the thrill of being the power behind the throne, the worrying satisfaction I had at making Vulciber squirm. Is it better that Oak is without those impulses or impossible for him to ever rule unless he has them?

And now that I have found in myself a taste for power, will I be loath to give it up?

I wipe wet hands over my face, pushing back those thoughts.

There is only now. There is only tomorrow and tonight and now and soon and never.

We start back, walking together as the dawn turns the sky gold. In the distance I hear the bellow of a deer and what sounds like drums.

Halfway there, the Ghost tips his head in a half bow. "You beat me tonight. I won't let that happen again."

"If you say so," I tell him with a grin.

By the time I get back to the palace, the sun is up and I want nothing more than sleep. But when I make it to my apartments, I find someone standing in front of the door.

My twin sister, Taryn.

"You've got a bruise coming up on your cheek," she says, the first words she's spoken to me in five months.

CHAPTER 4

Taryn's hair is dressed with a halo of laurel, and her gown is a soft brown, woven through with green and gold. She has dressed to accentuate the curves of her hips and chest, both unusual in Faerie, where bodies are thin to the point of attenuation. The clothes suit her, and there is something new in the set of her shoulders that suits her as well.

She is a mirror, reflecting someone I could have been but am not.

"It's late," I say clumsily, unlocking the door to my rooms. "I didn't expect anyone to be up." It's well past dawn by now. The whole palace is quiet and likely to stay so until the afternoon, when pages race through the halls and cooks light fires. Courtiers will rise from their beds much later, at full dark.

For all my wanting to see her, now that she is in front of me, I am unnerved. She must want something, to have put in this effort all of a sudden.

"I've come twice before," she says, following me inside. "You weren't here. This time I decided to wait, even if I waited all day."

I light the lamps; though it is bright outside, I am too deep in the palace to have windows in my rooms. "You look well."

She waves off my stiff politeness. "Are we going to fight forever? I want you to wear a flower crown and dance at my wedding. Vivienne is coming from the mortal world. She's bringing Oak. Madoc promises he won't argue with you. Please say you'll come."

Vivi is bringing Oak? I groan internally and wonder if there's a chance of talking her out of it. Maybe it's because she's my elder sister, but sometimes it's hard for her to take me particularly seriously.

I sink down on the couch, and Taryn does the same.

I consider again the puzzle of her being here. Of whether I should demand an apology or if I should let her skip past all that, the way she clearly wants.

"Okay," I tell her, giving in. I've missed her too much to risk losing her again. For the sake of us being sisters, I will try to forget what it felt like to kiss Locke. For my own sake, I will try to forget that she knew about the games he was playing with me during their courtship.

I will dance at her wedding, though I am afraid it will feel like dancing on knives.

She reaches into the bag by her feet and pulls out my stuffed cat and snake. "Here," she says. "I didn't think you meant to leave them behind."

They're relics of our old mortal life, talismans. I take them and press them to my chest, as I might a pillow. Right now, they feel like reminders of all my vulnerabilities. They make me feel like a child playing a grown-up game.

I hate her a little for bringing them.

They're a reminder of our shared past—a deliberate reminder, as though she couldn't trust me to remember on my own. They make me feel all my exposed nerves when I am trying so hard not to feel anything.

When I don't speak for a long moment, she goes on. "Madoc misses you, too. You were always his favorite."

I snort. "Vivi is his heir. His firstborn. The one he came to the mortal world to find. She's his *favorite.* Then there's you—who lives at home and didn't betray him."

"I'm not saying you're *still* his favorite," Taryn says with a laugh. "Although he was a little proud of you when you outmaneuvered him to get Cardan onto the throne. Even if it was stupid. I thought you hated Cardan. I thought we both hated him."

"I did," I say, nonsensically. "I do."

She gives me a strange look. "I thought you wanted to punish Cardan for everything he's done."

I think of his horror at his own desire when I brought my mouth to his, the dagger in my hand, edge against his skin. The toe-curling, corrosive pleasure of that kiss. It felt as though I *was* punishing him—punishing him and myself at the same time.

I hated him so much.

Taryn is dredging up every feeling I want to ignore, everything I want to pretend away.

"We made an agreement," I tell her, which is close to the truth. "Cardan lets me be his advisor. I have a position and power, and Oak is out of danger." I want to tell her the rest, but I don't dare. She might tell Madoc, might even tell Locke. I cannot share my secrets with her, even to brag.

And I admit that I desperately want to brag.

"And in return, you gave him the crown of Faerie. . . ." Taryn is looking at me as though struck by my presumption. After all, who was I, a mortal girl, to decide who should sit on the throne of Elfhame?

We get power by taking it.

Little does she know how much more presumptuous I have been. *I stole the crown of Faerie,* I want to tell her. *The High King, Cardan, our old enemy, is mine to command.* But of course I cannot say those words. Sometimes it seems dangerous even to think them. "Something like that," I say instead.

"It must be a demanding job, being his advisor." She looks around the room, forcing me to see it as she does. I have taken over these chambers, but I have no servants save for the palace staff, whom I seldom allow inside. Cups of tea rest on bookshelves, saucers lie on the floor along with dirty plates of fruit rinds and bread crusts. Clothes are scattered where I drop them after tugging them off. Books and papers rest on every surface. "You're unwinding yourself like a spool. What happens when there's no more thread?"

"Then I spin more," I say, carrying the metaphor.

"Let me help you," she says, brightening.

My brows rise. "You want to make thread?"

She rolls her eyes at me. "Oh, come on. I can do things you don't have time for. I see you in Court. You have perhaps two good jackets. I could bring some of your old gowns and jewels over—Madoc wouldn't notice, and even if he did, he wouldn't mind."

Faerie runs on debt, on promises and obligations. Having grown up here, I understand what she's offering—a gift, a boon, instead of an apology.

"I have *three* jackets," I say.

She raises both brows. "Well, then I guess you're all set."

I can't help wondering at her coming now, just after Locke has been made Master of Revels. And with her still in Madoc's house, I wonder where her political loyalties lie.

I am ashamed of those thoughts. I don't want to think of her the way I have to think about everyone else. She is my twin, and I missed her, and I hoped she would come, and now she has.

"Okay," I say. "If you want to, bringing over my old stuff would be great."

"Good!" Taryn stands. "And you ought to acknowledge what an enormous act of forbearance it was for me not to ask where you came from tonight or how you got hurt."

At that, my smile is instant and real.

She reaches out a finger to pet the plush body of my stuffed snake. "I love you, you know. Just like Mr. Hiss. And neither of us wants to be left behind."

"Good night," I tell her, and when she kisses my bruised cheek, I hug her to me, brief and fierce.

Once she's gone, I take my stuffed animals and seat them next to me on the rug. Once, they were a reminder that there was a time before Faerieland, when things were normal. Once, they were a comfort to me. I take a long last look, and then, one by one, I feed them to the fire.

I'm no longer a child, and I don't need comfort.

Once that is done, I line up little shimmering glass vials in front of me.

Mithridatism, it is called, the process by which one takes a little bit of poison to inoculate oneself against a full dose of it. I started a year ago, another way for me to correct my defects.

There are still side effects. My eyes shine too brightly. The half moons of my fingernails are bluish, as though my blood doesn't get quite enough oxygen. My sleep is strange, full of too-vivid dreams.

A drop of the bloodred liquid of the blusher mushroom, which causes potentially lethal paralysis. A petal of deathsweet, which can cause a sleep that lasts a hundred years. A sliver of wraithberry, which makes the blood race and induces a kind of wildness before stopping the heart. And a seed of everapple—*faerie fruit*—which muddies the minds of mortals.

I feel dizzy and a little sick when the poison hits my blood, but I would be sicker still if I skipped a dose. My body has acclimated, and now it craves what it should revile.

An apt metaphor for other things.

I crawl to the couch and lie there. As I do, Balekin's words wash over me: *I have heard that for mortals, the feeling of falling in love is very like the feeling of fear. Your heart beats fast. Your senses are heightened. You grow light-headed, maybe even dizzy. Is that right?*

I am not sure I sleep, but I do dream.

CHAPTER 5

I am tossing fitfully in a nest of blankets and papers and scrolls on the rug before the fire when the Ghost wakes me. My fingers are stained with ink and wax. I look around, trying to recall when I got up, what I was writing and to whom.

The Roach stands in the open panel of the secret passageway into my rooms, watching me with his reflecting, inhuman eyes.

My skin is sweaty and cold. My heart races.

I can still taste poison, bitter and cloying, on my tongue.

"He's at it again," the Ghost says. I do not have to ask whom he means. I may have tricked Cardan into wearing the crown, but I have not yet learned the trick of making him behave with the gravitas of a king.

While I was off getting information, he was off with Locke. I knew there would be trouble.

I scrub my face with the calloused heel of my hand. "I'm up," I say.

Still in my clothes from the night before, I brush off my jacket and hope for the best. Walking into my bedroom, I scrape my hair back, knotting it with a bit of leather and covering the mess with a velvet cap.

The Roach frowns at me. "You're wrinkled. His Majesty isn't supposed to go around with a seneschal who looks like she just rolled out of bed."

"Val Moren had sticks in his hair for the last decade," I remind him, taking a few partially dried mint leaves from my cabinet and chewing on them to take the staleness from my breath. The last High King's seneschal was mortal, as I am, fond of somewhat unreliable prophecy, and widely considered to be mad. "Probably the *same* sticks."

The Roach harrumphs. "Val Moren's a poet. Rules are different for poets."

Ignoring him, I follow the Ghost into the secret passage that leads to the heart of the palace, pausing only to check that my knives are still tucked away in the folds of my clothes. The Ghost's footfalls are so silent that when there's not enough light for my human eyes to see, I might as well be entirely alone.

The Roach does not follow us. He heads in the opposite direction with a grunt.

"Where are we going?" I ask the darkness.

"*His* apartments," the Ghost tells me as we emerge into a hall, a staircase below where Cardan sleeps. "There's been some kind of disturbance."

I have difficulty imagining what trouble the High King got into in his own rooms, but it doesn't take long to discover. When we arrive, I spot Cardan resting among the wreckage of his furniture. Curtains ripped from their rods, the frames of paintings cracked, their canvases kicked through, furniture broken. A small fire smolders in a corner, and everything stinks of smoke and spilled wine.

Nor is he alone. On a nearby couch are Locke and two beautiful faeries—a boy and a girl—one with ram's horns, the other with long ears that come to tufted points, like those of an owl. All of them are in an advanced state of undress and inebriation. They watch the room burn with a kind of grim fascination.

Servants cower in the hall, unsure if they should brave the king's wrath and clean up. Even his guards seem intimidated. They stand awkwardly in the hall outside his massive doors—one barely hanging from its hinges—ready to protect the High King from any threat that isn't himself.

"Carda—" I remember myself and sink into a bow. "Your *Infernal* Majesty."

He turns and, for a moment, seems to look through me, as though he has no idea who I am. His mouth is painted gold, and his pupils are large with intoxication. Then his lip lifts in a familiar sneer. "You."

"Yes," I say. "Me."

He gestures with a wineskin. "Have a drink." His wide-sleeved linen hunting shirt hangs open. His feet are bare. I guess I should be glad he's wearing pants.

"I have no head for liquor, my lord," I say, entirely truthfully, narrowing my eyes in warning.

"Am I not your king?" he asks, daring me to contradict him. Daring me to refuse him. Obediently, because we are in front of people, I take the skin and tip it against my closed lips, pretending to take a long swallow.

I can tell he's not fooled, but he doesn't push it.

"Everyone else may leave us." I indicate the faeries on the couch, including Locke. "You. Move. Now."

The two I do not know turn toward Cardan beseechingly, but he barely seems to notice them and does not countermand me. After a long moment, they sulkily unfold and see themselves out through the broken door.

Locke takes longer to get up. He smiles at me as he goes, an insinuating smile that I can't believe I ever found charming. He looks at me as though we share secrets, although we don't. We don't share anything.

I think of Taryn waiting in my rooms as this merriment began. I wonder if she could hear it. I wonder if she's used to staying up late with Locke, watching things burn.

The Ghost shakes his sandy head at me, eyes bright with amusement. He is in palace livery. To the knights in the hall and anyone else who might be looking, he is just another member of the High King's personal guard.

"I'll make sure everyone stays where they're put," the Ghost says, leaving through the doorway and issuing what sound like orders to the other knights.

"Well?" I say, looking around.

Cardan shrugs, sitting on the newly unoccupied couch. He picks at a piece of horsehair stuffing that is sticking out through the torn fabric. His every movement is languorous. It feels dangerous to rest my gaze on him for too long, as though he is so thoroughly debauched that it might be contagious. "There were more guests," he says, like that's any explanation. "They left."

"I can't imagine why," I say, voice as dry as I can make it.

"They told me a story," Cardan says. "Would you like to hear it? Once upon a time, there was a human girl stolen away by faeries, and because of that, she swore to destroy them."

"Wow," I say. "That really is a testament to how much you suck as a king, to believe your reign is capable of destroying Faerie."

Still, the words unnerve. I don't want my motives to be considered. I ought not to be thought of as influential. I ought not to be thought of at all.

The Ghost returns from the hall, leaning the door against the frame, closing it as much as is possible. His hazel eyes are shadowed.

I turn back to Cardan. "That little story is not why I was sent for. What happened?"

"This," he says, and staggers into the room with a bed in it. There, embedded deeply in the splintered wood of the headboard, are two black bolts.

"You're mad that one of your guests shot your bed?" I guess.

He laughs. "They weren't aiming for the bed." He pulls aside his shirt, and I see the hole in the cloth and a stripe of raw skin along his side.

My breath catches.

"Who did this?" the Ghost demands. And then, looking more closely at Cardan: "And why aren't the guards outside more upset? They don't behave as though they failed to prevent an assassination attempt."

Cardan shrugs. "I believe the guards think I was taking aim at my guests."

I take a step closer and notice a few drops of blood on one of the disarranged pillows. There are a few scattered white flowers, too, seeming to grow out of the fabric. "Did someone else get hit?"

He nods. "The bolt hit her leg, and she was screaming and not making very much in the way of sense. So you see how someone might conclude that I shot her when no one else was around. The actual shooter went back into the walls." He narrows his eyes at the Ghost and me, tilting his head, accusation burning in his gaze. "There seems to be some sort of secret passageway."

The Palace of Elfhame is built into a hill, with High King Eldred's old apartments at the very center, their walls crawling with roots and blooming vines. The whole Court assumed that Cardan would take those, but he moved to the farthest place possible from them, at the very peak of the hill, with crystal panes set into the earth like windows. Before his coronation, they had belonged to the least favored of the royal household. Now the residents of the palace scramble to rearrange themselves so they can be closer to the new High King. And Eldred's rooms—abandoned and too grand for anyone else to rightfully claim—remain empty.

I know of only a few ways into Cardan's rooms—a single, large, thick-glassed window enchanted never to break, a pair of double doors, and, apparently, a secret passage.

"It's not on the map of tunnels we have," I tell him.

"Ah," he says. I am not sure he believes me.

"Did you see who shot at you? And why didn't you tell your own guards what really happened?" I demand.

He gives me an exasperated look. "I saw a blur of black. And as to why I didn't correct the guards—I was protecting you and the Court of Shadows. I didn't think you would want the whole royal guard in your secret passageways!"

To that, I have no answer. The disturbing thing about Cardan is how well he plays the fool to disguise his own cleverness.

Opposite the bed is a cabinet built into the wall, taking the whole length of it. It has a painted clock face on the front, with constellations instead of numbers. The arms of the clock are pointed toward a configuration of stars prophesying a particularly amorous lover.

Inside, it appears merely a wardrobe overstuffed with Cardan's clothes. I pull them out, letting them fall to the floor in a pile of velvet cuffs, satin, and leather. From the bed, Cardan makes a sound of mock distress.

I press my ear to the wood backing, listening for the whistle of wind and feeling for a draft. The Ghost does the same on the other side. His fingers find a latch, and a thin door springs open.

Although I knew the palace was riddled with passageways, I never would have dreamed one was in Cardan's very bedroom. And yet...I should have combed over every inch of wall. I could have, at the least, asked one of the other spies to do so. But I avoided it, because I avoided being alone with Cardan.

"Stay with the king," I tell the Ghost, and, picking up a candle, head into the darkness beyond the wall, avoiding being alone with him again.

The tunnel is dim, lit throughout with golden hands holding torches that burn with a smokeless green flame. The stone floor is covered in a threadbare carpet, a strangely decorative detail for a secret passageway.

A few feet in, I find the crossbow. It is not the compact thing that I have carried. It's massive, more than half my size, obviously dragged here—I can see the way the carpet is rucked up in the direction whence it came.

Whoever shot it, shot it from here.

I jump over and keep going. I would expect a passageway like this to have many branches, but this one has none. It dips down at intervals, like a ramp, and turns in on itself, but it runs in only one direction—straight ahead. I hurry, faster and faster, my hand cupped around my candle flame to keep it from going out.

Then I come to a heavy wooden slab carved with the royal crest, the same one stamped in Cardan's signet ring.

I give it a push, and it shifts, clearly on a track. There's a bookshelf on the other side.

Until now, I have only heard stories of the great majesty of High King Eldred's rooms in the very heart of the palace, just above the brugh, the great branches of the throne itself snaking through his walls. Although I've never seen them before, the descriptions make it impossible to think I am anywhere else.

I walk through the enormous, cavernous rooms of Eldred's apartments, candle in one hand, a knife in the other.

And there, sitting on the High King's bed, her face stained with tears, is Nicasia.

Orlagh's daughter, Princess of the Undersea, fostered in the High King's Court as part of the decades-ago treaty of peace between Orlagh and Eldred, Nicasia was once part of the foursome made up of Cardan and his closest, most awful friends. She was also his beloved, until she betrayed him for Locke. I haven't seen her by Cardan's side as often since he ascended to the throne, but ignoring her hardly seems like a killing offense.

Is this what Balekin was whispering about with the Undersea? Is this the way Cardan was to be ruined?

"*You?*" I shout. "*You* shot Cardan?"

"Don't tell him!" She glares at me furiously, wiping wet eyes. "And put away that knife."

Nicasia wears a robe, heavily embroidered with phoenixes and wrapped tightly around herself. Three earrings shine along her lobes, snaking up the ears all the way to their bluish webbed points. Her hair has gotten darker since I saw it last. It was always the many colors of the sea, but now it is the sea in a storm—a deep greenish black.

"Are you out of your mind?" I yell. "You tried to assassinate the High King of Faerie."

"I didn't," she says. "I swear. I only meant to kill the girl he was with."

For a moment, I am too stunned by the cruelty and indifference to speak.

I take another look at her, at the robe she's clutching so tightly. With her words echoing in my head, I suddenly have a clear idea of what happened. "You thought to surprise him in his rooms."

"Yes," she says.

"But he wasn't alone. . . ." I continue, hoping she will take up the tale.

"When I saw the crossbow on the wall, it didn't seem it would be so difficult to aim," she says, forgetting the part about dragging it up through the passageway, though it's heavy and awkward and that couldn't have been easy. I wonder how angry she was, how unthinking in her rage.

Of course, perhaps she was thinking entirely clearly.

"It's treason, you know," I say aloud. I am shaking, I realize. The aftereffects of believing someone tried to assassinate Cardan, of realizing he could have died. "They'll execute you. They'll make you dance yourself to death in iron shoes heated hot as pokers. You'll be lucky if they put you in the Tower of Forgetting."

"I am a Princess of the Undersea," she says haughtily, but I can see the shock on her face as my words register. "Exempt from the laws of the land. Besides, I told you I wasn't aiming for him."

Now I understand the worst of her behavior in school: She thought she could never be punished.

"Have you ever used a crossbow before?" I ask. "You put his life at risk. He could have died. You idiot, *he could have died.*"

"I told you—" she starts to repeat herself.

"Yes, yes, the compact between the sea and the land," I interrupt her, still furious. "But it just so happens I know that your mother is intent on breaking the treaty. You see, she will say it was between Queen Orlagh and High King Eldred, not Queen Orlagh and High King Cardan. It doesn't apply any longer. Which means it won't protect you."

At that, Nicasia gapes at me, afraid for the first time. "How did you know that?"

I wasn't sure, I think. *Now I am.*

"Let's assume I know everything," I tell her instead. "Everything. Always. Yet I'm willing to make a deal with you. I'll tell Cardan and the guards and the rest of them that the shooter got away, if you do something for me."

"Yes," she says before I even lay out the conditions, making the depth of her desperation clear. For a moment, a desire for vengeance rises in me. Once, she laughed at my humiliation. Now I could gloat before hers.

This is what power feels like, pure unfettered power. It's *great.*

"Tell me what Orlagh is planning," I say, pushing those thoughts away.

"I thought you knew everything already," she returns sulkily, shifting so she can rise from the bed, one hand still clutching her robe. I guess she is wearing very little, if anything, underneath.

You should have just gone in, I want to tell her, suddenly. *You should have told him to forget the other girl. Maybe he would have.*

"Do you want to buy my silence or not?" I ask, sitting down on the edge of the cushions. "We have only a certain amount of time before someone comes looking for me. If they see you, it will be too late for denials."

Nicasia gives a long-suffering sigh. "My mother says he is a young and weak king, that he lets others influence him too much." With that, she gives me a hard look. "She believes he will give in to her demands. If he does, then nothing will change."

"And if he doesn't . . . ?"

Her chin comes up. "Then the truce between land and sea will be over, and it will be the land that suffers. The Isles of Elfhame will sink beneath the waves."

"And then what?" I ask. "Cardan is unlikely to make out with you if your mom floods the place."

"You don't understand. She wants us to be married. She wants me to be queen."

I am so surprised that, for a moment, I just stare at her, fighting down a kind of wild, panicky laughter. "You just *shot* him."

The look she gives me is beyond hatred. "Well, you murdered Valerian, did you not? I saw him the night he disappeared, and he was talking about you, talking about paying you back for stabbing him. People say he died at the coronation, but I don't think he did."

Valerian's body is buried on Madoc's estate, beside the stables, and if it was unearthed, I would have heard about it before now. She's guessing.

And so what if I did, anyway? I am at the right hand of the High King of Faerie. He can pardon my every crime.

Still, the memory of it brings back the terror of fighting for my life. And it reminds me how she would have delighted in my death the way she delighted in everything Valerian did or tried to do to me. The way she delighted in Cardan's hatred.

"Next time you catch *me* committing treason, you can force me to tell you *my* secrets," I say. "But right now I'd rather hear what your mother intends to do with Balekin."

"Nothing," Nicasia says.

"And here I thought the Folk couldn't lie," I tell her.

Nicasia paces the room. Her feet are in slippers, the points of which curl up like ferns. "I'm not! Mother believes Cardan will agree to her terms. She's just flattering Balekin. She lets him believe he's important, but he won't be. He won't."

I try to piece the plot together. "Because he's her backup plan if Cardan refuses to marry you."

My mind is reeling with the certainty that above all else, I cannot allow Cardan to marry Nicasia. If he did, it would be impossible to prize both of them from the throne. Oak would never rule.

I would lose everything.

Her gaze narrows. "I've told you enough."

"You think we're still playing some kind of game," I say.

"Everything's a game, Jude," she says. "You know that. And now it's your move." With those words, she heads toward the enormous doors and heaves one open. "Go ahead and tell them if you want, but you should know this—someone you trust has already betrayed you." I hear the slap of her slippers on stone, and then the heavy slam of wood against the frame.

My thoughts are a riot of confusion as I make my way back through the passageway. Cardan is waiting for me in the main room of his chambers, reclining on a couch with a shrewd look on his face. His shirt is still open, but a fresh bandage covers his wound. Across his fingers, a coin dances—I recognize the trick as one of the Roach's.

Someone you trust has already betrayed you.

From the shattered remains of the door, the Ghost looks in from where he stands with the High King's personal guard. He catches my eye.

"Well?" Cardan asks. "Have you discovered aught of my erstwhile murderer?"

I shake my head, not quite able to give speech to the lie. I look around at the wreckage of these rooms. There is no way for them to be secure, and they reek of smoke. "Come on," I say, taking Cardan's arm and pulling him unsteadily to his feet. "You can't sleep here."

"What happened to your cheek?" he asks, his gaze focusing blurrily on me. He's close enough that I can see his long lashes, the gold ring around the black of his iris.

"Nothing," I say.

He lets me squire him into the hall. As we emerge, the Ghost and the rest of the guards move immediately to stand at attention.

"At ease," says Cardan with a wave of his hand. "My seneschal is taking me somewhere. Worry not. I am sure she's got a plan of some kind."

His guards fall in line behind us, some of them frowning, as I half-lead him, half-carry him to my chambers. I hate taking him there, but I do not feel confident about his safety anywhere else.

He looks around in amazement, taking in the mess. "Where—Do you really sleep here? Perhaps you ought to set fire to your rooms as well."

"Maybe," I say, guiding him to my bed. It is strange to put my hand on his back. I can feel the warmth of his skin through the thin linen of his shirt, can feel the flex of his muscles.

It feels wrong to touch him as though he were a regular person, as though he weren't both the High King and also my enemy.

He needs no encouragement to sprawl on my mattress, head on the pillow, black hair spilling like crow feathers. He looks up at me with his night-colored eyes, beautiful and terrible all at once. "For a moment," he says, "I wondered if it wasn't you shooting bolts at me."

I make a face at him. "And what made you decide it wasn't?"

He grins up at me. "They missed."

I have said that he has the power to deliver a compliment and make it hurt. So, too, can he say something that ought to be insulting and deliver it in such a way that it feels like being truly seen.

Our eyes meet, and something dangerous sparks.

He hates you, I remind myself.

"Kiss me again," he says, drunk and foolish. "Kiss me until I am sick of it."

I feel those words, feel them like a kick to the stomach. He sees my expression and laughs, a sound full of mockery. I can't tell which of us he's laughing at.

He hates you. Even if he wants you, he hates you.

Maybe he hates you the more for it.

After a moment, his eyes flutter closed. His voice falls to a whisper, as though he's talking to himself. "If you're the sickness, I suppose you can't also be the cure."

He drifts off to sleep, but I am wide awake.

CHAPTER 6

All through the morning I sit on a chair tipped back against the wall of my own bedroom. My father's sword is across my lap. My mind keeps going over Nicasia's words.

You don't understand. She wants us to be married. She wants me to be queen.

Though I am across the floor from him, my gaze strays often to the bed and to the boy sleeping there.

His black eyes closed, his dark hair spilling over my pillow. At first, he could not seem to get comfortable, tangling his feet in the sheets, but eventually his breathing smoothed out and so did his movements. He is as ridiculously beautiful as ever, mouth soft, lips slightly parted, lashes so long that when his eyes are closed they rest against his cheek.

I am used to Cardan's beauty, but not to any vulnerability. It feels uncomfortable to see him without his fanciful clothes, without his acid tongue and malicious gaze for armor.

Over the five months of our arrangement, I have tried to anticipate the worst. I have issued commands to prevent him from avoiding, ignoring, or getting rid of me. I've figured out rules to prevent mortals from being tricked into years-long servitude and gotten him to proclaim them.

But it never seems like enough.

I recall walking with him in the gardens of the palace at dusk. Cardan's hands were clasped behind his back, and he stopped to sniff the enormous globe of a white rose tipped with scarlet, just before it snapped at the air. He grinned and lifted an eyebrow at me, but I was too nervous to smile back.

Behind him, at the edge of the garden, were a half dozen knights, his personal guard, to which the Ghost was already assigned.

Although I went over and over what I was about to tell him, I still felt like the fool who believes she can trick a dozen wishes from a single one if she just gets the phrasing right. "I am going to give you orders."

"Oh, indeed," he said. On his brow, the gold crown of Elfhame caught the light of the sunset.

I took a breath and began. "You're never to deny me an audience or give an order to keep me from your side."

"Whysoever would I want you to leave my side?" he asked, voice dry.

"And you may never order me arrested or imprisoned or killed," I said, ignoring him. "Nor hurt. Nor even detained."

"What about asking a servant to put a very sharp pebble in your boot?" he asked, expression annoyingly serious.

I gave him what I hoped was a scathing look in return. "Nor may you raise a hand against me yourself."

He made a gesture in the air, as though all of this was ridiculously obvious, as though somehow giving him the commands out loud was an act of bad faith.

I went doggedly on. "Each evening, you will meet me in your rooms before dinner, and we will discuss policy. And if you know of harm to be done to me, you must warn me. You must try to prevent anyone from guessing how I control you. And no matter how much you hate being High King, you must pretend otherwise."

"I don't," he said, looking up at the sky.

I turned to him, surprised. "What do you mean?"

"I don't hate being High King," he said. "Not always. I thought I would, and yet I do not. Make of that what you will."

I was unnerved, because it was a lot easier when I knew he was not just unsuitable for, but also uninterested in, ruling. Whenever I looked at the Blood Crown on his head, I had to pretend it away.

It didn't help how immediately he'd convinced the Gentry of his right to preside over them. His reputation for cruelty made them wary of crossing him. His license made them believe all delights were possible.

"So," I said. "You enjoy being my pawn?"

He grinned lazily, as though he didn't mind being baited. "For now."

My gaze sharpened. "For far longer than that."

"You've won yourself a year and a day," he told me. "But a lot can happen in a year and a day. Give me all the commands you want, but you'll never think of everything."

Once, I was the one to throw him off balance, the one to ignite his anger and shred his self-control, but somehow the tables turned. Every day since, I've felt the slippage.

As I gaze at him now, stretched out on my bed, I feel more off balance than ever.

The Roach sweeps into the room late that afternoon. On his shoulder is the hob-faced owl, once a messenger for Dain, now a messenger for the Court of Shadows. It goes by Snapdragon, although I don't know if that's a code name.

"The Living Council wants to see you," the Roach says. Snapdragon blinks sleepy black eyes at me.

I groan.

"In truth," he says, nodding toward the bed, "they want to see *him*, but it's you they can order around."

I stand and stretch. Then, strapping on the sheath, I head into the parlor of my apartments so as not to wake Cardan. "How's the Ghost?"

"Resting," the Roach says. "Lot of rumors flying around about last night, even among the palace guard. Gossips begin to spin their webs."

I head to my bath chamber to clean myself up. I gargle with salty water and scrub my face and armpits with a cloth slathered in lemony verbena soap. I brush out my tangles, too exhausted to manage anything more complicated than that. "I guess you checked the passageway by now," I call out.

"I did," the Roach says. "And I see why it wasn't on any of our maps—there's no connection to the other passageways at any point down the length of it. I'm not even sure it was built when they were."

I consider the painting of the clock and the constellations. The stars prophesying an amorous lover.

"Who slept there before Cardan?" I ask.

The Roach shrugs. "Several Folk. No one of particular note. Guests of the crown."

"Lovers," I say, finally putting it together. "The High King's lovers who weren't consorts."

"Huh." The Roach indicates Cardan with the lift of his chin in the direction of my bedroom. "And that's the place *our* High King chose to sleep?" The Roach gives me a significant look, as though I am supposed to know the answer to this puzzle, when I didn't realize it was a puzzle at all.

"I don't know," I say.

He shakes his head. "You best get to that Council meeting."

I can't say it's not a relief to know that when Cardan wakes, I won't be there.

CHAPTER 7

The Living Council was assembled during Eldred's time, ostensibly to help the High King make decisions, and they have calcified into a group difficult to oppose. It's not so much that the ministers have raw individual power—although many are themselves formidable—but as a collective, it has the authority to make many smaller decisions regarding the running of the kingdom. The kind of small decisions that, taken together, could put even a king in a bind.

After the disrupted coronation and the murder of the royal family, after the irregularity with the crown, the Council is skeptical of Cardan's youth and confused by my rise to power.

Snapdragon leads me to the meeting, beneath a braided dome of willow trees at a table of fossilized wood. The ministers watch me walk across the grass, and I look at them in turn—the Unseelie Minister, a troll with a thick head of shaggy hair with pieces of metal braided into it; the Seelie Minister, a green woman who looks like a mantis; the

Grand General, Madoc; the Royal Astrologer, a very tall, dark-skinned man with a sculpted beard and celestial ornaments in the long fall of his navy-blue hair; the Minister of Keys, a wizened old hob with ram's horns and goat eyes; and the Grand Fool, who wears pale lavender roses on his head to match his purple motley.

All along the table are carafes of water and wine, dishes of dried fruit.

I lean over to one of the servants and send them for a pot of the strongest tea they can find. I will need it.

Randalin, the Minister of Keys, sits in the High King's chair; the wooden back of the throne-like seat is burned with the royal crest. I note the move—and the assumptions inherent in it. In the five months since assuming the mantle of High King, Cardan has not come to the Council. Only one chair is empty—between Madoc and Fala, the Grand Fool. I remain standing.

"Jude Duarte," says Randalin, fixing me with his goat eyes. "Where is the High King?"

Standing in front of them is always intimidating, and Madoc's presence makes it worse. He makes me feel like a child, overeager to say or do something clever. A part of me wants nothing more than to prove I am more than what they suppose me to be—the weak and silly appointee of a weak and silly king.

To prove that there is another reason for Cardan to have chosen a mortal seneschal than because I can lie for him.

"I am here in his place," I say. "To speak in his stead."

Randalin's gaze is withering. "There is a rumor that he shot one of his paramours last night. Is it true?"

A servant sets the asked-for pot of tea at my elbow, and I am grateful both for the fortification and for an excuse not to immediately answer.

"Today courtiers told me that girl wore an anklet of swinging rubies sent to her in apology, but was unable to stand on her own," says Nihuar, the Seelie representative. She purses her small green lips. "I find everything about that to be in poor taste."

Fala the Fool laughs, clearly finding it to *his* taste. "Rubies for the spilling of her ruby-red blood."

That couldn't be true. Cardan would have had to arrange it in the time it took me to get from my rooms to the Council. But that doesn't mean someone else didn't arrange it on his behalf. Everyone is eager to help a king.

"You'd prefer he'd killed her outright?" I say. My skills in diplomacy are nowhere near as honed as my skills in aggravation. Besides, I'm tired.

"I wouldn't mind," says the Unseelie representative, Mikkel, with a chuckle. "Our new High King seems Unseelie through and through, and he will favor us, I think. We could give him a debauch better than the one his Master of Revels brags over, now that we know what he likes."

"There are other stories," continues Randalin. "That one of the guards shot High King Cardan to save that courtier's life. That she is bearing the royal heir. You must tell the High King that his Council stands ready to advise him so that his rule is not plagued by such tales."

"I'll be sure to do so," I say.

The Royal Astrologer, Baphen, gives me a searching look, as though reading correctly my intention not to talk to Cardan about any of this. "The High King is tied to the land and to his subjects. A king is a living symbol, a beating heart, a star upon which Elfhame's future is written." He speaks quietly, and yet somehow his voice carries. "Surely you have noticed that since his reign began, the isles are different. Storms come in faster. Colors are a bit more vivid, smells are sharper.

"Things have been seen in the forests," he goes on. "Ancient things, long thought gone from the world, come to peer at him.

"When he becomes drunk, his subjects become tipsy without knowing why. When his blood falls, things grow. Why, High Queen Mab called Insmire, Insmoor, and Insweal from the sea. All the isles of Elfhame, formed in a single hour."

My heart speeds faster the longer that Baphen talks. My lungs feel as though they cannot get enough air. Because none of this can be describing Cardan. He cannot be connected to the land so profoundly, cannot be able to do all that and yet be under my control.

I think of the blood on his coverlet—and beside it, the scattered white flowers.

When his blood falls, things grow.

"And so you see," says Randalin, unaware that I am freaking out, "the High King's every decision changes Elfhame and influences its inhabitants. During Eldred's reign, when children were born, they were perforce brought before him to pledge themselves to the kingdom. But in the low Courts, some heirs were fostered in the mortal world, growing up outside of Eldred's reach. Those changeling children returned to rule without making vows to the Blood Crown. At least one Court has made such a changeling its queen. And who knows how many wild Folk managed to avoid making vows. And the general of the Court of Teeth, Grima Mog, seems to have left her post. No one is sure what she intends. We can ill afford carelessness on the part of the High King."

I've heard of Grima Mog. She is terrifying, but not as terrifying as Orlagh.

"We need to watch the Queen of the Undersea, too," I say. "She's got a plan and is going to move against us."

"What's this?" Madoc says, interested in the conversation for the first time.

"Impossible," says Randalin. "How would you have heard such a thing?"

"Balekin has been meeting with her representatives," I say.

Randalin snorts. "And I suppose you have that from the prince's own lips?"

If I bit my tongue any harder, I'd bite clean through it. "I have it from more than one source. If their alliance was with Eldred, then it's over."

"The sea Folk have cold hearts," Mikkel says, which sounds at first as though he's agreeing with me, but the approving tone of his voice undermines it.

"Why doesn't Baphen consult his star charts?" Randalin says placatingly. "If he finds a threat prophesied there, we shall discuss further."

"I am telling you—" I insist, frustrated.

That is the moment that Fala jumps up on the table and begins to dance—interpretively, I think. Madoc grunts out a laugh. A bird alights on Nihuar's shoulder, and they begin gossiping back and forth in low whispers and trills.

It is clear that none of them wants to believe me. How could I know something they do not, after all? I am too young, too green, too mortal. "Nicasia—" I begin again.

Madoc smiles. "Your little friend from school."

I wish I could tell Madoc that the only reason he still sits on the

Council is because of me. Despite his running Dain through with his own hand, he is still the Grand General. I could say that I want to keep him busy, that he's a weapon better deployed by us than against us, that it's easier for my spies to watch him when I know where he is, but a part of me knows he is still Grand General because I couldn't bring myself to strip so much authority from my dad.

"There is still the matter of Grimsen," says Mikkel, moving on as though I have not spoken. "The High King has welcomed the Alderking's smith, maker of the Blood Crown. Now he dwells among us but does not yet labor for us."

"We must make him welcome," says Nihuar in a rare moment of sympathy between the Unseelie and Seelie factions. "The Master of Revels has made plans for the Hunter's Moon. Perhaps he can add an entertainment for Grimsen's benefit."

"Depends on what Grimsen's into, I guess," I say, giving up on convincing them that Orlagh is going to move against us. I am on my own.

"Rooting in the dirt, mayhap," Fala says. "Looking for trifles."

"Truffles," Randalin corrects automatically.

"Oh no," says Fala, wrinkling his nose. "Not those."

"I will endeavor to discover his preferred amusements." Randalin makes a small note on a piece of paper. "I have also been told that a representative from the Court of Termites will be attending the Hunter's Moon revel."

I try not to let my surprise show. The Court of Termites, led by Lord Roiben, was helpful in getting Cardan onto the throne. And for their efforts I promised that when Lord Roiben asked me for a favor, I'd do it. But I have no idea what he might want, and now isn't a good time for another complication.

Randalin clears his throat and turns, giving me a pointed look. "Convey our regrets to the High King that we were unable to advise him directly, and let him know we stand ready to come to his aid. If you fail to impress this upon him, we will find other means of doing so."

I make a short bow and no reply to what is clearly a threat.

As I leave, Madoc falls into step alongside me.

"I understand you've spoken with your sister," he says, thick eyebrows lowered in at least a mimicry of concern.

I shrug, reminding myself that he didn't speak a word on my behalf today.

He gives me an impatient look. "Don't tell me how busy you are with that boy king, though I imagine he takes some looking after."

Somehow, in just a few words, he has turned me into a sullen daughter and himself into her long-suffering father.

I sigh, defeated. "I've spoken with Taryn."

"Good," he says. "You're too much alone."

"Don't pretend at solicitude," I say. "It insults us both."

"You don't believe that I could care about you, even after you betrayed me?" He watches me with his cat eyes. "I'm still your father."

"You're my father's murderer," I blurt out.

"I can be both," Madoc says, smiling, showing those teeth.

I tried to rattle him, but I succeeded only in rattling myself. Despite the passage of months, the memory of his final aborted lunge once he realized he was poisoned is fresh in my mind. I remember his looking as though he would have liked to cleave me in half. "Which is why neither of us should pretend you're not furious with me."

"Oh, I'm angry, daughter, but I am also curious." He makes a dismissive gesture toward the Palace of Elfhame. "Is this really what you wanted? *Him?*"

As with Taryn, I choke on the explanation I cannot give.

When I do not speak, he comes to his own conclusions. "As I thought. I didn't appreciate you properly. I dismissed your desire for knighthood. I dismissed your capacity for strategy, for strength—and for cruelty. That was my mistake, and one I will not make again."

I am not sure if that's a threat or an apology.

"Cardan is the High King now, and so long as he wears the Blood Crown, I am sworn to serve him," he says. "But no oath binds you. If you regret your move, make another. There are games yet to play."

"I already won," I remind him.

He smiles. "We will speak again."

As he walks off I can't help thinking that maybe I was better off when he was ignoring me.

CHAPTER 8

I meet the Bomb in High King Eldred's old rooms. This time I am resolved to go over every inch of the chambers before Cardan is moved into them—and I am determined he should stay here, in the most secure part of the palace, whatever his preferences might be.

When I arrive, the Bomb is lighting the last of the fat candles above a fireplace, the runnels of wax so established that they make a kind of sculpture. It is strange to be in here now, without Nicasia to buttonhole or anything else to distract me from looking around. The walls shimmer with mica, and the ceiling is all branches and green vines. In the antechamber, the shell of an enormous snail glows, a lamp the size of a small table.

The Bomb gives me a quick grin. Her white hair is pulled back into braids knotted with a few shimmering silver beads.

Someone you trust has already betrayed you.

I try to put Nicasia's words out of my head. After all, that could mean anything. It's typical faerie bullshit, ominous but applicable so broadly that it could be the clue to a trap about to be sprung on me or a reference to something that happened when we were all taking lessons together. Maybe she is warning me that a spy is in my confidence or maybe she's alluding to Taryn's having it off with Locke.

And yet I cannot stop thinking about it.

"So the assassin got away through here?" the Bomb says. "The Ghost says you chased after them."

I shake my head. "There was no assassin. It was a romantic misunderstanding."

Her eyebrows go up.

"The High King is very bad at romance," I say.

"I guess so," she says. "So you want to toss the sitting room, and I'll take the bedroom?"

"Sure," I agree, heading toward it.

The secret passageway is beside a fireplace carved like the grinning mouth of a goblin. The bookshelf is still shifted to one side, revealing spiraling steps up into the walls. I close it.

"You really think you can get Cardan to move in here?" the Bomb calls from the other room. "It's such a waste to have all this glorious space go unused."

I lean down to start pulling books off the shelves, opening them and shaking them a bit to see if there's anything inside.

A few yellowing and disintegrating pieces of paper fall out, along with a feather and a carved-bone letter opener. Someone hollowed one of the books out, but nothing rests inside the compartment. Still another tome has been eaten away by insects. I throw that one out.

"The last room Cardan occupied caught fire," I call back to the Bomb. "Let me rephrase. It caught fire because *he lit it on fire*."

She laughs. "It would take him days to burn all this."

I look back at the books and am not so sure. They are dry enough to burst into flames just by my looking at them too long. With a sigh, I stack them and move on to the cushions, to pulling back the rugs. Underneath, I find only dust.

I dump out all the drawers onto the massive table-size desk: the metal nibs of quill pens, stones carved with faces, three signet rings, a long tooth of a creature I cannot identify, and three vials with the liquid inside dried black and solid.

In another drawer, I find jewels. A collar of black jet, a beaded bracelet with a clasp, heavy golden rings.

In the last I find quartz crystals, cut into smooth, polished globes and spears. When I lift one to the light, something moves inside it.

"Bomb?" I call, my voice a little high.

She comes into the room, carrying a jeweled coat so heavily encrusted that I am surprised anyone was willing to stand in it. "What's wrong?"

"Have you ever seen anything like this before?" I hold up a crystal ball.

She peers into it. "Look, there's Dain."

I take it back and look inside. A young Prince Dain sits on the back of a horse, holding a bow in one hand and apples in the other. Elowyn sits on a pony to one side of him, and Rhyia to the other. He throws three apples in the air, and all of them draw their bows and shoot.

"Did that happen?" I ask.

"Probably," she says. "Someone must have enchanted these orbs for Eldred."

I think of Grimsen's legendary swords, of the golden acorn that disgorged Liriope's last words, of Mother Marrow's cloth that could turn even the sharpest blade, and all the mad magic that High Kings are given. These were common enough to be stuffed away into a drawer.

I pull out each one to see what's inside. I see Balekin as a newborn child, the thorns already growing out of his skin. He squalls in the arms of a mortal midwife, her gaze glazed with glamour.

"Look into this one," the Bomb says with a strange expression.

It's Cardan as a very small child. He is dressed in a shirt that's too large for him. It hangs down like a gown. He is barefoot, his feet and shirt streaked with mud, but he wears dangling hoops in his ears, as though an adult gave him their earrings. A horned faerie woman stands nearby, and when he runs to her, she grabs his wrists before he can put his dirty hands on her skirts.

She says something stern and shoves him away. When he falls, she barely notices, too busy being drawn into conversation with other courtiers. I expect Cardan to cry, but he doesn't. Instead, he stomps off to a tree that an older boy is climbing. The boy says something, and Cardan grabs for his ankle. A moment later, the boy is on the ground, and Cardan's small, grubby hand is forming a fist. At the sound of the scuffle, the faerie woman turns and laughs, clearly delighted by his escapade.

When Cardan looks back at her, he's smiling, too.

I shove the crystal back into the drawer. Who would cherish this? It's horrible.

And yet, it's not *dangerous*. There's no reason to do anything with it but leave it where it was. The Bomb and I continue through the room together. Once we're satisfied it's safe, we head through a door carved with an owl, back into the king's bedchamber.

A massive half-tester bed rests in the center, curtained in green, with the symbol of the Greenbriar line stitched in gleaming gold. Thick spider-silk blankets are smoothed out over a mattress that smells as though it has been stuffed with flowers.

"Come on," says the Bomb, flopping down on the bed and rolling over so that she is looking up at the ceiling. "Let's make sure it's safe for our new High King, just in case."

I suck in a surprised breath, but follow. My weight on the mattress makes it dip, and the heady scent of roses overwhelms my senses.

Spreading out on the King of Elfhame's coverlets, breathing in the air that perfumed his nights, has an almost hypnotic quality. The Bomb pillows her head in her arms as though it's no big thing, but I remember High King Eldred's hand on my head and the slight jolt of nerves and pride I felt each time he acknowledged me. Lying on his bed feels like wiping my dirty peasant feet on the throne.

And yet, how could I not?

"Our king is a lucky duck," the Bomb says. "I'd like a bed like this, big enough to have a guest or two."

"Oh yeah?" I ask, teasing her as I would have once teased my sisters. "Anyone in particular?"

She looks away, embarrassed, which makes me pay attention. I push myself up on one elbow. "Wait! Is it someone I know?"

For a moment, she doesn't answer, which is long enough.

"It is! The Ghost?"

"Jude!" she says. "No."

I frown at her. "The Roach?"

The Bomb sits up, long fingers pulling the coverlet to her. Since she cannot lie, she only sighs. "You don't understand."

The Bomb is beautiful, delicate features and warm brown skin, wild white hair and luminous eyes. I think of her as possessing some combination of charm and skill that means she could have anyone she wanted.

The Roach's black tongue and his twisted nose and the tuft of furlike hair at the top of his scalp add up to his being impressive and terrifying, but even according to the aesthetics of Faerieland, even in a place where inhuman beauty is celebrated along with almost opulent ugliness, I am not sure even he would guess that the Bomb longs for him.

I would never have guessed it.

I don't know how to say that to her without sounding as though I am insulting him, however.

"I guess I don't," I concede.

She draws a pillow onto her lap. "My people died in a brutal, internecine Court war a century ago, leaving me on my own. I went into the human world and became a small-time crook. I wasn't particularly good at it. Mostly I was just using glamour to hide my mistakes. That's when the Roach spotted me. He pointed out that while I might not be much of a thief, I was a dab hand at concocting potions and bombs. We went around together for decades. He was so affable, so dapper and charming, that he'd con people right to their faces, no magic required."

I smile at the thought of him in a derby hat and a vest with a pocket watch, amused by the world and everything in it.

"Then he had this idea we were going to steal from the Court of Teeth in the North. The con went wrong. The Court carved us up and filled us full of curses and geases. Changed us. Forced us to serve them." She snaps her fingers, and sparks fly. "Fun, right?"

"I bet it wasn't," I say.

She flops back and keeps talking. "The Roach—Van, I can't call him the Roach while I'm talking like this. Van's the one who got me through being there. He told me stories, tales of Queen Mab's imprisoning a frost giant, of binding all the great monsters of yore, and winning the High Crown. Stories of the impossible. Without Van, I don't know if I could have survived.

"Then we screwed up a job, and Dain got hold of us. He had a scheme for us to betray the Court of Teeth and join him. So we did. The Ghost was already by his side, and the three of us made a formidable team. Me with explosives. The Roach stealing anything or anyone. And the Ghost, a sharpshooter with a light step. And here we are, somehow, safe in the Court of Elfhame, working for the High King himself. Look at me, sprawled across his royal bed, even. But here there's no reason for Van to take my hand or sing to me when I am hurting. There is no reason for him to bother with me at all."

She lapses into silence. We both stare up at the ceiling.

"You should tell him," I say. Which is not bad advice, I think. Not advice I would take myself, but that doesn't necessarily make it bad.

"Perhaps." The Bomb pushes herself up off the bed. "No tricks or traps. You think it's safe to let our king in here?"

I think of the boy in the crystal, of his proud smile and his balled fist. I think of the horned faerie woman, who must have been his mother, shoving him away from her. I think of his father, the High King, who didn't bother to intervene, didn't even bother to make sure he was clothed or his face wiped. I think of how Cardan avoided these rooms.

I sigh. "I wish I could think of a place he'd be safer."

At midnight, I am expected to attend a banquet. I sit several seats from the throne and pick at a course of crisped eels. A trio of pixies sings a cappella for us as courtiers try to impress one another with their wit. Overhead, chandeliers drip wax in long strands.

High King Cardan smiles down the table indulgently and yawns like a cat. His hair is messy, as though he did no more than finger-comb it since rising from my bed. Our eyes meet, and I am the one who looks away, my face hot.

Kiss me until I am sick of it.

Wine is brought in colored carafes. They glow aquamarine and sapphire, citrine and ruby, amethyst and topaz. Another course comes, with sugared violets and frozen dew.

Then come domes of glass, under which little silvery fish sit in a cloud of pale blue smoke.

"From the Undersea," says one of the cooks, dressed for the occasion. She bows.

I look across the table at Randalin, Minister of Keys, but he is pointedly ignoring me.

All around me, the domes rise, and the smoke, redolent of peppercorns and herbs, fills the room.

I see that Locke has seated himself beside Cardan, drawing the girl whose seat it was onto his lap. She kicks up her hooved feet and throws back her horned head in laughter.

"Ah," says Cardan, lifting up a gold ring from his plate. "I see my fish has something in its belly."

"And mine," says a courtier on his other side, picking out a single shiny pearl as large as a thumbnail. She laughs with delight. "A gift from the sea."

Each silvery fish contains a treasure. The cooks are summoned, but they give stammering disavowals, swearing the fish were fresh-caught and fed nothing but herbs by the kitchen Folk. I frown at my plate, at the beads of sea glass I find beneath my fish's gills.

When I look up, Locke holds a single gold coin, perhaps part of a lost mortal ship's hoard.

"I see you staring at him," Nicasia says, sitting down beside me. Tonight she wears a gown of gold lacework. Her dark tourmaline hair is pulled up with two golden combs the shape of a shark jaw, complete with golden teeth.

"Perhaps I am looking only at the trinkets and gold with which your mother thinks she can buy this Court's favor," I say.

She picks up one of the violets from my plate and places it delicately on her tongue.

"I lost Cardan's love for Locke's easy words and easier kisses, sugared like these flowers," she says. "Your sister lost *your* love to get Locke's, didn't she? But we all know what you lost."

"Locke?" I laugh. "Good riddance."

Her brows knit together. "Surely it's not the High King himself you were gazing at."

"Surely not," I echo, but I don't meet her eyes.

"Do you know why you didn't tell anyone my secret?" she asks. "Perhaps you tell yourself that you enjoy having something over my head. But in truth, I think it's that you knew no one would ever believe you. I belong in this world. You don't. And you know it."

"You don't even belong on *land*, sea princess," I remind her. And yet, I cannot help recalling how the Living Council doubted me. I cannot help how her words crawl under my skin.

Someone you trust has already betrayed you.

"This will never be your world, *mortal*," she says.

"This *is* mine," I say, anger making me reckless. "My land and my king. And I will protect them both. Say the same, go on."

"He cannot love you," she says to me, her voice suddenly brittle.

She obviously doesn't like the idea of my claiming Cardan, obviously is still infatuated with him, and just as obviously has no idea what to do about it.

"What do you want?" I ask her. "I was just sitting here, minding my own business, eating my dinner. You're the one who came up to me. You're the one accusing me of... I'm not even sure what."

"Tell me what you have over him," Nicasia says. "How did you trick him into putting you at his right hand, you whom he despised and reviled? How is it that you have his ear?"

"I will tell you, if you tell me something in return." I turn toward her, giving her my full attention. I have been puzzling over the secret passageway in the palace, over the woman in the crystal.

"I've told you all that I am willing to—" Nicasia begins.

"Not that. Cardan's mother," I say, cutting her off. "Who was she? Where is she now?"

She tries to turn her surprise into mockery. "If you're such good friends, why don't you ask him?"

"I never said we were friends."

A servant with a mouth full of sharp teeth and butterfly wings on his back brings the next course. The heart of a deer, cooked rare and stuffed with toasted hazelnuts. Nicasia picks up the meat and tears into it, blood running over her fingers.

She runs her tongue over red teeth. "She wasn't anyone, just some girl from the lower Courts. Eldred never made her a consort, even after she'd borne him a child."

I blink in obvious surprise.

She looks insufferably pleased, as though my not knowing has proved once and for all how unsuitable I am. "Now it's your turn."

"You want to know what I did to make him raise me up?" I ask, leaning toward her, close enough that she can feel the warmth of my breath. "I kissed him on the mouth, and then I threatened to kiss him some more if he didn't do exactly what I wanted."

"Liar," she hisses.

"If you're such good friends," I say, repeating her own words back to her with malicious satisfaction, "why don't you ask him?"

Her gaze goes to Cardan, his mouth stained red with heart's blood, crown at his brow. They appear two of a kind, a matched set of monsters. He doesn't look over, busy listening to the lutist who has composed, on the spot, a rollicking ode to his rule.

My king, I think. *But only for a year and a day, and five months are already gone.*

CHAPTER 9

Tatterfell is waiting for me when I get back to my rooms, her beetle eyes disapproving as she picks up the High King's trousers from my couch.

"So this is how you've been living," the little imp grumbles. "A worm in a butterfly's cocoon."

Something about being scolded is comfortingly familiar, but that doesn't mean I like it. I turn away so she can't see my embarrassment at how untidy I've let things get. Not to mention what it looks like I've been doing, and with whom.

Sworn into Madoc's service until she worked off some old debt of honor, Tatterfell could not have come here without his knowledge. She may have taken care of me since I was a child—brushed my hair and mended my dresses and strung rowan berries to keep me from being enchanted—but it is Madoc who has her loyalty. It's not that I don't think she was fond of me, in her way, but I've never mistaken that for love.

I sigh. The castle servants would have cleaned my rooms if I let them, but then they'd notice my odd hours and be able to rifle through my papers, not to mention my poisons. No, better to bar the door and sleep in filth.

My sister's voice comes from my bedroom. "You're back early." She sticks her head out, holding up a few garments.

Someone you trust has already betrayed you.

"How did you get in?" I ask. My key turned, met resistance. The tumblers moved. I have been taught the humble art of lock picking, and though I am no prodigy, I can at least tell when a door is locked in the first place.

"Oh," Taryn says, and laughs. "I posed as you and got a copy of your key."

I want to kick a wall. Surely everyone knows I have a twin sister. Surely everyone knows mortals can lie. Ought someone not have at least asked a question she might find tricky to answer before handing over access to palace rooms? To be fair, though, I have myself lied again and again and gotten away with it. I can hardly begrudge Taryn for doing the same.

It's my bad luck that tonight is when she chooses to barge in, with Cardan's clothing scattered over my rug and a heap of his bloody bandages still on a low table.

"I persuaded Madoc to gift the remainder of Tatterfell's debt to you," Taryn announces. "And I've brought you all your coats and dresses and jewels."

I look into the imp's inkdrop eyes. "You mean Madoc has her spying for him."

Tatterfell's lip curls, and I am reminded how sharply she pinches. "Aren't you a sly and suspicious girl? You ought to be ashamed, saying such a thing."

"I am grateful for the times you were kind," I say. "If Madoc has given your debt to me, consider it paid long ago."

Tatterfell frowns unhappily. "Madoc spared my lover's life when he could have taken it by right. I pledged him a hundred years of my service, and that time is nearly up. Do not dishonor my vow by thinking it can be dismissed with a wave of *your* hand."

I am stung by her words. "Are you sorry he sent you?"

"Not yet," she says, and goes back to work.

I head toward my bedroom, picking up Cardan's bloody rags before Tatterfell can. As I pass the hearth, I toss them into the flames. The fire flares up.

"So," I ask my sister, "what did you bring me?"

She points to my bed, where she has spread my old things on my newly rumpled sheets. It's odd to see the clothes and jewels I haven't had in months, the things Madoc bought for me, the things Oriana approved. Tunics, gowns, fighting gear, doublets. Taryn even brought the homespun I used to sneak around Hollow Hall and the clothes we wore when we snuck to the mortal world.

When I look at it all, I see a person who is both me and not. A kid who went to classes and didn't think the stuff she was learning would be all that important. A girl who wanted to impress the only dad she knew, who wanted a place in the Court, who still believed in honor.

I am not sure I fit in these clothes anymore.

Still, I hang them in my closet, beside my two black doublets and a single pair of high boots.

I open a box of my jewels. Earrings given to me for birthdays, a golden cuff, three rings—one with a ruby that Madoc gave me on a Blood Moon revel, one with his crest that I don't even remember receiving, and a thin gold one that was a present from Oriana. Necklaces of moonstone, chunks of quartz, carved bone. I slide the ruby ring onto my left hand.

"And I brought some sketches," she says, taking out a pad of paper and sitting cross-legged on my bed. Neither of us is a great artist, but her drawings of clothing are easy to understand. "I want to take them to my tailor."

She's imagined me in a lot of black jackets with high collars, the skirts slashed up the sides for easy movement. The shoulders look as though they're armored, and, in a few cases, she has drawn what appears to be a single shiny sleeve of metal.

"They can measure me," she says. "You won't even have to go to the fittings."

I give her a long look. Taryn doesn't like conflict. Her manner of dealing with all the terror and confusion in our lives has been to become immensely adaptable, like one of those lizards that change color to match their surroundings. She's the person who knows what to wear and how to behave, because she studies people carefully and mimics them.

She's good at picking out clothes to send a certain message—even if the message of her drawings appears to be "stay away from me or I will chop off your head"—and it's not like I don't think she wants to help me, but the effort she's put into this, especially as her own marriage is imminent, seems extraordinary.

"Okay," I say. "What do you want?"

"What do you mean?" she asks, all innocence.

"You want us to be friends again," I say, sliding into more modern diction with her. "I appreciate that. You want me to come to your wedding, which is great, because I want to be there. But this—this is too much."

"I can be nice," she says, but does not meet my eyes.

I wait. For a long moment, neither of us speaks. I know she saw Cardan's clothes tossed on the floor. Her not immediately asking about that should have been my first clue that she wanted something.

"Fine." She sighs. "It's not a big deal, but there is a thing I want to talk to you about."

"No kidding," I say, but I can't help smiling.

She shoots me a look of vast annoyance. "I don't want Locke to be Master of Revels."

"You and me both."

"But you could do something about it!" Taryn winds her hands in her skirts. "Locke craves dramatic experiences. And as Master of Revels, he can create these—I don't even know what to call them—*stories*. He doesn't so much think of a party as food and drinks and music, but rather a dynamic that might create conflict."

"Okay…" I say, trying to imagine what that means for politics. Nothing good.

"He wants to see how I'll react to the things he does," she says.

That's true. He wanted to know, for instance, if Taryn loved him enough to let him court me while she stood by, silent and suffering. I think he'd have been interested in finding out the same about me, but I turned out to be very prickly.

She goes on. "And Cardan. And the Circles of the Court. He's already been talking to the Larks and the Grackles, finding their weaknesses, figuring out which squabbles he can inflame and how."

"Locke might do the Larks some good," I say. "Give them a ballad to write." As for the Grackles, if he can compete with their debauches, I guess he ought to have at it, although I am clever enough not to say that out loud.

"The way he talks, for a moment, it all seems like it's fun, even if it's a terrible idea," Taryn says. "His being Master of Revels is going to be awful. I don't care about him taking lovers but I hate him being away from me. Jude, please. Do something. I know you want to say you told me so, but I don't care."

I have bigger problems, I want to tell her.

"Madoc would almost certainly say you don't have to marry him. Vivi'd say that, too, I bet. In fact, I bet they have."

"But you know me too well to bother." She shakes her head. "When I'm with him, I feel like the hero of a story. Of *my* story. It's when he's not there that things don't feel right."

I don't know what to say to that. I could point out that Taryn seems to be the one making up the story, casting Locke in the role of the protagonist and herself as the romantic interest who disappears when she's not on the page.

But I do remember being with Locke, feeling special and chosen and pretty. Now, thinking about it, I just feel dumb.

I guess I *could* order Cardan to strip the title from Locke, but Cardan would resent my using my power for something so petty and personal. It would make me seem weak. And Locke would figure out that the stripping of his title was my fault, since I haven't made my dislike a secret. He'd know that I had more power over Cardan than quite made sense.

And everything Taryn is complaining about would still happen. Locke doesn't need to be the High King's Master of Revels to get into this kind of trouble; the title just allows him to manage it on a grander scale.

"I'll talk to Cardan about it," I lie.

Her gaze goes to where his clothes were scattered across my floor, and she smiles.

CHAPTER 10

As the Hunter's Moon approaches, the level of debauchery in the palace increases. The tenor of the parties changes—they become more frenetic, more wild. No longer is Cardan's presence necessary for such license. Now that rumors paint him as someone who would shoot a lover for sport, his legend grows from there.

Recollections of his younger days—of the way he rode a horse into our lessons, the fights he had, the cruelties he perpetrated—are picked over. The more horrible the story, the more it is cherished. Faeries may not be able to lie, but stories grow here as they do anywhere, fed on ambition and envy and desire.

In the afternoons, I step over sleeping bodies in the halls. Not all of them are courtiers. Servants and guards seem to have fallen prey to the same wild energy and can be found abandoning their duties to pleasure. Naked Folk run across the gardens of Elfhame, and troughs once used to water horses now run with wine.

I meet with Vulciber, seeking more information about the Undersea, but he has none. Despite knowing that Nicasia was trying to bait me, I go over the list of people who may have betrayed me. I fret over who and to what end, over the arrival of Lord Roiben's ambassador, over how to extend my year-and-a-day lease on the throne. I wish I'd asked Cardan for his true name back when I had a crossbow trained on him. I study my moldering papers and drink my poisons and plan a thousand parries to blows that may never come.

Cardan has moved to Eldred's old chambers, and the rooms with the burnt floor are barred from the inside. If it makes him uncomfortable to sleep where his father slept, he gives no sign. When I arrive, he is lounging nonchalantly as servants remove tapestries and divans to make room for a new bed carved to his specifications.

He is not alone. A small circle of courtiers is with him—a few I don't know, plus Locke, Nicasia, and my sister, currently pink with wine and laughing on the rug before the fire.

"Go," he says to them when he sees me at the threshold.

"But, Your Majesty," begins a girl. She's all cream and gold, in a light blue gown. Long pale antennae rise from the outer edges of her eyebrows. "Surely such dull news as your seneschal brings will require the antidote of our cheer."

I've thought carefully about commanding Cardan. Too many orders and he'd chafe under them, too few and he'd duck beneath them easily. But I am glad to have made sure he'd never deny me admittance. I am especially glad that he can never countermand me.

"I am sure I will call you back swiftly enough," Cardan says, and the courtiers troop out merrily. One of them carries a mug, obviously stolen from the mortal world and filled to the brim with wine. *I RULE*, it reads. Locke shoots me a curious glance. My sister grabs hold of my hand as she goes, squeezing it hopefully.

I go to a chair and sit down without waiting for an invitation. I want to remind Cardan that over me, he has no authority.

"The Hunter's Moon revel is tomorrow night," I say.

He sprawls in a chair opposite mine, watching me with his black eyes as though I am the one to be wary of. "If you wish to know details, you ought to have kept Locke behind. I know little. It is to be another one of my performances. I shall caper while you scheme."

"Orlagh of the Undersea is watching you—"

"Everyone's watching me," Cardan says, fingers fiddling restlessly with his signet ring, turning it round and round again.

"You don't seem to mind," I say. "You said yourself that you don't hate being king. Maybe you're even enjoying it."

He gives me a suspicious look.

I try to give him a genuine smile in return. I hope I can be convincing. I need to be convincing. "We can both have what we want. You can rule for a lot longer than a year. All you have to do is extend your vow. Let me command you for a decade, for a score of years, and together—"

"I think not," he says, cutting me off. "After all, you know how dangerous it would be to have Oak sit in my place. He is only a year older than he was. He's not ready. And yet, in only a few months, you will have to order me to abdicate in favor of him or make an arrangement that will require us to trust each other—rather than my trusting you without hope of being trusted in return."

I am furious with myself for thinking he might agree to keeping things the way they are.

He gives me his sweetest smile. "Perhaps then you could be my seneschal in earnest."

I grit my teeth. Once, a position as grand as seneschal would have been beyond my wildest dreams. Now it seems a humiliation. Power is infectious. Power is greedy.

"Have a care," I tell him. "I can make the months that remain go slowly indeed."

His smile doesn't falter. "Any other commands?" he asks. I ought to tell him more about Orlagh, but the thought of his crowing over her offer is more than I can bear. I cannot let that marriage happen, and right now I don't want to be teased about it.

"Don't drink yourself to death tomorrow," I say. "And watch out for my sister."

"Taryn seemed well enough tonight," he says. "Roses in her cheeks and merriment on her lips."

"Let's be sure she stays that way," I say.

His brows rise. "Would you like me to seduce her away from Locke? I could certainly try. I promise nothing in the way of results, but you might find amusement in the attempt."

"No, no, absolutely not, do not do that," I say, and do not examine the hot spike of panic his words induce. "I just mean try to keep Locke from being his worst self when she's around, that's all."

He narrows his eyes. "Shouldn't you encourage just the opposite?"

Perhaps it *would* be better for Taryn to discover unhappiness with Locke as soon as possible. But she's my sister, and I never want to be the cause of her pain. I shake my head.

He makes a vague gesture in the air. "As you wish. Your sister will be wrapped in satin and sackcloth, as protected from herself as I can make her."

I stand. "The Council wants Locke to arrange some amusement to please Grimsen. If it's nice, perhaps the smith will make you a cup that never runs out of wine."

Cardan gives me a look up through his lashes that I find hard to interpret and then rises, too. He takes my hand. "Nothing is sweeter," he says, kissing the back of it, "but that which is scarce."

My skin flushes, hot and uncomfortable.

When I go out, his little circle is in the hall, waiting to be allowed back into his rooms. My sister looks a bit queasy, but when she sees me, she pastes on a wide, fake smile. One of the boys has put a limerick to music, playing it again and again, faster and faster. Their laughter floods the hallway, sounding like the cawing of crows.

Heading through the palace, I pass a chamber where a few courtiers have gathered. There, toasting an eel in the flames of a massive fireplace, sitting on a rug, is the old High King Eldred's Court Poet and Seneschal, Val Moren.

Faerie artists and musicians sit around him. Since the death of most of the royal family, he's found himself at the center of one of the Court factions, the Circle of Larks. Brambles are coiled in his hair, and he sings softly to himself. He's mortal, like me. He's also probably mad.

"Come drink with us," one of the Larks says, but I demur.

"Pretty, petty Jude." The flames dance in Val Moren's eyes when he looks my way. He begins picking off burnt skin and eating the soft white flesh of the eel. Between bites, he speaks. "Why haven't you come to me for advice yet?"

It's said that he was High King Eldred's lover, once. He's been in the Court since long before the time my sisters and I came here. Despite that, he never made common cause of our mortality. He never tried to help us, never tried to reach out to us to make us feel less alone. "Do you have some?"

He gazes at me and pops one of the eyes of the eel into his mouth. It sits, glistening, on his tongue. Then he swallows. "Maybe. But it matters little."

I am so tired of riddles. "Let me guess. Because when I ask you for advice, you're not going to give it to me?"

He laughs, a dry, hollow sound. I wonder how old he is. Under the brambles, he looks like a young man, but mortals won't grow old so long as they don't leave Elfhame. Although I cannot see age in lines on his face, I can see it in his eyes. "Oh, I will give you the finest advice anyone's ever given you. But you will not heed it."

"Then what good are you?" I demand, about to turn away. I don't have time for a few lines of useless doggerel for me to interpret.

"I'm an excellent juggler," he says, wiping his hands on his pants, leaving stains behind. He reaches into his pocket, coming up with a stone, three acorns, a piece of crystal, and what appears to be a wishbone. "Juggling, you see, is just tossing two things in the air at the same time."

He begins to toss the acorns back and forth, then adds the wishbone. A few of the Larks nudge one another, whispering delightedly. "No matter how many things you add, you've got only two hands, so you can only toss two things. You've just got to throw faster and faster, higher and higher." He adds the stone and the crystal, the things flying between his hands fast enough that it's hard to see what he's tossing. I suck in a breath.

Then everything falls, crashing to the stone floor. The crystal shatters. One of the acorns rolls close to the fire.

"My advice," says Val Moren, "is that you learn to juggle better than I did, seneschal."

For a long moment, I am so angry that I can't move. I feel incandescent with it, betrayed by the one person who ought to understand how hard it is to be what we are, here.

Before I do something I will regret, I turn on my heels and walk away.

"I foretold you wouldn't take my advice," he calls after me.

CHAPTER 11

The evening of the Hunter's Moon, the whole Court moves to the Milkwood, where the trees are shrouded in masses of silk coverings that look, to my mortal eyes, like nothing so much as the egg sacks of moths, or perhaps the wrapped-up suppers of spiders.

Locke has had a structure of flat stones built up the way a wall might be, into the rough shape of a throne. A massive slab of rock serves for a back, with a wide stone for a seat. It towers over the grove. Cardan sits on it, crown gleaming at his brow. The nearby bonfire burns sage and yarrow. For a distorted moment, he seems larger than himself, moved into myth, the true High King of Faerie and no one's puppet.

Awe slows my step, panic following at my heels.

A king is a living symbol, a beating heart, a star upon which Elfhame's future is written. Surely you have noticed that since his reign began, the isles are different. Storms come in faster. Colors are a bit more vivid, smells are sharper. . . . When he becomes drunk, his subjects become tipsy without knowing why. When his blood falls, things grow.

I just hope he doesn't see any of this on my face. When I am in front of him, I bow my head, grateful for an excuse not to meet his eyes.

"My king," I say.

Cardan rises from the throne, unclasping a cape made entirely of gleaming black feathers. A new ring glimmers on his pinkie finger, red stone catching the flames of the bonfire. A very familiar ring. *My* ring.

I recall that he took my hand in his rooms.

I grind my teeth, stealing a glance at my own bare hand. He stole my ring. He stole it and I didn't notice. The Roach taught him how to do that.

I wonder if Nicasia would count that as a betrayal. It sure feels like one.

"Walk with me," he says, taking my hand and guiding me through the crowd. Hobs and grigs, green skin and brown, tattered wings and sculpted bark garments—all the Folk of Elfhame have come out tonight in their finery. We pass a man in a coat stitched with golden leaves and another in a green leather vest with a cap that curls up like a fern. Blankets cover the ground and are piled with trays of grapes the size of fists and ruby-bright cherries.

"What are we doing?" I ask as Cardan steers me to the edge of the woods.

"I find it tedious to have my every conversation remarked on," he says. "I want you to know your sister isn't here tonight. I made sure of it."

"So what does Locke have planned?" I ask, unwilling to be grateful and refusing to compliment him on his sleight of hand. "He's certainly staked his reputation on this evening."

Cardan makes a face. "I don't worry my pretty head about that kind of thing. You're the ones who are supposed to be doing the work. Like the ant in the fable who labors in the dirt while the grasshopper sings the summer away."

"And has nothing left for winter," I say.

"I need for nothing," he says, shaking his head, mock-mournful. "I am the Corn King, after all, to be sacrificed so little Oak can take my place in the spring."

Overhead, orbs have been lit and glow with warm, magical light as they drift through the night air, but his words send a shiver of dread through me.

I look into his eyes. His hand slides to my hip, as though he might pull me closer. For a dizzy, stupid moment, something seems to shimmer in the air between us.

Kiss me until I am sick of it.

He doesn't try to kiss me, of course. He hasn't been shot at, isn't delirious with drink, isn't filled with enough self-loathing.

"You ought not to be here tonight, little ant," he says, letting go of me. "Go back to the palace." Then he is cutting back through the crowd. Courtiers bow as he passes. A few, the most brazen, catch hold of his coat, flirt, try to pull him into the dance.

And he, who once ripped a boy's wing from his back because he wouldn't bow, now allows all this familiarity with a laugh.

What has changed? Is he different because I have forced him to be? Is it because he is away from Balekin? Or is he no different at all and I am only seeing what I want to see?

I still feel the warm pressure of his fingers against my skin. Something is really wrong with me, to want what I hate, to want someone who despises me, even if he wants me, too. My only comfort is that he doesn't know what I feel.

Whatever debauchery Locke has planned, I must stay to find the representative from the Court of Termites. The sooner my favor to their Lord Roiben is dismissed, the sooner I have one less debt hanging over my head. Besides, they can hardly offend me more than they have.

Cardan makes it back to the throne as Nicasia arrives with Grimsen, a moth pin holding his cloak.

Grimsen begins a speech that doubtlessly is flattering and produces something from a pocket. It looks like an earring—a single drop, which Cardan lifts to the light and admires. I guess he has made his first magical object in Elfhame's service.

In the tree to the left of them, I see the hob-faced owl, Snapdragon, blinking down. Although I can't spot them, the Ghost and several more spies are nearby, watching the revel from enough distance that if a move is made, they will be there.

A centaur-like musician with the body of a deer has come forward—one carrying a lyre carved in the shape of a pixie, her wings forming the top curve of the instrument. It is strung with what appears to be thread of many colors. The musician begins to play, the carving to sing.

Nicasia saunters over to where the smith is sitting. She wears a dress of purple that is peacock blue when it catches the light. Her hair is woven into a braid that circles her head, and at her brow is a chain from which dangle dozens upon dozens of beads in sparkling purples and blues and amber.

When Grimsen turns toward her, his expression lightens. I frown.

Jugglers begin tossing a series of objects—from live rats to shiny swords—into the air. Wine and honeyed cakes are passed around.

Finally, I spot Dulcamara from the Court of Termites, her red-as-poppies hair bound up into coils and a two-handed blade strapped across her back, a silver dress blowing around her. I walk over, trying not to seem intimidated.

"Welcome," I say. "To what do we owe the honor of your visit? Has your king found something I could do—"

She cuts me off with a glance toward Cardan. "Lord Roiben wants you to know that even in the low Courts, we hear things."

For a moment, my mind goes through an anxious inventory of all the things Dulcamara might have heard, then I remember that the Folk have been whispering that Cardan shot one of his lovers for his own amusement. The Court of Termites is one of the few Courts to have both Seelie and Unseelie members; I'm not sure if they'd mind about the hurt courtier or just the possibility of an unstable High King.

"Even without liars, there can still be lies," I say carefully. "Whatever rumors you heard, I can explain what really happened."

"Because I ought to believe you? I think not." She smiles. "We can call in our marker anytime we like, mortal girl. Lord Roiben may send me to you, for instance, to be your personal guard." I wince. By *guard* she obviously means *spy*. "Or perhaps we will borrow your smith, Grimsen. He could make Lord Roiben a blade that cuts clean through vows."

"I haven't forgotten my debt. Indeed, I hoped you would let me repay it now," I say, drawing myself up to my full authority. "But Lord Roiben shouldn't forget—"

She cuts me off with a snarl. "See that *you* don't forget." With that, she stalks off, leaving me to think of all the smarter things I should have said. I still owe a debt to the Court of Termites, and I still have no way to extend my power over Cardan. I still have no idea who might have betrayed me or what to do about Nicasia.

At least this revel does not seem particularly worse than any other, for all of Locke's braggadocio. I wonder if it might be possible for me to do what Taryn wants and get him ousted as Master of Revels after all, just for being boring.

As though Locke can read my thoughts, he claps his hands together, silencing the crowd. Music stutters to a stop, and with it the dancing and juggling, even the laughter.

"I have another amusement for you," he says. "It is time to crown a monarch tonight. The Queen of Mirth."

One of the lutists plays a merry improvisation. There is scattered laughter from the audience.

A chill goes through me. I have heard of the game, although I have never seen it played. It is simple enough: Steal away a mortal girl, make her drunk on faerie wine and faerie flattery and faerie kisses, then convince her she is being honored with a crown—all the time heaping insults on her oblivious head.

If Locke has brought some mortal girl here to have fun at her expense, he will have me to reckon with. I will lash him to the black rocks of Insweal for the mermaids to devour.

While I am still thinking that, Locke says, "But surely only a king can crown a queen."

Cardan stands up from the throne, stepping down the stones to be beside Locke. His long, feathered cape slithers after him.

"So where is she?" the High King asks, brows raised. He doesn't seem amused, and I am hopeful he will end this before it begins. What possible satisfaction could he find in the game?

"Haven't you guessed? There is only one mortal among our company," Locke says. "Why, our Queen of Mirth is none other than Jude Duarte."

For a moment, my mind goes entirely blank. I cannot think. Then I see Locke's grin and the grinning faces of the Folk of the Court, and all my feelings curdle into dread.

"Let's have a cheer for her," says Locke.

They cry out in their inhuman voices, and I have to choke down panic. I look over at Cardan and find something dangerous glittering in his eyes—I will get no sympathy there.

Nicasia is smiling exultantly, and beside her, the smith, Grimsen, is clearly diverted. Dulcamara, at the edge of the woods, watches to see what I will do.

I guess Locke has done something right at last. He promised the High King delights, and I am entirely sure that Cardan is thoroughly delighted.

I could order him to stop whatever happens next. He knows it, too, which means that he supposes I will hate what he's about to do, but not enough to command him and reveal all.

Of course, there's a lot I would endure before I did that.

You will regret this. I don't say the words, but I look at Cardan and think them with such force that it feels as though I am shouting.

Locke gives a signal, and a group of imps comes forward carrying an ugly, tattered dress, along with a circle of branches. Affixed to the makeshift crown are foul little mushrooms, the kind that produce a putrid-smelling dust.

I swear under my breath.

"New raiment for our new queen," Locke says.

There is some scattered laughter and gasps of surprise. This is a cruel game, meant to be played on mortal girls when they're glamoured so they don't know they're being laughed at. That's the fun of it, their foolishness. They delight over dresses that appear like finery to them. They exult greedily over crowns seeming to gleam with jewels. They swoon at the promise of true love.

Thanks to Prince Dain's geas, faerie glamours do not work on me, but even if they did, every member of the Court expects the High King's human seneschal to be wearing a charm of protection—a strand of rowan berries, a tiny bundle of oak, ash, and thorn twigs. They know I see the truth of what Locke is giving me.

The Court watches me with eager, indrawn breaths. I am sure they have never watched a Queen of Mirth who knew she was being mocked before. This is a new kind of game.

"Tell us what you think of our lady," Locke asks Cardan loudly, with a strange smile.

The High King's expression stiffens, only to smooth out a moment later when he turns toward the Court. "I have too often been troubled by dreams of Jude," he says, voice carrying. "Her face features prominently in my most frequent nightmare."

The courtiers laugh. Heat floods my face because he's telling them a secret and using that secret to mock me.

When Eldred was High King, his revels were staid, but a new High King isn't just a renewal of the land, but of the Court itself. I can tell he delights them with his caprices and his capacity for cruelty. I was a fool to be tempted into thinking he's any different than he's always been. "Some among us do not find mortals beautiful. In fact, some of you might swear that Jude is unlovely."

For a moment, I wonder if he *wants* me to be furious enough to order him to stop and reveal our bargain to the Court. But no, it's only that with my heart thundering in my head, I can barely think.

"But I believe it is only that her beauty is... unique." Cardan pauses for more laughter from the crowd, greater jeering. "Excruciating. Alarming. *Distressing*."

"Perhaps she needs new raiment to bring out her true allure," Locke says. "Greater finery for one so fine."

The imps move to pull the tattered, threadbare rag gown over my own to the delight of the Folk.

More laughter. My whole body feels hot. Part of me wants to run away, but I am caught by the desire to show them I cannot be cowed.

"Wait," I say, pitching my voice loud enough to carry. The imps hesitate. Cardan's expression is unreadable.

I reach down and catch hold of my hem, then pull the dress I am wearing over my head. It's a simple thing—no corset, no clasps—and it comes off just as simply. I stand in the middle of the party in my underwear, daring them to say something. Daring Cardan to speak.

"*Now* I am ready to put on my new gown," I say. There are a few cheers, as though they don't understand the game is humiliation. Locke, surprisingly, appears delighted.

Cardan steps close to me, his gaze devouring. I am not sure I can bear his cutting me down again. Luckily, he seems at a loss for words.

"I hate you," I whisper before he can speak.

He tilts my face to his.

"Say it again," he says as the imps comb my hair and place the ugly, stinking crown on my head. His voice is low. The words are for me alone.

I pull out of his grip, but not before I see his expression. He looks as he did when he was forced to answer my questions, when he admitted his desire for me. He looks as though he's confessing.

A flush goes through me, confusing because I am both furious and shamed. I turn my head.

"Queen of Mirth, time for your first dance," Locke tells me, pushing me toward the crowd.

Clawed fingers close on my arms. Inhuman laughter rings in my ears as the music starts. When the dance begins anew, I am in it. My feet slap down on the dirt in time with the pounding rhythm of the drums, my heart speeds with the trill of a flute. I am spun around, passed hand to hand through the crowd. Pushed and shoved, pinched and bruised.

I try to pull against the compulsion of the music, try to break away from the dance, but I cannot. When I try to drag my feet, hands haul me along until the music catches me up again. Everything becomes a wild blur of sound and flying cloth, of shiny inkdrop eyes and too-sharp teeth.

I am lost to it, out of my own control, as though I were a child again, as though I hadn't bargained with Dain and poisoned myself and stolen the throne. This is not glamour. I cannot stop myself from dancing, cannot stop my body from moving even as my terror grows. I will not stop. I will dance through the leather of my shoes, dance until my feet are bloody, dance until I collapse.

"Cease playing!" I shout as loudly as I can, panic giving my voice the edge of a scream. "As your Queen of Mirth, as the seneschal of the High King, you will allow me to choose the dance!"

The musicians pause. The footfalls of the dancers slow. It is only perhaps a moment's reprieve, but I wasn't sure I could get even that.

I am shaking all over with fury and fear and the strain of fighting my own body.

I draw myself up, pretending with the rest of them that I am decked out in finery instead of rags. "Let's have a reel," I say, trying to imagine the way my stepmother, Oriana, would have spoken the words. For once, my voice comes out just the way I want, full of cool command. "And I will dance it with my king, who has showered me with so many compliments and gifts tonight."

The Court watches me with their glistening, wet eyes. These are words they might expect the Queen of Mirth to say, the ones I am sure countless mortals have spoken before under different circumstances.

I hope it unnerves them to know I am lying.

After all, if the insult to me is pointing out that I am mortal, then this is my riposte: I live here, too, and I know the rules. Perhaps I even know them better than you since you were born into them, but I had to learn. Perhaps I know them better than you because you have greater leeway to break them.

"Will you dance with me?" I ask Cardan, sinking into a curtsy, acid in my voice. "For I find you every bit as beautiful as you find me."

A hiss goes through the crowd. I have scored a point on Cardan, and the Court is not sure how to feel about it. They like unfamiliar things, like surprises, but perhaps they are wondering if they will like this one.

Still, they seem riveted by my little performance.

Cardan's smile is unreadable.

"I'd be delighted," he says as the musicians begin to play again. He sweeps me into his arms.

We danced once before, at the coronation of Prince Dain. Before the murdering began. Before I took Cardan prisoner at knifepoint. I wonder if he is thinking of it when he spins me around the Milkwood.

He might not be particularly practiced with a blade, but as he promised the hag's daughter, he's a skilled dancer. I let him steer me through steps I doubtlessly would have fumbled on my own. My heart is racing, and my skin is slicked with sweat.

Papery moths fly above our heads, circling up as though tragically drawn to the light of the stars.

"Whatever you do to me," I say, too angry to stay quiet, "I can do worse to you."

"Oh," he says, fingers tight on mine. "Do not think I forget that for a moment."

"Then *why*?" I demand.

"You believe I planned your humiliation?" He laughs. "Me? That sounds like work."

"I don't care if you did or not," I tell him, too angry to make sense of my feelings. "I just care that you enjoyed it."

"And why shouldn't I delight to see you squirm? You tricked me," Cardan says. "You played me for a fool, and now I am the King of Fools."

"The *High* King of Fools," I say, a sneer in my voice. Our gazes meet, and there's a shock of mutual understanding that our bodies are pressed too closely. I am conscious of my skin, of the sweat beading on my lip, of the slide of my thighs against each other. I am aware of the warmth of his neck beneath my twined fingers, of the prickly brush of his hair and how I want to sink my hands into it. I inhale the scent of him—moss and oakwood and leather. I stare at his treacherous mouth and imagine it on me.

Everything about this is wrong. Around us, the revel is resuming. Some of the Court glance our way, because some of the Court always look to the High King, but Locke's game is at an end.

Go back to the palace, Cardan said, and I ignored the warning.

I think of Locke's expression while Cardan spoke, the eagerness in his face. It wasn't me he was watching. I wonder for the first time if my humiliation was incidental, the bait to his hook.

Tell us what you think of our lady.

To my immense relief, at the end of the reel, the musicians pause again, looking to the High King for instructions.

I pull away from him. "I am overcome, Your Majesty. I would like your permission to withdraw."

For a moment, I wonder what I will do if Cardan denies me permission. I have issued many commands, but none about sparing my feelings.

"You are free to depart or stay, as you like," Cardan says magnanimously. "The Queen of Mirth is welcome wheresoever she goes."

I turn away from him and stumble out of the revel to lean against a tree, sucking in breaths of cool sea air. My cheeks are hot, my face is burning.

At the edge of the Milkwood, I watch waves beating against the black rocks. After a moment, I notice shapes on the sand, as though shadows were moving on their own. I blink again. Not shadows. Selkies, rising from the sea. A score, at least. They cast off their sleek sealskins and raise silver blades.

The Undersea has come to the Hunter's Moon revel.

CHAPTER 12

I rush back, tearing the long gown on thorns and briars in my haste. I go immediately to the nearest member of the guard. He looks startled when I run up, out of breath, still clad in the rags of the Queen of Mirth.

"The Undersea," I manage. "Selkies. They're coming. Protect the king."

He doesn't hesitate, doesn't doubt me. He calls together his knights and moves to flank the throne. Cardan looks at their movement in confusion, and then with a brief, bright spark of panic. No doubt he is recalling how Madoc ordered the circling of the guards around the dais at Prince Dain's coronation ceremony, just before Balekin started murdering people.

Before I can explain, out of the Milkwood step the selkies, their sleek bodies bare except for long ropes of seaweed and pearls around their throats. The playing of instruments ceases. Laughter gutters out.

Reaching to my thigh, I take out the long knife holstered there.

"What is this?" Cardan demands, standing.

A female selkie bows and steps to one side. Behind them come the Gentry of the Undersea. Walking on legs I am not sure they possessed an hour before, they sweep through the grove in soaking-wet gowns and doublets and hose, seeming not at all discomfited. They look ferocious even in their finery.

My eyes search the crowd for Nicasia, but neither she nor the smith are there. Locke sits on one of the arms of the throne, looking for all the world as though he takes for granted that if Cardan is High King, then being High King cannot be so special.

"Your Majesty," says a gray-skinned man in a coat that appears to be made from the skin of a shark. He has a strange voice, one that seems hoarse with disuse. "Orlagh, Queen of the Undersea, sends us with a message for the High King. Grant us permission to speak."

The half circle of knights around Cardan tightens.

Cardan does not immediately answer. Instead, he sits. "The Undersea is welcome at this Hunter's Moon revel. Dance. Drink. Never let it be said that we are not generous hosts, even to uninvited guests."

The man kneels, but his expression is not at all humble. "Your munificence is great. And yet, we may not partake of it until our lady's message is delivered. You must hear us."

"Must I? Very well," the High King says after a moment. He makes an airy gesture. "What has she to say?"

The gray-skinned man beckons a girl in a wet blue dress, her hair up in braids. When she opens her mouth, I see that her teeth are thin, viciously pointed, and oddly translucent. She intones the words in a singsong:

The Sea needs a bridegroom,
The Land needs a bride.
Cleave together lest
You face the rising tide.
Spurn the Sea once,
We will have your blood.
Spurn the Sea twice,
We will have your clay.
Spurn the Sea thrice,
Your crown will away.

The gathered Folk of the land, courtiers and petitioners, servants and Gentry, grow wide-eyed at the words.

"Is that a proposal?" Locke asks. I think he means to speak so that only Cardan hears him, but in the silence, his voice carries.

"A threat, I'm afraid," Cardan returns. He glares at the girl, at the gray-skinned man, at everyone. "You've delivered your message. I have no bit of doggerel to send back—my own fault for having a seneschal who cannot double as my Court Poet—but I will be sure to crumple up some paper and drop it into the water when I do."

For a moment, everyone stays as they were, exactly in their places.

Cardan claps his hands, startling the sea Folk. "Well?" he shouts. "Dance! Make merry! Isn't that what you came for?"

His voice rings with authority. He no longer just *looks* like the High King of Elfhame; he *sounds* like the High King.

A shiver of premonition goes through me.

The Undersea courtiers, in their sodden garments and gleaming pearls, watch him with pale, cold eyes. Their faces are unexpressive enough that I cannot tell if his shouting upset them. But when the music begins again, they take one another's webbed hands and sweep away into the revel, to leap and cavort as though this was something they did for pleasure themselves beneath the waves.

My spies have remained hidden through this encounter. Locke melts away from the throne to whirl with two mostly naked selkies. Nicasia remains nowhere to be seen, and when I look for Dulcamara, I cannot spot her, either. Dressed as I am, I cannot bear to speak with anyone in an official capacity. I tear the stinking crown from my head and toss it into the grass.

I think about shimmying out of the tattered gown, but before I can decide to actually do it, Cardan waves me over to the throne.

I do not bow. Tonight, after all, I am a ruler in my own right. The Queen of Mirth, who is not laughing.

"I thought you were leaving," he snaps.

"And I thought the Queen of Mirth was welcome wheresoever she goes," I hiss back.

"Assemble the Living Council in my rooms in the palace," he tells me, voice cold and remote and royal. "I will join you as soon as I can get away."

I nod and am halfway through the crowd when I realize two things: One, he gave me an order; and two, I obeyed it.

Once at the palace, I send out pages to summon the Council. I send Snapdragon with a message for my spies to discover where Nicasia has gone. I would have thought that she'd make herself available to hear

Cardan's answer, but given that she was uncertain enough about Cardan's feelings to shoot a rival lover, maybe she's reluctant to hear it.

Even if she believes he'd choose her over a war, that's not saying much.

In my rooms, I strip off my clothes quickly and wash myself. I want to be rid of the perfume of the mushrooms, the stink of the fire, and the humiliation. It feels like a blessing to have my old clothing there. I tug on a dull brown dress, too simple for my current position but comforting all the same. I pull back my hair with ruthless severity.

Tatterfell is no longer around, but it's obvious she's been by. My rooms are tidy, my things pressed and hung.

And sitting on my desk, a note addressed to me: *From the Grand General of the High King's Army to His Majesty's Seneschal.*

I rip it open. The note is shorter than what is written on the envelope:

Come to the war room immediately.
Do not wait for the Council.

My heart thuds dully. I consider pretending I didn't get the message and simply not going, but that would be cowardice.

If Madoc still has hopes of scheming Oak onto the throne, he can't let a marriage to the Undersea happen. He has no reason to know that, in this at least, I am entirely on his side. This is a good opportunity to get him to show his hand.

And so, I head reluctantly to his war room. It's familiar; I played here as a child under a large wooden table covered in a map of Faerie, with little carved figures to represent its Courts and armies. His "dolls," as Vivi used to call them.

When I let myself in, I find it dimly lit. Candles burn low on a desk beside a few stiff chairs.

I recall reading a book curled up in one of those chairs while beside me violent plots were hatched.

Looking up from the very same chair, Madoc rises and gestures for me to sit opposite him, as though we are equals. He is being interestingly careful with me.

On the strategy board, there are only a few figures. Orlagh and Cardan, Madoc and a figure I do not recognize until I study it more carefully. It is myself I am looking at, rendered in carved wood. Seneschal. Spymaster. Kingmaker.

I am abruptly afraid of what I have done to make it onto that board.

"I got your note," I tell him, settling into a chair.

"After tonight, I thought you might be finally reconsidering some of the choices you made," he says.

I begin to speak, but he holds up a clawed hand to stop my words. "Were I you," he goes on, "my pride might lead me to pretend otherwise. The Folk cannot tell lies, as you know, not with our tongues. But we can deceive. And we are as capable of self-deceit as any mortal."

I am stung by his knowing I was crowned Queen of Mirth and laughed at by the Court. "You don't think I know what I'm doing?"

"Well," he says carefully, "not for certain. What I see is you humiliating yourself with the youngest and most foolish of princes. Did he promise you something?"

I bite the inside of my cheek to keep from snapping at him. No matter how low I already feel, if he thinks me a fool, then a fool I must allow myself to be. "I am seneschal to the High King, am I not?"

It's just hard to dissemble with the laughter of the Court still ringing in my ears. With the foul dust of those mushrooms still in my hair and the memory of Cardan's obnoxious words.

Excruciating. Alarming. Distressing.

Madoc sighs and spreads his hands in front of him. "Do you know why Eldred had no interest in his youngest son? Baphen saw ill fortune in his stars from the moment of his birth. Yet so long as Cardan wears the Blood Crown, I am sworn to him as surely as I was to his father, as surely as I would have been to Dain or even Balekin. The opportunity that presented itself at the coronation—the opportunity to change the course of destiny—is lost to me."

He pauses. However he phrases it, the meaning is the same. The opportunity was lost because I stole it from him. I am the reason Oak is not the High King and Madoc isn't using his influence to remake Elfhame in his image.

"But you," Madoc says, "who are not bound by your words. Whose promises can be forsworn..."

I think of what he said to me after the last Living Council meeting, as we walked: *No oath binds you. If you regret your move, make another. There are games yet to play.* I see he has chosen this moment to expand upon his theme.

"You want me to betray Cardan," I say, just to make things clear.

He stands and beckons me to the strategy table. "I don't know what knowledge you have of the Queen of the Undersea from her daughter, but once, the Undersea was a place much like the land. It had many fiefdoms, with many rulers among the selkies and merfolk.

"When Orlagh came into power, she hunted down each of the smaller rulers and murdered them, so the whole Undersea would answer only to her. There are yet a few rulers of the sea she hasn't brought beneath her thumb, a few too powerful and a few more too remote. But if she marries her daughter to Cardan, you can be sure she will push Nicasia to do the same on land."

"Murder the heads of the smaller Courts?" I ask.

He smiles. "Of all the Courts. Perhaps at first it will seem like a series of accidents—or a few foolish orders. Or maybe it will be another bloodbath."

I study him carefully. After all, the last bloodbath was at least partially his doing. "And do you disagree with Orlagh's philosophy? Would you have done much the same were you the power behind the throne?"

"I wouldn't have done it on behalf of the sea," he says. "She means to have the land as her vassal." He reaches for the table and picks up a small figurine, one carved to represent Queen Orlagh. "She believes in the forced peace of absolute rule."

I look at the board.

"You wanted to impress me," he says. "You guessed, rightly, that I would not see your true potential until you bested me. Consider me impressed, Jude. But it would be better for both of us to stop fighting each other and focus on our common interest: power."

That hangs in the air ominously. A compliment delivered in the form of a threat. He goes on. "But now, come back to my side. Come back before I move against you in earnest."

"What does coming back look like?" I ask.

He gives me an evaluating stare, as though wondering just how much to say out loud. "I have a plan. When the time comes, you can help me implement it."

"A plan I didn't help make and that you won't tell me much about?" I ask. "What if I'm more interested in the power I already have?"

He smiles, showing his teeth. "Then I guess I don't know my daughter very well. Because the Jude I knew would cut out that boy's heart for what he did to you tonight."

At the shame of having the revel thrown in my face, I snap. "You let me be humiliated in Faerie from the time I was a child. You've let Folk hurt me and laugh at me and mutilate me." I hold up the hand with the missing fingertip, where one of his own guards bit it clean off. Another scar is at its center, from where Dain forced me to stick a dagger through my hand. "I've been glamoured and carried into a revel, weeping and alone. As far as I can tell, the only difference between tonight and all the other nights when I endured indignities without complaint is that those benefited you, and when I endure this, it benefits me."

Madoc looks shaken. "I didn't know."

"You didn't want to know," I return.

He turns his gaze to the board, to the pieces on it, to the little figurine that represents me. "That argument's a fine strike, right at my liver, but I am not so sure it does as well as a parry. The boy is unworthy—"

He would have kept on talking, but the door opens and Randalin is there, peering in, his robes of state looking hastily tugged on. "Oh, both of you. Good. The meeting is about to begin. Make haste."

As I start to follow, Madoc grabs my arm. His voice is pitched low. "You tried to tell us that this was going to happen. All I ask from you tonight is that you use your power as seneschal to block any alliance with the Undersea."

"Yes," I say, thinking of Nicasia and Oak and all my plans. "That I can guarantee."

CHAPTER 13

The Living Council gathers in the High King's enormous chambers, around a table inlaid with the symbol of the Greenbriar line, flowers and thorns with coiling roots.

Nihuar, Randalin, Baphen, and Mikkel are seated, while Fala stands in the middle of the floor singing a little song:

Fishies. Fishies. Putting on their feet.
Marry a fish and life will be sweet.
Fry her in a pan and pick out her bones.
Fishy blood is cold 'top a throne.

Cardan throws himself onto a nearby couch with dramatic flair, disdaining the table entirely. "This is ridiculous. Where is Nicasia?"

"We must discuss this offer," says Randalin.

"*Offer?*" scoffs Madoc, taking a seat. "The way it was delivered, I am not sure how he could marry the girl without seeming as though the land feared the sea and capitulated to its demands."

"Perhaps it was a trifle heavy-handed," says Nihuar.

"Time for us to prepare," Madoc says. "If it's war she wants, it is war we will give her. I will pull the salt from the sea before I let Elfhame tremble over Orlagh's wrath."

War, exactly what I feared Madoc would rush us into, and yet now it arrives without his instigation.

"Well," says Cardan, closing his eyes as though he is going to nap right there. "No need for me to do a thing, then."

Madoc's lip curls. Randalin looks slightly discomposed. For so long, he wanted Cardan at meetings of the Living Council, but now he isn't quite sure what to do with his actual presence.

"You could take Nicasia as your consort instead of your bride," says Randalin. "Get an heir on her fit to rule over land and sea."

"Now I am not to marry at Orlagh's command, only breed?" Cardan demands.

"I want to hear from Jude," Madoc says, to my enormous surprise.

The rest of the Council turns toward me. They seem utterly baffled by Madoc's words. In meetings, my only value has been as a conduit between themselves and the High King. Now, with his representing himself, I might as well be one of the little wooden figures on a strategy board for all they expect me to speak.

"Whatever for?" Randalin wants to know.

"Because we didn't heed her before. She told us that the Queen of the Undersea was going to move against the land. Had we attended her, we might not now be scrambling for strategy."

Randalin winces.

"That's true enough," says Nihuar, as though she is trying to think of a way to explain away this troubling sign of competence.

"Perhaps she will tell us what else she knows," Madoc says.

Mikkel's eyebrows rise.

"Is there more?" Baphen asks.

"Jude?" prompts Madoc.

I weigh my next words. "As I said, Orlagh has been communicating with Balekin. I don't know what information he's passed on to her, but the sea sends Folk to the land with gifts and messages for him."

Cardan looks surprised and clearly unhappy. I realize that I neglected to tell him about Balekin and the Undersea, despite informing the Council. "Did you know about Nicasia as well?" he asks.

"I, uh—" I begin, foundering.

"She likes to keep her own counsel on the Council," Baphen says with a sly look.

As though it's my fault none of them listens to me.

Randalin glowers. "You never explained how you learned any of this."

"If you're asking whether I have secrets, I could easily ask the same of you," I remind him. "Previously, you weren't interested in any of mine."

"Prince of the land, prince under the waves," says Fala. "Prince of prisons, prince of knaves."

"Balekin's no strategist," Madoc says, which is as close to admitting he was behind Eldred's execution as he's ever done. "He's ambitious, though. And proud."

"*Spurn the Sea once, we will have your blood,*" says Cardan. "That's Oak, I imagine."

Madoc and I share a swift look. The one thing we agree on is that

Oak will be kept safe. I am glad he's far from here, inland, with both spies and knights looking out for him. But if Cardan is correct about what the line means, I wonder if he will need even more protection than that.

"If the Undersea is planning to steal Oak, then perhaps they promised Balekin the crown," says Mikkel. "Safer for there to be only two in the bloodline, when one is needed to crown the other. Three is superfluous. Three is dangerous."

Which is a roundabout way of saying somebody should kill Balekin before he tries to assassinate Cardan.

I wouldn't mind seeing Balekin dead, either, but Cardan has been stubbornly against the execution of his brother. I think of the words he said to me in the Court of Shadows: *I may be rotten, but my one virtue is that I'm not a killer.*

"I will take that under advisement, advisors," says Cardan. "Now, I wish to speak with Nicasia."

"But we still haven't decided . . ." Randalin says, trailing off when he sees the scorching glare Cardan levels at him.

"Jude, go fetch her," says the High King of Elfhame. Another order.

I get up, grinding my teeth, and go to the door. The Ghost is waiting for me. "Where's Nicasia?" I ask.

It turns out that she's been put in my rooms, with the Roach. Her dove-gray dress is arranged on my divan as though she's posing for a painting. I wonder if the reason she rushed off was so she could change clothing for this audience.

"Look what the wind blew in," she says when she sees me.

"The High King requires your presence," I tell her.

She gives me a strange smile and rises. "If only that were true."

Down the hall we go, knights watching her pass. She looks majestic and miserable at once, and when the huge doors to Cardan's apartments open, she goes inside with her head high.

While I was gone, a servant brought in tea. It steeps in a pot at the center of a low table. A cup of it steams in the cage of Cardan's slender fingers.

"Nicasia," he drawls. "Your mother has sent a message for us both."

She frowns, taking in the other councilors, the lack of an invitation to sit, and the lack of an offer to take tea. "This was her scheme, not mine."

He leans forward, no longer sleepy or bored but every bit the terrifying faerie lord, empty-eyed and incalculably powerful. "Perhaps, but you knew she'd do it, I'll wager. Do not play with me. We know each other too well for tricks."

Nicasia looks down, eyelashes brushing her cheeks. "She desires a different kind of alliance." Perhaps the Council might see her as meek and humbled, but I am not yet so foolish.

Cardan stands, hurling his teacup at the wall, where it shatters. "Tell the Queen of the Undersea that if she threatens me again, she will find her daughter my prisoner instead of my bride."

Nicasia looks stricken.

Randalin finally finds his voice. "It is not meet to throw things at the daughter of the Undersea."

"Little fishie," says Fala, "take off your legs and swim away."

Mikkel barks out a laugh.

"We must not be hasty," says Randalin helplessly. "Princess, let the High King take more time to consider."

I worried that Cardan would be amused or flattered or tempted. Instead, he's clearly furious.

"Let me speak with my mother." Nicasia looks around the room, at the councilors, at me, before seeming to decide that she's not going to persuade Cardan to send us away. She does the next best thing, turning her gaze only to him and speaking as though we're not there. "The sea is harsh, and so are Queen Orlagh's methods. She demands when she ought to request, but that doesn't mean there isn't wisdom in what she wants."

"Would you marry me, then? Tie the sea to the land and bind us together in misery?" Cardan gazes at her with all the scorn he once reserved for me. It feels as though the world has been turned upside down.

But Nicasia does not back down. Instead, she takes a step closer. "We would be legends," she tells him. "Legends need not concern themselves with something as small as happiness."

And then, without waiting to be dismissed, she turns and goes out. Without being ordered, the guards part to let her by.

"Ah," says Madoc. "That one behaves as though she is queen already."

"Out," says Cardan, and then when no one reacts, he makes a wild gesture in the air. "Out! Out. I am certain you wish to deliberate further as though I am not in the room, so go do it where I am not in the room. Go and trouble me no more."

"Your pardon," says Randalin. "We meant only—"

"Out!" he says, at which point even Fala heads for the door.

"Except Jude," he calls. "You, tarry a moment."

You. I turn toward him, the humiliation of the night still hot on my skin. I think of all my secrets and plans, and of what it will mean if we go to war with the Undersea, of what I've risked and what is already forever lost.

I let the others leave, waiting until the last of the Living Council is out of the room.

"Give me an order again," I say, "and I will show you true shame. Locke's games will be as nothing to what I make you do."

With that, I follow the others into the hall.

In the Court of Shadows, I consider what moves are possible.

Murder Balekin. Mikkel wasn't wrong that it would make it harder for the Undersea to wrest the crown from Cardan's head.

Marry Cardan to someone else. I think of Mother Marrow and almost regret interfering. If Cardan had a hag's daughter for a bride, perhaps Orlagh wouldn't have engaged in such martial matchmaking.

Of course, I would have had other problems.

A headache starts up behind my eyes. I rub my fingers over the bridge of my nose.

With Taryn's wedding so close, Oak will be here in mere days. I don't like the thought of it with Orlagh's threat hanging over Elfhame. He is too valuable a piece on the strategy board, too necessary for Balekin, too dangerous for Cardan.

I recall the last time I saw Balekin, the influence he had over the guard, the way he behaved as though he were the king in exile. And all my reports from Vulciber suggest that not much has changed. He demands luxuries, he entertains visitors from the sea who leave puddles and pearls behind. I wonder what they've told him, what promises he's been made. Despite Nicasia's belief that he won't be necessary, he must be hoping just the opposite.

And then I recall something else—the woman who wanted to tell me about my mother. She's been there the whole time, and if she's willing to sell one kind of information for her freedom, maybe she's willing to sell another.

As I think over what I'd like to know, it occurs to me how much more useful it would be to send information *to* Balekin, instead of getting information out of him.

If I let that prisoner believe I was temporarily freeing her to tell me about my mother, then I could drop some information in her ear. Something about Oak, something about his whereabouts or vulnerability. She wouldn't be lying when she passed it on; she would believe she'd heard true and spoke truth.

I puzzle further and realize, no, it's too soon for that. What I need now is to give the prisoner simpler information that she can pass on, information I can control and verify, so that I can be sure she's a good source.

Balekin wanted to send Cardan a message. I will find a way to let him.

The Court of Shadows has begun to formalize the scribing of documents on the denizens of Elfhame, but none of the current scrolls deal with any prisoners in the Tower but Balekin. Walking down the hall, I go to the Bomb's newly dug office.

She's there, throwing daggers at a painting of a sunset.

"You didn't like it?" I ask, pointing to the canvas.

"I liked it well enough," she says. "Now I like it better."

"I need a prisoner from the Tower of Forgetting. Do we have enough uniforms to dress up some of our new recruits? The knights there have seen my face. Vulciber can help smooth things over, but I'd rather not risk it. Better to forge some papers and have her out with fewer questions."

She frowns in concentration. "Whom do you want?"

"There's a woman." I take a piece of paper and grid out the bottom floor as well as I can. "She was up the staircase. Here. All on her own."

The Bomb frowns. "Can you describe her?"

I shrug. "Thin face, horns. Pretty, I guess. You're all pretty."

"What kind of horns?" the Bomb asks, tilting her head to one side as though she's considering something. "Straight? Curved?"

I gesture to the top of my head where I remember hers being. "Little ones. Goatish, I guess. And she had a tail."

"There aren't that many Folk in the Tower," the Bomb explains. "The woman you're describing..."

"Do you know her?" I ask.

"I've never spoken a word to her," the Bomb says. "But I know who she is—or who she was: one of Eldred's lovers who begot him a son. That's Cardan's mother."

CHAPTER 14

I drum my fingernails against Dain's old desk as the Roach leads the prisoner in.

"Her name is Asha," he says. "*Lady* Asha."

Asha is thin and so pale that she seems a little gray. She does not look much like the laughing woman I saw in the crystal globe.

She is looking around the room in an ecstasy of confusion. It's clear that she's pleased to be away from the Tower of Forgetting. Her eyes are hungry, drinking in every detail of even this rather dull room.

"What was her crime?" I ask, downplaying my knowledge. I hope she will set the game and show more of herself that way.

The Roach grunts, playing along. "She was Eldred's consort, and when he tired of her, she got tossed into the Tower."

There was doubtlessly more to it than that, but all I have discovered is that it concerned the death of another lover of the High King's and, somehow, Cardan's involvement.

"Hard luck," I say, indicating the chair in front of my desk. The one to which, five long months ago, Cardan had been tied. "Come sit."

I can see his face in hers. They share those ridiculous cheekbones, that soft mouth.

She sits, gaze turning sharply to me. "I have a powerful thirst."

"Do you, now?" the Roach asks, licking a corner of his lip with his black tongue. "Perhaps a cup of wine would restore you."

"I am chilled, too," she tells him. "Cold down to the bone. Cold as the sea."

The Roach shares a look with me. "You tarry here with our own Shadow Queen, and I will see to the rest."

I do not know what I did to deserve such an extravagant title and fear it has been bestowed upon me as one might bestow an enormous troll with the moniker "Tiny," but it does seem to impress her.

The Roach steps out, leaving us alone. My gaze follows him for a moment, thinking of the Bomb and her secret. Then I turn to Lady Asha.

"You said you knew my mother," I remind her, hoping to draw her out with that, until I can figure out how to move on to what I really must know.

Her expression is of slight surprise, as though she is so distracted by her surroundings that she forgot her reason for being here. "You resemble her very strongly."

"Her secrets," I prompt. "You said you knew secrets about her."

Finally, she smiles. "Eva found it tedious to have to do without *everything* from her old life. Oh, it was fun for her at first to be in Faerieland—it always is, but eventually they get homesick. We used to sneak across the sea to be among mortals and take back little things she missed.

Bars of waxy chocolate. Perfume. Pantyhose. That was before Justin, of course."

Justin and Eva. Eva and Justin. My mother and my father. My stomach lurches at the thought of their being two people Asha knew better than I ever did.

"Of course," I echo anyway.

She leans forward, across the desk. "You look like her. You look like them both."

And you look like him, I think.

"You've heard the story, I'll wager," Asha says. "How one or both of them killed a woman and burned the body to hide your mother's disappearance from Madoc. I could tell you about that. I could tell you how it happened."

"I brought you here so you could do just that," I tell her. "So you could tell me everything you know."

"Then have me thrown back in the Tower? No. My information is worth a price."

Before I can answer, the door opens, and the Roach comes in carrying a tray piled with cheese and brown bread and a steaming cup of spiced wine. He wears a cape over his shoulders, and after setting down the food, he sweeps it onto her like a blanket.

"Any other requests?" he asks.

"She was just getting to that," I tell him.

"Freedom," she says. "I wish to be away from the Tower of Forgetting, and I wish safe passage away from Insmoor, Insweal, and Insmire. Moreover, I want your promise that the High King of Elfhame will never become aware of my release."

"Eldred is dead," I tell her. "You have nothing to worry about."

"I know who the High King is," she corrects sharply. "And I don't want to be discovered by him once I am free."

The Roach's eyebrows rise.

In the silence, she takes a big swallow of wine. She bites off a hunk of cheese.

It occurs to me that Cardan very likely knows where his mother was sent. If he has done nothing to get her out, nothing to so much as see her since becoming High King, that's intentional. I think of the boy in the crystal orb and the worshipful way he stared after her, and I wondered what changed. I barely remember my mother, but I would do a lot to see her again, even just for a moment.

"Tell me something of value," I say. "And I will consider it."

"So I am to have nothing today?" she wants to know.

"Have we not fed you and clothed you in our own garments? Moreover, you may take a turn around the gardens before you return to the Tower. Drink in the scents of the flowers and feel the grass beneath your feet," I tell her. "Let me make myself clear: I do not beg for comforting reminiscences or love stories. If you have something better to give me, then perhaps I will find something for you. But do not think I need you."

She pouts. "Very well. There was a hag who came across Madoc's land when your mother was pregnant with Vivienne. The hag was given to prophecy and divined futures in eggshells. And do you know what the hag said? That Eva's child was destined to be a greater weapon than Justin could ever forge."

"Vivi?" I demand.

"Her child," says Asha. "Although she must have thought of the one in her belly right then. Perhaps that's why she left. To protect the child from fate. But no one can escape fate."

I am silent, my mouth a grim line. Cardan's mother takes another drink of wine.

I will not let any of what I feel show on my face. "Still not enough," I say, keeping myself focused on the hope this information will find itself to Balekin, on the hope that I have found a path to outwitting him. "If you think of something better, you can send me a message. Our spies monitor notes going in and out of the Tower of Forgetting—usually at the point they're passed to the palace. Whatever you send, no matter to whom it is addressed, if it leaves the hand of the guard, we will see it. It will be easy to let me know if your memory comes up with anything of more value."

With that, I get up and step out of the room. The Roach follows me into the hall and puts a hand on my arm.

For a long moment, I stand there wordlessly trying to marshal my thoughts.

He shakes his head. "I asked her some questions on the way here. It sounds as though she was entranced by palace life, besotted with the High King's regard, glorying in the dancing and the singing and the wine. Cardan was left to be suckled by a little black cat whose kittens came stillborn."

"He survived on cat milk?" I exclaim. The Roach gives me a look, as though I've missed the point of his story entirely.

"After she was sent to the Tower, Cardan was sent to Balekin," he says.

I think again of the globe I held in Eldred's study, of Cardan dressed in rags, looking to the woman in my chamber for approval, which came only when he was awful. An abandoned prince, weaned on cat milk and cruelty, left to roam the palace like a little ghost. I think of myself, huddling in a tower of Hollow Hall, watching Balekin enchant a mortal into beating his younger brother for poor swordsmanship.

"Take her back to the Tower," I tell the Roach.

He raises his eyebrows. "You don't want to hear more about your parents?"

"She gets too much satisfaction in the telling. I'll have the information from her without so many bargains." Besides, I have planted a more important seed. Now I have only to see if it grows.

He gives me a half smile. "You like it, don't you? Playing games with us? Pulling our strings and seeing how we dance?"

"The Folk, you mean?"

"I imagine you'd like it as well with mortals, but we're what you're practiced in." He doesn't sound disapproving, but it still feels like being skewered on a pin. "And perhaps some of us offer a particular savor."

He looks down his curved goblin nose at me until I answer. "Is that meant to be a compliment?"

At that, his smile blooms. "It's no insult."

CHAPTER 15

Gowns arrive the next day, boxes of them, along with coats and cunning little jackets, velvet pants and tall boots. They all look as though they belong to someone ferocious, someone both better and worse than me.

I dress myself, and before I am done, Tatterfell comes in. She insists on sweeping back my hair and catching it up in a new comb, one carved in the shape of a toad with a single cymophane gem for an eye.

I look at myself in a coat of black velvet tipped with silver and think of the care with which Taryn chose the piece. I want to think about that and nothing else.

Once, she said that she hated me a little for being witness to her humiliation with the Gentry. I wonder if that's why I have such a hard time forgetting about what happened with Locke, because she saw it, and whenever I see her, I remember all over again how it felt to be made a fool.

When I look at my new clothes, though, I think of all the good things that come from someone knowing you well enough to understand your hopes and fears. I may not have told Taryn all the awful things I've done and the terrible skills I've acquired, but she's dressed me as though I had.

In my new clothes, I make my way to a hastily called Council meeting and listen as they debate back and forth whether Nicasia took Cardan's angry message back to Orlagh and whether fish can fly (that's Fala).

"Whether or not she did doesn't matter," says Madoc. "The High King has made his position clear. If he won't marry, then we have to assume that Orlagh is going to fulfill her threats. Which means she's going to go after his blood."

"You are moving very fast," says Randalin. "Ought we not yet consider that the treaty might still hold?"

"What good does it do to consider that?" asks Mikkel with a sidelong glance at Nihuar. "The Unseelie Courts do not survive on wishes."

The Seelie representative purses her small insect-like mouth.

"The stars say that this is a time of great upheaval," says Baphen. "I see a new monarch coming, but whether that's a sign of Cardan deposed or Orlagh overturned or Nicasia made queen, I cannot say."

"I have a plan," says Madoc. "Oak will be here in Elfhame very soon. When Orlagh sends her people after him, I mean to catch her out."

"No," I say, surprising everyone into looking my way. "You're not going to use Oak as bait."

Madoc doesn't seem particularly offended by my outburst. "It may seem that's what I am doing—"

"Because you are." I glare at him, remembering all the reasons I didn't want Oak to be High King in the first place, with Madoc as his regent.

"If Orlagh plans to hunt Oak, then it's better we know when she will strike than wait for her to move. And the best way to know is to engineer an opportunity."

"How about *removing* opportunity instead?" I say.

Madoc shakes his head. "That's nothing but the wishes Mikkel cautioned against. I've already written to Vivienne. They plan to arrive within the week."

"Oak can't come here," I say. "It was bad enough before, but not now."

"You think the mortal world is safe?" Madoc scoffs. "You think the Undersea cannot reach him there? Oak is my son, I am the Grand General of Elfhame, and I know my business. Make any arrangement you like for protecting him, but leave the rest to me. This is no time for an attack of nerves."

I grind my teeth. "Nerves?"

He gives me a steady look. "It's easy to put your own life on the line, isn't it? To make peace with danger. But a strategist must sometimes risk others, even those we love." He gives me a significant look, perhaps to remind me that I once poisoned him. "For the good of Elfhame."

But I bite my tongue again. This is not a conversation that I am likely to get anywhere with in front of the entire Council. Especially since I'm not sure I'm right.

I need to find out more of the Undersea's plans, and I need to do so quickly. If there's any alternative to risking Oak, I mean to find it.

Randalin has more questions about the High King's personal guard. Madoc wants the lower Courts to send more than their usual allotment of troops. Both Nihuar and Mikkel have objections. I let the words wash over me, trying to corral my thoughts.

As the meeting breaks up, a page comes to me with two messages.

One is from Vivi, delivered to the palace, asking me to come and bring her and Oak and Heather to Elfhame for Taryn's wedding in a day's time—sooner even than Madoc suggested. The second is from Cardan, summoning me to the throne room.

Cursing under my breath, I start to leave. Randalin catches my sleeve.

"Jude," he says. "Allow me to give you a word of advice."

I wonder if I am about to be scolded.

"The seneschal isn't just the voice of the king," he says. "You're his hands as well. If you don't like working with General Madoc, find a new Grand General, one who hasn't previously committed treason."

I knew that Randalin was often at odds with Madoc in Council meetings, but I had no idea he wanted to eliminate him. And yet, I don't trust Randalin any more than I do Madoc.

"An interesting thought," I say in what I hope is a neutral manner before making my escape.

Cardan is lounging sideways on the throne when I come in, one long leg hanging over an armrest.

Sleepy revelers party yet in the great hall, around tables still piled high with delights. The smell of freshly turned earth and freshly spilled wine hangs in the air. As I make my way to the dais, I see Taryn asleep on a rug. A pixie boy I do not know slumbers beside her, his tall dragonfly wings twitching occasionally, as though in dreams of flight.

Locke is wide awake, sitting on the edge of the dais, yelling at musicians.

Frustrated, Cardan shifts, legs falling to the floor. "What exactly is the problem here?"

A boy with the lower half of a deer steps forward. I recognize him from the Hunter's Moon revel, where he played. His voice shakes when he speaks. "Your pardon, Your Majesty. It is only that my lyre was stolen."

"So what are we debating?" Cardan says. "A lyre is either here or gone, is it not? If it's gone, let a fiddler play."

"He stole it." The boy points to one of the other musicians, this one with hair like grass.

Cardan turns toward the thief with an impatient frown.

"*My* lyre was strung with the hair of beautiful mortals who died tragically young," sputters the grass-haired faerie. "It took me decades to assemble and was not easy to maintain. The mortal voices sang mournfully when I played. It could have made even yourself cry, begging your pardon."

Cardan makes an impatient gesture. "If you are done with bragging, what is the meat of this matter? I have not asked you about *your* instrument, but *his*."

The grass-haired faerie seems to blush, his skin turning a darker green—which I suppose is not actually the color of his flesh but of his blood. "He borrowed it of an eve," he says, pointing toward the deer-boy. "After that, he became obsessed and would not rest until he'd destroyed it. I only took *his* lyre in recompense, for though it is inferior, I must play something."

"You ought to punish them both," says Locke. "For bringing such a trivial concern before the High King."

"Well?" Cardan turns back to the boy who first claimed his lyre was stolen. "Shall I render my judgment?"

"Not yet, I beg of you," says the deer-boy, his ears twitching with nerves. "When I played his lyre, the voices of those who had died and whose hair made the strings spoke to me. They were the true owners of the lyre. And when I destroyed it, I was saving them. They were trapped, you see."

Cardan flops onto his throne, tipping back his head in frustration, knocking his crown askew. "Enough," he says. "You are both thieves, and neither of you particularly skilled ones."

"But you don't understand the torment, the screaming—" Then the deer-boy presses a hand over his mouth, recalling himself in the presence of the High King.

"Have you never heard that virtue is its *own* reward?" Cardan says pleasantly. "That's because there's no *other* reward in it."

The boy scuffs his hoof on the floor.

"You stole a lyre and your lyre was stolen in turn," Cardan says softly. "There's some justice in that." He turns to the grass-haired musician. "And you took matters into your own hands, so I can only assume they were arranged to your satisfaction. But both of you have irritated me. Give me that instrument."

Both look displeased, but the grass-haired musician comes forward and surrenders the lyre to a guard.

"Each of you will have a chance to play it, and whosoever plays most sweetly, you will have it. For art is more than virtue or vice."

I make my careful way up the steps as the deer-boy begins his playing. I didn't expect Cardan to care enough to hear out the musicians, and I can't decide if his judgment is brilliant or if he is just a jerk. I worry that once again I am reading what I want to be true into his actions.

The music is haunting, thrumming across my skin and down to my bones.

"Your Majesty," I say. "You sent for me?"

"Ah, yes." His raven's-wing hair falls over one eye. "So are we at war?"

For a moment, I think he is talking about us. "No," I say. "At least not until the next full moon."

"You can't fight the sea," Locke says philosophically.

Cardan gives a little laugh. "You can fight anything. Winning, though, that's something else again. Isn't that right, Jude?"

"Jude is a real winner," Locke says with a grin. Then he looks out at the players and claps his hands. "Enough. Switch."

When Cardan doesn't contradict his Master of Revels, the deer-boy reluctantly turns over the lyre to the grass-haired faerie. A fresh wash of music rushes through the hill, a wild tune to speed my heart.

"You were just going," I tell Locke.

He grins. "I find I am very comfortable here," Locke says. "Surely there's nothing you have to say to the king that is so very personal or private."

"It's a shame you'll never find out. Go. Now." I think about Randalin's advice, his reminder that I have power. Maybe I do, but I am still unable to get rid of a Master of Revels for a half hour, no less a Grand General who is also, more or less, my father.

"Leave," Cardan tells Locke. "I didn't summon her here for *your* pleasure."

"You are most ungenerous. If you truly cared for me, you would have," Locke says as he hops down from the dais.

"Take Taryn home," I call after him. If it wasn't for her, I would punch him right in the face.

"He likes you this way, I think," Cardan says. "Flush-cheeked and furious."

"I don't care what he likes," I spit out.

"You seem to *not* care quite a lot." His voice is dry, and when I look at him, I cannot read his face.

"Why am I here?" I ask.

He kicks his legs off the side of the throne and stands. "You." He points to the deer-boy. "Today you are fortunate. Take the lyre. See that neither of you draw my notice again." As the deer-boy bows and the grass-haired faerie begins to sulk, Cardan turns to me. "Come."

Ignoring his high-handed manner with some difficulty, I follow him behind the throne and off the dais, where a small door is set against the stone wall, half hidden by ivy. I've never been here before.

Cardan sweeps aside the ivy, and we go in.

It is a small room, clearly intended for intimate meetings and assignations. Its walls are covered in moss, with small glowing mushrooms climbing them, casting a pale white light on us. There's a low couch, upon which people could sit or recline, as the situation called for.

We are alone in a way we have not been alone for a long time, and when he takes a step toward me, my heart skips a beat.

Cardan's eyebrows rise. "My brother sent me a message." He unfolds it from his pocket:

> *If you want to save your neck, pay me a visit.*
> *And put your seneschal on a leash.*

"So," he says, holding it out to me. "What have you been about?"

I let out a sigh of relief. It didn't take long for Lady Asha to pass the information I gave her to Balekin, and it didn't take long for Balekin to act on it. One point to me.

"I stopped you from getting some messages," I admit.

"And you decided not to mention them." Cardan looks at me without particular rancor but is not exactly pleased. "Just as you declined to tell me about Balekin's meetings with Orlagh or Nicasia's plans for me."

"Look, of course Balekin wants to see you," I say, trying to redirect the conversation away from his sadly incomplete list of stuff I haven't told him. "You're his brother, whom he kept in his own house. You're the only person with the power to free him who might actually do it. I figured if you were in a forgiving mood, you could talk to him anytime you wanted. You didn't need his exhortations."

"So what changed?" he asks, waving the piece of paper at me. Now he does sound angry. "Why was I permitted to receive this?"

"I gave him a source of information," I say. "One it's possible for me to compromise."

"And I am supposed to reply to this little note?" he asks.

"Have him brought to you in chains." I take the paper from him and jam it into my pocket. "I'd be interested to know what he thinks he can get from you with a little conversation, especially since he doesn't know you're aware of his ties to the Undersea."

Cardan's gaze narrows. The worst part is that I am deceiving him again right now, deceiving by omission. Hiding that my source of information, the one I can now compromise, is his own mother.

I thought you wanted me to do this on my own, I want to say. *I thought I was supposed to rule and you were supposed to be merry and that was supposed to be that.*

"I suspect he will try to shout at me until I give him what he wants,"

Cardan says. "It might be possible to goad him into letting something slip. Possible, not likely."

I nod, and the scheming part of my brain, honed on strategy games, supplies me with a move. "Nicasia knows more than she's saying. Make her say the rest of it, and then use that against Balekin."

"Yes, well, I don't think it would be politically expedient to put thumbscrews to a princess of the sea."

I look at him again, at his soft mouth and his high cheekbones, at the cruel beauty of his face. "Not thumbscrews. You. You go to Nicasia and charm her."

His eyebrows go up.

"Oh, come on," I say, the plan coming together in my mind as I am speaking, a plan that I hate as surely as I know it will be effective. "You're practically draped in courtiers every time I see you."

"I'm the *king*," he says.

"They've been draped over you for longer than that." I am frustrated having to explain this. Surely he's aware of the response of the Folk to him.

He makes an impatient gesture. "You mean back when I was merely the *prince*?"

"Use your wiles," I say, exasperated and embarrassed. "I'm sure you've got some. She wants you. It shouldn't be difficult."

His eyebrows, if anything, climb higher. "You're seriously suggesting I do this."

I take a breath, realizing that I am going to have to convince him that it will work. And that I know something that might. "Nicasia's the one who came through the passageway and shot that girl you were kissing," I say.

"You mean she tried to kill me?" he asks. "Honestly, Jude, how many secrets are you keeping?"

I think of his mother again and bite my tongue. Too many. "She was shooting at the girl, not you. She found you in bed with someone, got jealous, and shot twice. Unfortunately for you, but fortunately for everyone else, she's a terrible shot. Now do you believe me that she wants you?"

"I know not what to believe," he says, clearly angry, maybe at her, maybe at me, probably at both of us.

"She thought to surprise you in your bed. Give her what she wants, and get the information we need to avoid a war."

He stalks toward me, close enough that I can feel his breath stirring my hair. "Are you commanding me?"

"No," I say, startled and unable to meet his gaze. "Of course not."

His fingers come to my chin, tilting my head so I am looking up into his black eyes, the rage in them as hot as coals. "You just think I ought to. That I can. That I'd be good at it. Very well, Jude. Tell me how it's done. Do you think she'd like it if I came to her like this, if I looked deeply into her eyes?"

My whole body is alert, alive with sick desire, embarrassing in its intensity.

He knows. I know he knows.

"Probably," I say, my voice coming out a little shakily. "Whatever it is you usually do."

"Oh, come now," he says, his voice full of barely controlled fury. "If you want me to play the bawd, at least give me the benefit of your advice."

His beringed fingers trace over my cheek, trace the line of my lip and down my throat. I feel dizzy and overwhelmed. "Should I touch her like this?" he asks, lashes lowered. The shadows limn his face, casting his cheekbones into stark relief.

"I don't know," I say, but my voice betrays me. It's all wrong, high and breathless.

He presses his mouth to my ear, kissing me there. His hands skim over my shoulders, making me shiver. "And then like this? Is this how I ought to seduce her?" I can feel his mouth shape the light words against my skin. "Do you think it would work?"

I dig my fingernails into the meat of my palm to keep from moving against him. My whole body is trembling with tension. "Yes."

Then his mouth is against mine, and my lips part. I close my eyes against what I'm about to do. My fingers reach up to tangle in the black curls of his hair. He doesn't kiss me as though he's angry; his kiss is soft, yearning.

Everything slows, goes liquid and hot. I can barely think.

I've wanted this and feared it, and now that it's happening, I don't know how I will ever want anything else.

We stumble back to the low couch. He leans me against the cushions, and I pull him down over me. His expression mirrors my own, surprise and a little horror.

"Tell me again what you said at the revel," he says, climbing over me, his body against mine.

"What?" I can barely think.

"That you hate me," he says, his voice hoarse. "Tell me that you hate me."

"I hate you," I say, the words coming out like a caress. I say it again, over and over. A litany. An enchantment. A ward against what I really feel. "I hate you. I hate you. I hate you."

He kisses me harder.

"I hate you," I breathe into his mouth. "I hate you so much that sometimes I can't think of anything else."

At that, he makes a harsh, low sound.

One of his hands slides over my stomach, tracing the shape of my skin. He kisses me again, and it's like falling off a cliff. Like a mountain slide, building momentum with every touch, until there is only crashing destruction ahead.

I have never felt anything like this.

He begins to unbutton my doublet, and I try not to freeze, try not to show my inexperience. I don't want him to stop.

It feels like a geas. It has all the sinister pleasure of sneaking out of the house, all the revolting satisfaction of stealing. It reminds me of the moment before I slammed a blade through my hand, amazed at my own capacity for self-betrayal.

He leans up to pull off his own jacket, and I try to wriggle out of mine. He looks at me and blinks, as through a fog. "This is an absolutely terrible idea," he says with a kind of amazement in his voice.

"Yes," I tell him, kicking off my boots.

I am wearing hose, and I don't think there's an elegant way to strip them off. Certainly, I don't find it. Tangled in the fabric, feeling foolish, I realize I could stop this now. I could gather up my things and go. But I don't.

He shucks his cuffed white shirt over his head in a single elegant gesture, revealing bare skin and scars. My hands are shaking. He captures them and kisses my knuckles with a kind of reverence.

"I want to tell you so many lies," he says.

I shudder, and my heart hammers as his hands skim over my skin, one sliding between my thighs. I mirror him, fumbling with the buttons of his breeches. He helps me push them down, his tail curling against his leg then twisting to coil against mine, soft as a whisper. I reach over to slide my hand over the flat plane of his stomach. I don't let myself hesitate, but my inexperience is obvious. His skin is hot under my palm, against my calluses. His fingers are too clever by half.

I feel as though I am drowning in sensation.

His eyes are open, watching my flushed face, my ragged breathing. I try to stop myself from making embarrassing noises. It's more intimate than the way he's touching me, to be looked at like that. I hate that he knows what he's doing and I don't. I hate being vulnerable. I hate that I throw my head back, baring my throat. I hate the way I cling to him, the nails of one hand digging into his back, my thoughts splintering, and the single last thing in my head: that I like him better than I've ever liked anyone and that of all the things he's ever done to me, making me like him so much is by far the worst.

CHAPTER 16

One of the hardest things to do as a spy, as a strategist, or even just as a person, is wait. I recall the Ghost's lessons, making me sit for hours with a crossbow in my hand without my mind wandering, waiting for the perfect shot.

So much of winning is waiting.

The other part, though, is taking the shot when it comes. Unleashing all that momentum.

In my rooms again, I remind myself of that. I can't afford to be distracted. Tomorrow, I need to get Vivi and Oak from the mortal world, and I need to come up with either a scheme better than Madoc's or a way to make Madoc's scheme safer for Oak.

I concentrate on what I am going to say to Vivi, instead of thinking of Cardan. I do not want to consider what happened between us. I do not want to think about the way his muscles moved or how his skin felt or the soft gasping sounds he made or the slide of his mouth against mine.

I definitely don't want to think about how hard I had to bite my own lip to keep quiet. Or how obvious it was that I'd never done any of the things we did, no less the things we didn't do.

Every time I think of any of it, I shove the memory away as fiercely as possible. I shove it along with the enormous vulnerability I feel, the sensation of being exposed down to my raw nerves. I do not know how I will face Cardan again without behaving like a fool.

If I cannot attack the problem of the Undersea and I cannot attack the problem of Cardan, then perhaps I can take care of something else.

It is a relief to don a suit of dark fabric and high leather boots, to holster blades at my wrists and calves. It is a relief to do something physical, heading through the woods and then slyfooting my way into a poorly guarded house. When one of the residents comes in, my knife is at his throat faster than he can speak.

"Locke," I say sweetly. "Are you surprised?"

He turns to me, dazzling smile faltering. "My blossom. What is this?"

After an astonished moment, I realize that he thinks I am Taryn. Can he really not tell the difference between us?

A bitter pit where my heart should be is pleased by the thought.

"If you think my sister would put a knife to your throat, perhaps you should delay your nuptials," I tell him, taking a step back and indicating a chair with the point. "Go ahead. Sit."

He sits down just as I kick the chair, sending it backward and him sprawling to the floor. He rolls over, glaring at me with indignation. "Unchivalrous," is all he says, but there's something in his face that wasn't there before.

Fear.

For five months I have tried to use every bit of restraint I learned over a lifetime of keeping my head down. I have tried to behave as though I had only dribs and drabs of power, an important servant's power, and still keep in my head that I was in charge. A balancing act that makes me think of Val Moren's lesson in juggling.

I have allowed the Locke situation to get out of hand.

I place my foot on his chest, pressing down a little to remind him that if I kicked hard, it could shatter bone.

"I am done with being polite. We're not going to play word games or make up riddles. Humiliating the High King is a bad idea. Humiliating me is a terrible idea. Running around on my sister is just dumb. Maybe you thought I was too *busy* to take my revenge? Well, Locke, I want you to understand that for you, I will *make time*."

His face pales. He's obviously not sure what to make of me right now. He knows I stabbed Valerian once, but he doesn't know I killed him, nor that I have killed since then. He has no idea I became a spy and then a spymaster. Even the sword fight with Taryn was something he only heard about.

"Making you Queen of Mirth was a jest," Locke says, gazing up at me from the floor with a kind of fondness in his fox eyes, a little smile on the corner of his mouth, as though he's willing me to grin along with him. "Come on, Jude, let me up. Am I really to believe you'd harm me?"

My voice is mock-sweet. "You once accused me of playing the great game. What was it you called it: 'the game of kings and princes, of queens and crowns'? But to play it well, I must be pitiless."

He begins to get up, but I press down harder with my foot and shift the grip on my knife. He stops moving. "You always liked stories," I remind him. "You said you wanted to create the sparks of stories. Well, the tale of a twin who murders her sister's betrothed is a good one, don't you think?"

He closes his eyes and holds out his empty hands. "Peace, Jude. Perhaps I overplayed my hand. But I cannot believe you want to murder me for it. Your sister would be devastated."

"Better she never be a bride than wind up a widow," I say, but take my foot off his chest. He gets up slowly, dusting himself off. Once on his feet, he looks around the room as though he doesn't quite recognize his own manor now that he's seen it from the vantage of the floor.

"You're right," I continue. "I don't want to harm you. We are to be family. You will be my brother and I your sister. Let us make friends. But to do that, I need you to do some things for me.

"First, stop trying to make me uncomfortable. Stop trying to turn me into a character in one of your dramas. Pick another target to weave stories around.

"Second, whatever your issue is with Cardan, whatever pushed you to make such a meal of toying with him, whatever made you think it was fun to steal his lover and then throw her over for a mortal girl—as though you wanted him to know the thing dearest to him was worth nothing to you—let it go. Whatever made you decide to make me Queen of Mirth to torment him with the feelings you suspected he had, leave off. He's the High King, and it's too dangerous."

"Dangerous," he says, "but *fun*."

I don't smile. "Humiliate the king before the Court, and the courtiers will spread rumors and his subjects will forget to be afraid. Soon, the lesser Courts will think they can go against him."

Locke tries to right the broken chair, leaning it against a nearby table when it becomes clear it will no longer stand on its own. "Oh, fine, you're angry with me. But think. You may be Cardan's seneschal and you've obviously fascinated him with your hips and lips and warm mortal skin, but I know that in your heart, whatever he has promised you, you still hate him. You'd love to see him brought low in front of his entire Court. Why, if you hadn't been dressed in rags and been laughed at, you'd probably have forgiven me for every wrongdoing I've ever committed against you, just for engineering that."

"You're wrong," I say.

He smiles. "Liar."

"Even if I did like it," I say, "it must end."

He seems to be evaluating how serious I am and of what I am capable. I am sure he is seeing the girl he brought home, the one he kissed and tricked. He is wondering, probably not for the first time, how I lucked into being made seneschal, how I managed to get my hands on the crown of Elfhame to orchestrate my little brother's putting it on Cardan's head.

"The last thing is this," I say. "You're going to keep faith with Taryn. Once you're wed, if you want to take other lovers, she better be with you when you do it and she better be into it. If it's not fun for everyone, it's not happening."

He stares at me blankly. "Are you accusing me of not caring for your sister?" he asks.

"If I truly believed you didn't care for Taryn, we wouldn't be having this conversation."

He gives a long sigh. "Because you'd murder me?"

"If you're playing with Taryn, Madoc will murder you; I won't even get a chance."

I sheathe my knife and head toward the door.

"Your ridiculous family might be surprised to find that not everything is solved by murder," Locke calls after me.

"We *would* be surprised to find that," I call back.

CHAPTER 17

In the five months that Vivi and Oak have been gone, I have visited the mortal world only twice. Once to help them set up their apartment, and the second time for a wine party Heather threw for Vivi's birthday. At it, Taryn and I sat awkwardly on the edge of a couch, eating cheese with oily olives, being allowed little sips of Shiraz by college girls because we were "too young to legally drink." My nerves were on edge the whole night, wondering what trouble was happening in my absence.

Madoc had sent Vivi a present, and Taryn had faithfully carried it across the sea—a golden dish of salt that never emptied. Turn it over, and it's full again. I found it to be a nervous-making present, but Heather had only laughed, as though it was some kind of novelty with a trick bottom.

She didn't believe in magic.

How Heather was going to react to Taryn's wedding was anyone's guess. All I hoped was that Vivienne had warned her about at least some of what was going to happen. Otherwise, the news that mermaids were *real* was going to come along with the news that mermaids were *out to get us*. I didn't think "all at once" was the ideal way to hear any of that news.

After midnight, the Roach and I go across the sea in a boat made of river rushes and breath. We carry a cargo of mortals who have been tunneling out new rooms in the Court of Shadows. Taken from their beds just after dusk, they will be returned just before dawn. When they wake, they will find gold coins scattered in their sheets and filling their pockets. Not faerie gold, which blows away like dandelion puffs off leaves and stones, but real gold—a month's wages for a single stolen night.

You might think I am heartless to allow this, no less order it. Maybe I am. But they made a bargain, even if they didn't understand with whom they were making it. And I can promise that besides the gold, all they are left with in the morning is exhaustion. They will not remember their journey to Elfhame, and we will not take them twice.

On the trip over, they sit quietly on the boat, lost in dreams as the swells of the sea and the wind propel us whitherward. Overhead, Snapdragon keeps pace, looking for trouble. I gaze at the waves and think of Nicasia, imagine webbed hands on the sides of the vessel, imagine sea Folk clawing their way aboard.

You can't fight the sea, Locke said. I hope he's wrong.

Near the shore, I climb out, stepping into the shock of icy water at my calves and black rocks under my feet, then clamber over them, leaving the boat to come apart as the Roach's magic fades from it. Snapdragon heads off to the east to scout for future workers.

The Roach and I put each mortal to bed, occasionally beside a sleeping lover we take care not to wake as we ply them with gold. I feel like a faerie in a story, slyfooting my way through homes, able to drink the cream off the milk or put knots in a child's hair.

"This is usually a lonely business," the Roach says when we're finished. "Your company was a pleasure. There's hours yet between dawn and waking—come sup with me."

It's true that it's still too early to pick up Vivi and Heather and Oak. It's also true that I am hungry. I have a tendency these days to put off eating until I am ravenous. I feel a little like a snake, either starved or swallowing a mouse whole. "Okay."

The Roach suggests we go to a diner. I do not tell him I've never been to one. Instead, I follow him through the woods. We come out near a highway. Across the road rests a building, brightly lit and shiny with chrome. Beside it is a sign proclaiming it to be open twenty-four hours, and the parking lot is enormous, big enough even for several trucks already parked there. This early in the morning, there is barely any traffic, and we are able to cross the highway easily.

Inside, I slide obediently into the booth he chooses. He snaps his fingers, and the little box beside our table springs to life, blaring music. I flinch, surprised, and he laughs.

A waitress comes by the table, a pen with a thoroughly chewed cap stuck behind her ear, like in the movies. "Something to drink?" she says, the words running together so that it takes a moment to understand she's asked a question.

"Coffee," the Roach says. "Black as the eyes of the High King of Elfhame."

The waitress just stares at him for a long blink, then scratches something on her pad and turns to me.

"Same," I say, not sure what else they have.

When she's gone, I open the menu and look at the pictures. It turns out they have *everything*. Piles of food. Chicken wings, bright and gleaming with glaze beside little pots of white sauce. A pile of chopped potatoes, fried to a turn, topped with crisped sausages and bubbling eggs. Wheat cakes larger than my spread hand, buttered and glistening with syrup.

"Did you know," the Roach inquires, "your people once believed the Folk came and took the wholesomeness out of mortal food?"

"Did they?" I ask with a grin.

He shrugs. "Some tricks may be lost to time. But I grant that mortal food does possess a great deal of substance."

The waitress comes back with hot coffees, and I warm my hands on the cup while the Roach orders fried pickles and buffalo wings, a burger, and a milkshake. I order an omelet with mushrooms and something called pepper jack cheese.

We sit in silence for a time. I watch the Roach rip sugar packets and dump them into his cup. I don't do anything to mine. I am used to the whipped-cream-topped drinks Vivi used to bring me, but there is something satisfyingly bracing about drinking coffee this way, hot and bitter.

Black as the eyes of the king of Elfhame.

"So," says the Roach. "When will you tell the king about his mother?"

"She doesn't want me to," I say.

The Roach frowns. "You've made improvements in the Court of Shadows. You're young, but you're ambitious in the way that perhaps only the young can be. I judge you by three things and three things only—how square you are with us, how capable, and what you want for the world."

"Where does Lady Asha come into any of that?" I ask, just as the waitress returns with our food. "Because I can already sense that she does. You didn't open with that question for nothing."

My omelet is enormous, an entire henhouse of eggs. My mushrooms are identically shaped, as though someone had ground up real mushrooms and then made cookie-cutter versions. They taste that way, too. With the Roach's food piled up on the other side, soon the table is full to groaning.

He takes a bite of a wing and licks his lips with his black tongue. "Cardan is part of the Court of Shadows. We may play the world, but we don't play one another. Hiding messages from Balekin is one thing. But his mother—does he even know she's not dead?"

"You're writing a tragedy for him without cause," I say. "We have no reason to believe he doesn't know. And he's not one of us. He's no spy."

The Roach bites off the last piece of gristle from the chicken bones, cracking it between his teeth. He's finished the whole plate of them and, pushing it aside, starts on the pickles. "You made a bargain for me to train him, and I've taken him under my wing. Sleight of hand. Pick-pocketing. Little magics. He's good at it."

I think of the coin playing across his long fingers while he slouched in the burnt remains of his rooms. I glare at the Roach.

He only laughs. "Don't look at me like that. 'Twas you who made the bargain."

I barely recall that part, so intent was I on getting Cardan to agree to a year and a day of service. So long as he pledged to me, I could put him on the throne. I would have promised him much more than lessons in spycraft.

But when I think of the night he was shot at, the night he did coin tricks, I can't help recalling him gazing up from my bed, intoxicated and disturbingly intoxicating.

Kiss me until I am sick of it.

"And now he's playacting, isn't he?" the Roach goes on. "Because if he's the true High King of Elfhame, whom we are to follow to the end of days, then we've been a mite disrespectful, running the kingdom for him. But if he is playacting, then he's a spy for sure and better than most of us. Which makes him part of the Shadow Court."

I drink down my coffee in a scalding swallow. "We can't talk about this."

"Not at home we can't," the Roach says with a wink. "Which is why we're here."

I asked him to seduce Nicasia. Yes, I guess I have been a "mite disrespectful" to the High King of Elfhame. And the Roach is right: Cardan didn't behave as though he was too royal for my request. That wasn't his reason for taking offense.

"Fine," I say in defeat. "I'll figure out a way to tell him."

The Roach grins. "The food's good here, right? Sometimes I miss the mortal world. But for good or ill, my work in Elfhame is not yet done."

"Hopefully for good," I say, and take a bite of the shredded potato cake that came with my omelet.

The Roach snorts. He's moved on to his milkshake, the other plates bare and stacked up to one side of him. He lifts his mug in a salute. "To the triumph of goodness, just not before we get ours."

"I want to ask you something," I say, clinking my mug against his. "About the Bomb."

"Leave her out of this," he says, studying me. "And if you can, leave her out of your schemes against the Undersea. I know you're always sticking your neck out as though you're enamored of the axe, but if there must be a neck on the chopping block beside you, choose a less comely one."

"Including your own?" I ask.

"Much better," he agrees.

"Because you love her?" I ask.

The Roach frowns at me. "And if I did? Would you lie to me about my chances?"

"No—" I begin, but he cuts me off.

"I love a good lie," he says, standing and setting down little stacks of silver coins on the table. "I love a good liar even better, which is to your benefit. But some lies are not worth the telling."

I bite my lip, unable to say anything else without spilling the Bomb's secrets.

After the diner, we part ways, both of us with ragwort in our pockets. I watch him go, thinking of his claim on Cardan. I had been trying so hard not to think of him as the rightful High King of Elfhame that I had entirely missed asking myself whether *he* considered himself to be High King. And, if he didn't, whether that meant he thought of himself as one of my spies instead.

I make my way to my sister's apartment. Though in the past I've donned mortal clothing to walk around the mall and tried to behave in such a way as would be above suspicion, it turns out that arriving in Maine in a doublet and riding boots draws a few stares but no fear that I have come from another world.

Perhaps I am part of a medieval festival, a girl suggests as I pass her. She went to one a few years ago and enjoyed the joust very much. She had a large turkey leg and tried mead for the first time.

"It goes to your head," I tell her. She agrees.

An elderly man with a newspaper remarks that I must be doing Shakespeare in the park. A few louts on some steps call out to me that Halloween is in October.

The Folk doubtlessly learned this lesson long ago. They do not need to deceive humans. Humans will deceive themselves.

It is with this fresh in my mind that I cross a lawn full of dandelions, go up the steps to my sister's door, and knock.

Heather opens it. Her pink hair is freshly dyed for the wedding. For a moment, she looks taken aback—probably by my outfit—and then smiles, opening the door wide. "Hi! Thanks for being willing to drive. Everything's mostly packed. Is your car big enough?"

"Definitely," I lie, looking around the kitchen for Vivi with a kind of desperation. How is my big sister thinking this is going to go if she hasn't told Heather *anything*? If she believes I have a *car* instead of *ragwort stalks*.

"Jude!" Oak yells, hopping down from his seat at the table. He throws his arms around me. "Can we go? Are we going? I made everyone presents at school."

"Let's see what Vivi says," I tell him, and give him a squeeze. He's more solid than I remembered. Even his horns seem slightly longer, although he can't have grown that much in just a few months, can he?

Heather throws a switch, and the coffeepot starts chugging away. Oak climbs onto a chair and pours candy-colored cereal into a bowl and begins eating it dry.

I sidle past and head into the next room. There's Heather's desk, piled with sketches and markers and paints. Prints of her work are taped to the wall above.

Besides making comics, Heather works part time at a copy shop to help cover bills. She believes Vivi has a job, too, which may or may not be a fiction. There are jobs for the Folk in the mortal world, just not the sort of jobs one tells one's human girlfriend about.

Especially if one has conveniently never mentioned one isn't human.

Their furniture is a collection of stuff from garage sales, salvage places, and the side of the road. Covering the walls are old plates with funny, big-eyed animals; cross-stitches with ominous phrases; and Heather's collection of disco memorabilia, more of her art, and Oak's crayon drawings.

In one, Vivi and Heather and Oak are together, rendered as he sees them—Heather's brown skin and pink hair, Vivi's pale skin and cat eyes, Oak's horns. I bet Heather thinks it's adorable, how Oak made himself and Vivi into monsters. I bet she thinks it's a sign of his creativity.

This is going to suck. I am prepared for Heather to yell at my sister—Vivi more than deserves it. But I don't want Heather to hurt Oak's feelings.

I find Vivi in her bedroom, still packing. It is small by comparison to the rooms we grew up in, and much less tidy than the rest of the apartment. Her clothes are everywhere. Scarves are draped over the headboard, bangles threaded on the pole of the footboard, shoes peeking out from underneath the bed.

I sit down on the mattress. "Where does Heather think she's going today?"

Vivi gives me a big grin. "You got my message—looks like it's possible to enchant birds to do useful things after all."

"You don't need me," I remind her. "You are perfectly capable of making all the ragwort horses you could ever need—something I can't do."

"Heather believes we are attending the wedding of my sister Taryn, which we are, on an island off the coast of Maine, which we also are. See? Not a single lie was told."

I begin to understand why I was roped in. "And when she wanted to drive, you said your sister would come pick you up."

"Well, she assumed there would be a ferry, and I could hardly agree or disagree with that," Vivi says with the breezy honesty that I've always liked and also been exasperated with.

"And now you're going to have to tell the truthier truth," I say. "Or—I have a proposal. Don't. Keep putting it off. Don't come to the wedding."

"Madoc said you'd say that," she tells me, frowning.

"It's too dangerous—for complicated reasons I know you don't care about," I say. "The Queen of the Undersea wants her daughter to marry Cardan, and she's working with Balekin, who has his own agenda. She's probably playing him, but since she's better at being worse than him, that's not good."

"You're right," Vivi says. "I don't care. Politics are boring."

"Oak is in danger," I say. "Madoc wants to use him as bait."

"There's always danger," Vivi says, throwing a pair of boots on top of some crumpled dresses. "Faerie is one big mousetrap of danger. But if I let that keep us away, how could I look my stalwart father in the face?

"Not to mention my stalwart sister, who is going to keep us safe while Father schemes his schemes," Vivi continues. "At least, according to him."

I groan. Just like him to cast me in a role I can't deny, but which serves his purpose. And just like her to ignore me and believe that she knows best.

Someone you trust has already betrayed you.

I have trusted Vivi more than anyone else. I have trusted her with Oak, with the truth, with my plan. I have trusted her because she is my older sister, because she doesn't care about Faerie. But it occurs to me that if she betrayed me, I would be undone.

I wish she wouldn't keep reminding me she was talking to Madoc. "And you trust Dad? That's a change."

"He's not good at a lot of things, but he knows about scheming," Vivi says, which is not that reassuring. "Come on. Tell me about Taryn. Is she actually excited?"

How do I even answer? "Locke got himself made Master of Revels. She's not exactly pleased about his new title or behavior. I think half the reason he likes to screw around is to get under her skin."

"This is not boring," Vivi says. "Go on."

Heather comes into the room with two cups of coffee. We stop talking as she passes one to me and one to Vivi. "I didn't know how you took it," she says. "So I made it like Vee's."

I take a sip. It's very sweet. I've already had plenty of coffee this morning, but I drink some more anyway.

Black as the eyes of the High King of Elfhame.

Heather leans against the door. "You done packing?"

"Almost." Vivi eyes her suitcase and then throws in a pair of rain boots. Then she looks around the room, as though she's wondering what other stuff she can cram in.

Heather frowns. "You're bringing all that for a week?"

"It's just the top layer that's clothes," Vivi says. "Underneath, it's mostly stuff for Taryn that's hard to get on the... *island*."

"Do you think what I'm planning on wearing will be okay?"

I can understand why Heather is worried, since she's never met my family. She believes our dad is strict. She has no idea.

"Sure," Vivi says, and then looks at me. "It's a hot silver dress."

"Wear anything you want. Really," I tell Heather, thinking of how gowns and rags and nakedness are all acceptable in Faerie. She's about to have much bigger problems.

"Hurry up. We don't want to get stuck in traffic," Heather says, and goes out again. In the other room, I hear her talking to Oak, asking him if he wants some milk.

"So," Vivi says. "You were saying..."

I let out a long sigh and gesture with my coffee cup toward the door, bugging out my eyes.

Vivi shakes her head. "Come on. You won't be able to tell me any of this once we're there."

"You know already," I say. "Locke is going to make Taryn unhappy. But she doesn't want to hear that, and she especially doesn't want to hear it from me."

"You did once have a sword fight over him," Vivi points out.

"Exactly," I say. "I'm not objective. Or I don't seem objective."

"You know what I wonder about, though," she says, closing her suitcase and sitting on it to squish it down. She looks up at me with her cat eyes, twin to Madoc's. "You've manipulated the High King of Faerie into obeying you, but you can't find a way to manipulate one jerk into keeping our sister happy?"

Not fair, I want to say. Practically the last thing I did before I came here was threaten Locke, ordering him not to mess with Taryn after they got married—or else. Still, her words rankle. "It's not that simple."

She sighs. "I guess nothing ever is."

CHAPTER 18

Oak holds my hand, and I carry his small suitcase down the steps toward the empty parking lot.

I look back up at Heather. She's dragging a bag behind her and some bungee cords she says we can use if we have to put one of the suitcases on the roof rack. I haven't told her there isn't even a car.

"So," I say, looking at Vivi.

Vivi smiles, reaching out her hand toward me. I take the ragwort stalks out of my pocket and hand them over.

I can't look at Heather's face. I turn back to Oak. He's picking four-leaf clovers from the grass, finding them effortlessly, making a bouquet.

"What are you doing?" Heather asks, puzzled.

"We're not going to take a car. We're going to fly instead," says Vivi.

"We're going to the airport?"

Vivi laughs. "You'll love this. Steed, rise and bear us where I command."

A choked gasp behind me. Then Heather screams. I turn despite myself.

The ragwort steeds are there in front of the apartment complex—starved-looking yellow ponies with lacy manes and emerald eyes, like sea horses on land, weeds come to snorting, snuffling life. And Heather, hands over her mouth.

"Surprise!" says Vivi, continuing to behave as though this is a small thing. Oak, clearly anticipating this moment, chooses it to rip off his own glamour, revealing his horns.

"See, Heather," he says. "We're magic. Are you surprised?"

She looks at Oak, at the monstrous ragwort ponies, and then sinks down to sit on her suitcase. "Okay," she says. "This is some kind of bullshit practical joke or something, but one of you is going to tell me what's going on or I am going to go back inside the house and lock you all out."

Oak looks crestfallen. He'd really expected her to be delighted. I put my arm around him, rubbing his shoulder. "Come on, sweets," I say. "Let's get the stuff loaded up, and they can come after. Mom and Dad are so excited to see you."

"I miss them," he tells me. "I miss you, too."

I kiss him on one soft cheek as I lift him onto the horse's back. He looks over my shoulder at Heather.

Behind me, I can hear Vivi start to explain. "Faerie is real. Magic is real. See? I'm not human, and neither is my brother. And we're going to take you away to a magic island for the whole week. Don't be afraid. We're not the scary ones."

I manage to get the bungee cords from Heather's numb hands while Vivi shows off her pointed ears and cat eyes and tries to explain away never telling her any of it before.

We are definitely the scary ones.

Some hours later, we are in Oriana's parlor. Heather, still looking bewildered and upset, walks around, staring at the strange art on the walls, the ominous pattern of beetles and thorns in the weave of draperies.

Oak sits on Oriana's lap, letting her cradle him in her arms as though he is very small again. Her pale fingers fuss with his hair—which she thinks is too short—and he tells her a long, rambling story about school and the way the stars are different in the mortal world and what peanut butter tastes like.

It hurts a little to watch, because Oriana no more gave birth to Oak than to me or Taryn, but she is very clearly Oak's mother while she has steadfastly refused to be ours.

Vivi pulls presents from her suitcase. Bags of coffee beans, glass earrings in the shape of little leaves, tins of *dulce de leche.*

Heather walks over to me. "This is all real."

"Really, really real," I confirm.

"And it's true that these people are elves, that Vee is an elf, like from a story?" Heather looks around the room again, warily, as though she is expecting a rainbow-colored unicorn to burst through the plaster and lath.

"Yup," I say. She seems freaked out, but not actually angry at Vivi, which is something. Maybe the news is too big for anger, at least yet.

Or maybe Heather's honestly pleased. Maybe Vivi was right about the way to tell her, and it was only that the delight took a few minutes to kick in. What do I know about love?

"And this place is . . ." She stops herself. "Oak is some kind of prince? He's got horns. And Vivi has those eyes."

"Cat eyes like her father," I say. "It's a lot, I'm sure."

"He sounds scary," Heather says. "Your dad. Sorry, I mean Vee's dad. She says he's not really your father."

I flinch, although I am sure Vivi didn't mean it that way. Maybe she didn't even say it that way.

"Because you're human," Heather tries to clarify. "You are human, right?"

I nod, and the relief on her face is clear. She laughs a little.

"It's not easy to be human in Faerie," I tell her. "Come walk with me. I want to tell you some stuff."

She tries to catch Vivi's eye, but Vivi is still sitting on the rug, rooting through her suitcase. I see more trinkets, packages of licorice, hair ribbons, and a large package covered in white paper with a golden bow, stamped with *Congratulations* all along its length.

Unsure of what else to do, Heather follows me. Vivi doesn't even seem to notice.

It is strange to be back in the house where I grew up. Tempting to run up the stairs and throw open the doors to my old room, to see if there's any trace of me there. Tempting to go into Madoc's study and go through his papers like the spy that I am.

Instead, I head out onto the lawn and start toward the stables. Heather takes a deep breath. Her eyes are drawn to the towers visible above the tree line.

"Did Vee talk to you about rules?" I ask as we walk.

Heather shakes her head, clearly puzzled. "Rules?"

Vivi has come through for me plenty of times when no one else did, so I know she cares. Still, it feels like willful blindness to have overlooked how hard Taryn and I had it as mortals, how careful we had to be, and how careful Heather ought to be while she's here.

"She said I should stick by her," Heather says, probably seeing the frustration on my face and wanting to defend Vivi. "That I shouldn't wander off without one of her family members."

I shake my head. "Not good enough. Listen, the Folk can glamour things to look different than they do. They can mess with your mind—charm you, persuade you to do things you wouldn't consider normally. And then there's everapple, the fruit of Faerie. If you taste it, all you'll think of is getting more."

I sound like Oriana.

Heather is looking at me in horror and possibly disbelief. I wonder if I went too far. I try again with a slightly calmer tone. "We're at a disadvantage here. The Folk, they're ageless, immortal, and magical. And they're not all fond of humans. So don't let your guard down, don't make any bargains, and keep some specific things on your person at all times—rowan berries and salt."

"Okay," she says.

In the distance, I can see Madoc's two riding toads out on the lawn, being tended by grooms.

"You're taking this really well," I say.

"I have two questions." Something in her voice or her manner makes me realize she is maybe having a harder time than I thought. "One, what are rowan berries? And two, if Faerieland is the way you say, why do you live here?"

I open my mouth, and then shut it. "It's home," I say finally.

"It doesn't have to be," she says. "If Vee can leave, so can you. Like you said, you're not one of them."

"Come to the kitchens," I tell her, veering back toward the house.

Once there, Heather is transfixed by the enormous cauldron, big enough for both of us to bathe in. She stares at the plucked bodies of partridges, resting on the counter beside dough rolled out for a pie.

I go over to the glass jars of herbs and draw out a few rowan berries. I take out a thick thread for sewing stuffing inside hens, and I use that and a bit of cheesecloth to make her a small knot of them.

"Put this in your pocket or in your bra," I tell her. "Keep it on you while you're here."

"And this will keep me safe?" Heather asks.

"Safer," I say, sewing her up a bag of salt. "Sprinkle this on whatever you eat. Don't forget."

"Thank you." She takes my arm, giving it a quick squeeze. "I mean, this doesn't feel real. I know that must sound ridiculous. I'm standing in front of you. I can smell herbs and blood from those weird little birds. If you stuck me with that needle, it would hurt. But it still doesn't feel real. Even though it makes sense of all of Vee's stupid evasions about normal stuff like where she went to high school. But it means the whole world is upside down."

When I've been over there—at the mall, in Heather's apartment—the difference between them and us has seemed so vast that I can't imagine how Heather is managing to bridge it. "Nothing you could say would sound ridiculous to me," I tell her.

Her gaze, as she takes in the stronghold, as she drinks in a breath of late-afternoon air, is full of hopeful interest. I have an uncomfortable memory of a girl with stones in her pockets and am desperately relieved that Heather is willing to accept her world being turned over.

Back in the parlor, Vivi grins at us. "Did Jude give you the grand tour?"

"I made her a charm," I say, my tone making it clear that she should have been the one to do it.

"Good," Vivi says happily, because it's going to take much more than a slightly aggrieved tone to get under her skin when things are going her way. "Oriana tells me you haven't been around much lately. Your feud with dear old Dad sounds pretty serious."

"You know what it cost him," I say.

"Stay for dinner." Oriana rises, pale as a ghost, to look at me with her ruby eyes. "Madoc would like that. I would, too."

"I can't," I tell her, actually feeling regretful about it. "I've dallied here more than I should have, but I will see you all at the wedding."

"Things are always super *dramatic* around here," Vivi tells Heather. "Epic. Everyone acts as though they just stepped out of a murder ballad."

Heather looks at Vivi as though, perhaps, she just stepped out of a ballad, too.

"Oh," Vivi says, reaching into her suitcase again, coming up with another squishy-looking package wrapped with a black bow. "Can you take this to Cardan? It's a 'congratulations on being king' present."

"He's the *High King of Elfhame*," Oriana says. "Whether or not you played together, you cannot call him as you did when you were children."

I stand there stupidly for a long moment, not reaching for the package. I knew Vivi and Cardan were friendly. After all, Vivi's the one who told Taryn about his tail, having seen it while swimming together with one of his sisters.

I just forgot.

"Jude?" Vivi asks.

"I think you better give it to him yourself," I say, and with that, I make my escape from my old house before Madoc returns home and I am overcome with nostalgia.

I pass by the throne room where Cardan sits at one of the low tables, his head bent toward Nicasia's. I cannot see his face, but I can see hers as she throws back her head with laughter, showing the long column of her throat. She looks incandescent with joy, his attention the light in which her beauty shines especially bright.

She *loves* him, I realize uncomfortably. She loves him, and she betrayed him with Locke and is terrified he will never love her again.

His fingers trace their way down her arm to the back of her wrist, and I remember vividly the feeling of those hands on me. My skin heats at the memory, a blush that starts at my throat and keeps going from there.

Kiss me until I am sick of it, he said, and now he has most certainly gorged on my kisses. Now he is most certainly sick of them.

I hate seeing him with Nicasia. I hate the thought of his touching her. I hate that this is my plan, that I have no one to be angry with but myself.

I am an idiot.

Pain makes you strong, Madoc once told me, making me lift a sword again and again. *Get used to the weight.*

I force myself to watch no more. Instead, I meet with Vulciber to coordinate bringing Balekin to the palace for his audience with Cardan.

Then I go down to the Court of Shadows and hear information about courtiers, hear rumors of Madoc's marshaling his forces as though preparing for the war I still hope to avoid. I send two spies to the lower Courts with the largest number of unsworn changelings to see what they can learn. I talk to the Bomb about Grimsen, who has crafted Nicasia a gem-encrusted brooch that allows her to summon gauzy wings from her back and fly.

"What do you think he wants?" I ask.

"Praise, flattery," says the Bomb. "Perhaps to find a new patron. Probably he wouldn't mind a kiss."

"Do you think he's interested in Nicasia for Orlagh's sake or her own?" I want to know.

The Bomb shrugs. "He is interested in Nicasia's beauty and Orlagh's power. Grimsen went into exile with the first Alderking; I believe that the next time he swears fealty, he will be very sure of the monarch to whom he swears."

"Or maybe he doesn't want to swear fealty ever again," I say, determining to pay him a visit.

Grimsen chose to live as well as work in the old forge Cardan gave him, though it was overgrown with rosebushes and not in the best repair.

A thin plume of smoke spirals up from the chimney as I approach. I rap three times on the door and wait.

A few moments later, he opens the door, letting out a blast of heat hot enough for me to take a step back.

"I know you," he says.

"Queen of Mirth," I acknowledge, getting it out of the way.

He laughs, shaking his head. "I knew your mortal father. He made a knife for me once, traveled all the way to Fairfold to ask me what I thought of it."

"And what *did* you think?" I wonder if this was before Justin arrived at Elfhame, before my mother.

"He had real talent. I told him that if he practiced for fifty years he might make the greatest blade ever made by a mortal man. I told him that if he practiced for a *hundred* years, he might craft one of the finest blades made by anyone. None of it satisfied him. Then I told him that I would give him one of my secrets: He could learn the practice of a hundred years in a single day, if only he would make a bargain with me. If only he would part with something he didn't want to lose."

"And did he make the bargain?" I ask.

He appears delighted. "Oh, wouldn't you like to know? Come in."

With a sigh, I do. The heat is nearly unbearable, and the stink of metal overwhelms my senses. In the dim room, what I see most is fire. My hand goes to the knife in my sleeve.

Thankfully, we move through the forge and into the living quarters of the house. It is untidy, all the surfaces littered with beautiful things—gems, jewelry, blades, and other ornaments. He pulls out a small wooden chair for me and then sits on a low bench.

He has a worn, leathery face, and his silvery hair stands on end, as though he has been tugging on it as he worked. Today he is not clad in jeweled jackets; he wears a worn leather smock over a gray shirt smeared with ash. Seven heavy gold hoops hang from his large, pointed ears.

"What brings you to my forge?" he asks.

"I was hoping to find a gift for my sister. She is getting married in just a few days."

"Something special, then," he says.

"I know you are a legendary smith," I tell him. "So I thought it was possible you no longer sold your wares."

"No matter my fame, I am still a tradesman," he says, covering his heart. He looks pleased to be flattered. "But it's true that I no longer deal in coins, only in barter."

I should have figured there was some trick. Still, I blink at him, all innocence. "What can I give you that you don't already have?"

"Let's find out," he says. "Tell me about your sister. Is this a love match?"

"It must be," I say, thinking that over. "Since there's no practical value in it."

His eyebrows rise. "Yes, I see. And does your sister resemble you?"

"We're twins," I say.

"Blue stones, then, for your coloring," he says. "Perhaps a necklace of tears to weep so that she won't have to? A pin of teeth to bite annoying husbands? No." He continues to walk through the small space. He lifts a ring. "To bring on a child?" And then, seeing my face, lifts a pair of earrings, one in the shape of a crescent moon and the other in the shape of a star. "Ah, yes. Here. This is what you want."

"What do they do?" I ask.

He laughs. "They are beautiful—isn't that enough?"

I give him a skeptical look. "It would be enough, considering how exquisite they are, but I bet it isn't all."

He enjoys that. "Clever girl. They are not only beautiful, but they add to beauty. They make someone more lovely than they were, painfully lovely. Her husband will not leave her side for quite some time."

The look on his face is a challenge. He believes I am too vain to give such a gift to my sister.

How well he knows the selfish human heart. Taryn will be a beautiful bride. How much more do I, her twin, want to put myself in her shadow? How lovely can I bear her to be?

And yet, what better gift for a human girl wedded to the beauty of the Folk?

"What would you take for them?" I ask.

"Oh, any number of little things. A year of your life. The luster of your hair. The sound of your laugh."

"My laugh is not such a sweet sound as all that."

"Not sweet, but I bet it's rare," he says, and I wonder at his knowing that.

"What about my tears?" I ask. "You could make another necklace."

He looks at me, as though evaluating how often I weep. "I will take a single tear," he says finally. "And you will take an offer to the High King for me."

"What kind of offer?" I counter.

"It is known that the Undersea has threatened the land. Tell your king that if he declares war, I will make him armor of ice to shatter every blade that strikes it and that will make his heart too cold to feel pity. Tell him I will make him three swords that, when used in the same battle, will fight with the might of thirty soldiers."

I am shocked. "I will tell him. But why would you want that?"

He grimaces, taking out a cloth to polish the earrings. "I have a reputation to rebuild, my lady, and not just as a maker of trinkets. Once, kings and queens came to me as supplicants. Once, I forged crowns and blades to change the world. It stands within the High King's power to restore my fame, and it stands within my power to add to his power."

"What happens if he likes the world the way it is?" I ask. "Unchanged."

He gives a little laugh. "Then I will make you a little glass in which to suspend time."

The tear is taken out of the corner of my eye with a long siphon. Then I leave, holding Taryn's earrings and more questions.

Back in my own rooms, I hold the jewels to my own ears. Even in the mirror, they make my eyes look liquid and luminous. My mouth seems redder, my skin glows as though I have just risen from a bath.

I wrap them up before I think better of it.

CHAPTER 19

I spend the rest of the night in the Court of Shadows, preparing plans to keep Oak safe. Winged guards who can sweep him up into the air if he is lured by the delights of the waves he once played in. A spy disguised as a nanny, to follow him and dote on him and sample anything before he can taste it. Archers in the trees, the tips of their arrows trained on anyone who comes too close to my brother.

As I am trying to anticipate what Orlagh might do and how to know as soon as it happens, there's a knock on my door.

"Yes?" I call, and Cardan walks in.

I jerk to my feet in surprise. I don't expect him to be here, but he is, dressed in disarranged finery. His lips are slightly swollen, his hair mussed. He looks as though he came straight from a bed and not his own.

He tosses a scroll down on my desk.

"Well?" I ask, my voice coming out as cold as I could ever wish.

"You were right," he says, and it sounds like an accusation.

"What?" I ask.

He leans against the doorjamb. "Nicasia gave up her secrets. All it took was some kindness and a few kisses."

Our eyes meet. If I look away, then he will know I am embarrassed, but I fear he can tell anyway. My cheeks go hot. I wonder if I will ever be able to look at him again without remembering what it was like to touch him.

"Orlagh will act during the wedding of Locke and your sister."

I sit back down in my chair, looking at all the notes in front of me. "You're sure?"

He nods. "Nicasia said that as mortal power grows, land and sea ought to be united. And that they would be, either in the way she hoped or the way I should fear."

"Ominous," I say.

"It seems I have a singular taste for women who threaten me."

I cannot think of what to say to that, so instead I tell him about Grimsen's offer to forge him armor and swords to carry him to victory. "So long as you're willing to fight the Undersea."

"He wants me to have a war to restore him to his former glory?" Cardan asks.

"Pretty much," I say.

"Now, that's ambition," Cardan says. "There might be only a floodplain and several pine trees still on fire remaining, but the four Folk huddling together in a damp cave would have heard the name Grimsen. One must admire the focus. I don't suppose you told him that declaring war was your call, not mine."

If he's the true High King of Elfhame, whom we are to follow to the end of days, then we've been a mite disrespectful, running the kingdom for him. But if he's playacting, then he's a spy for sure and better than most of us.

"Of course not," I say.

For a moment, there is silence between us.

He takes a step toward me. "The other night—"

I cut him off. "I did it for the same reason that you did. To get it out of my system."

"And is it?" he asks. "Out of your system?"

I look him in the face and lie. "Yes."

If he touches me, if he even takes another step toward me, my deceit will be exposed. I don't think I can keep the longing off my face. Instead, to my relief, he gives a thin-lipped nod and departs.

From the next room, I hear the Roach call out to Cardan, to offer to teach him the trick of levitating a playing card. I hear Cardan laugh.

It occurs to me that maybe desire isn't something overindulging helps. Maybe it is not unlike mithridatism; maybe I took a killing dose when I should have been poisoning myself slowly, one kiss at a time.

I am unsurprised to find Madoc in his strategy room in the palace, but he is surprised by me, unused to my slyfooting.

"Father," I say.

"I used to think I wanted you to call me that," he says. "But it turns out that when you do, good things seldom come after."

"Not at all," I say. "I came to tell you that you were right. I hate the idea of Oak's being in danger, but if we can engineer when the Undersea's strike comes, that's safer for Oak."

"You've been planning out the guarding of him while he's here." He grins, showing his sharp teeth. "Hard to cover every eventuality."

"Impossible." I sigh, walking deeper into the room. "So I'm on board. Let me help misdirect the Undersea. I have resources." He's been a general a long time. He planned Dain's murder and got away with it. He's better at this than I am.

"What if you only want to thwart me?" he asks. "You can hardly expect me to take it on faith that now you are in earnest."

Although Madoc has every reason to distrust me, it stings. I wonder what it would have been like if he had shared his plans for putting Oak on the throne before I was witness to the coronation bloodbath. Had he trusted me to be a part of his scheme, I wonder if I would have waved away my doubts. I don't like to think of that being possible, but I fear it might be.

"I wouldn't put my brother at risk," I say, half in response to him, half in response to my own fears.

"Oh?" he asks. "Not even to save him from my clutches?"

I guess I deserve that. "You said you wanted me to come back to your side. Here's your chance to show me what it would be like to work with you. Persuade me."

While I control the throne, we can't ever truly be on the same side, but maybe we could work together. Maybe he can channel his ambition into beating the Undersea and forget about the throne, at least until Oak comes of age. By then, at least, things will be different.

He indicates the table with a map of the islands and his carved figurines. "Orlagh has a week to strike, unless she means to set a trap back in the mortal world in Oak's absence. You have guards on Vivienne's apartment—ones you've engaged outside the military and who do not look like knights. Clever. But nothing and no one is infallible. I think the place most advantageous for us to tempt them into striking—"

"The Undersea is going to make its move during Taryn's wedding."

"What?" He gives me a narrow-eyed evaluation. "How do you know that?"

"Nicasia," I say. "And I think I can narrow things more if we work fast. I have a way to get information to Balekin, information that he will believe."

Madoc's eyebrows rise.

I nod. "A prisoner. I've already sent information through her successfully."

He turns away from me to pour himself a finger of some dark liquor and flop back into a leather chair. "These are the resources you mentioned?"

"I do not come to you empty-handed," I say. "Aren't you at least a little pleased you decided to trust me?"

"I could claim that it was *you* who finally decided to trust *me*. Now it remains to be seen how well we will work together. There are many more projects on which we could collaborate."

Like taking the throne. "One misadventure at a time," I caution him.

"Does he know?" Madoc asks, grinning in a slightly terrifying yet paternal fashion. "Does our High King have any idea how good you are at running his kingdom for him?"

"Keep hoping he doesn't," I say, trying for a breezy confidence that I don't feel when it comes to anything to do with Cardan or our arrangement.

Madoc laughs. "Oh, I shall, daughter, much as I hope you will realize how much better it would be if you were running it for your own family."

Cardan's audience with Balekin takes place the next day. My spies tell me Cardan spent the night alone—no riotous parties, no drunken revels, no contests for lyres. I do not know how to interpret that.

Balekin is led into the throne room in chains, but he walks with his head up, in clothing far too fine for the Tower. He flaunts his ability to obtain luxuries, flaunts his arrogance, as though Cardan is to be awed by this instead of annoyed.

For his part, Cardan looks especially formidable. He wears a coat of mossy velvet, embroidered all over in bright gold. The earring given to him by Grimsen dangles from his lobe, catching the light as he turns his head. No revelers are here today, but the room is not empty. Randalin and Nihuar stand together near the dais to one side, near three guards. I am on the other, standing near a patch of shadows. Servants linger nearby, ready to pour wine or play harps, as suits the High King's pleasure.

I arranged with Vulciber for Lady Asha to get a note just as Balekin was being brought up the stairs and out of the Tower for this audience.

The note read:

> I have thought over your requests and want to negotiate. There's a way to get you off the island, immediately after my sister's wedding. For his safety, my little brother is being brought back by boat because flying

made him ill. You can go, too, without the High King being the wiser, as the journey is, of necessity, secret. If you agree that this will suffice, send me word back and we will meet again to discuss my past and your future. —J

There is some chance that she will say nothing to Balekin when he returns to his cell, but since she has passed on information to him already and since he doubtlessly saw her get the note, I believe he will not stand for hearing there was nothing to it, especially as, being a faerie, she must engage in evasions rather than outright lies.

"Little brother," Balekin says without waiting to be acknowledged. He wears the chained cuffs on his wrists as though they are bracelets, as though they add to his status instead of marking him as a prisoner.

"You requested an audience with the crown," Cardan says.

"No, brother, it was you I wanted to speak with, not the ornament on your head." Balekin's sly disrespect makes me wonder why he wanted this audience in the first place.

I think of Madoc and how around him, I am perpetually a child. It's no small thing to pass judgment on the person who raised you, no matter what else they have done. This confrontation is less about this moment and more about the vast sweep of their past, the warp and weft of old resentments and alliances between them.

"What is it you want?" Cardan asks. His voice remains mild but empty of the bored authority he usually wields.

"What does any prisoner want?" Balekin says. "Let me out of the Tower. If you mean to succeed, you need my help."

"If you've been trying to see me only to say that, your efforts have been to no purpose. No, I will not release you. No, I do not need you." Cardan sounds certain.

Balekin smiles. "You've locked me away for fear of me. After all, you hated Eldred more than I did. You despised Dain. How can you punish me for deaths you do not regret?"

Cardan looks at Balekin in disbelief, half-rising from the throne. His fists are balled. His face is that of a person who has forgotten where he is. "What of Elowyn? What of Caelia and Rhyia? If all I cared for were my own feelings, their deaths would be enough reason for me to revenge myself on you. They were our sisters, and they would have been better rulers than either you or I."

I thought Balekin would back down at that, but he doesn't. Instead, an insidious little smile grows on his mouth. "Did they intercede for you? Did any one of your dear sisters take you in? How can you think they cared for you when they wouldn't go against Father for your sake?"

For a moment, I think Cardan is going to strike him. My hand goes to the hilt of my own sword. I will get in front of him. I will fight Balekin. It would be my pleasure to fight Balekin.

Instead, Cardan slumps back down onto the throne. The fury leaves his face, and he speaks as though Balekin's last words went unheard. "But you are locked away neither because I fear you nor for revenge. I did not indulge myself with your punishment. You are in the Tower because it is just."

"You can't do this alone," Balekin says, looking around the room. "You've never cared for work, never cared to flatter diplomats or follow duty instead of pleasure. Give me the difficult tasks, instead of giving them to some mortal girl to whom you feel indebted and who will only fail you."

The eyes of Nihuar and Randalin and a few of the guards go to me, but Cardan watches his brother. After a long moment, he speaks. "You would be my regent, though I am of age? You come before me not as a penitent, but as before a stray dog you would call to heel."

Finally, Balekin looks discomfited. "Although I have sometimes been harsh with you, it was because I sought to make you better. Do you think that you can be indolent and self-indulgent and yet succeed here, as a ruler? Without me, you would be nothing. Without me, you *will* be nothing."

The idea that Balekin can say those words without believing them a lie is shocking.

Cardan, for his part, wears a small smile, and when he speaks, his voice is light. "You threaten me, you praise yourself. You give away your desires. Even were I considering your offer, after that little speech, I would be sure you were no diplomat."

Balekin takes a furious step toward the throne, and guards close the space between them. I can see Balekin's physical urge to punish Cardan.

"You are playing at being king," Balekin says. "And if you don't know it, then you are the only one. Send me back to prison, lose my help, and lose the kingdom."

"That," Cardan says. "The second option, the one that doesn't involve you. That's the one I choose." He turns to Vulciber. "This audience is over."

As Vulciber and the other guards move to escort Balekin back to the

Tower of Forgetting, his gaze goes to me. And in his eyes, I see a well of hate so deep that I fear that if we're not careful, all of Elfhame may drown in it.

Two nights before my sister's wedding, I stand in front of the long mirror in my rooms and slowly draw Nightfell. I move through the stances, the ones Madoc taught me, the ones I learned in the Court of Shadows.

Then I raise my blade, presenting it to my opponent. I salute her in the mirror.

Back and forth, I dance across the floor, fighting her. I strike and parry, parry and strike. I feint. I duck. I watch sweat bead on her forehead. I battle on until perspiration stains her shirt, until she's shaking with exhaustion.

It's still not enough.

I can never beat her.

CHAPTER 20

The trap for Orlagh is set. I spend the day with Madoc going over the particulars. We created three specific times and places where the Undersea could strike with some confidence:

The boat itself, carrying a decoy, is obvious. It requires a hob to pretend to be Oak, huddling in a cloak, and the boat itself to be enchanted to fly.

Before that, there is a moment during Taryn's reception when Oak is to wander off on his own into the maze. A section of the greenery will be replaced with treefolk, who will remain unseen until they need to strike.

And even before that, upon arrival at Locke's estate for the wedding, Oak will seem to step out of the carriage onto an open patch of land visible from the ocean. We will employ the decoy there as well. I will wait with the real Oak in the carriage while the rest of the family goes out and—hopefully—the sea strikes. Then the carriage will pull around, and we will climb straight through a window. In this case, the trees near the shore will be full of sprites, ready to spot the denizens of the Undersea, and a net has been buried under the sand to trap them.

Three chances to catch the Undersea in an attempt to harm Oak. Three chances to make them regret trying.

We do not neglect protecting Cardan, either. His personal guard is on high alert. He has his own coterie of archers who will follow his every move. And, of course, our spies.

Taryn wants to spend her last night before the wedding with her sisters, so I pack up a dress and Taryn's earrings in a rucksack and tie it to the back of the same horse I once took to Insweal. I strap Nightfell across one saddlebag. Then I ride to Madoc's estate.

The night is beautiful. A breeze runs through the trees, fragrant with the scent of pine needles and everapple. Distantly, I hear hoofbeats. Foxes make their odd screaming calls to one another. The trill of flute music comes from somewhere far off, along with the sound of mermaids singing their high-pitched, wordless songs out on the rocks.

Then, abruptly, the hoofbeats are no longer distant. Through the woods come riders. Seven of them, mounted on the backs of pearl-eyed, emaciated horses. Their faces are covered, their armor splashed with white paint. I can hear their laughter as they split apart to come at me from different angles. For a moment, I think there must be some mistake.

One of them draws an axe, which shines under the light of the first-quarter moon, putting a chill into my blood. No, there is no mistake. They have come to kill me.

My experience fighting on horseback is limited. I thought I would be a knight in Elfhame, defending some royal's body and honor, not riding into battles like Madoc.

Now, as they close in on me, I think about who was aware of that particular vulnerability. Certainly Madoc knew. Perhaps this is his method of repaying me for my betrayal. Perhaps trusting me was a ruse. After all, he knew I was headed to his stronghold tonight. And we spent the afternoon planning traps just like this.

Regretfully, I think of the Roach's warning: *Next time, take a member of the royal guard. Take one of us. Take a cloud of sprites or a drunken spriggan. Just take someone.*

But it's just me. Alone.

I urge my horse to greater speed. If I can make it through the woods and get close enough to the house, then I'll be safe. There are guards there, and whether or not Madoc put the riders up to this, he would never let a guest, not to mention his ward, be slain on his own lands.

That wouldn't be playing by the rules of courtesy.

All I have to do is make it.

The hoofbeats pound behind me as we streak through the woods. I look back, wind in my face, hair blowing into my mouth. They're riding far apart, trying to get enough ahead of me to herd me away from Madoc's, toward the coast, where there's nowhere to hide.

Closer and closer they come. I can hear them calling to one another, but the words are lost in the wind. My horse is fast, but theirs flow like water through the night. As I look back, I see one of them has drawn a bow with black-fletched arrows.

I wheel my mount to one side, only to find another rider there, cutting off my escape.

They are armored, with weapons in hand. I have only a few knives on me and Nightfell back with my saddlebags, along with a small crossbow in the pack itself. I walked through these woods hundreds of times in my childhood; I never thought I would need to be armored for battle here.

An arrow whizzes past me as another rider closes, brandishing a blade.

There is no way I will outrun them.

I stand up in the stirrups, a trick I am not sure is going to work, and then grab hold of the next sturdy branch I pass. One of the white-eyed steeds bares its teeth and bites down on the flank of my own mount. My poor animal whinnies and bucks. In the moonlight, I think I make out amber eyes as a rider's long sword swings through the air.

I vault up, hauling myself onto the branch. For a moment, I just hold on to it, breathing hard, as the riders pass beneath me. They wheel around. One takes a swig from a flask, leaving a golden stain on his lips.

"Little cat up in a tree," another calls. "Come down for the foxes!"

I push myself to my feet, mindful of the Ghost's lessons as I run along the branch. Three riders circle below me. There's a flash in the air as the axe flies in my direction. I duck, trying not to slip. The weapon whirls past me, biting into the trunk of the tree.

"Nice try," I call, trying to sound anything but terrified. I've got to get away from them. I've got to get higher. But then what? I can't fight seven of them. Even if I wanted to try, my sword is still tied to my horse. All I have are a few knives.

"Come down, human girl," says one with silvery eyes.

"We heard of your viciousness. We heard of your ferocity," says another in a deep, melodious voice that might be female. "Do not disappoint us."

A third notches another black-tipped arrow.

"If I am to be a cat, let me give you a scratch," I say, pulling two leaf-shaped knives from my sides and sending them in two shining arcs toward the riders.

One misses, and the other hits armor, but I hope it's enough of a distraction for me to tug the axe from the wood. Then I move. I jump from branch to branch as arrows fly all around, grateful for everything the Ghost ever taught me.

Then an arrow takes me in the thigh.

I am unable to bite back a cry of pain. I start moving again, pushing through the shock, but my speed is gone. The next arrow hits so near my side that it's only luck that saves me.

They can see too well, even in the dark. They can see so much better than I can.

The riders have all the advantages. Up in the trees, so long as I can't hide, all I am presenting is a slightly tricky target, but the fun kind of tricky. And the more tired I get, the more I bleed, the more I hurt, the slower I will become. If I don't change the game, I am going to lose.

I have to even the odds. I have to do something they won't expect. If I can't see, then I must trust my other senses.

Sucking in a deep breath, ignoring the pain in my leg and the arrow still sticking out of it, axe in hand, I take a running jump off the branch with a howl.

The riders try to turn their horses to get away from me.

I catch a rider in the chest with the axe. The point of it folds his armor inward. Which is quite a trick—or would have been if I didn't lose my balance a moment later. The weapon comes out of my hand as I fall. I hit the dirt hard, knocking the breath out of me. Immediately, I roll to avoid hoof strikes. My head is ringing, and my leg feels as though it's on fire when I push myself to my feet. I cracked the spine of the arrow sticking out of me, but I drove the point deeper.

The rider I struck is hanging in his saddle, his body limp and his mouth bubbling red.

Another rider wheels to the side while a third comes straight on. I draw a knife as the archer coming toward me attempts to switch back to his sword.

Six to one is much better odds, especially when four of the riders are hanging back, as though they hadn't considered that they could get hurt, too.

"Ferocious enough for you?" I shout at them.

The silver-eyed rider comes at me, and I throw my knife. It misses him but hits the horse in the flank. The animal rears up. But as he tries to get his mount back under control, another barrels toward me. I grab for the axe, take a deep breath, and focus.

The skeletal horse watches me with its pupil-less white eyes. It looks hungry.

If I die here in the woods because I wasn't better prepared, because I was too distracted to bother to strap on my own stupid sword, I will be absolutely furious with myself.

I brace as another rider bears down on me, but I am not sure I can withstand the charge. Frantically, I try to come up with another option.

When the horse is close, I drop to the ground, fighting every instinct for survival, every urge to run from the huge animal. It rushes over me, and I lift the axe and chop upward. Blood spatters my face.

The creature runs a little farther, and then drops with a vicious keening sound, trapping its rider's leg underneath its bulk.

I push to my feet, wiping my face, just in time to see the silver-eyed knight preparing to charge. I grin at him, lifting the bloody axe.

The amber-eyed rider heads toward his fallen comrade, calling for the others. The silver-eyed knight wheels around at the sound, heading toward his companions. The trapped rider struggles as I watch the other two knights pulling him free and up onto one of the other horses. Then the six wheel away through the night, no more laughter following them.

I wait, afraid they might double back, afraid that something worse is about to leap from the shadows. Minutes slip by. The loudest sound is my ragged breath and the roaring of blood in my ears.

Shakily, painfully, I walk on through the woods, only to find my own steed lying in the grass, being devoured by the dead rider's horse. I wave my axe, and it runs away. Nothing makes my poor horse any less dead, though.

My pack is gone from her back. It must have fallen off during the ride, taking my clothing and crossbow with it. My knives are gone, too, littering the forest after I threw them, probably lost in the brush. At least Nightfell is still here, tied to the saddle. I unstrap my father's sword with cramping fingers.

Using it as a cane, I manage to drag myself the rest of the way to Madoc's stronghold and wash off the blood in the pump outside.

Inside, I find Oriana sitting near a window, sewing on an embroidery hoop. She looks at me with her pink eyes and does not bother to smile, as a human might, to put me at ease. "Taryn is upstairs with Vivi and her lover. Oak sleeps and Madoc schemes." She takes in my appearance. "Did you fall in a lake?"

I nod. "Stupid, right?"

She takes another stitch. I head for the stairs, and she speaks again before my foot can hit the first step.

"Would it be so terrible for Oak to stay with me in Faerie?" she asks. There is a long pause, and then she whispers, "I do not wish to lose his love."

I hate that I have to say what she already knows. "Here, there would be no end to courtiers pouring poison in his ear, whispers of the king he would be if only Cardan was out of the way—and that, in turn, might make those loyal to Cardan desirous of getting Oak out of the way. And that's not even thinking about the biggest threats. So long as Balekin lives, Oak's safest far from Faerie. Plus there's Orlagh."

She nods, expression bleak, and turns back to the window.

Maybe she just needs someone else to be the villain, someone to be responsible for keeping them apart. Good luck for her that I am someone she already doesn't much like.

Still, I remember what it was like to miss where I grew up, miss the people who raised me.

"You'll never lose his love," I say, my voice coming out as quietly as hers did. I know she can hear me, but still she doesn't turn.

With that, I go up the stairs, leg aching. I am at the landing when Madoc comes out of his office and looks up at me. He sniffs the air. I wonder if he smells the blood still running down my leg, if he smells dirt and sweat and cold well water.

A chill goes to my bones.

I go into my old room and shut the door. I reach beneath my headboard and am grateful to find that one of my knives is still there, sheathed and a little dusty. I leave it where it was, feeling a little safer.

I limp over to my old tub, bite the inside of my cheek against the pain, and sit down on the edge. Then I slice my pants and inspect what remains of the arrow embedded in my leg. The cracked shaft is willow, stained with ash. What I can see of the arrowhead is made of jagged antler.

My hands start to shake, and I realize how fast my heart is beating, how fuzzy my head feels.

Arrow wounds are bad, because every time you move, the wound worsens. Your body can't heal with a sharp bit cutting up tissue, and the longer it's there, the harder it is to get out.

Taking a deep breath, I slide my finger down to the arrowhead and press on it lightly. It hurts enough that I gasp and go light-headed for a moment, but it doesn't seem lodged in bone.

I brace myself, take the knife, and cut about an inch down the skin of my leg. It's excruciating, and I am breathing in shallow huffs by the time I work my fingers into the skin and pull the arrowhead free. There's a lot of blood, a scary amount. I press my hand against it, trying to stop the flow.

For a while, I am too dizzy to do anything but sit there.

"Jude?" It's Vivi, opening the door. She takes a look at me, and then at the tub. Her cat eyes widen.

I shake my head. "Don't tell anyone."

"You're bleeding," she says.

"Get me..." I start and then stop, realizing that I need to stitch up the wound, that I didn't think of that. Maybe I'm not as okay as I thought I was. Shock doesn't always hit right away. "I need a needle and thread—not thin stuff, embroidery floss. And a cloth to keep putting pressure on the wound."

She frowns at the knife in my hand, the freshness of the wound. "Did you do that to yourself?"

That snaps me out of my daze for a moment. "Yes, I shot *myself* with an arrow."

"Okay, okay." She hands me a shirt from the bed and then goes out of the room. I press the fabric against my wound, hoping to slow the bleeding.

When she gets back, she's holding white thread and a needle. That thread is not going to be white for long.

"Okay," I say, trying to concentrate. "You want to hold or sew?"

"Hold," she says, looking at me as though she wished there was a third option. "Don't you think I should get Taryn?"

"The night before her wedding? Absolutely not." I try to thread the needle, but my hands are shaking badly enough that it's difficult. "Okay, now push the sides of the wound together."

Vivi kneels down and does, making a face. I gasp and try not to pass out. Just a few more minutes and I can sit down and relax, I promise myself. Just a few more minutes and it will be like this never happened.

I stitch. It hurts. It hurts and hurts and hurts. After I'm done, I wash the leg with more water and rip off the cleanest section of the shirt to wrap around it.

She comes closer. "Can you stand?"

"In a minute." I shake my head.

"What about Madoc?" she asks. "We could tell—"

"No one," I say, and, gripping the edge of the tub, kick my leg over, biting back a scream.

Vivi turns on the taps, and water splashes out, washing away the blood. "Your clothes are soaked," she says, frowning.

"Hand me a dress from over there," I say. "Look for something sack-like."

I force myself to limp over to a chair and sink into it. Then I pull off my jacket and the shirt underneath it. Naked to my waist, I can't go any further without pain stopping me.

Vivi brings over a dress—one so old that Taryn didn't bother to take it to me—and bunches it up so she can lift it over my head, then guides my hands through the armholes as though I were a child. Gently, she takes off my boots and the remains of my pants.

"You could lie down," she says. "Rest. Heather and I can distract Taryn."

"I am going to be fine," I say.

"You don't have to do anything else, is all I'm saying." Vivi looks as though she's reconsidering my warnings about coming here. "Who did this?"

"Seven riders—maybe knights. But who was actually behind the attack? I don't know."

Vivi gives a long sigh. "Jude, come back to the human world with me. This doesn't have to be normal. This isn't normal."

I get up out of the chair. I would rather walk on the wounded leg than listen to more of this.

"What would have happened if I hadn't come in here?" she demands.

Now that I am up, I have to keep moving or lose momentum. I head for the door. "I don't know," I say. "But I do know this. Danger can find me in the mortal world, too. My being *here* lets me make sure you and Oak have guards watching you *there*. Look, I get that you think what I am doing is stupid. But don't act like it's useless."

"That's not what I meant," she says, but by then I am in the hall. I jerk open the door to Taryn's room to find her and Heather laughing at something. They stop when we come in.

"Jude?" Taryn asks.

"I fell off my horse," I tell her, and Vivi doesn't contradict me. "What are we talking about?"

Taryn is nervous, roaming around the room to touch the gauzy gown she will wear tomorrow, to hold up the circlet woven with greenery grown in goblin gardens and fresh as the moment they were plucked.

I realize that the earrings I bought for Taryn are gone, lost with the rest of the pack. Scattered among leaves and underbrush.

Servants bring wine and cakes, and I lick the sweet icing and let the conversation wash over me. The pain in my leg is distracting, but more distracting yet is the memory of the riders laughing, the memory of their closing in beneath the tree. The memory of being wounded and frightened and all alone.

When I wake the day of Taryn's wedding, it is in the bed of my childhood. It feels like coming up from a deep dream, and for a moment, it's not that I don't know where I am—it's that I don't remember *who* I am. For those few moments, blinking in the late-morning sunlight, I am Madoc's loyal daughter, dreaming of becoming a knight in the Court. Then the last half year comes back to me like the now-familiar taste of poison in my mouth.

Like the sting of the sloppily done stitches.

I push myself up and unwrap the cloth to look at the wound. It's ugly and swollen, and the needlework is poor. My leg is stiff, too.

Gnarbone, an enormous servant with long ears and a tail, comes into my room with a belated knock. He is carrying a tray with breakfast on it. Quickly, I flip the blankets over my lower body.

He puts the tray on the bed without comment and goes into the bath area. I hear the rush of water and smell crushed herbs. I sit there, braced, until he leaves.

I could tell him I'm hurt. It would be a simple thing. If I asked Gnarbone to send for a military surgeon, he'd do it. He'd tell Oriana and Madoc, of course. But my leg would be stitched up well and I'd be safe from infection.

Even if Madoc had sent the riders, I believe he'd still take care of me. Courtesy, after all. He'd take it to be a concession, though. I'd be admitting that I needed him, that he won. That I'd come home for good.

And yet, in the light of the morning, I am fairly sure it wasn't Madoc who sent the riders, even if it was the sort of trap he favors. He would have never sent assassins who hung back and who rode off when the numbers were still on their side.

Once Gnarbone goes out, I drink the coffee greedily and make my way to the bath.

It's milky and fragrant, and only under the water can I allow myself to weep. Only under the water can I admit that I almost died and that I was terrified and that I wish there was someone to whom I could tell all that. I hold my breath until there's no more breath to hold.

After the bath, I wrap myself in an old robe and make it to the bed. As I try to decide if it's worth sending a servant back to the palace to get me another dress or if I should just borrow something of Taryn's, Oriana comes into the room, holding a silvery piece of cloth.

"The servants tell me you brought no luggage," she says. "I assume you forgot that your sister's wedding would require a new gown. Or a gown at all."

"At least one person is going to be naked," I say. "You know it's true. I've never been to a single revel in Faerie where *everyone* had clothes on."

"Well, if that's your plan," she says, turning on her heels. "Then I suppose all you need is a pretty necklace."

"Wait," I say. "You're right. I don't have a dress, and I need one. Please don't go."

When Oriana turns, a hint of a smile is on her face. "How unlike you, to say what you actually mean and have it be something other than hostile."

I wonder how it is for her to live in Madoc's house, to be Madoc's obedient wife and have had a hand in all his schemes being undone. Oriana is capable of more subtlety than I would have given her credit for.

And she has brought me a dress.

That seems like a kindness until she spreads it out on my bed.

"It's one of mine," she says. "I believe it will fit."

The gown is silver and reminds me a little of chain mail. It's beautiful, with trumpet sleeves slashed along the length of the arm to show skin, but it has a plunging neckline, which would look one way on Oriana and a totally different way on me.

"It's a little, uh, daring for a wedding, don't you think?" There's no way to wear it with a bra.

She just looks at me for a moment, with a puzzled, almost insect-like stare.

"I guess I can try it on," I say, remembering that I had joked about being naked just a moment ago.

This being Faerie, she makes no move to leave. I turn around, hoping that will be enough to draw attention away from my leg as I strip. Then I pull the gown over my head and let it slither over my hips. It sparkles gorgeously, but as I suspected, it shows a lot of my chest. Like, *a lot.*

Oriana nods, satisfied. "I will send someone to do your hair."

A short while later, a willowy pixie girl has braided my hair into ram's horns and wrapped the tips with silver ribbon. She paints the lids of my eyes and my mouth with more silver.

Then, dressed, I go downstairs to join the rest of the family in Oriana's parlor, as though the last few months haven't happened.

Oriana is dressed in a gown of pale violet with a collar of fresh petals that rises to her powdery jawline. Vivi and Heather are both in mortal clothes, Vivi in a fluttery fabric with a pattern of eyes printed on the cloth, and Heather in a short pink dress with little silver spangles all over it. Heather's hair is pulled back in sparkling pink clips. Madoc is wearing a deep plum tunic, Oak in a matching tone.

"Hey," Heather says. "We're both in silver."

Taryn isn't there yet. We sit around the parlor, drinking tea and eating bannocks.

"Do you really think she's going to go through with this?" Vivi asks.

Heather gives her a scandalized look, swats at her leg.

Madoc sighs. "It is said we learn more from our failures than our successes," he says with a pointed look in my direction.

Then Taryn finally comes down. She's been bathed in lilac dew and wears a gown of incredibly fine layers of cloth on top of one another, herbs and flowers trapped between them to give the impression that she's this beautiful, floating figure and a living bouquet at the same time.

Her hair is braided into a crown with green blooms all through it.

She looks beautiful and painfully human. In all that pale fabric, she looks like a sacrifice instead of a bride. She smiles at all of us, shy and glowingly happy.

We all rise and tell her how beautiful she looks. Madoc takes her hands and kisses them, looking at her like any proud father. Even though he thinks she's making a mistake.

We get into the carriage, along with the small hob who is going to be Oak's double, who switches jackets once we're inside, and then sits worriedly in a corner.

On our way to Locke's estate, Taryn leans forward and catches my hand. "Once I am married, things will be different."

"Some things," I say, not entirely sure what she's talking about.

"Dad has promised to keep him in line," she whispers.

I recall Taryn's appeal to me to have Locke dismissed from his position as Master of Revels. Curbing Locke's indulgences is likely to keep Madoc busy, which seems like no bad thing.

"Are you happy for me?" she asks. "Truly?"

Taryn has been closer to me than any other person in the world. She has known the tide and undertow of my feelings, my hurts, both small and large, for most of my life. It would be stupid to let anything interfere with that.

"I want *you* to be happy," I say. "Today and always."

She gives me a nervous smile, and her fingers tighten on mine.

I am still holding her hand when the hedge maze comes into view. I see three pixie girls in diaphanous gowns fly over the greenery, giggling together, and beyond them other Folk already beginning to mill. As Master of Revels, Locke has organized a wedding worthy of the title.

CHAPTER 21

The first trap goes unsprung. The decoy climbs out with my family while Oak and I duck down in the carriage. He grins at me at first, when we huddle down in the space between the cushioned benches, but the grin slips off his face a moment later, replaced by worry.

I take his hand and squeeze it. "Ready to climb through a window?"

That delights him anew. "From the carriage?"

"Yes," I say, and wait for it to pull around. When it does, there's a knock. I peek out and see the Bomb inside the estate. She winks at me, and then I lift up Oak and feed him, hooves first, through the carriage window and into her arms.

I climb after, inelegantly. My dress is ridiculously revealing, and my leg is still stiff, still hurting, when I fall onto Locke's stone floor.

"Anything?" I ask, looking up at the Bomb.

She shakes her head, extending a hand to me. "That was always the long shot. My bet is on the maze."

Oak frowns, and I rub his shoulders. "You don't have to do this," I tell him, although I am not sure what we'll do if he says he won't.

"I'm okay," he says without looking into my eyes. "Where's my mom?"

"I'll find her for you, twigling," says the Bomb, and puts her arm over his thin shoulder to lead him out. At the doorway, she looks back at me and fishes something out of her pocket. "You seem to have hurt yourself. Good thing I don't just cook up explosives."

With that, she tosses me something. I catch it without knowing what it is, and then turn it over in my hand. A pot of ointment. I look back up to thank her, but she's already gone.

Unstoppering the little pot, I breathe in the scent of strong herbs. Still, once I spread it over my skin, my pain diminishes. The ointment cools the heat of what was probably imminent infection. The leg is still sore, but nothing as it was.

"My seneschal," Cardan says, and I nearly drop the ointment. I tug down my dress, turning. "Are you ready to welcome Locke into your family?"

The last time we were in this house, in the maze of the gardens, his mouth was streaked with golden nevermore, and he watched me kiss Locke with a simmering intensity that I thought was hatred.

Now he studies me with a not-dissimilar look, and all I want to do is walk into his arms. I want to drown my worries in his embrace. I want him to say something totally unlike himself, about things being okay.

"Nice dress," he says instead.

I know the Court must already think I am besotted with the High King to endure being crowned Queen of Mirth and still serve as his seneschal. Everyone must think, as Madoc does, that I am his creature. Even after he humiliated me, I came crawling back.

But what if I actually *am* becoming besotted with him?

Cardan is more knowledgeable than I am at love. He could use that against me, just as I asked him to use it against Nicasia. Perhaps he found a way to turn the tables after all.

Kill him, a part of me says, a part I remember from the night I took him captive. *Kill him before he makes you love him.*

"You shouldn't be alone," I say, because if the Undersea is going to strike, then we must not give it any easy targets. "Not tonight."

Cardan grins. "I hadn't planned on it."

The offhand implication that he's not alone most nights bothers me, and I hate that it does. "Good," I say, swallowing that feeling, though it feels like swallowing bile. "But if you're planning on taking someone to bed—or better yet, several someones—choose guards. And then have yourselves guarded by more guards."

"A veritable orgy." He seems delighted by the idea.

I keep thinking of the steady way he looked at me when we were both naked, before he pulled on his shirt and fastened those elegant cuffs. *We should have called truce*, he'd said, brushing back his ink-black hair impatiently. *We should have called truce long before this.*

But neither of us called it, not then, not after.

Jude, he'd said, running a hand up my calf, *are you afraid of me?*

I clear my throat, forcing the memories away. "I command you not to allow yourself to be alone from tonight's sundown to tomorrow's sunup."

He draws back, as though bitten. He no longer expects me to deliver orders in this high-handed way, as though I don't trust him.

The High King of Elfhame makes a shallow bow. "Your *wish*—no, strike that. Your *command* is my command," he says.

I cannot look at him as he goes out. I am a coward. Maybe it's the pain in my leg, maybe it's worry over my brother, but a part of me wants to call after him, wants to apologize. Finally, when I am sure he's gone, I head toward the party. A few steps and I am in the hallway.

Madoc leans against the wall. His arms are crossed over his chest, and he shakes his head at me. "It never made sense to me. Until now."

I stop. "What?"

"I was coming in to get Oak when I heard you speaking with the High King. Forgive me for eavesdropping."

I can barely think through the thundering in my ears. "It's not what you thin—"

"If it wasn't, you wouldn't know what I thought," Madoc counters. "Very clever, daughter. No wonder you weren't tempted by anything I offered you. I said I wouldn't underestimate you, and yet I did. I underestimated you, and I underestimated both your ambition and your arrogance."

"No," I say. "You don't understand—"

"Oh, I think I do," he says, not waiting for me to explain about Oak's not being ready for the throne, about my desire to avoid bloodshed, about how I don't even know if I can hang on to what I have for longer than a year and a day. He's too angry for any of that. "At last, I finally understand. Orlagh and the Undersea we will vanquish together. But when they are gone, it will be us staring across a chessboard at each other. And when I best you, I will make sure I do it as thoroughly as I would any opponent who has shown themselves to be my equal."

Before I can think of what to say to that, he grabs hold of my arm, marching us together onto the green. "Come," he says. "We have roles yet to play."

Outside, blinking in the late-afternoon sun, Madoc leaves me to go speak with a few knights standing in a tight knot near an ornamental pool. He gives me a nod when he departs, the nod of someone acknowledging an opponent.

A shiver goes through me. When I confronted him in Hollow Hall after poisoning his cup, I thought I had made us enemies. But this is far worse. He knows I stand between him and the crown, and it matters little whether he loves or hates me—he will do whatever it takes to wrest that power from my hands.

With no other options, I head into the maze, toward the celebration at its center.

Three turns and it seems that the partygoers are farther away. Sounds grow muffled, and faint laughter comes from every direction. The boxwoods are high enough to be disorienting.

Seven turns and I am truly lost. I start back, only to find the maze has changed itself around. The paths are not where they were before.

Of course. It can't just be a normal maze. No, it's got to be out to get me.

I remember that among this foliage are the treefolk, waiting to keep Oak safe. Whether they're the ones messing with me now, I do not know, but at least I can be sure something is listening when I speak.

"I will slice my way clean through you," I say to the leafy walls. "Let's start playing fair."

Branches rustle behind me. When I turn, there's a new path.

"This better be the way to the party," I grumble, starting on it. I hope this doesn't lead to the secret oubliette reserved for people who threaten the maze.

Another turn and I come to a stretch of little white flowers and a stone tower built in miniature. From inside, I hear a strange sound, half growl and half cry.

I draw Nightfell. Not many things weep in Faerie. And the weeping things that are more common here—like banshees—are very dangerous.

"Who's in there?" I say. "Come out or I'm coming in."

I am surprised to see Heather shuffle into view. Her ears have grown furred and long, like that of a cat. Her nose is differently shaped, and the stubs of whiskers are growing above her eyebrows and from the apples of her cheeks.

Worse, since I can't see through it, it's not a glamour. It's a real spell of some kind, and I don't think it's done with her. As I watch, a light dusting of fur grows along her arms in a patterning not unlike a tortoiseshell cat.

"What—what happened?" I stammer.

She opens her mouth, but instead of an answer, a piteous yowling comes out.

Despite myself, I laugh. Not because it's funny, but because I'm startled. Then I feel awful, especially when she hisses.

I squat down, wincing at the pulling of my stitches. "Don't panic. I'm sorry. You just took me by surprise. This is why I warned you to keep that charm on you."

She makes another hissing yowl.

"Yeah," I say, sighing. "No one likes to hear 'I told you so.' Don't worry. Whatever jerk thought this was going to be a fun prank is about to have a lot of regrets. Come on."

She follows me, shivering. When I try to put an arm around her, she flinches away with another hiss. At least she remains upright. At least she is human enough to stay with me and not run off.

We plunge into the hedges, and this time the maze doesn't mess with us. In three turns, we are standing among guests. A fountain splashes gently, the sound of it mixing with conversation.

I look around, searching for someone I know.

Taryn and Locke aren't there. Most likely, they have gone to a bower, where they will make private vows to each other—their true faerie marriage, unwitnessed and mysterious. In a land where there are no lies, promises need not be public to be binding.

Vivi rushes over to me, taking Heather's hands. Her fingers have curled under in a paw-like manner.

"What's happened?" Oriana demands.

"Heather?" Oak wants to know. She looks at him with eyes that match my sister's. I wonder if that was the heart of the jest. A cat for a cat-eyed girl.

"Do something," Vivi says to Oriana.

"I am no deft hand at enchantments," she says. "Undoing curses was never my specialty."

"Who did this? *They* can undo it." My voice has a growl to it that makes me sound like Madoc. Vivi looks up with a strange expression on her face.

"Jude," Oriana cautions, but Heather points with her knuckles.

Standing by a trio of flute-playing fauns is a boy with cat ears. I stride across the maze toward him. One hand goes to the hilt of my sword; all the frustration I feel over everything I cannot control bends toward fixing this one thing.

My other hand knocks the goblet of green wine out of his grip. The liquid pools on the clover before sinking into the earth under our feet.

"What is this?" he demands.

"You put a curse on that girl over there," I tell him. "Fix her *immediately.*"

"She admired my ears," the boy says. "I was only giving her what she desired. A party favor."

"That's what I am going to say after I gut you and use your entrails as streamers," I tell him. "*I was only giving him what he wanted. After all, if he didn't want to be eviscerated, he would have honored my very reasonable request.*"

With furious looks at everyone, he stomps across the grass and speaks a few words. The enchantment begins to dissipate. Heather weeps anew, though, as her humanity returns. Huge sobbing gasps shake her.

"I want to go," she says finally in a quavering, wet voice. "I want to go home right now and never come back."

Vivi should have prepared her better, should have made sure she always wore a charm—or better yet, two. She should never have let Heather wander off alone.

I fear that, in some measure, this is my fault. Taryn and I hid from Vivi the worst of what it was to be human in Faerie. I think Vivi believed that because her sisters were fine, Heather would be, too. But we were never fine.

"It's going to be okay," Vivi is saying, rubbing Heather's back in soothing circles. "You're okay. Just a little weirdness. Later, you're going to think it was funny."

"She's not going to think it was funny," I say, and Vivi flashes me an angry look.

The sobbing continues. Finally, Vivi puts her finger under Heather's chin, raising her face to look fully into it.

"You're okay," Vivi says again, and I can hear the glamour in her voice. The magic makes Heather's whole body relax. "You don't remember the last half hour. You've been having a lovely time at the wedding, but then took a spill. You were crying because you bruised your knee. Isn't that silly?"

Heather looks around, embarrassed, and then wipes her eyes. "I feel a little ridiculous," she says with a laugh. "I guess I was just surprised."

"Vivi," I hiss.

"I know what you're going to say," Vivi tells me under her breath. "But it's just this one time. And before you ask, I've never done it before. But she doesn't need to remember all of that."

"Of course she does," I say. "Or she won't be careful next time."

I am so angry that I can barely speak, but I need to make Vivi understand. I need to make her realize that even terrible memories are better than weird gaps or the hollowness of your feelings not making sense.

But before I can begin, the Ghost is at my shoulder. Vulciber, beside him. They are both in uniform.

"Come with us," the Ghost says, uncharacteristically blunt.

"What is it?" I ask them, my voice sharp. I am still thinking about Vivi and Heather.

The Ghost is as grim as I've ever seen him. "The Undersea made its move."

I look around for Oak, but he is where I left him moments before, with Oriana, watching Heather insist that she's fine. A small frown creases the space between his brows, but he seems otherwise utterly safe from everything but bad influence.

Cardan stands on the other side of the green, near where Taryn and Locke have just come back from swearing their vows. Taryn looks shy, with roses in her cheeks. Folk rush over to kiss her—goblins and grigs, Court ladies and hags. The sky is bright overhead, the wind sweet and full of flowers.

"The Tower of Forgetting. Vulciber insists you ought to see it," the Bomb says. I didn't even notice her walking up. She's all in black, her hair pulled into a tight bun. "Jude?"

I turn back to my spies. "I don't understand."

"We will explain on the way," Vulciber says. "Are you ready?"

"Just a second." I should congratulate Taryn before I leave. Kiss her cheeks and say something nice, and then she'll know I was here, even if I had to go. But as I look toward her, evaluating how swiftly I can do that, my gaze catches on her earrings.

Dangling from her lobes are a moon and a star. The same ones I bargained for from Grimsen. The ones I lost in the wood. She wasn't wearing them when we got in the carriage, so she must have got them...

Beside her, Locke is smiling his fox smile, and when he walks, he has a slight limp.

For a moment, I just stare, my mind refusing to acknowledge what I'm seeing. Locke. It was Locke with the riders, Locke and his friends on the night before he was to be married. A bachelor party of sorts. I guess he decided to pay me back for threatening him. That, or perhaps he knew he could never stay faithful and decided to go after me before I came back for him.

I take one last look at them and realize I can do nothing now.

"Pass the news about the Undersea on to the Grand General," I tell the Bomb. "And make sure—"

"I'll watch over your brother," she reassures me. "And the High King."

Turning my back on the wedding, I follow Vulciber and the Ghost. Yellow horses with long manes are nearby, already saddled and bridled. We swing up onto them and ride to the prison.

From the outside, the only evidence that something might be wrong is the waves striking higher than I've ever seen them. Water has pooled on the uneven flagstones.

Inside, I see the bodies. Knights, lying pale and still. The few on their backs have water filling their mouths as though their lips were the edges of cups. Others lie on their sides. All their eyes have been replaced with pearls.

Drowned on dry land.

I rush down the stairs, terrified for Cardan's mother. She is there, though, alive, blinking out at me from the gloom. For a moment, I just stand in front of her cell, hand on my chest in relief.

Then I draw Nightfell and cut straight down between bar and lock. Sparks fly, and the door opens. Asha looks at me suspiciously.

"Go," I say. "Forget our bargains. Forget everything. Get out of here."

"Why are you doing this?" she asks me.

"For Cardan," I say. I leave unsaid the second part: *Because his mother is still alive and mine is not, because even if he hates you, at least he should get a chance to tell you about it.*

With one baffled look back at me, she begins to ascend.

I need to know if Balekin is still imprisoned, if he's still alive. I head lower, picking my way through the gloom with one hand against the wall and the other holding my blade.

The Ghost calls my name, probably because of Asha's abrupt arrival in front of him, but I am intent on my purpose. My feet grow swifter and more sure on the spiral steps.

I find Balekin's cell is empty, the bars bent and broken, his opulent rugs wet and covered in sand.

Orlagh took Balekin. Stole a prince of Faerie from right under my nose.

I curse my own shortsightedness. I knew they were meeting, knew they were scheming together, but I was sure, because of Nicasia, that Orlagh truly wanted Cardan to be the bridegroom of the sea. It didn't occur to me that Orlagh would act before hearing an answer. And I didn't think that when she threatened to take blood, she meant Balekin.

Balekin. It would be difficult to get the crown of Faerie on his head without Oak putting it there. But should Cardan ever abdicate, that would mean a period of instability, another coronation, another chance for Balekin to rule.

I think of Oak, who is not ready for any of this. I think of Cardan, who must be persuaded to pledge himself to me again, especially now.

I am still swearing when I hear a wave strike the rocks, hard enough to reverberate through the Tower. The Ghost shouts my name again, from closer by than I expect.

I turn as he steps into view on the other side of the room. Beside him are three of the sea Folk, watching me with pale eyes. It takes me a moment to put the image together, to realize the Ghost is not restrained nor even menaced. To realize this is a betrayal.

My face goes hot. I want to feel angry, but instead I feel a roaring in my head that overwhelms everything else.

The sea crashes against the shore again, slamming into the side of the Tower. I am glad Nightfell is already in my hand.

"Why?" I ask, hearing Nicasia's words pounding in my ears like the surf: *Someone you trust has already betrayed you.*

"I served Prince Dain," the Ghost says. "Not you."

I begin to speak, when there is a rustle behind me. Then pain in the back of my skull and nothing more.

Book Two

They stole little Bridget
For seven years long;
When she came down again
Her friends were all gone.
They took her lightly back,
Between the night and morrow,
They thought that she was fast asleep,
But she was dead with sorrow.
They have kept her ever since
Deep within the lake,
On a bed of flag-leaves,
Watching till she wake.

—William Allingham,
"The Fairies"

CHAPTER 22

I wake at the bottom of the sea.

At first, I panic. I have water in my lungs and a terrible pressure on my chest. I open my mouth to scream, and a sound comes out, but not the one I expect. It startles me enough to stop and realize that I am not drowning.

I am alive. I am breathing water, heavily, laboriously, but I am breathing it.

Beneath me is a bed shaped from reef coral and padded with kelp, long tendrils of which flutter with the current. I am inside a building, which seems also of coral. Fish dart through the windows.

Nicasia floats at the end of my bed, her feet replaced by a long tail. It feels like seeing her for the first time to see her in the water, to see her blue-green hair whorl around her and her pale eyes shine metallic under the waves. She was beautiful on land, but here she looks elemental, terrifying in her beauty.

"This is for Cardan," she says, just before she balls up her fist and hits me in the stomach.

I wouldn't have thought it possible to get the momentum needed to strike someone underwater, but this is her world, and she connects just fine.

"Ouch," I say. I try to touch where she hit me, but my wrists are restrained in heavy cuffs and won't move that far. I turn my head, seeing boulders anchoring me to the floor. A fresh panic grips me, bringing with it a sense of unreality.

"I don't know what trick you performed on him, but I will discover it," she says, unnerving me with how close her guess comes to the mark. Still, it means she doesn't *know* anything.

I force myself to concentrate on that, on the here and now, on discovering what I can do and making a plan. But it's hard when I am so very angry—angry at the Ghost for betraying me, angry at Nicasia and at myself, myself, always myself, more than anyone else. Furious at myself for winding up in this position. "What happened to the Ghost?" I spit out. "Where is he?"

Nicasia gives me a narrow-eyed look. "What?"

"He helped you kidnap me. Did you pay him?" I ask, trying to sound calm. What I most want to know is what I cannot ask—does she know the Ghost's plans for the Court of Shadows? But to find out and stop him, I must escape.

Nicasia puts her hand against my cheek, smooths back my hair. "Worry about yourself."

Maybe she only wants me here for reasons of personal jealousy. Maybe I can still get out of this.

"You think I performed a trick because Cardan likes me better than you," I say. "But you shot at him with a crossbow bolt. Of course he likes me better."

Her face goes pale, her mouth opening in surprise and then curling into rage when she realizes what I am implying—that I told him. Maybe it's not a great idea to goad her into fury when I am powerless, but I hope she will be goaded into telling me why I am here.

And how long I must stay. Already, time has passed while I was unconscious. Time when Madoc is free to scheme toward war with his new knowledge of my influence over the crown, when Cardan is entirely free to do whatever his chaotic heart desires, when Locke may make a mockery of everyone he can and draw them into his dramatics, when the Council may push for capitulation to the sea, and I can do nothing to stop any of it.

How much more time will I spend here? How long before all five months of work is undone? I think of Val Moren tossing things in the air and letting them crash down around him. His human face and his unsympathetic human eyes.

Nicasia seems to have regained her composure, but her long tail swishes back and forth. "Well, you're ours now, mortal. Cardan will regret the day he put any trust in you."

She means me to be more afraid, but I feel a little relief. They don't think I have any special power. They think I have a special vulnerability. They think they can control me as they would any mortal.

Still, relief is the last thing I ought to show. "Yeah, Cardan should definitely trust you more. You seem really trustworthy. It's not like you're actually currently betraying him."

Nicasia reaches into a bandolier across her chest and draws a blade—a shark's tooth. Holding it, she gazes at me. "I could hurt you, and you wouldn't remember."

"But you would," I say.

She smiles. "Perhaps that would be something to cherish."

My heart thunders in my chest, but I refuse to show it. "Want me to show you where to put the point?" I ask. "It's delicate work, causing pain without doing permanent damage."

"Are you too stupid to be afraid?"

"Oh, I'm scared," I tell her. "Just not of you. Whoever brought me here—your mother, I presume, and Balekin—has a use for me. I am afraid of what *that* is, but not of you, an inept torturer who is irrelevant to everyone's plans."

Nicasia says a word, and suffocating pain crashes in on my lungs. I can't breathe. I open my mouth, and the agony only intensifies.

Better it's over fast, I tell myself. But it's not fast enough.

The next time I wake, I am alone.

I lie there, water flowing around me, lungs clear. Although the bed is still beneath me, I am aware of floating above it.

My head hurts, and there is a pain in my stomach that is some combination of hunger and soreness after being punched. The water is cold, a deep chill that seeps into my veins, making my blood sluggish. I am not sure how long I've been unconscious, not sure how long it's been since I was taken from the Tower. As time slips by and fish come to pluck at my feet and hair, at the stitches around my wound, anger drains away and despair fills me. Despair and regrets.

I wish I'd kissed Taryn's cheek before I left. I wish I'd made sure Vivi understood that if she loved a mortal, she had to be more careful with her. I wish I'd told Madoc that I always intended for Oak to have the throne.

I wish I'd planned more plans. I wish I'd left more instructions. I wish I had never trusted the Ghost.

I hope Cardan misses me.

I am not sure how long I float like that, how many times I panic and pull against my chains, how many times the weight of the water over me feels oppressive and I choke on it. A merman swims into the room. He moves through the water with immense grace. His hair is a kind of striped green, and the same stripes continue down his body. His large eyes flash in the indifferent light.

He moves his hands and makes a few sounds I don't understand. Then, obviously adjusting his expectations, he speaks again. "I am here to prepare you to join Queen Orlagh for dinner. If you give me any trouble, I can equally easily render you unconscious. That's how I'd hoped to find you."

I nod. "No trouble. Got it."

More merfolk come into the room, ones with green tails and yellow tails and black-tipped tails. They swim around me, staring with their large, shining eyes.

One unshackles me from the bed, and another guides my body upright. I have almost no weight in the water. My body goes where it is pushed.

When they begin undressing me, I panic again, a kind of animal response. I twist in their arms, but they hold me firm and pull a diaphanous gown over my head. It is both short and thin, barely a garment at all. It flows around me, and I am sure most of my body is visible through it. I try not to look down, for fear that I will blush.

Then I am wrapped in ropes of pearls, my hair pulled back with a crown of shells and a net of kelp. The wound on my leg is dressed with a bandage of seagrass. Finally, I am guided through the vast coral palace, its dim light punctuated by glowing jellyfish.

The merfolk lead me into a banquet room without a ceiling, so that when I look up, I see schools of fish and even a shark above me, and above that, the glimmering light of what must be the surface.

I guess it's daytime.

Queen Orlagh sits on an enormous throne-like chair at one end of the table, the body of it encased with barnacles and shells, crabs and live starfish crawling over it, fanlike coral and bright anemones moving in the current.

She herself is impossibly regal. Her black eyes rake over me, and I flinch, knowing that I am looking at someone who has ruled longer than the span of generations of mortal lives.

Beside her sits Nicasia, in an only slightly less impressive chair. And at the other end of the table is Balekin, in a chair much diminished from either of theirs.

"Jude Duarte," he says. "Now you know how it feels to be a prisoner. How is it to rot in a cell? To think you will die there?"

"I don't know," I tell him. "I always knew I was getting out."

At that, Queen Orlagh tips back her head and laughs. "I suppose you have, in a manner of speaking. Come to me." I hear the glamour in her voice and remember what Nicasia said about my not remembering whatever she did to me. Truly, I should be glad she didn't do worse.

My flimsy gown makes it clear I am not wearing any charms. They do not know the geas Dain put on me. They believe I am entirely susceptible to glamours.

I can pretend. I can do this.

I swim over, keeping my face carefully blank. Orlagh gazes deeply into my eyes, and it's excruciatingly hard not to look away, to keep my face open and sincere.

"We are your friends," Orlagh says, stroking my cheek with long nails. "You love us very much, but you must never tell anyone how much outside this room. You are loyal to us and would do absolutely anything for us. Isn't that right, Jude Duarte?"

"Yes," I say readily.

"What would you do for me, little minnow?" she asks.

"Anything, my queen," I tell her.

She looks down the table at Balekin. "You see? That's how it's done."

He appears sullen. He thinks a lot of himself and mislikes being put in his place. The eldest of Eldred's children, he resented his father for not seriously considering him for the throne. I am sure he hates the way Orlagh talks to him. If he didn't need this alliance, and if he weren't in her domain, I doubt he would allow it.

Perhaps here is a divide for me to exploit.

Soon a parade of dishes is brought out in cloches full of air, so that even under the water, they are dry until about to be eaten.

Raw fish, cut into artful rosettes and cunning shapes. Oysters, perfumed with roasted kelp. Roe, glistening red and black.

I don't know if I may eat without being explicitly granted permission, but I am hungry and willing to risk being reprimanded.

The raw fish is mild and mixed in some peppery green. I didn't anticipate liking it, but I do. I quickly swallow three pink strips of tuna.

My head still hurts, but my stomach starts to feel better.

As I eat, I think about what I must do: listen carefully and act in every way as though I trust them, as though I am loyal to them. To do that, I must imagine myself into at least the shadow of that feeling.

I look over at Orlagh and imagine that it was she instead of Madoc who brought me up, that I was Nicasia's sort-of sister, who was sometimes mean but ultimately looked out for me. At Balekin, my imaginings balk, but I try to think of him as a new member of the family, someone I was coming to trust because everyone else did. I turn a smile on them, a generous smile that almost doesn't feel like a lie.

Orlagh looks over at me. "Tell me about yourself, little minnow."

The smile almost wavers, but I concentrate on my full stomach, on the wonder and beauty of the landscape.

"There's little to know," I say. "I'm a mortal girl who was raised in Faerie. That's the most interesting thing about me."

Nicasia frowns. "Did you kiss Cardan?"

"Is that important?" Balekin wants to know. He is eating oysters, spearing them one after another with a tiny fork.

Orlagh doesn't answer, just nods toward Nicasia. I like that she does that, putting her daughter above Balekin. It's good to have something to like about her, something to concentrate on to keep the warmth in my voice real.

"It's important if it's the reason he didn't agree to an alliance with the Undersea," Nicasia says.

"I don't know if I am supposed to answer," I say, looking around in what I hope appears like honest confusion. "But yes."

Nicasia's expression crumples. Now that I am "glamoured," she doesn't seem to think of me as a person in front of whom she has to pretend stoicism. "More than once? Does he love you?"

I didn't realize how much she'd hoped I was lying when I'd told her I kissed him. "More than once, but no. He doesn't love me. Nothing like it."

Nicasia looks at her mother, inclining her head, indicating she got the answers she wanted.

"Your father must be very angry with you for ruining all his plans," Orlagh says, turning the conversation to other things.

"He is," I say. Short and sweet. No lies I don't have to tell.

"Why didn't the general tell Balekin about Oak's parentage?" she continues. "Wouldn't that have been easier than scouring Elfhame for Prince Cardan after taking the crown?"

"I am not in his confidence," I say. "Not then and definitely not now. All I know is that he had a reason."

"Doubtless," Balekin says, "he meant to betray me."

"If Oak was High King, then it would really be Madoc who ruled Elfhame," I say, because it's nothing that they don't know.

"And you didn't want that." A servant comes in with a little silken handkerchief filled with fish. Orlagh spears one with a long fingernail, causing a thin ribbon of blood to snake toward me in the water. "Interesting."

Since it's not a question, I don't have to answer.

A few other servants begin to clear the plates.

"And would you take us to Oak's door?" Balekin asks. "Take us to the mortal world and take him from your big sister, carry him back to us?"

"Of course," I lie.

Balekin shoots a look toward Orlagh. If they took Oak, they could foster him under the sea, they could marry him to Nicasia, they could have a Greenbriar line of their own, loyal to the Undersea. They would have options beyond Balekin for access to the throne, which cannot please him.

A long game, but in Faerie, that's a reasonable way to play.

"This Grimsen creature," Orlagh asks her daughter. "You really believe he can make a new crown?"

My heart feels for a moment as though it's stuttered to a stop. I am glad no one was looking at me, because in that moment, I do not believe I could have hidden my horror.

"He made the Blood Crown," says Balekin. "If he made that, surely he can make another."

If they don't need the Blood Crown, then they don't need Oak. They don't need to foster him, don't need him to place the crown on Balekin's head, don't need him alive at all.

Orlagh gives him a look that's a reprimand. She waits for Nicasia's answer.

"He's a smith," Nicasia says. "He cannot forge beneath the sea, so he will always favor the land. But with the death of the Alderking, he craves glory. He wishes to have a High King who will give him that."

This is their plan, I tell myself to try to stifle the panic I feel. *I know their plan.* If I can escape, then I can stop it.

A knife in Grimsen's back before he finishes the crown. I sometimes doubt my effectiveness as a seneschal, but never as a killer.

"Little minnow," Orlagh says, her attention returning to me. "Tell me what Cardan promised you to help him."

"But she—" Nicasia begins, but Orlagh's look silences her.

"Daughter," says the Queen of the Undersea, "you do not see what is right beneath your nose. Cardan got a throne from this girl. Stop searching for what she has over him—and start looking for what he had over her."

Nicasia turns a petulant look on me. "What do you mean?"

"You've said that Cardan didn't much care for her. And yet she made him High King. Consider that perhaps he realized she'd be useful and exploited that usefulness, through kisses and flattery, much as you've cultivated the little smith."

Nicasia looks puzzled, as though all her ideas of the world are upset. Perhaps she didn't think of Cardan as someone capable of scheming. Still, I can see something about this pleases her. If Cardan has seduced me to his side, then she need no longer worry that he cares for me. Instead, she need only worry over my usefulness.

"What did he promise you for getting him the crown of Elfhame?" Orlagh asks me with exquisite gentleness.

"I always wanted a place in Faerie. He told me he would make me his seneschal and put me at his right hand, like Val Moren in Eldred's Court. He'd make sure I was respected and even feared." It's a lie, of course. He never promised me anything, and Dain promised far less than that. But, oh, if someone had—if Madoc had—it would have been very hard to turn down.

"You're telling me that you betrayed your father and put that fool on the throne in exchange for a *job*?" Balekin demands incredulously.

"Being the High King of Elfhame is also a job," I return. "And look at what has been sacrificed to get that." For a moment, I pause, wondering if I have spoken too harshly for them to believe I am still glamoured, but Orlagh only smiles.

"True, my dear," she says after a pause. "And aren't we putting our faith in Grimsen, even as we offer him a not particularly dissimilar reward."

Balekin looks unhappy, but he doesn't dispute it. Far easier to believe that Cardan was the mastermind than a mortal girl.

I manage to eat three more slices of fish and drink some kind of toasted rice and seaweed tea through a clever straw that leaves it unmixed with seawater before I am led to a sea cave. Nicasia accompanies the merfolk guards taking me there.

This is no bedchamber, but a cage. Once I am pushed through, however, I discover that while I am still soaking wet, my surroundings are dry and filled with air I abruptly can't breathe.

I choke, my body spasming. And up from my lungs comes all that water, along with a few pieces of partially digested fish.

Nicasia laughs.

Then, glamour heavy in her voice, she speaks. "Isn't this a beautiful room?"

What I see is only a rough stone floor, no furniture, no nothing.

Her voice is dreamy. "You'll love the four-poster bed, wrapped in coverlets. And the cunning little side tables and your own pot of tea, still steaming. It will be perfectly warm and delicious whenever you try it."

She sets down a glass of seawater on the floor. I guess that's the tea. If I drink it, as she suggests, my body will become quickly dehydrated. Mortals can go for a few days without fresh water, but since I was breathing seawater, I may already be in trouble.

"You know," she says as I pretend to admire the room, turning around in it in awe, feeling foolish, "nothing I could do to you will be as terrible as what you'll do to yourself."

I turn to her, frowning in the pretense of puzzlement.

"No matter," she says, and leaves me to spend the rest of the evening tossing and turning on the hard floor, trying to seem as though I feel it is the height of comfort.

CHAPTER 23

I wake to terrible cramps and dizziness. Cold sweat beads on my brow, and my limbs shiver uncontrollably.

For the better part of a year, I have been poisoning my body every day. My blood is used to the doses, far higher than they were when I began. Addicted to them. Now I can't do without the poison.

I lie on the stone floor and try to marshal my thoughts. Try to remember the many times Madoc was on a campaign and tell myself that he was uncomfortable on each one. Sometimes he slept stretched out on the ground, head pillowed on a clump of weeds and his own arms. Sometimes he was wounded and fought on anyway. He didn't die.

I am not going to die, either.

I keep telling myself that, but I am not sure I believe it.

For days, no one comes.

I give up and drink the seawater.

Sometimes I think about Cardan while I am lying there. I think about what it must have been like to grow up as an honored member of the royal family, powerful and unloved. Fed on cat milk and neglect. To be arbitrarily beaten by the brother you most resembled and who most seemed to care for you.

Imagine all those courtiers bowing to you, allowing you to hiss and slap at them. But no matter how many of them you humiliated or hurt, you would always know someone had found them worthy of love, when no one had ever found you worthy.

Despite growing up among the Folk, I do not always understand the way they think or feel. They are more like mortals than they believe, but the moment I allow myself to forget they're not human, they will do something to remind me. For that reason alone, I would be stupid to think I knew Cardan's heart from his story. But I wonder at it.

I wonder what would have happened if I'd admitted he wasn't out of my system.

They come for me eventually. They allow me a little water, a little food. By then, I am too weak to worry about pretending to be glamoured.

I tell them the details I remember about Madoc's strategy room and what he thinks about Orlagh's intentions. I go over the murder of my parents in visceral detail. I describe a birthday, pledge my loyalty, explain how I lost my finger and how I lied about it.

I even lie to them, at their command.

And then I have to pretend to forget when they tell me to forget. I have to pretend to feel full when they have told me I feasted and to be drunk on imaginary wine when all I've had is a goblet of water.

I have to allow them to slap me.

I can't cry.

Sometimes, when lying on the cold stone floor, I wonder if there's a limit to what I will let them do, if there is something that would make me fight back, even if it dooms me.

If there is, that makes me a fool.

But maybe if there isn't, that makes me a monster.

"Mortal girl," Balekin says one afternoon when we're alone in the watery chambers of the palace. He does not like using my name, perhaps because he doesn't like having to recall it, finding me as disposable as all the human girls who have come through Hollow Hall.

I am weak with dehydration. They regularly forget to give me fresh water and food, enchanting me illusory sustenance when I beg for it. I am having difficulty concentrating on anything.

Despite the fact that Balekin and I are alone in a coral chamber, with guards swimming patrols at intervals that I count automatically, I do not even try to fight and flee. I have no weapon and little strength. Even were I able to kill Balekin, I am not a strong enough swimmer to make it to the surface before they caught me.

My plan has narrowed to endurance, to surviving hour by hour, sunless day by day.

Perhaps I cannot be glamoured, but that doesn't mean I cannot be broken.

Nicasia has said that her mother has many palaces in the Undersea and that this, built into the rock of Insweal and along the seafloor beneath it, is only one of them. But for me, it is a constant torment to be so close to home and yet leagues beneath it.

Cages hang in the water all through the palace, some of them empty, but many of them containing mortals with graying skin, mortals who seem as though they ought to be dead but occasionally move in ways that suggest they are not. The *drowned ones*, the guards sometimes call them, and more than anything, that's what I fear becoming. I remember thinking I'd spotted the girl I pulled out of Balekin's house at Dain's coronation, the girl who threw herself into the sea, the girl who'd certainly drowned. Now I am not so sure I was wrong.

"Tell me," Balekin says today. "Why did my brother steal my crown? Orlagh thinks she understands, because she understands the craving for power, but she doesn't understand Cardan. He never much cared for hard work. He liked charming people. He liked making trouble, but he despaired of real effort. And whether or not Nicasia would admit it, she doesn't understand, either. The Cardan she knows might have manipulated you, but not into this."

This is a test, I think nonsensically. A test where I have to lie, but I am afraid my ability to make sense has deserted me.

"I am no oracle," I say, thinking of Val Moren and the refuge he's found in riddles.

"Then guess," he says. "When you paraded in front of my cell in the Tower of Forgetting, you suggested it was because I'd had a firm hand with him. But you of all people must believe he lacked discipline and that I sought his improvement."

He must be remembering the tournament that Cardan and I fought and the way he tormented me. I am tangled up in memories, in lies. I am too exhausted to make up stories. "In the time I knew him, he drunkenly rode a horse through a lesson from a well-respected lecturer, tried to feed me to nixies, and attacked someone at a revel," I say. "He did not seem to be disciplined. He seemed to have his way all the time."

Balekin seems surprised. "He sought Eldred's attention," he says finally. "For good or for ill, and mostly for ill."

"Then perhaps he wants to be High King for Eldred's sake," I say. "Or to spite his memory."

That seems to draw Balekin's attention. Though I said it only to suggest something that would misdirect him from thinking too much about Cardan's motives, once it comes out of my mouth, I ponder whether there isn't some truth to it.

"Or because he was angry with you for chopping off Eldred's head. Or being responsible for the deaths of all his siblings. Or because he was afraid you might murder him, too."

Balekin flinches. "Be quiet," he says, and I go gratefully silent. After a moment, he looks down at me. "Tell me which of us is worthy of being High King, myself or Prince Cardan?"

"You are," I say easily, giving him a look of practiced adoration. I do not point out that Cardan is no longer a prince.

"And would you tell him that yourself?" he asks.

"I would tell him whatever you wish," I say with all the sincerity I can wearily muster.

"Would you go to him in his rooms and stab him again and again until his red blood ran out?" Balekin asks, leaning closer. He says the words softly, as though to a lover. I cannot control the shudder that runs through me, and I hope he will believe it is something other than disgust.

"For you?" I ask, shutting my eyes against his closeness. "For Orlagh? It would be my pleasure."

He laughs. "Such savagery."

I nod, trying to rein in overeagerness at the thought of being sent on a mission away from the sea, at having the opportunity for escape. "Orlagh has given me so much, treated me like a daughter. I want to repay her. Despite the loveliness of my chambers and the delicacies I am given, I was not made to be idle."

"A pretty speech. Look at me, Jude."

I open my eyes and gaze up at him. Black hair floats around his face, and here, under the water, the thorns on his knuckles and running up his arms are visible, like the spiky fins of a fish.

"Kiss me," he says.

"What?" My surprise is genuine.

"Don't you want to?" he asks.

This is nothing, I tell myself, *certainly better than being slapped.* "I thought you were Orlagh's lover," I tell him. "Or Nicasia's. Won't they mind?"

"Not in the least," he tells me, watching carefully.

Any hesitation on my part will seem suspicious, so I move toward him in the water, pressing my lips against his. The water is cold, but his kiss is colder.

After what I hope is a sufficient interval, I pull back. He wipes his mouth with the back of his hand, clearly disgusted, but when he stares down at me, there's greed in his eyes. "Now kiss me as though I were Cardan."

To buy myself a moment of reflection, I gaze into his owl eyes, run my hands up his thorned arms. It is clearly a test. He wants to know how much control he has over me. But I think he wants to know something else, too, something about his brother.

I force myself to lean forward again. They have the same black hair, the same cheekbones. All I have to do is pretend.

The next day, they bring me a pitcher of clear river water, which I guzzle gratefully. The day after that, they begin to prepare me to return to the surface.

The High King has made a bargain to get me back.

I think over the many commands I gave him, but none was specific enough to have ordered his paying a ransom for my safe return. He had been free of me, and now he is willingly bringing me back.

I do not know what that means. Perhaps politics demanded it; perhaps he really, really didn't like going to meetings.

All I know is that I am giddy with relief, wild with terror that this is some kind of a game. If we do not go to the surface, I fear I will not be able to hide the pain of disappointment.

Balekin "glamours" me again, making me repeat my loyalty to them, my love, my murderous intent toward Cardan.

Balekin comes to the cave, where I am pacing back and forth, each scuff of my bare feet on the stone loud in my ears. I have never been so much alone, and I have never had to play a role for this long. I feel hollowed out, diminished.

"When we return to Elfhame, we won't be able to see each other often," he says, as though this is something I will greatly miss.

I am so jumpy that I do not trust myself to speak.

"You will come to Hollow Hall when you can."

I wonder at the idea that he anticipates living in Hollow Hall, that he doesn't expect to be put in the Tower. I suppose his freedom is part of the price of my release, and I am surprised all over again that Cardan agreed to pay it.

I nod.

"If I need you, I will give you a signal, a red cloth dropped in your path. When you see it, you must come immediately. I expect that you will be able to fabricate some excuse."

"I will," I say, my voice coming out too loud in my ears.

"You must regain the High King's trust, get him alone, and then find a way to kill him. Do not attempt it if people are around. You must be clever, even if it takes more than one meeting. And perhaps you can find out more of your father's schemes. Once Cardan is dead, we will need to move fast to secure the military."

"Yes," I say. I take a breath and then dare ask what I really want to know. "Do you have the crown?"

He frowns. "Very nearly."

For a long moment, I do not speak. I let the silence linger.

Into it, Balekin speaks. "Grimsen needs you to finish your work before he can make it. He needs my brother dead."

"Ah," I say, my mind racing. Once, Balekin risked himself to save Cardan, but now that Cardan stands between him and the crown, he seems willing enough to sacrifice his brother. I try to make sense of that, but I can't focus. My thoughts keep spiraling away.

Balekin smiles a shark's grin. "Is something the matter?"

I am almost broken.

"I feel a little faint," I say. "I don't know what could be wrong. I remember eating. At least I think I remember eating."

He gives me a concerned look and calls for a servant. In a few moments, I am brought a platter of raw fish, oysters, and inky roe. He watches in disgust as I devour it.

"You will avoid all charms, do you understand? No rowan, no bundles of oak, ash, and thorn. You will not wear them. You will not so much as touch them. If you are given one, you will cast it into a fire as soon as you can conceal doing so."

"I understand," I say. The servant has brought no more fresh water for me, but wine instead. I drink it greedily with no care for the strange aftertaste or how it goes to my head.

Balekin gives me more commands, and I try to listen, but by the time he leaves, I am dizzy from the wine, exhausted and sick.

I curl up on the cold floor of my cell, and for a moment, right before I close my eyes, I can almost believe I am in the grand room they have been conjuring for me with their glamours. Tonight, the stone feels like a feather bed.

CHAPTER 24

The next day my head pounds as I am once again dressed, and my hair is braided. Merfolk put me in my own clothes—the silver dress I wore to Taryn's wedding, now faded from exposure to salt and frayed from being picked at by Undersea creatures. They even strap Nightfell onto me, although the scabbard is rusted, and the leather looks as though something has been feasting on it.

Then I am taken to Balekin, dressed in the colors and wearing the sigil of the Undersea. He looks me over and hangs new pearls in my ears.

Queen Orlagh has assembled a huge procession of sea Folk. Merfolk, riders on enormous turtles and sharks, the selkies in their seal form, all cutting through the water. The Folk on the turtles carry long red banners that fan behind them.

I am seated on a turtle, beside a mermaid with two bandoliers of knives. She grips me firmly, and I do not struggle, though it is hard to keep still. Fear is terrible, but the combination of hope and fear is worse. I careen between the two, my heart beating so fast and my breaths coming so quickly that my insides feel bruised.

When we begin to rise, up and up and up, a sense of unreality grips me.

We crest the surface in the narrow stretch between Insweal and Insmire.

On the shore of the island, Cardan sits in a fur-lined cloak, regal on a dappled gray steed. He is surrounded by knights in armor of gold and green. To one side of him is Madoc, on a sturdy roan. To the other is Nihuar. The trees are full of archers. The hammered gold of the oak leaves on Cardan's crown seems to glow in the dimming light of sunset.

I am shaking. I feel I may shake apart.

Orlagh speaks from her place at the center of our procession. "King of Elfhame, as we agreed, now that you have paid my price, I have secured the safe return of your seneschal. And I bring her to you escorted by the new Ambassador of the Undersea, Balekin, of the Greenbriar line, son of Eldred, your brother. We hope this choice will please you, since he knows so many customs of the land."

Cardan's face is impossible to read. He doesn't look at his brother. Instead, his gaze goes to me. Everything in his demeanor is icy.

I am small, diminished, powerless.

I look down, because if I don't, I am going to behave stupidly. *You have paid my price*, Orlagh said to him. What might he have done for my return? I try to recall my commands, to recall whether I forced his hand.

"You promised her whole and hale," says Cardan.

"And you can see she is so," Orlagh says. "My daughter Nicasia, Princess of the Undersea, will help her to the land with her own royal hands."

"Help her?" says Cardan. "She ought to need no help. You have kept her in the damp and the cold for too long."

"Perhaps you no longer want her," Orlagh says. "Perhaps you would bargain for something else in her place, King of Elfhame."

"I will have her," he says, sounding both possessive and contemptuous at once. "And my brother will be your ambassador. It shall all be as we agreed." He nods toward two knights, who wade out to where I am sitting and help me down, help me to walk. I am ashamed of my unsteady legs, of my weakness, of the ridiculousness of still being dressed in Oriana's utterly unsuitable dress for a party long over.

"We are not yet at war," says Orlagh. "Nor are we yet at peace. Consider well your next move, king of the land, now that you know the cost of defiance."

The knights guide me onto the land and past the other Folk. Neither Cardan nor Madoc turn as I pass them. A carriage is waiting a little ways into the trees, and I am loaded inside.

One knight removes her helm. I have seen her before, but I do not know her. "The general has instructed me to take you to his home," she says.

"No," I say. "I have to go to the palace."

She does not contradict me, nor does she relent. "I must do as he says."

And although I know I ought to fight, that once upon a time I would have, I don't. I let her shut the door of the carriage. I lean back against the seats and close my eyes.

When I wake, the horses are kicking up dust in front of Madoc's stronghold. The knight opens the door, and Gnarbone lifts me bodily from the carriage as easily as I might have lifted Oak, as though I am made of twigs and leaves instead of earthly flesh. He carries me to my old bedroom.

Tatterfell is waiting for us. She takes down my hair and strips off my dress, carrying away Nightfell and putting me into a shift. Another servant sets down a tray holding a pot of hot tea and a plate of venison bleeding onto toast. I sit on the rug and eat it, using the buttered bread to sop up the meat juices.

I fall asleep there, too. When I wake, Taryn is shaking me.

I blink hazily and stumble to my feet. "I'm up," I say. "How long was I lying there?"

She shakes her head. "Tatterfell says that you've been out for the whole day and night. She worried that you had a human illness—that's why she sent for me. Come on, at least get in bed."

"You're married now," I say, recalling it suddenly. With that comes the memory of Locke and the riders, the earrings I was supposed to give her. It all feels so far away, so distant.

She nods, putting her wrist to my forehead. "And you look like a wraith. But I don't think you have a fever."

"I'm fine," I say, the lie coming automatically to my lips. I have to get to Cardan and warn him about the Ghost. I have to see the Court of Shadows.

"Don't act so proud," she says, and there are tears in her eyes. "You disappeared on my wedding night, and I didn't even know you were gone until morning. I've been so frightened.

"When the Undersea sent word it had you, well, the High King and Madoc blamed each other. I wasn't sure what was going to happen. Every morning, I went to the edge of the water and looked down, hoping I could see you. I asked all the mermaids if they could tell me if you were okay, but no one would."

I try to imagine the panic she must have felt, but I can't.

"They seem to have worked through their differences," I say, thinking of them together at the beach.

"Something like it." She makes a face, and I try to smile.

Taryn helps me into my bed, arranging the cushions behind me. I feel bruised all over, sore and ancient and more mortal than ever before.

"Vivi and Oak?" I ask. "Are they okay?"

"Fine," she says. "Back home with Heather, who seems to have gotten through her visit to Faerieland without much drama."

"She was glamoured," I say.

For a moment, I see anger cross her face, raw and rare. "Vivi shouldn't do that," Taryn says.

I am relieved not to be the only one to feel that way. "How long have I been gone?"

"A little over a month," she says, which seems impossibly brief. I feel as though I have aged a hundred years beneath the sea.

Not only that, but now I am more than halfway through the year and a day Cardan promised. I sink back on the cushions and close my eyes. "Help me get up," I say.

She shakes her head. "Let the kitchens send up more soup."

It isn't difficult to persuade me. As a concession, Taryn helps me dress in clothes that were once too tight and now hang on me. She stays to feed me spoonfuls of broth.

When she's ready to go, she pulls up her skirts and takes a long hunting knife out of a sheath attached to a garter. In that moment, it's clear we grew up in the same house.

She puts the knife onto the coverlets beside a charm she takes from her pocket. "Here," she says. "Take them. I know they'll make you feel safer. But you must rest. Tell me you won't do anything rash."

"I can barely stand on my own."

She gives me a stern look.

"Nothing rash," I promise her.

She embraces me before she goes, and I hang a little too long on her shoulders, drinking in the human smell of sweat and skin. No ocean, no pine needles or blood or night-blooming flowers.

I doze off with my hand on her knife. I am not sure when I wake, but it's to the sound of arguing.

"Whatsoever the Grand General's orders, I am here to see the High King's seneschal and I won't be put off with any more excuses!" It's a woman's voice, one I half-recognize. I roll off the bed, heading dizzily out into the hall, where I can look down from the balcony. I spot Dulcamara from the Court of Termites. She looks up at me. There is a fresh cut on her face.

"Your pardon," she calls in a way that makes it clear she means nothing of the sort. "But I must have an audience. In fact, I am here to remind you of your obligations, including that one."

I recall Lord Roiben with his salt-white hair and the promise I made him for supporting Cardan half a year ago. He pledged to the crown and the new High King, but on a specific condition.

Someday, I will ask your king for a favor, he said.

What did I say in return? I tried to bargain: *Something of equal value. And within our power.*

I guess he's sent Dulcamara to call in that favor, though I do not know what use I am to be when I am like this.

"Is Oriana in her parlor? If not, show Dulcamara to it, and I will speak with her there," I say, gripping the railing so that I don't fall. Madoc's guards look unhappy, but they don't contradict me.

"This way," says one of the servants, and with a last hostile look at me, Dulcamara follows.

This leaves me time to make my unsteady way down the stairs.

"Your father's orders were that you not go out," one of the guards says, used to my being a child to be minded and not the High King's seneschal with whom one might behave with more formality. "He wanted you to rest."

"By which you mean he didn't order me *not* to have audiences here, but only because he didn't think of it." The guard doesn't contradict me, only frowns. "His concerns—and yours—are noted."

I manage to make it to Oriana's parlor without falling over. And if I hold slightly too long to the wooden trim around windows or to the edges of tables, that's not so awful.

"Bring us some tea, please, as hot as you can make it," I say to a servant who watches me a little too closely.

Steeling myself, I let go of the wall and walk into the parlor, give Dulcamara a nod, and sink into a chair, although she has remained standing, hands clasped behind her back.

"Now we see what your High King's loyalty looks like," she says, taking a step toward me, her face hostile enough that I wonder if her purpose is more than speaking.

Instinct wants to push me to my feet. "What happened?"

At that, she laughs. "You know very well. Your king gave the

Undersea permission to attack us. It came two nights ago, out of nowhere. Many of our people were slain before we understood what was happening, and now we are being forbidden from retaliating."

"Forbidden from retaliating?" I think of what Orlagh said about not being at war, but how can the land not be at war if the sea has already attacked? As the High King, Cardan owes his subjects the might of his military—of Madoc's army—when they are under threat. But to deny permission of striking back was unheard of.

She bares her teeth. "Lord Roiben's consort was hurt," she says. "Badly."

The green-skinned, black-eyed pixie who spoke as though she were mortal. The one whom the terrifying leader of the Court of Termites deferred to, laughed with.

"Is she going to live?" I ask, my voice gone soft.

"You best hope so, mortal," Dulcamara says. "Or Lord Roiben will bend his will to the destruction of your boy king, despite the vows he made."

"We'll send you knights," I say. "Let Elfhame rectify our mistake."

She spits on the floor. "You don't understand. Your High King did this for you. Those were the terms under which Queen Orlagh would return you. Balekin chose the Court of Termites as the target, the Undersea attacked us, and your Cardan let her. There was no mistake."

I close my eyes and pinch the bridge of my nose. "No," I say. "That's not possible."

"Balekin has long had a grudge against us, daughter of dirt."

I flinch at the insult, but I do not correct her. She may rail at me all she likes. The High Court has failed the Court of Termites because of me.

"We should never have joined the High Court. We should never have pledged to your fool of a king. I have come to deliver that message and one message more. You owe Lord Roiben a favor, and it best be granted."

I worry over what he might ask me for. An unnamed favor is a dangerous thing to give, even for a mortal who cannot be forced to honor it.

"We have our own spies, seneschal. They tell us you're a good little murderer. Here is what we want—*kill Prince Balekin.*"

"I can't do that," I say, too astonished to weigh my words. I am not insulted by her praise of my skill at killing, but setting me an impossible task is hardly flattery, either. "He's the Ambassador of the Undersea. If I killed him, we'd be at war."

"Then go to war." With that, she sweeps from the room, leaving me sitting in Oriana's parlor when the steaming tray of tea comes in.

Once she is gone and the tea is cold, I climb the steps to my room. There, I take up Taryn's knife and the other one hidden under my bed. I take the edge of one to the pocket of my dress, slicing through it so I can strap the knife to my thigh and draw it swiftly. There are plenty of weapons in Madoc's house—including my own Nightfell—but if I start looking for them and belting them on properly, the guards are sure to notice. I need them to believe I have gone docilely back to bed.

Padding to the mirror, I look to see if the knife is concealed beneath my dress. For a moment, I don't know the person looking back at me. I am horrified at what I see—my skin has a sickly pallor, and my weight has dropped enough to make my limbs look frail and sticklike, my face gaunt.

I turn away, not wanting to look anymore.

Then I go out onto the balcony. Normally, it would be no small thing to climb over the railing and scale the wall down to the lawn. But as I put one leg over, I realize how rubbery my legs and arms have become. I don't think I can manage the climb.

So I do the next best thing: I jump.

CHAPTER 25

I get up, grass stains on my knees, my palms stinging and dirty. My head feels unsteady, as though I am still expecting to move with the current even though I am on land.

Taking a few deep breaths, I drink in the feeling of the wind on my face and the sounds of it rustling the leaves of the trees. I am surrounded by the scents of land, of Faerie, of home.

I keep thinking about what Dulcamara said: that Cardan refused to retaliate for the sake of my safe return. That can't have made his subjects happy with him. I am not sure even Madoc would think it was a good strategy. Which is why it's difficult to imagine why he agreed to it, especially since, if I stayed stuck in the Undersea, he'd be out of my control. I never thought he liked me enough to save me. And I am not sure I'll still believe it unless I hear his reasons from his lips.

But for whatever reason he brought me back, I need to warn him about the Ghost, about Grimsen and the crown, about Balekin's plan to make me into his murderer.

I start toward the palace on foot, sure it will take the guards far longer to realize I have gone than it would take the stable hands to discover a missing mount. Still, I am breathing hard soon after I start. Halfway there I have to stop and rest on a stump.

You're fine, I tell myself. *Get up.*

It takes me a long time to make it to the palace. As I walk toward the doors, I square my shoulders and try not to show just how exhausted I am.

"Seneschal," one of the guards at the gate says. "Your pardon, but you are barred from the palace."

You're never to deny me an audience or give an order to keep me from your side. For a delirious moment, I wonder if I've been in the Undersea for longer than Taryn told me. Maybe a year and a day is up. But that's impossible. I narrow my gaze. "By whose command?"

"Apologies, my lady," another knight says. His name is Diarmad. I recognize him as a knight Madoc has his eye on, someone he would trust. "The general, your father, gave the order."

"I have to see the High King," I say, trying for a tone of command, but instead a note of panic creeps into my voice.

"The Grand General told us to call you a carriage if you came and, if necessary, ride in it with you. Do you expect you will require our presence?"

I stand there, furious and outmaneuvered. "No," I say.

Cardan *couldn't* refuse me an audience, but he could *allow* someone else to give the order. So long as Madoc didn't ask for Cardan's permission, it didn't contradict my commands. And it wouldn't be so hard to figure out the sort of things I might have commanded Cardan—after all, most of it was stuff Madoc would probably have ordered himself.

I knew that Madoc wanted to rule Faerie from behind the throne. It didn't occur to me that he might find his way to Cardan's side and cut me out.

They played me. Either together or separately, they played me.

My stomach churns with anxiety.

The feeling of being fooled, the shame of it, haunts me. It tangles up my thoughts.

I recall Cardan sitting atop the dappled gray horse on the beach, his impassive face, furred cloak, and crown highlighting his resemblance to Eldred. I may have tricked him into his role, but I didn't trick the land into receiving him. He has real power, and the longer he's on the throne, the greater his power will become.

He's become the High King, and he's done it without me.

This is everything I feared when I came up with this stupid plan in the first place. Perhaps Cardan didn't want this power at first, but now that he has it, it belongs to him.

But the worst part is that it makes sense that Cardan is out of my reach, for him to be inaccessible to me. Diarmad and the other knights stopping me at the palace doors is the fulfillment of a fear I've had since the crown was placed on Cardan's head. And as terrible as it feels, it also seems more reasonable than what I've been trying to convince myself of for months—that I am the seneschal of the High King of Faerie, that I have real power, that I can keep this game going.

The only thing I wonder is why not let me languish beneath the sea?

Turning away from the palace, I head through the trees to where there's an entrance into the Court of Shadows. I just hope I won't run into the Ghost. If I do, I am not sure what will happen. But if I can get to the Roach and the Bomb, then maybe I can rest awhile. And get the information I need. And send someone to slit Grimsen's throat before he has completed making the new crown.

When I get there, though, I realize the entrance is collapsed. No, as I look at it more carefully, that's not exactly right—there's evidence of an explosion. Whatever destroyed this entrance did more damage than that.

I cannot breathe.

Kneeling in the pine needles, I try to understand what I am looking at, because it seems as though the Court of Shadows has been *buried.* This must have been the Ghost's work—betrayal on top of betrayal. I just hope the Roach and the Bomb are alive.

Please let them be alive.

And yet, without a way to find them, I am more trapped than ever. Numbly, I wander back toward the gardens.

A group of faerie children has gathered around a lecturer. A Lark boy picks blue roses from the royal bushes, while Val Moren wanders beside him, smoking a long pipe, his scald crow perched on one shoulder.

His hair is unbrushed around his head, matted in places and braided with bright cloth and bells in others. Laugh lines crease the corners of his mouth.

"Can you get me inside the palace?" I ask him. It's a long shot, but I don't care about embarrassment anymore. If I can get inside, I can discover what happened to the Court of Shadows. I can get to Cardan.

Val Moren's eyebrows rise. "Do you know what they are?" he asks me, waving a vague hand toward the boy, who turns to give us both a sharp-eyed look.

Maybe Val Moren cannot help me. Maybe Faerie is a place where a madman can play the fool and seem like a prophet—but maybe he is only a madman.

The Lark boy continues picking his bouquet, humming a tune.

"Faeries . . . ?" I ask.

"Yes, yes." He sounds impatient. "The Folk of the Air. Insubstantial, unable to hold one shape. Like the seeds of flowers launched into the sky."

The scald crow caws.

Val Moren takes a long pull on his pipe. "When I met Eldred, he rode up on a milk-white steed, and all the imaginings of my life were as dust and ashes."

"Did you love him?" I ask.

"Of course I did," he tells me, but he sounds as though he's talking about long ago, an old tale that he only needs to tell the way it was told before. "Once I met him, all the duty I felt for my family was rendered as frayed and worn as an old coat. And the moment his hands were on my skin, I would have burned my father's mill to the ground to have him touch me again."

"Is that love?" I ask.

"If not love," he says, "something very like it."

I think of Eldred as I knew him, aged and bent. But I also recall the way he seemed younger when the crown was taken from his head. I wonder how much younger he would have grown had he not been cut down.

"Please," I say. "Just help me get into the palace."

"When Eldred rode up on his milk-white steed," he says again, "he made me an offer. 'Come with me,' he said, 'to the land under the hill, and I will feed you on apples and honey wine and love. You will never grow old, and all you wish to know, you may discover.' "

"That sounds pretty good," I admit.

"Never make a bargain with them," he tells me, taking my hand abruptly. "Not a wise one or a poor one, not a silly one or a strange one, but especially not one that sounds pretty good."

I sigh. "I've lived here nearly all my life. I know that!"

My voice startles his crow, which leaps from his shoulder to fly up into the sky.

"Then know this," Val Moren says, looking at me. "I may not help you. It was one of the things I gave up. I promised Eldred that once I became his, I would renounce all of humanity. I would never choose a mortal over a faerie."

"But Eldred is dead," I insist.

"And yet my promise remains." He holds his hands in front of him in acknowledgment of his helplessness.

"We're human," I say. "We can lie. We can break our word." But the look he turns on me is pitying, as though I am the one who is mistaken.

Watching him walk off, I make a decision. Only one person has a reason to help me, only one person I can be sure of.

You will come to Hollow Hall when you can, Balekin told me. Now is as good a time as any.

I force myself to walk, though the path through the Milkwood is not a direct one, and it passes too close to the sea for my comfort. When I look out at the water, a shudder comes over me. It will not be easy to live on an island if I am tormented by waves.

I pass by the Lake of Masks. When I look down, I see three pixies staring back at me with apparent concern. I plunge my hands in and scrub my face with the fresh water. I even drink a little, though it's magical water and I'm not sure it's safe. Still, fresh water was too dear for me to pass up an opportunity to have it.

Once Hollow Hall is in sight, I pause for a moment, to get breath and courage both.

I walk up to the door as boldly as I can. The knocker on the door is a piercing through the nose of a sinister carved face. I lift my hand to touch the ring, and the carving's eyes open.

"I remember you," says the door. "My prince's lady."

"You're mistaken," I say.

"Seldom." The door swings open with a slight creak that indicates disuse. "Hail and welcome."

Hollow Hall is empty of servants and guards. No doubt it is difficult for Prince Balekin to cozen any of the Folk to serve him when he is so clearly a creature of the Undersea. And with the new rules Cardan passed, Balekin's ability to trick mortals into endless servitude has also been curtailed. I walk through echoing rooms to a parlor, where Balekin is drinking wine surrounded by a dozen thick pillar candles. Above his head, red moths dance. He left them behind in the Undersea, but now that he's back, they circle around him like a candle flame.

"Did anyone see you?" he asks.

"I don't believe so," I say with a curtsy.

He stands, going to a long trestle table and lifting a small blown-glass vial. "I don't suppose you've managed to murder my brother?"

"Madoc has ordered me away from the palace," I say. "I think he fears my influence over the High King, but I can do nothing to Cardan if I am not allowed to see him."

Balekin takes another sip of his wine and walks to me. "There's to be a ball, a masquerade to honor one of the lower Court lords. It will be tomorrow, and so long as you are able to steal away from Madoc, I will find a way to get you in. Can you acquire a costume and mask yourself, or will you need that from me as well?"

"I can costume myself," I say.

"Good." He holds up the vial. "Stabbing would be very dramatic at such a public function. Poison is ever so much easier. I want you to carry this with you until you have a moment alone with him, and then you must add it to his wine in secret."

"I will," I vow.

Then he takes my chin, glamour in his voice. "Tell me that you're mine, Jude."

When he places the vial in my hand, my fingers close over it.

"I am your creature, Prince Balekin," I say, looking into his eyes and lying with my whole broken heart. "Do with me what you will. I am yours."

CHAPTER 26

As I am about to leave Hollow Hall, I am suddenly beset by a wave of exhaustion. I sit down on the steps, light-headed, and wait until the feeling passes. A plan is growing in my mind, a plan that requires the cover of dark and my being well-rested and reasonably well-equipped.

I could go to Taryn's house, but Locke would be there, and he did try to kill me that one time.

I could return to Madoc's, but if I do, it's likely that the servants have been instructed to roll me up in fuzzy blankets and hold me in cushioned captivity until Cardan is no longer under my command, but sworn to obey his Grand General.

Horrifyingly, I wonder if the best thing to do is to stay *here*. There are no servants, no one to bother me but Balekin, and he is preoccupied. I doubt he would even notice my presence in this enormous and echoing house.

I mean to be practical, but it's hard to fight against the instinct to run as far and as fast from Balekin as I can. But I've exhausted myself already.

Having snuck through Hollow Hall enough times before, I know the way to the kitchens. I drink more water from the pump just beyond it, finding myself desperately thirsty. Then I wend my way up the steps to where Cardan once slept. The walls are as bare as I remember; the half-tester bed dominates the room with its carvings of dancing, bare-breasted cat girls.

He had books and papers—now gone—but the closet is still full of extravagant and abandoned clothes. I suppose they are no longer ridiculous enough for the High King. But more than a few are black as night, and there's hose that will be easy to move in. I crawl into Cardan's bed, and although I fear I will toss and turn with nerves, I surprise myself by slipping immediately into a deep and dreamless sleep.

Upon waking in the moonlight, I go to his closet and dress myself in the simplest of his clothes—a velvet doublet whose collar and cuffs I rip pearls from, along with a pair of plain, soft leggings.

I set out again, feeling less wobbly. When I pass through the kitchens, I find little in the way of food, but there's a corner of hard bread that I gnaw on as I walk through the dark.

The Palace of Elfhame is a massive mound with most of the important chambers—including the enormous throne room—underground. At the peak is a tree, its roots worming down more deeply than could come from anything but magic. Just beneath the tree, however, are the few rooms that have panes of thin crystal letting in light. They are unfashionable rooms, like the one Cardan once set fire to the floor of and where Nicasia popped out of his wardrobe to shoot him.

That room is now sealed, the double doors locked and barred so that the passage to the royal chambers cannot be accessed. It would be impossible to get inside from within the palace.

But I am going to climb the hill.

Quietly, stealthily, I set off, sinking my two knives into the dirt, pulling myself up, wedging my feet on rocks and roots, and then doing it again. Higher and higher I go. I see bats circling overhead and freeze, willing them not to be anyone's eyes. An owl calls from a nearby tree, and I realize how many things could be observing me. All I can do is go faster. I am nearly to the first set of windows when weakness hits me.

I grit my teeth and try to ignore the shaking of my hands, the unsteadiness of my step. I am breathing too fast, and all I want to do is give myself a rest. I am sure, though, that if I do, my muscles will stiffen up, and I won't be able to start again. I keep going, although my whole body hurts.

Then I stab one of the knives into the dirt and try to lever myself up, but my arm is too weak. I can't do it. I stare down the steep, rocky hill, at the twinkling lights around the entrance to the brugh. For a moment, my vision blurs, and I wonder what would happen if I just let go.

Which is a stupid thought. What would happen is that I would roll down the hill, hit my head, and hurt myself really badly.

I hold on, scrabbling my way toward the glass panes. I have looked at the maps of the palace enough times that I only have to peer into three panes before I find the correct one. It looks down on only darkness, but I get to work, chipping at the crystal with my knife until it cracks.

I wrap my hands in the sleeve of the doublet and break off pieces of it. Then I drop through into the darkness of the rooms that Cardan abandoned. The walls and furnishings still stink of smoke and sour wine. I make my way by touch to the wardrobe.

From there it is easy to open the passage and pad down the hall, down the spiraling path to the royal chamber.

I slip into Cardan's room. Though it is not yet dawn, I am lucky. The room is empty of revelry. No courtiers doze on the cushions or in his bed. I walk to where he sleeps and press my hand over his mouth.

He wakes, fighting against my grip. I press down hard enough that I can feel his teeth against my skin.

He grabs for my throat, and for a moment, I am scared that I'm not strong enough, that my training isn't good enough. Then his body relaxes utterly, as though realizing who I am.

He shouldn't relax like that. "He sent me to kill you," I whisper against his ear.

A shiver goes through his body, and his hand goes to my waist, but instead of pushing me away, he pulls me into the bed with him, rolling my body across him onto the heavily embroidered coverlets.

My hand slips from his mouth, and I am unnerved to find myself here, in the new High King's new bed—one I am still too human to lie in, beside someone who terrifies me the more I feel for him.

"Balekin and Orlagh are planning your murder," I say, flustered.

"Yes," he says lazily. "So why did I wake up at all?"

I am awkwardly conscious of his physicality, of the moment when he was half awake and pulled me against him. "Because I am difficult to charm," I say.

That makes him give a soft laugh. He reaches out and touches my hair, traces the hollow of my cheekbone. "I could have told my brother that," he says, with a softness in his voice I am utterly unprepared for.

"If you hadn't allowed Madoc to bar me from seeing you, I might have told you all this sooner. I have information that cannot wait."

Cardan shakes his head. "I know not of what you speak. Madoc told me that you were resting and that we should let you heal."

I frown. "I see. And in the interim, Madoc would no doubt take my place as your advisor," I tell Cardan. "He gave your guards orders to keep me out of the palace."

"I will give them different orders," Cardan says. He sits up in the bed. He's bare to the waist, his skin silvery in the soft glow of the magical lights. He continues looking at me in this strange way, as though he's never seen me before or as though he thought he might never see me again.

"Cardan?" I say, his name tasting strange on my tongue. "A representative from the Court of Termites came to see me. She told me something—"

"What they asked in exchange for you," he says. "I know all the things you will say. That it was foolish to agree to pay their price. That it destabilizes my rule. That it was a test of my vulnerabilities, and that I failed it. Even Madoc believed it was a betrayal of my obligations, although his alternatives weren't exactly diplomatic, either. But you do not know Balekin and Nicasia as I do—better they think you are important to me than to believe what they do to you is without consequences."

I consider how they treated me when they believed me to be valuable and shudder.

"I have thought and thought since you were gone, and there is something I wish to say." Cardan's face is serious, almost grave, in a way that he seldom allows himself to be. "When my father sent me away, at first I tried to prove that I was nothing like he thought me. But when that didn't work, I tried to be exactly what he believed I was instead. If he thought I was bad, I would be worse. If he thought I was cruel, I would be horrifying. I would live down to his every expectation. If I couldn't have his favor, then I would have his wrath.

"Balekin did not know what to do with me. He made me attend his debauches, made me serve wine and food to show off his tame little prince. When I grew older and more ill-tempered, he grew to like having someone to discipline. His disappointments were my lashings, his insecurities my flaws. And yet, he was the first person who saw something in me he liked—himself. He encouraged all my cruelty, inflamed all my rage. And I got worse.

"I wasn't kind, Jude. Not to many people. Not to you. I wasn't sure if I wanted you or if I wanted you gone from my sight so that I would stop feeling as I did, which made me even more unkind. But when you were gone—truly gone beneath the waves—I hated myself as I never have before."

I am so surprised by his words that I keep trying to find the trick in them. He can't truly mean what he's saying.

"Perhaps I am foolish, but I am not a fool. You like something about me," he says, mischief lighting his face, making its planes more familiar. "The challenge? My pretty eyes? No matter, because there is more you do not like and I know it. I can't trust you. Still, when you were gone, I had to make a great many decisions, and so much of what I did right was imagining you beside me, Jude, giving me a bunch of ridiculous orders that I nonetheless obeyed."

I am robbed of speech.

He laughs, his warm hand going to my shoulder. "Either I've surprised you or you are as ill as Madoc claimed."

But before I can say anything, before I can even figure out what I might say, a crossbow is suddenly lowered at me. Behind it stands the Roach, with the Bomb at his heels, twin daggers in her hands.

"Your Majesty, we tracked her. She came from your brother's house, and she's here to kill you. Please step out of the bed," says the Bomb.

"That's ridiculous," I say.

"If that's true, show me what charms you're wearing," says the Roach. "Rowan? Is there even salt in your pockets? Because the Jude I know wouldn't go around with nothing."

My pockets are empty, of course, since Balekin would check for anything, and I don't need it anyway. But it doesn't leave me a lot of options in terms of proof. I could tell them about the geas from Dain, but they have no reason to believe me.

"Please get out of the bed, Your Majesty," repeats the Bomb.

"I should be the one to get out—it's not my bed," I say, moving toward the footboard.

"Stay where you are, Jude," says the Roach.

Cardan slips out of the sheets. He's naked, which is briefly shocking, but he goes and pulls on a heavily embroidered dressing gown with no apparent shame. His lightly furred tail twitches back and forth in annoyance. "She woke me," he says. "If she was intent on murder, that's hardly the way to go about it."

"Empty your pockets," the Roach tells me. "Let's see your weapons. Put everything on the bed."

Cardan settles himself in a chair, his dressing gown enfolding him like a robe of state.

I have little. The heel of bread, gnawed but unfinished. Two knives, crusted with dirt and grass. And the stoppered vial.

The Bomb lifts it up and looks at me, shaking her head. "Here we go. Where did you get this?"

"From Balekin," I say, exasperated. "Who tried to glamour me to murder Cardan because he needs him dead to persuade Grimsen to make him his own crown of Elfhame. And that is what I came to tell the High King. I would have told you first, but I couldn't get to the Court of Shadows."

The Bomb and the Roach share a disbelieving look.

"If I was really glamoured, would I have told you any of that?"

"Probably not," says the Bomb. "But it would make for a quite clever piece of misdirection."

"I can't be glamoured," I admit. "It's part of a bargain I made with Prince Dain, in exchange for my service as a spy."

The Roach's eyebrows go up. Cardan gives me a sharp look, as though sure that anything to do with Dain can't be good. Or perhaps he's just surprised that I have yet another secret.

"I wondered what he gave you to make you throw in your lot with us ne'er-do-wells," the Bomb says.

"Mostly a purpose," I say, "but also the ability to resist glamour."

"You could still be lying," says the Roach. He turns to Cardan. "Try her."

"Your pardon?" Cardan says, drawing himself up, and the Roach seems to suddenly remember to whom he's speaking in such an offhanded way.

"Don't be such a prickly rose, Your Majesty," the Roach says with a shrug and a grin. "I'm not giving you an order. I'm suggesting that if you tried to glamour Jude, we could find out the truth."

Cardan sighs and walks toward me. I know this is necessary. I know that he doesn't intend to hurt me. I know he *can't* glamour me. And yet I draw back automatically.

"Jude?" he asks.

"Go ahead," I say.

I hear the glamour enter his voice, heady and seductive and more powerful than I expected. "Crawl to me," he says with a grin. Embarrassment pinks my cheeks.

I stay where I am, looking at all their faces. "Satisfied?"

The Bomb nods. "You're not charmed."

"Now tell me why I ought to trust you," I say to her and the Roach. "The Ghost came, with Vulciber, to take me to the Tower of Forgetting. Urged me to go alone, led me right to where I was to be captured, and I still don't know why. Were either of you in on it with him?"

"We didn't know the Ghost had betrayed us until it was too late," the Roach says.

I nod. "I saw the old forest entrance to the Court of Shadows."

"The Ghost activated some of our own explosives." He dips his head toward the Bomb.

"Collapsed part of the castle, along with the lair of the Court of Shadows, not to mention the old catacombs where Mab's bones lie," Cardan says.

"He's been planning this for a while. I was able to keep it from being worse," the Bomb says. "A few of us got out unscathed—Snapdragon is well and spotted you climbing the hill of the palace. But many were hurt in the blast. The sluagh—Niniel—got badly burned."

"What about the Ghost?" I ask.

"He's in the wind," the Bomb says. "Gone. We know not where."

I remind myself that so long as the Bomb and the Roach are okay, things could have been a lot worse.

"Now that we're all on the same dreary page," Cardan says, "we must discuss what to do next."

"If Balekin thinks he can get me into the masquerade, then let him bend his will toward that aim. I'll play along." I stop and turn to Cardan. "Or I could just kill him."

The Roach claps his hand on the back of my neck with a laugh. "You did good, kid, you know that? You came out of the sea even tougher than you went in."

I have to look down because I am surprised by how much I wanted to hear someone say that. When I glance back up, Cardan is watching me carefully. He looks stricken.

I shake my head, to keep him from saying whatever he's thinking.

"Balekin is the Ambassador of the Undersea," he says instead, an echo of my own words to Dulcamara. I am grateful for a return to the subject. "He's protected by Orlagh. And she has Grimsen and a mighty desire to test me. If her ambassador was killed, she would be very angry."

"Orlagh attacked the land already," I remind him. "The only reason she hasn't declared outright war is that she's seeking every advantage. But she will. So let the first blow be ours."

Cardan shakes his head.

"He wants to have *you* killed," I insist. "Grimsen has made that a condition of Balekin getting the crown."

"You should have the hands of the smith," the Bomb says. "Cut them off at the wrists so he can make no more trouble."

The Roach nods. "I will find him tonight."

"The three of you have one solution to every problem. *Murder.* No key fits every lock." Cardan gives us all a stern look, holding up a long-fingered hand with my stolen ruby ring still on one finger. "Someone tries to betray the High King, *murder.* Someone gives you a harsh look, *murder.* Someone disrespects you, *murder.* Someone ruins your laundry, *murder.*

"I find the more I listen, the more I am reminded that I have been awakened after very little sleep. I am going to send for some tea for myself and some food for Jude, who looks a bit pale."

Cardan stands and sends a servant for oatcakes, cheese, and two enormous pots of tea, but he does not allow anyone else into the room. He carries the large carved-wood-and-silver tray from the door himself, setting it down on a low table.

I am too hungry to resist making a sandwich from the cakes and cheese. After I eat a second one and wash it down with three cups of tea, I do feel steadier.

"The masquerade tomorrow," Cardan says. "It is to honor Lord Roiben of the Court of Termites. He has come all this way to yell at me, so we ought to let him. If Balekin's assassination attempt keeps him busy until after that, so much the better.

"Roach, if you can spirit away Grimsen to somewhere he won't cause any trouble, that would be most helpful. It's time for him to choose sides and bend his knee to one of the players in this little game. But I do not want Balekin dead."

The Roach takes a sip of tea and raises one bushy brow. The Bomb sighs audibly.

Cardan turns to me. "Since you were taken, I've gone over all the history I could find on the relationship of the land and the sea. From when the first High Queen, Mab, summoned the isles of Elfhame from the depths, our Folk have occasionally skirmished, but it seems clear that should we fight in earnest, there will be no victor. You said that you thought Queen Orlagh was waiting for an advantage to declare war. Instead, I think she is trying a new ruler—one she hopes she can trick or replace with another indebted to her. She thinks me young and feckless and means to take my measure."

"So what?" I ask. "Our choice is to endure her games, no matter how deadly, or engage in a war we cannot win?"

Cardan shakes his head and drinks another cup of tea. "We show her that I am no feckless High King."

"And how do we do that?" I ask.

"With great difficulty," he says. "Since I fear she is right."

CHAPTER 27

It would be a small thing to smuggle one of my own dresses out of my rooms, but I don't want Balekin to guess I've been inside the palace. Instead, I head to the Mandrake Market on the tip of Insmoor to find something suitable for the masquerade.

I've been to the Mandrake Market twice before, both times long past and accompanying Madoc. It is exactly the sort of place that Oriana warned Taryn and me away from—entirely too full of Folk eager to make bargains. It's open only in the misty mornings, when most of Elfhame is asleep, but if I can't get a gown and a mask there, I will have to steal one out of a courtier's wardrobe.

I walk through the stalls, a little queasy from the smell of oysters smoking on a bed of kelp, the scent reminding me forcefully of the Undersea. I pass trays of spun-sugar animals, little acorn cups filled with wine, enormous sculptures of horn, and a stall where a bent-backed woman takes a brush and draws charms on the soles of shoes. It takes some wandering, but I finally find a collection of sculpted leather masks. They are pinned to a wall and cunningly shaped like the faces of strange animals or laughing goblins or boorish mortals, painted gold and green and every other color imaginable.

I find one that is of a human face, unsmiling. "This one," I say to the shopkeeper, a tall woman with a hollow back. She gives me a dazzling smile.

"Seneschal," she says, recognition lighting her eyes. "Let it be my gift to you."

"That's very kind," I say, a little desperately. All gifts come with a price, and I am already struggling to pay my debts. "But I'd prefer—"

She winks. "And when the High King compliments your mask, you will let me make him one." I nod, relieved that what she wants is straightforward. The woman takes the mask from me, laying it down on the table and pulling out a pot of paint from beneath a desk. "Let me make a little alteration."

"What do you mean?"

She takes out a brush. "So she looks more like you." And with a few swipes of the brush, the mask does bear my likeness. I stare at it and see Taryn.

"I will remember your kindness," I say as she packs it up.

Then I depart and look for the fluttering cloth that marks a dress shop. I find a lace-maker instead and get a little turned around in a maze of potion-makers and tellers of fortunes. As I attempt to find my way back, I pass a stall occupied by a small fire. A hag sits on a little stool before it.

She stirs the pot, and from it comes the scent of stewing vegetables. When she glances in my direction, I recognize her as Mother Marrow.

"Come and sit by my fire?" she says.

I hesitate. It doesn't do to be rude in Faerie, where the highest laws are those of courtesy, but I am in a hurry. "I am afraid that I—"

"Have some soup," she says, picking up a bowl and shoving it toward me. "It is only that which is most wholesome."

"Then why offer it to me?" I ask.

She gives a delighted laugh. "If you had not cost my daughter her dreams, I might well like you. Sit. Eat. Tell me, what have you come to the Mandrake Market for?"

"A dress," I say, moving to perch by the fire. I take the bowl, which is filled with an unappetizing thin brown liquid. "Perhaps you could consider that your daughter might not have liked a princess of the sea for a rival. I spared her that, at least."

She gives me an evaluating look. "She was spared you, moreover."

"Some might say that was a prize above price," I tell her.

Mother Marrow gestures to the soup, and I, who can afford no more enemies, bring it to my lips. It tastes of a memory I cannot quite place, warm afternoons and splashing in pools and kicking plastic toys across the brown grass of summer lawns. Tears spring to my eyes.

I want to spill it out in the dirt.

I want to drink it down to the dregs.

"That'll fix you right up," she says as I blink back everything I was feeling and glare at her. "Now, about that dress. What would you give me for one?"

I take off the pair of pearl earrings from the Undersea. "How about these? For the dress and the soup." They are worth more than the price of ten dresses, but I do not want to engage in any more bargaining, especially with Mother Marrow.

She takes them, sliding her teeth over the nacre, then tucking them away in a pocket. "Well enough." Out of another pocket, she takes a walnut and holds it out to me.

I raise my eyebrows.

"Don't you trust me, girl?" she asks.

"Not as far as I can throw you," I return, and she lets out another cackle.

Still, *something* is in the walnut, and it's probably *some* kind of gown, because otherwise she wouldn't be honoring the terms of the agreement. And I will not play the naive mortal for her, demanding to know how everything works. With that thought, I stand.

"I don't much like you," she says, which is not an enormous surprise, although it stings. "But I like the sea Folk far less."

Thusly dismissed, I take the walnut and my mask and make the trek back to Insmire and Hollow Hall. I look out at the waves all around us, the expanse of ocean in every direction with its constant, restless, white-tipped waves. When I breathe, salt spray catches me in the back of my throat, and when I walk, I must avoid tide pools with little crabs in them.

It seems hopeless to fight something so vast. It seems ridiculous to believe we can win.

Balekin is sitting in a chair near the stairs when I come into Hollow Hall. "And where did you spend the night?" he asks, all insinuation.

I go over to him and lift my new mask. "Costuming."

He nods, bored again. "You may ready yourself," he says, waving vaguely to the stairs.

I go up. I am not sure which room he intends for me to use, but I go again to Cardan's. There, I bathe. Then I sit on the rug before the unlit grate and crack open the walnut. Out spills pale apricot muslin, frothing quantities of it. I shake the dress. It has an empire waist and wide, gathered sleeves that start just above the elbow so that my shoulders are bare. It hangs down to the floor in more gathered pleats.

When I put it on, I realize the fabric is the perfect complement to my complexion, although nothing can make me look less starved. No matter how the dress flatters me, I can't get away from the feeling that my skin doesn't fit. Still, it will do well for the night.

As I adjust it, however, I realize the dress has several cunningly hidden pockets. I transfer the poison to one. I transfer the smallest of my knives to another.

Then I attempt to make myself presentable. I find a comb among Cardan's things and attempt to fix my hair. I have nothing to put it up with, so I wear it loose around my shoulders. I wash out my mouth. Then, tying the mask on, I head back to where Balekin waits.

Up close, I am likely to be recognized by those who know me well, but otherwise I think I will be able to pass unnoticed through the larger crowd.

When he sees me, he has no visible reaction but impatience. He stands. "You know what to do?"

Sometimes lying is a real pleasure.

I take the stoppered vial from my pocket. "I was a spy for Prince Dain. I have been a part of the Court of Shadows. You can trust me to kill your brother."

That brings a smile to his face. "Cardan was an ungrateful child to imprison me. He ought to have put me beside him. He ought to have made me seneschal. Really, he ought to have given me the crown."

I say nothing, thinking of the boy I saw in the crystal. The boy who still hoped he might be loved. Cardan's admission of who he has become since haunts me: *If he thought I was bad, I would be worse.*

How well I know that feeling.

"I will mourn my youngest brother," Balekin says, seeming to cheer himself a bit at the thought. "I may not mourn the others, but I will have songs composed in his honor. He alone will be remembered."

I think of Dulcamara's exhortation to kill Prince Balekin, that he was the one who ordered the attack on the Court of Termites. Maybe he was responsible for the Ghost setting explosives in the Court of Shadows. I recall him under the sea, exultant in his power. I think of all that he's done and all he intends to do and am glad I am masked.

"Come," he says, and I follow him out the door.

Only Locke would make the ridiculous choice of arranging a *masquerade* for a grave affair of state such as hosting Lord Roiben after an attack on his lands. And yet, when I sweep into the brugh on Balekin's arm, such a thing appears under way. Goblins and grigs, pixies and elves all cavort in endless intertwined circle dances. Honey wine flows freely from horns, and tables are stacked with ripe cherries, gooseberries, pomegranates, and plums.

I walk from Balekin toward the empty dais, scanning the crowd for Cardan, but he is nowhere to be seen. I catch sight of salt-white hair instead. I am partway to the convocation from the Court of Termites when I pass Locke.

I swing toward him. "You tried to kill me."

He startles. Maybe he doesn't remember the way he limped on his wedding day, but surely he must have known I would see the earrings in Taryn's ears. Perhaps since the consequences took so long in coming, he supposed they wouldn't come at all.

"It wasn't supposed to be so serious," he says, reaching for my hand, a ridiculous grin coming to his face. "I only wanted you to be afraid the way you'd frightened me."

I jerk my fingers from his grip. "I have little time for you now, but I will *make time* for you anon."

Taryn, dressed in a gorgeous panniered ball gown all robin's-egg blue, embroidered with delicate roses, and wearing a lacy mask over her eyes, sweeps up to us. "Make time for Locke? Whatever for?"

He raises his brows, then throws an arm over his wife's shoulders. "Your twin is upset with me. She had a gift all planned out for you, but I was the one to present the gift in her stead."

That's accurate enough that it's hard to contradict him, especially given the suspicious way that Taryn is looking at me.

"What gift?" she wants to know. I ought to just tell her about the riders, about how I hid the fight in the forest from her because I didn't want her to be upset on her wedding day, about how I lost the earrings, about how I cut one of the riders down and threw a dagger at her husband. About how, whether or not he wanted me dead, he was certainly willing to let me die.

But if I say all that, will she believe me?

As I am trying to decide how to respond, Lord Roiben moves in front of us, looking down at me with his shining silver eyes.

Locke bows. My sister sinks into a beautiful curtsy, and I copy her as best I can.

"An honor," she says. "I've heard many of your ballads."

"Hardly mine," he demurs. "And largely exaggerated. Though blood does bounce on ice. That line is very true."

My sister looks momentarily discomfited. "Did you bring your consort?"

"Kaye, yes, she's in plenty of those ballads as well, isn't she? No, I am afraid she didn't come this time. Our last journey to the High Court was not quite what I promised her it would be."

Dulcamara said she was badly hurt, but he is taking care to avoid saying so—interesting care. Not a single lie, but a web of misdirection.

"The coronation," Taryn says.

"Yes," he goes on. "Not quite the minibreak either of us envisioned."

Taryn smiles a little at that, and Lord Roiben turns toward me. "You will excuse Jude?" he asks Taryn. "We have something pressing to discuss."

"Of course," she says, and Roiben escorts me away, toward one of the darker corners of the hall.

"Is she well?" I ask. "Kaye?"

"She will live," he says tersely. "Where is your High King?"

I scan the hall again, my gaze going to the dais and the empty throne. "I don't know, but he'll be here. Only last night, he expressed his regret over your losses and his desire to speak with you."

"We both know who was behind this attack," Roiben says. "Prince Balekin blames me for throwing my weight and influence behind you and your princeling when you got him a crown."

I nod, glad of his calm.

"You made me a promise," he says. "Now it is time to determine if a mortal is truly as good as her word."

"I will fix things," I vow. "I will find a way to fix things."

Lord Roiben's face is calm, but his silver eyes are not, and I am forced to remember that he murdered his way to his own throne. "I will speak to your High King, but if he cannot give me satisfaction, then I must call in my debt."

And with that, he departs in a swirl of his long cloak.

Courtiers cover the floor, executing intricate steps—a circle dance that turns in on itself, splits into three, and re-forms. I see Locke and Taryn out there, together, dancing. Taryn knows all the steps.

I will have to do something about Locke eventually, but not tonight.

Madoc sweeps into the room, Oriana on his arm. He is dressed in black, and she in white. They look like chess pieces on opposite sides of the board. Behind them come Mikkel and Randalin. A quick scan of the room and I spot Baphen speaking with a horned woman it takes me a moment to recognize. When I do, it comes with a jolt.

Lady Asha. Cardan's mother.

I knew she was a courtier before, saw it in the crystal globe on Eldred's desk, but now it is as though I am seeing her for the first time. She wears a high-skirted gown, so that her ankles show along with little shoes cunningly made to resemble leaves. Her whole dress is in shades of autumn, leaves and blossoms of more cloth stitched over the length of it. The tips of her horns have been painted with copper, and she wears a copper circlet, which is not a crown but reminiscent of one.

Cardan said nothing to me about her, and yet somehow they must have effected a reconciliation. He must have pardoned her. As another courtier leads her out to the dance, I am uncomfortably aware that she is likely to acquire both power and influence quickly—and that she will do nothing good with either.

"Where is the High King?" Nihuar asks. I didn't notice the Seelie representative until she was beside me, and I startle.

"How ought I to know?" I demand. "I wasn't even allowed inside the palace until today."

It is just then that Cardan finally enters the room. Ahead of him are two members of his personal guard, who step away from him once they've escorted him safely to the brugh.

A moment later, Cardan falls. He sprawls across the floor in all his fantastic robes of state, then begins to laugh. He laughs and laughs as though this is the most amazing trick he's ever performed.

He's obviously drunk. Very, very drunk.

My heart falls. When I look over at Nihuar, she is expressionless. Even Locke, staring over from the dance floor, looks discomfited.

Meanwhile, Cardan gets up and snatches a lute from the hands of an amazed goblin musician. He leaps unsteadily onto a long banquet table.

Strumming the strings, he begins a song so vulgar that the entire Court stops their dancing to listen and titter. Then, as one, they join in the madness. The courtiers of Faerie are not shy. They begin to dance again, now to the High King's song.

I didn't even know he could play.

When the song is over, he falls off the table, landing awkwardly on his side. His crown tilts forward so it's hanging over one of his eyes. His guards rush over to help him up off the floor, but he waves them away. "How is that for an introduction?" he demands of Lord Roiben, although they have in fact met before. "I am no dull monarch."

I look over at Balekin, who is wearing a satisfied smirk. Lord Roiben's face is like stone, unreadable. My gaze goes to Madoc, who watches Cardan with disgust as he fixes his crown.

Grimly, Roiben goes through the motions of what he's come here to do. "Your Majesty, I have come to ask you to allow me vengeance for my people. We were attacked and now we wish to respond." I have seen many people unable to humble themselves, but Lord Roiben does it with great grace.

And yet, with a look at Cardan, I know it won't matter.

"They say you're a specialist in bloodshed. I suppose you want to show off your skills." Cardan wags a finger in Roiben's direction.

The Unseelie king grimaces at that. A part of him must want to show off *immediately*, but he makes no comment.

"Yet that you must forgo," Cardan says. "I'm afraid you've come a long way for nothing. At least there's wine."

Lord Roiben turns his silvery gaze on me, and there's a threat in it.

This is not going at all the way I hoped.

Cardan waves his hand toward a table of refreshments. The skins of the fruit curl back from the flesh, and a few globes burst, spilling out seeds and startling nearby courtiers. "I've been practicing a skill of my own," he says with a laugh.

I go toward Cardan to try to intercede when Madoc catches my hand. His lip curls. "Is this going according to your plan?" he demands under his breath. "Get him out of here."

"I'll try," I say.

"I have stood by long enough," Madoc says, his cat eyes staring into mine. "Get your puppet to abdicate the throne in favor of your brother or face the consequences. I won't ask you again. It's now or never."

I pitch my voice low to match his. "After barring me from the palace?"

"You were ill," he returns.

"Working with you will always be working *for* you," I say. "So, never."

"You would really choose *that* over your own family?" he sneers, his gaze going to Cardan before cutting back to me.

I wince, but no matter how right he is, he's also wrong. "Whether you believe me or not, this *is* for my family," I tell him, and lay my hand on Cardan's shoulder, hoping I can guide him out of the room without anything else going wrong.

"Oh ho," he says. "My darling seneschal. Let us take a turn around the room." He grabs me and pulls me toward the dance.

He can barely stand. Three times he stumbles, and three times I have to hold most of his weight to keep him upright.

"Cardan," I hiss. "This is no meet behavior for the High King."

He giggles at that. I think of how serious he was last night in his rooms and how far he seems from that person.

"Cardan," I try again. "You must not do this. I order you to pull yourself together. I command you to drink no more liquor and to attempt sobriety."

"Yes, my sweet villain, my darling god. I will be as sober as a stone carving, just as soon as I can." And with that, he kisses me on the mouth.

I feel a cacophony of things at once. I am furious with him, furious and resigned that he is a failure as High King, corrupt and fanciful and as weak as Orlagh could have hoped. Then there is the public nature of the kiss; parading this before the Court is shocking, too. He's never been willing to seem to want me in public. Perhaps he can take it back, but in this moment, it is known.

But there is also a weakness in me, because I dreamed of him kissing me for all my time in the Undersea, and now with his mouth on mine, I want to sink my nails into his back.

His tongue brushes my lower lip, the taste heady and familiar.

Wraithberry.

He's not drunk; he's been poisoned.

I pull back and look into his eyes. Those familiar eyes, black, rimmed in gold. His pupils are blown wide.

"Sweet Jude. You are my dearest punishment." He dances away from me and immediately falls to the ground again, laughing, arms flung wide as though he would embrace the whole room.

I watch in astonished horror.

Someone poisoned the High King, and he is going to laugh and dance himself to death in front of a Court that will veer between delight and disgust. They will think him ridiculous as his heart stops.

I try to concentrate. Antidotes. There must be one. Water, certainly, to flush the system. Clay. The Bomb would know more. I look around for her, but all I see is the dizzying array of courtiers.

I turn to one of the guards instead. "Get me a pail, a lot of blankets, two pitchers of water, and put them in my rooms. Yes?"

"As you wish," he says, turning to give orders to the other knights. I turn back to Cardan, who has, predictably, headed in the worst direction possible. He's walking straight toward the councilors Baphen and Randalin, where they stand with Lord Roiben and his knight, Dulcamara, doubtlessly trying to smooth the situation over.

I can see the faces of the courtiers, the glitter of their eyes as they regard him with a kind of greedy scorn.

They watch as he lifts a carafe of water, tipping it back to cascade over his laughing mouth till he chokes on it.

"Excuse us," I say, wrapping my arm through his.

Dulcamara greets this with disdain. "We have come all this way to have an audience with the High King. Surely he means to stay longer than this."

He's been poisoned. The words are on my tongue when I hear Balekin say to them instead, "I fear the High King is not himself. I believe he's been poisoned."

And then, too late, I understand the scheme.

"You," he says to me. "Turn out your pockets. You are the only one here not bound by a vow."

Had I been truly glamoured, I would have had to pull out the stoppered vial. And once the Court saw it and found wraithberry inside, any protest would come to nothing. Mortals are liars, after all.

"He's drunk," I say, and am gratified by Balekin's shocked expression. "However, you are unbound as well, Ambassador. Or, shall I say, not bound to the land."

"Have I drunk too much? Merely a cup of poison for my breakfast and another for my dinner," Cardan says.

I give him a look but say no more as I guide the stumbling High King across the floor.

"Where are you taking him?" asks one of the guards. "Your Majesty, do you wish to depart?"

"We all dance at Jude's command," he says, and laughs.

"Of course he doesn't wish to go," Balekin says. "Attend to your other duties, seneschal, and let me look after my brother. He has duties to perform tonight."

"You will be sent for if you're needed," I tell him, trying to bluff through this. My heart speeds. I am not sure if anyone here would be on my side, if it came to that.

"Jude Duarte, you will leave the High King's side," Balekin says.

At that tone, Cardan's focus narrows. I can see him straining to concentrate. "She will not," he says.

Since no one can gainsay him, even in this state, I am able to finally lead him out. I bear up the heavy weight of the High King as we move through the passageways of the palace.

CHAPTER 28

The High King's personal guard follows us at a distance. Questions run through my mind—how was he poisoned? Who actually put whatever he drank in his hand? When did it happen?

Grabbing a servant in the hall, I send out runners for the Bomb and, if they are unable to find her, an alchemist.

"You're going to be okay," I say.

"You know," he says, hanging on to me, "that ought to be reassuring. But when mortals say it, it doesn't mean the same thing as when the Folk do, does it? For you, it's an appeal. A kind of hopeful magic. You say I will be well because you fear I won't be."

For a moment, I don't speak. "You're poisoned," I say finally. "You know that, right?"

He doesn't startle. "Ah," he says. "Balekin."

I say nothing, just set him down before the fire in my rooms, his back against my couch. He looks odd there, his beautiful clothes a contrast to the plain rug, his face pale with a hectic flush in his cheeks.

He reaches up and presses my hand to his face. "It's funny, isn't it, how I mocked you for your mortality when you're certain to outlive me."

"You're not going to die," I insist.

"Oh, how many times have I wished that you couldn't lie? Never more than now."

He lolls to one side, and I grab one of the pitchers of water and pour a glassful. I bring it to his lips. "Cardan? Get down as much as you can."

He doesn't reply and seems about to fall asleep. "No." I pat his cheek with increasing force until it's more of a smack. "You've got to stay awake."

His eyes open. His voice is muzzy. "I'll just sleep for a little while."

"Unless you want to wind up like Severin of Fairfold, encased in glass for centuries while mortals line up to take pictures with his body, you're going to stay awake."

He shifts into a more upright sitting position. "Fine," he says. "Talk to me."

"I saw your mother tonight," I say. "All dressed up. The time I saw her before that was in the Tower of Forgetting."

"And you're wondering if I forgot her?" he says airily, and I am pleased that he's paying enough attention to deliver one of his typical quips.

"Glad you're up to mocking."

"I hope it's the last thing about me to go. So tell me about my mother."

I try to think of something to say that isn't entirely negative. I go for carefully neutral. "The first time I met her, I didn't know who she was. She wanted to trade me some information for getting her out of the Tower. And she was afraid of you."

"Good," he says.

My eyebrows go up. "So how did she wind up a part of your Court?"

"I suppose I have some fondness for her yet," he admits. I pour him some more water, and he drinks it more slowly than I'd like. I refill the glass as soon as I can.

"There are so many questions I wish I could ask my mom," I admit.

"What would you ask?" The words slur together, but he gets them out.

"Why she married Madoc," I say, pointing to the glass, which he obediently brings to his mouth. "Whether she loved him and why she left him and whether she was happy in the human world. Whether she actually murdered someone and hid her body in the burnt remains of Madoc's original stronghold."

He looks surprised. "I always forget that part of the story."

I decide a subject change is in order. "Do you have questions like that for your father?"

"Why am I the way I am?" His tone makes it clear he's proposing something I might suggest he ask, not really wondering about it. "There are no real answers, Jude. Why was I cruel to Folk? Why was I awful to you? Because I could be. Because I liked it. Because, for a moment, when I was at my worst, I felt powerful, and most of the time, I felt powerless, despite being a prince and the son of the High King of Faerie."

"That's an answer," I say.

"Is it?" And then, after a moment, "You should go."

"Why?" I ask, annoyed. For one, this is my room. For another, I am trying to keep him alive.

He looks at me solemnly. "Because I am going to retch."

I grab for the bucket, and he takes it from me, his whole body convulsing with the force of vomiting. The contents of his stomach appear like matted leaves, and I shudder. I didn't know wraithberry did that.

There's a knock on the door, and I go to it. The Bomb is there, out of breath. I let her in, and she moves past me, straight to Cardan.

"Here," she says, pulling out a little vial. "It's clay. It may help draw out and contain the toxins."

Cardan nods and takes it from her, swallowing the contents with a grimace. "It tastes like dirt."

"It *is* dirt," she informs him. "And there's something else. Two things, really. Grimsen was already gone from his forge when we tried to capture him. We have to assume the worst—that he's with Orlagh.

"Also, I was given this." She takes a note from her pocket. "It's from Balekin. Cannily phrased, but breaks down to this—he's offering the antidote to you, Jude, if you will bring him the crown."

"The crown?" Cardan opens his eyes, and I realize he must have closed them without my noticing.

"He wants you to take it to the gardens, near the roses," the Bomb says.

"What happens if he doesn't get the antidote?" I ask.

The Bomb puts the back of her hand against Cardan's cheek. "He's the High King of Elfhame—he has the strength of the land to draw on. But he's very weak already. And I don't think he knows how to do it. Your Majesty?"

He looks at her with benevolent incomprehension. "Whatever do you mean? I just took a *mouthful* of the land at your behest."

I think about what she's saying, about what I know of the High King's powers.

Surely you have noticed that since his reign began, the isles are different. Storms come in faster. Colors are a bit more vivid, smells are sharper.

But all that was done without trying. I am certain he didn't notice the land altering itself to better suit him.

Look at them all, your subjects, he'd said to me at a revel months ago. *A shame not a one knows who their true ruler is.*

If Cardan doesn't believe himself to be the true High King of Elfhame, if he doesn't allow himself to access his own power, it will be my fault. If wraithberry kills him, it will be because of me.

"I'll get that antidote," I say.

Cardan lifts the crown from his head and looks at it for a moment, as though somehow he cannot fathom how it came into his hand. "This can't pass to Oak if you lose it. Although I admit the succession gets tricky if I die."

"I already told you," I say. "You're not going to die. And I am not going to take that crown." I go in the back and change around the contents of my pockets. I tie on a cloak with a deep hood and a new mask. I am so furious that my hands shake. Wraithberry, which I was once invulnerable to, thanks to careful mithridatism. If I had been able to keep up the doses, I could have perhaps tricked Balekin as I once tricked Madoc. But after my imprisonment in the Undersea, I have one less advantage and far higher stakes. I have lost my immunity. I am as vulnerable to poison as Cardan is.

"You'll stay with him?" I ask the Bomb, and she nods.

"No," says Cardan. "She goes with you."

I shake my head. "The Bomb knows about potions. She knows about magic. She can make sure you don't get worse."

He ignores me and takes her hand. "Liliver, as your king, I command you," he says with great dignity for someone sitting on the floor beside the bucket he's retched in. "Go with Jude."

I turn to the Bomb, but I see in her face that she won't disobey him—she's made her oath and even given him her name. He's her king.

"Damn you," I whisper to one or maybe both of them.

I vow that I will get the antidote swiftly, but that doesn't make it any easier for me to leave when I know the wraithberry could yet stop his heart. His searing gaze follows us out the door, blown pupils and crown still clenched in his hand.

Balekin is in the garden as he promised, near a blooming tree of silver-blue roses. When I get there, I note figures not too distant from where we stand, other courtiers going for midnight strolls. It means he cannot attack me, but neither can I attack him.

At least not without others knowing about it.

"You are a great disappointment," he says.

It's such a shock that I actually laugh. "You mean because I wasn't glamoured. Yes, I can see how that would be very sad for you."

He glowers, but he doesn't even have Vulciber beside him now to threaten me. Perhaps being the Ambassador of the Undersea makes him believe he's untouchable.

All I can think about is that he poisoned Cardan, he tormented me, he pushed Orlagh to raid the land. I am shaking with anger, but trying to bite back that fury so I can get through what must be done.

"Did you bring me the crown?" he asks.

"I've got it nearby," I lie. "But before I hand it over, I want to see the antidote."

He pulls a vial from his coat, nearly the twin of the one he gave me, which I take out of my pocket. "They would have executed me if they'd found me with this poison," I say, shaking it. "That's what you intended, wasn't it?"

"Someone may execute you yet," he says.

"Here's what we're going to do." I take the stopper out of the bottle. "I am going to drink the poison, and then you're going to give me the antidote. If it works on me, then I'll bring out the crown and trade it to you for the bottle. If not, then I guess I'll die, but the crown will be lost forever. Whether Cardan lives or dies, that crown is hidden well enough that you won't find it."

"Grimsen can forge me another," Balekin says.

"If that's true, then what are we here for?"

Balekin grimaces, and I consider the possibility that the little smith isn't with Orlagh after all. Maybe he's disappeared after doing his best to set us at one another's throats.

"You stole that crown from me," he says.

"True enough," I admit. "And I'll hand it over to you, but not for nothing."

"I can't lie, mortal. If I say I will give you the antidote, I will do it. My word is enough."

I give him my best scowl. "Everyone knows to beware when bargaining with the Folk. You deceive with your every breath. If you truly have the antidote, what does it harm you to let me poison myself? I would think it would be a pleasure."

He gives me a searching look. I imagine he's angry that I am not glamoured. He must have had to scramble when I hustled Cardan out of the throne room. Was he always ready with the antidote? Did he think he could persuade Cardan to crown him? Was he arrogant enough to believe that the Council wouldn't have stood in his way?

"Very well," he says. "One dose of antidote for you, and the rest for Cardan."

I unstopper the bottle he gave me and toss it back, drinking all the contents with a pronounced wince. I am angry all over again, thinking of how sick I made myself taking tiny doses of poison. All for nothing.

"Do you feel the wraithberry working on your blood? It will work far faster on you than on one of us. And you took such a large dose." He watches me with such a fierce expression that I can tell he wishes he could leave me to die. If he could justify walking away right now, he would. For a moment, I think he might.

Then he crosses toward me and unstoppers the bottle in his own hand. "Please do not believe that I will put it into your hand," he says. "Open your mouth like a little bird, and I will drop in your dose. Then you will give me the crown."

I open my mouth obediently and let him pour the thick, bitter, honey-like stuff onto my tongue. I duck away from him, returning the distance between us, making sure I am closer to the entrance of the palace.

"Satisfied?" he asks.

I spit the antidote into the glass bottle, the one he gave me, the one that once contained wraithberry but, until a few moments before, was filled only with water.

"What are you doing?" he asks.

I stopper it again and toss it through the air to the Bomb, who catches it handily. Then she is gone, leaving him to gape at me.

"What have you done?" he demands.

"I tricked you," I tell him. "A bit of misdirection. I dumped out your poison and washed out the vial. As you keep forgetting, I grew up here and so am also dangerous to bargain with—and, as you see, I *can* lie. And, like you reminded me so long ago, I am short on time."

He draws the sword at his side. It's a thin, long blade. I don't think it's the one he used to fight Cardan in his tower room, but it might be.

"We're in public," I remind him. "And I am still the High King's seneschal."

He looks around, taking in the sight of the other courtiers nearby. "Leave us," he shouts at them. A thing it did not occur to me that anyone could do, but he is used to being a prince. He is used to being obeyed.

And indeed, the courtiers seem to melt into the shadows, clearing the room for the sort of duel we definitely ought not to have. I slip my hand into my pocket, touching the hilt of a knife. The range on it is nothing like a sword. As Madoc explained more than once: *A sword is a weapon of war, a dagger is a weapon of murder.* I'd rather have the knife than be unarmed, but more than anything, I wish I had Nightfell.

"Are you suggesting a duel?" I ask. "I am sure you wouldn't want to bring dishonor to your name with me so outmatched in weaponry."

"You expect me to believe you have any honor?" he asks, which is, unfortunately, a fair point. "You are a coward. A coward like the man who raised you."

He takes a step toward me, ready to cut me down whether I have a weapon or not.

"Madoc?" I draw my knife. It's not small, but it's still less than half the length of the blade he is leveling at me.

"It was Madoc's plan that we should strike during the coronation. It was his plan that once Dain was out of the way, Eldred would see clear to put the crown on my head. It was all his plan, but he stayed Grand General and I went to the Tower of Forgetting. And did he lift a finger to help me? He did not. He bent his head to my brother, whom he despises. And you're just like him, willing to beg and grovel and lower yourself to anyone if it gets you power."

I doubt putting Balekin on the throne was ever part of Madoc's true plan, whatever he allowed Balekin to believe, but that doesn't make the words sting any less. I have spent a lifetime making myself small in the hopes I could find an acceptable place in Elfhame, and then, when I pulled off the biggest, grandest coup imaginable, I had to hide my abilities more than ever.

"No," I say. "That's not true."

He looks surprised. Even in the Tower of Forgetting, when he was a prisoner, I still *let* Vulciber strike me. In the Undersea, I pretended to have no dignity at all. Why should he think I see myself any differently than he sees me?

"You are the one who bent your head to Orlagh instead of to your own brother," I say. "You're the coward and a traitor. A murderer of your own kin. But worse than all that, you're a fool."

He bares his teeth as he advances on me, and I, who have been pretending to subservience, remember my most troublesome talent: pissing off the Folk.

"Go ahead," he says. "Run like the coward you are."

I take a step back.

Kill Prince Balekin. I think of Dulcamara's words, but I don't hear her voice. I hear my own, rough with seawater, terrified and cold and alone.

Madoc's words of long ago come back to me. *What is sparring but a game of strategy, played at speed?*

The point of a fight is not to have a good fight; it's to win.

I am at a disadvantage against a sword, a bad disadvantage. And I am still weak from my imprisonment in the Undersea. Balekin can hang back and take his time while I can't get past the blade. He will take me apart slowly, cut by cut. My best bet is closing the distance fast. I need to get inside his guard, and I don't have the luxury of taking his measure before I do it. I am going to have to rush him.

I have one shot to get this right.

My heart thunders in my ears.

He lunges toward me, and I slam my knife against the base of his sword with my right hand, then grab his forearm with my left, twisting as though to disarm him. He pulls against my grip. I drive the knife toward his neck.

"Hold," Balekin shouts. "I surr—"

Arterial blood sprays my arm, sprays the grass. It glistens on my knife. Balekin slumps over, sprawling on the ground.

It all happens so fast.

It happens too fast.

I want to have some reaction. I want to tremble or feel nauseated. I want to be the person who begins to weep. I want to be anyone but the person I am, who looks around to be sure no one saw, who wipes off my knife in the dirt, wipes off my hand on his clothes, and gets out of there before the guards come.

You're a good little murderer, Dulcamara said.

When I look back, Balekin's eyes are still open, staring at nothing.

Cardan is sitting on the couch. The bucket is gone and so is the Bomb.

He looks at me with a lazy smile. "Your dress. You put it back on."

I look at him in confusion; the consequences of what I've just done—including having to tell Cardan—are hard to think past. But the dress I am wearing is the one I wore before, the one I got from Mother Marrow's walnut. There's blood on one sleeve of it now, but it is otherwise the same.

"Did something happen?" I ask again.

"I don't know?" he asks, puzzled. "Did it? I granted the boon you wanted. Is your father safe?"

Boon?

My father?

Madoc. Of course. Madoc threatened me, Madoc was disgusted by Cardan. But what has he done and what has it to do with dresses?

"Cardan," I say, trying to be as calm as I can. I go over to the sofa and sit down. It's not a small couch, but his long legs are on it, blanketed and propped up on pillows. No matter how far from him I sit, it feels too close. "You've got to tell me what happened. I haven't been here for the last hour."

His expression grows troubled.

"The Bomb came back with the antidote," he says. "She said you'd be right behind her. I was still so dizzy, and then a guard came, saying that there was an emergency. She went to see. And then *you* came in, just like she said you would. You said you had a plan. . . ."

He looks at me, as though waiting for me to jump in and tell the rest of the story, the part I remember. But, of course, I don't.

After a moment, he closes his eyes and shakes his head. "Taryn."

"I don't understand," I say, because I don't want to understand.

"Your plan was that your father was going to take half the army, but for him to function independently, he needed to be freed of his vows to the crown. You had on one of your doublets—the ones you always wear. And these odd earrings. Moon and a star." He shakes his head.

A cold chill goes through me.

As children in the mortal world, Taryn and I would switch places to play tricks on our mother. Even in Faerie, we would sometimes pretend to be each other to see what we could get away with. Would a lecturer be able to tell the difference? Could Oriana? Madoc? Oak? What about the great and mighty Prince Cardan?

"But how did she make you agree?" I demand. "She has no power. She could pretend to be me, but she couldn't force you—"

He puts his head in his long-fingered hands. "She didn't have to command me, Jude. She didn't have to use any magic. I trust you. I trusted you."

And I trusted Taryn.

While I was murdering Balekin, while Cardan was poisoned and disoriented, Madoc made his move against the crown. Against me. And he did it with his daughter Taryn by his side.

CHAPTER 29

The High King is restored to his own chamber so he may rest. I feed my bloodstained dress to the fire, put on a robe, and plan. If none of the courtiers saw my face before Balekin sent them away, then wrapped in my cloak, I might not have been identified. And, of course, I can lie. But the question of how to avoid blame for the murder of the Undersea's ambassador pales beside the question of what to do about Madoc.

With half the army gone along with the general, if Orlagh decides to strike, I have no idea how to repel her. Cardan will have to choose another Grand General and quickly.

And he will have to inform the lower Courts of Madoc's defection, to make sure it is known he doesn't speak with the voice of the High King. There must be a way to drive Madoc back to the High Court. He is proud but practical. Perhaps the answer lies in something to do with

Oak. Perhaps it means I ought to make my hopes for Oak's rule less opaque. I am thinking over all this when a knock comes to my door.

Outside, a messenger, a lilac-skinned girl in royal livery. "The High King requires your presence. I am to conduct you to his chambers."

I take an unsteady breath. No one else might have seen me, but Cardan cannot fail to guess. He knows whom I went to meet and how late I returned from that meeting. He saw the blood on my sleeve. *You command the High King, not the other way around*, I remind myself, but the reminder feels hollow.

"Let me change," I say.

The messenger shakes her head. "The king made it clear I was to ask you to come at once."

When I get to the royal chambers, I find Cardan alone, dressed simply, sitting in a throne-like chair. He looks wan, and his eyes still shine a bit too much, as though maybe poison lingers in his blood.

"Please," he says. "Sit."

Warily, I do.

"Once, you had a proposal for me," he says. "Now I have one for you. Give me back my will. Give me back my freedom."

I suck in a breath. I'm surprised, although I guess I shouldn't be. No one wants to be under the control of another person, although the balance of power between us, in my view, has careened back and forth, despite his vow. My having command of him has felt like balancing a knife on its point, nearly impossible and probably dangerous. Still, to give it up would mean giving up any semblance of power. It would be giving up *everything*. "You know I won't do that."

He doesn't seem particularly put off by my refusal. "Hear me out.

What you want from me is obedience for longer than a year and a day. More than half your time is gone. Are you ready to put Oak on the throne?"

I don't speak for a moment, hoping he might think his question was rhetorical. When it becomes clear that's not the case, I shake my head.

"And so you thought to extend my vow. Just how were you imagining doing that?"

Again, I have no answer. Certainly no good one.

It's his turn to smile. "You thought I had nothing to bargain with."

Underestimating him is a problem I've had before, and I fear I will have again. "What bargain is possible?" I ask. "When what I want is for you to make the vow again, for at least another year, if not a decade, and what you want is for me to rescind the vow entirely?"

"Your father and sister tricked me," Cardan says. "If Taryn had given me a command, I would have known it wasn't you. But I was sick and tired and didn't want to refuse you. I didn't even ask why, Jude. I wanted to show you that you could trust me, that you didn't need to give me orders for me to do things. I wanted to show you that I believed you'd thought it all through. But that's no way to rule. And it's not really even trust, when someone can order you to do it anyway.

"Faerie suffered with us at each other's throats. You attempted to make me do what you thought needed to be done, and if we disagreed, we could do nothing but manipulate each other. That wasn't working, but simply giving in is no solution. We cannot continue like this. Tonight is proof of that. I need to make my own decisions."

"You said you didn't mind so much, listening to my orders." It's a paltry attempt at humor, and he doesn't smile.

Instead, he looks away, as though he can't quite meet my eyes. "All the more reason not to allow myself that luxury. You made me the High King, Jude. Let me *be* the High King."

I fold my arms protectively over my chest. "And what will I be? Your servant?" I hate that he's making sense, because there is no way I can give him what he's asking. I can't step aside, not with Madoc out there, not with so many threats. And yet I cannot help recalling what the Bomb said about Cardan's not knowing how to invoke his connection to the land. Or what the Roach said, about Cardan's thinking of himself as a spy pretending to be a monarch.

"Marry me," he says. "Become the Queen of Elfhame."

I feel a kind of cold shock come over me, as though someone has told a particularly cruel joke, with me its target. As though someone looked into my heart and saw the most ridiculous, most childish desire there and used it against me. "But you can't."

"I *can*," he says. "Kings and queens don't often marry for something other than a political alliance, true, but consider this a version of that. And were you queen, you wouldn't need my obedience. You could issue all your own orders. And I would be free."

I can't help thinking of how mere months ago I fought for a place in the Court, hoping desperately for knighthood, and didn't even get that.

The irony that it's Cardan, who insisted that I didn't belong in Faerie at all, offering me *this* makes it all the more shocking.

He goes on. "Moreover, it's not as though we'd be married forever. Marriages between kings and queens must last as long as they rule, but in our case, that's not so long. Only until Oak is old enough to rule, assuming that's what he wants. You could have everything you want at the price of merely releasing me from my vow of obedience."

My heart is pounding so hard that I fear it will stutter to a stop.

"You're serious?" I manage.

"Of course I am. In earnest as well."

I look for the trick, because this must be one of those faerie bargains that sound like one thing but turn out to be something very different. "So let me guess, you want me to release you from your vow for your promise to marry me? But then the marriage will take place in the month of never when the moon rises in the west and the tides flow backward."

He shakes his head, laughing. "If you agree, I will marry you tonight," he says. "Now, even. Right here. We exchange vows, and it is done. This is no mortal marriage, to require being presided over and witnessed. I cannot lie. I cannot deny you."

"It's not long until your vow is up," I say, because the idea of taking what he's offering—the idea that I could not only be part of the Court, but the head of it—is so tempting that it's hard not to just agree, no matter the consequences. "Surely the idea of a few more months tied to me can't be such a hardship that you'd like to tie yourself to me for years."

"As I said before, a lot can happen in a year and a day. Much has happened in half that time."

We sit silently for a moment as I try to think. For the last seven months, the question of what would happen after a year and a day has haunted me. This is a *solution*, but it doesn't feel at all practical. It's the stuff of absurd daydream, imagined while dozing in a mossy glen, too embarrassing to even confess to my sisters.

Mortal girls do not become queens of Faerieland.

I imagine what it would be like to have my own crown, my own power. Maybe I wouldn't have to be afraid to love him. Maybe it would be okay. Maybe I wouldn't have to be scared of all the things I've been scared of my whole life, of being diminished and weak and lesser. Maybe I would become a little bit magic.

"Yes," I say, but my voice fails me. It comes out all breath. "Yes."

He leans forward in the chair, eyebrows raised, but he doesn't wear his usual arrogant mien. I cannot read his expression. "To what are you agreeing?"

"Okay," I say. "I'll do it. I'll marry you."

He gives me a wicked grin. "I had no idea it would be such a sacrifice."

Frustrated, I flop over on the couch. "That's not what I mean."

"Marriage to the High King of Elfhame is largely thought to be a prize, an honor of which few are worthy."

I suppose his sincerity could last but only so long. I roll my eyes, grateful that he's acting like himself again, so I can better pretend not to be overawed by what's about to happen. "So what do we do?"

I think of Taryn's wedding and the part of the ceremony we did not witness. I think of my mother's wedding, too, the vows she must have made to Madoc, and abruptly a shiver goes through me that I hope has nothing to do with premonition.

"It's simple," he says, moving to the edge of the chair. "We pledge our troth. I'll go first—unless you wish to wait. Perhaps you imagined something more romantic."

"No," I say quickly, unwilling to admit to imagining anything to do with marriage at all.

He slides my ruby ring off his finger. "I, Cardan, son of Eldred, High King of Elfhame, take you, Jude Duarte, mortal ward of Madoc, to be my bride and my queen. Let us be wed until we wish for it to be otherwise and the crown has passed from our hands."

As he speaks, I begin to tremble with something between hope and fear. The words he's saying are so momentous that they're surreal, especially here, in Eldred's own rooms. Time seems to stretch out. Above us, the branches begin to bud, as though the land itself heard the words he spoke.

Catching my hand, he slides the ring on. The exchange of rings is not a faerie ritual, and I am surprised by it.

"Your turn," he says into the silence. He gives me a grin. "I'm trusting you to keep your word and release me from my bond of obedience after this."

I smile back, which maybe makes up for the way that I froze after he finished speaking. I still can't quite believe this is happening. My hand tightens on his as I speak. "I, Jude Duarte, take Cardan, High King of Elfhame, to be my husband. Let us be wed until we don't want to be and the crown has passed from our hands."

He kisses the scar of my palm.

I still have his brother's blood under my fingernails.

I don't have a ring for him.

Above us, the buds are blooming. The whole room smells of flowers.

Drawing back, I speak again, pushing away all thoughts of Balekin, of the future in which I am going to have to tell him what I've done. "Cardan, son of Eldred, High King of Elfhame, I forsake any command over you. You are free of your vow of obedience, for now and for always."

He lets out a breath and stands a bit unsteadily. I can't quite wrap my head around the idea that I am . . . I can't even think the words. Too much has happened tonight.

"You look as if you've barely rested." I rise to be sure that if he falls over, I can grab for him before he hits the floor, although I am not so sure of myself, either.

"I will lie down," he says, letting me guide him toward his enormous bed. Once there, he does not let go of my hand. "If you lie with me."

With no reason to object, I do, the sense of unreality heightening. As I stretch out on the elaborately embroidered comforter, I realize that I have found something far more blasphemous than spreading out on the bed of the High King, far more blasphemous than sneaking Cardan's signet onto my finger, or even sitting on the throne itself.

I have become the Queen of Faerie.

We trade kisses in the darkness, blurred by exhaustion. I don't expect to sleep, but I do, my limbs tangled with his, the first restful sleep I've had since my return from the Undersea. When I am awakened, it is to a banging on the door.

Cardan is already up, playing with the vial of clay the Bomb brought, tossing it from hand to hand. He's still dressed, his rumpled aspect giving him only an air of dissipation. I pull my robe more tightly around me. I am embarrassed to be so obviously sharing his bed.

"Your Majesty," says the messenger—a knight. "Your brother is dead. There was a duel, from what we've been able to determine."

"Ah," Cardan says.

"And the Queen of the Undersea." The knight's voice trembles. "She's here, demanding justice for her ambassador."

"I just bet she is." Cardan's voice is dry, clipped. "Well, we can hardly keep her waiting. You. What's your name?"

The knight hesitates. "Rannoch, Your Majesty."

"Sir Rannoch, assemble a group of knights to escort me to the water. Wait in the courtyard."

"But the general..." he begins.

"Is not here right now," Cardan finishes for him.

"I will do it," the knight says. I hear the door close, and Cardan rounds the corner, expression haughty.

"Well, wife," he says to me, a chill in his voice. "It seems you have kept at least one secret from your dowry. Come, we must dress for our first audience together."

My heart drops, but there is no time to explain and no good explanation, either.

I am left to rush through the halls in my robe. Back in my rooms, I call for my sword and throw on my velvets, all the while wondering what it will mean to have this newfound status and what Cardan will do now that he is unchecked.

CHAPTER 30

Orlagh waits for us in a choppy ocean, accompanied by her daughter and a pod of knights mounted on seals and sharks and all manner of sharp-toothed sea creatures. She herself sits on an orca and is dressed as though ready for battle. Her skin is covered in shiny silvery scales that seem both to be metallic and to have grown from her skin. A helmet of bone and teeth hides her hair.

Nicasia is beside her, on a shark. She has no tail today, her long legs covered in armor of shell.

All along the edge of the beach are clumps of kelp, washed up as though from a storm. I think I see other things out in the water. The back of a large creature swimming just below the waves. The hair of drowned mortals, blowing like seagrass. The Undersea's forces are larger than they seem at first glance.

"Where is my ambassador?" Orlagh demands. "Where is your brother?"

Cardan is seated on his gray steed, in black clothes and a cloak of scarlet. Beside him are two dozen mounted knights and both Mikkel and Nihuar. On the ride over, they tried to determine what Cardan had planned, but he has kept his own counsel from them and, more troublingly, from me. Since hearing of the death of Balekin, he's said little and avoided looking in my direction. My stomach churns with anxiety.

He looks at Orlagh with a coldness that I know from experience comes from either fury or fear. In this case, possibly both. "As you well know, he's dead."

"It was your responsibility to keep him safe," she says.

"Was it?" Cardan asks with exaggerated astonishment, touching his hand to his breast. "I thought my obligation was not to move against him, not to keep him from the consequences of his own risk-taking. He had a little duel, from what I hear. Dueling, as I am sure you know, is dangerous. But I neither murdered him nor did I encourage it. In fact, I quite *dis*couraged it."

I attempt to not let anything I am feeling show on my face.

Orlagh leans forward as though she senses blood in the water. "You ought not to allow such disobedience."

Cardan shrugs nonchalantly. "Perhaps."

Mikkel shifts on his horse. He's clearly uncomfortable with the way Cardan is speaking, carelessly, as though they are merely having a friendly conversation and Orlagh hasn't come to chisel away his power, to weaken his rule. And if she knew Madoc was gone, she might attack outright.

Looking at her, looking at Nicasia's sneer and the selkies and merfolk's strange, wet eyes, I feel powerless. I have given up command of

Cardan, and for it, I have his vow of marriage. But without anyone's knowing, it seems less and less as though it ever happened.

"I am here to demand justice. Balekin was my ambassador, and if you don't consider him to be under your protection, I do consider him to be under mine. You must give his murderer to the sea, where she will find no forgiveness. Give us your seneschal, Jude Duarte."

For a moment, I feel as though I can't breathe. It's as though I am drowning again.

Cardan's eyebrows go up. His voice stays light. "But she's only just returned from the sea."

"So you don't dispute her crime?" asks Orlagh.

"Why should I?" asks Cardan. "If she's the one with whom he dueled, I am certain she would win; my brother supposed himself expert with the sword—a great exaggeration of abilities. But she's mine to punish or not, as I see fit."

I hate hearing myself spoken of as though I am not *right there* when I have his pledge of troth. But his queen killing an ambassador does seem like a worse political problem.

Orlagh's gaze doesn't go to me. I doubt very much she cares about anything but that Cardan gave up a lot for my return and by threatening me, she believes she can get more. "King of the land, I am not here to fight your sharp tongue. My blood is cold and I prefer blades. Once, I considered you as a partner for my daughter, the most precious thing in the sea. She would have brokered a true peace between us."

Cardan looks at Nicasia, and although Orlagh leaves him an opening, for a long moment, he does not speak. And when he does, he only says, "Like you, I am not skilled at forgiveness."

Something in Queen Orlagh's manner changes. "If it's war you want, you would be unwise to declare it on an island." Around her, waves grow more violent, their white caps of froth larger. Whirlpools coalesce just off the edge of the land, small ones, deepening, only to spin themselves out as new ones form.

"War?" He peers at her as though she's said something particularly puzzling and it vexes him. "Do you mean for me to really believe you want to fight? Are *you* challenging *me* to a duel?"

He's obviously baiting her, but I cannot imagine to what benefit.

"And if I was?" she asks. "What then, boy?"

The smile that curves his lip is voluptuous. "Beneath every bit of your sea is land. Seething, volcanic land. Go against me, and I will show you what this boy will do, my lady."

He stretches out his hand, and something seems to rise to the top of the water around us, like a pale scrum. Sand. Floating sand.

Then, all around the Court of the Undersea, water begins to churn.

I stare at him, hoping to catch his eye, but he is concentrating. Whatever magic he is doing, this is what Baphen meant when he said the High King was tied to the land, was the beating heart and the star upon whom Elfhame's future was written. This is power. And to see Cardan wield it is to understand just how inhuman he is, how transformed, how far outside my control he's moved.

"Stop!" Orlagh shouts as the churning turns to boiling. A stretch of ocean bubbles and seethes as the Folk of the Undersea scream and scatter, swimming out of range. Several seals come up on the black rocks near the land, calling to one another in their language.

Nicasia's shark is spun sideways, and she plunges into the water.

Steam billows up from the waves, blowing hot. A huge white cloud rolls across my vision. When it clears, I can see that new earth is coalescing from the depths, hot stone cooling as we watch.

With Nicasia kneeling on the growing isle, her expression half amazement and half terror. "Cardan?" she calls.

One corner of his mouth is turned up in a little smile, but his gaze is unfocused. He believed that he needed to convince Orlagh that he wasn't feckless.

Now I see he's come up with a plan to do that. Just as he came up with a plan to throw off the yoke of my control.

During my month in the Undersea, he changed. He began scheming schemes. And he has become disturbingly effective at them.

I am thinking of that as I watch grass grow between Nicasia's toes and wildflowers spring up all along the gently rising hills, as I notice the trees and brambles sprout, and as the trunk of a tree begins to form around Nicasia's body.

"Cardan!" she screams as bark wraps around her, closing over her waist.

"What have you done?" Orlagh cries as the bark moves higher, as branches unfold, budding with leaves and fragrant blossoms. Petals blow out onto the waves.

"Will you flood the land now?" Cardan asks Orlagh with perfect calm, as though he didn't just cause a fourth island to rise from the sea. "Send salt water to corrupt the roots of our trees and make our streams and lakes brackish? Will you drown our berries and send your merfolk to slit our throats and steal our roses? Will you do it if it means your daughter will suffer the same? Come, I dare you."

"Release Nicasia," says Orlagh, defeat heavy in her voice.

"I am the High King of Elfhame," Cardan reminds her. "And I

mislike being given orders. You attacked the land. You stole my seneschal and freed my brother, who was imprisoned for the murder of our father, Eldred, with whom you had an alliance. Once, we respected each other's territory.

"I have allowed you too much disrespect, and you have overplayed your hand.

"Now, Queen of the Undersea, we will have a truce as you had with Eldred, as you had with Mab. We will have a truce or we will have a war, and if we fight, I will be unsparing. Nothing and no one you love will be safe."

Orlagh pauses, and I suck in my breath, not at all sure what will come next. "Very well, High King. Let us have an alliance. Give me my daughter, and we will go."

I exhale. He was wise to push her, even though it was terrifying. After all, once she found out about Madoc, she might press her advantage. Better to bring this moment to its crisis.

And it worked. I look down to hide my smile.

"Let Nicasia stay here and be your ambassador in Balekin's stead," Cardan says. "She has grown up on these islands, and many who love her are here."

That wipes the smile off my face. On the new island, the bark is pulling away from Nicasia's skin. I wonder what he's playing at, bringing her back to Elfhame. With her will inevitably come trouble.

And yet, maybe it's the sort of trouble he wants.

"If she wishes to stay, she may. Are you satisfied?" Orlagh asks.

Cardan inclines his head. "I am. I will not be led by the sea, no matter how great its queen. As the High King, I must lead. But I must also be just."

Here he pauses. And then he turns to me. "And today I will dispense justice. Jude Duarte, do you deny you murdered Prince Balekin, Ambassador of the Undersea and brother to the High King?"

I am not sure what he wants me to say. Would it help to deny it? If so, surely he would not put it to me in such a way—a way that makes it clear he believes I did kill Balekin. Cardan has had a plan all along. All I can do is trust that he has a plan now.

"I do not deny that we had a duel and that I won it," I say, my voice coming out more uncertain than I'd like.

All the eyes of the Folk are on me, and for a moment, as I look out at their pitiless faces, I feel Madoc's absence keenly. Orlagh's smile is full of sharp teeth.

"Hear my judgment," Cardan says, authority ringing in his voice. "I exile Jude Duarte to the mortal world. Until and unless she is pardoned by the crown, let her not step one foot in Faerie or forfeit her life."

I gasp. "But you can't do that!"

He looks at me for a long moment, but his gaze is mild, as though he's expecting me to be fine with exile. As though I am nothing more than one of his petitioners. As though I am nothing at all. "Of course I can," he replies.

"But I'm the Queen of Faerie," I shout, and for a moment, there is silence. Then everyone around me begins to laugh.

I can feel my cheeks heat. Tears of frustration and fury prick my eyes as, a beat too late, Cardan laughs with them.

At that moment, knights clap their hands on my wrists. Sir Rannoch pulls me down from the horse. For a mad moment I consider fighting him as though two dozen knights aren't around us.

"Deny it, then," I yell. "Deny me!"

He cannot, of course, so he does not. Our eyes meet, and the odd smile on his face is clearly meant for me. I remember what it was to hate him with the whole of my heart, but I've remembered too late.

"Come with me, my lady," Sir Rannoch says, and there is nothing I can do but go.

Still, I cannot resist looking back. When I do, Cardan is taking the first step onto the new island. He looks every bit the ruler his father was, every bit the monster his brother wanted to become. Crow-black hair blown back from his face, scarlet cape swirling around him, eyes reflecting the flat gray emptiness of the sky.

"If Insweal is the Isle of Woe, Insmire, the Isle of Might, and Insmoor, the Isle of Stone," he says, his voice carrying across the newly formed land, "then let this be Insear, Isle of Ash."

EPILOGUE

I lie on the couch in front of the television. In front of me, a plate of microwaved fish sticks grows cold. On the screen, a cartoon ice-skater is sulking. *He is not a very good skater*, I think. *Or maybe he's a great skater*. I keep forgetting to read the subtitles.

It's hard to concentrate on pretty much anything these days.

Vivi comes into the room and flops down on the couch. "Heather won't text me back," she says.

I turned up on Vivi's doorstep a week before, exhausted, my eyes red with weeping. Rannoch and his coterie had carried me across the sky on one of their horses and dumped me on a random street in a random town. I'd walked and walked until I had blisters on my feet, and I began to doubt my ability to navigate by the stars. Finally, I stumbled into a gas station with a taxi refueling and was startled to remember taxis existed. By then, I didn't care that I had no money with me and that Vivi was probably going to pay him with a handful of glamoured leaves.

But I didn't expect to arrive and find Heather gone.

When she and Vivi came back from Faerie, I guess she had a lot of questions. And then she'd had *more* questions, and finally, Vivi admitted to glamouring her. That's when everything totally unraveled.

Vivi removed the glamour, and Heather got her memories back. Heather moved out.

She's sleeping at her parents' house, so Vivi keeps hoping she might still come back. Some of her stuff is here. Clothes. Her drafting table. A set of unused oil paints.

"She'll text you when she's ready," I say, although I am not sure I believe it. "She's just trying to get her head straight." Just because I am bitter about romance doesn't mean everyone else needs to be.

For a while, we just sit on the couch together, watching the cartoon skater fail to land jumps and fall in helpless and probably unrequited love with his coach.

Soon, Oak will come home from school, and we will pretend that things are normal. I will take him into the wooded part of the apartment complex and drill him on the sword. He doesn't mind, but to him it's only messing around, and I don't have the heart to scare him into seeing swordplay differently.

Vivi takes a fish stick off my plate and dredges it through the ketchup. "How long you going to keep sulking? You were exhausted from being locked up in the Undersea. You were off your game. He got one over on you. It happens."

"Whatever," I say as she eats my food.

"If you hadn't gotten captured, you would have mopped the floor with him."

I am not even sure what that means, but it's nice to hear.

She turns to me with her cat eyes, eyes just like her father's. "I wanted you to come to the mortal world. Now you're here. Maybe you'll love it. Give it a chance."

I nod noncommittally.

"And if you don't love it," she says, lifting an eyebrow, "you can always join Madoc."

"I can't," I say. "He tried and tried to recruit me, but I kept turning him down. That ship sailed."

She shrugs. "He wouldn't—okay, he *would* care. He'd make you grovel a lot, and he'd bring it up awkwardly in war councils for the next couple of decades. But he'd take you."

I give her a stern look. "And what? Work to put Oak on the throne? After everything we've done to keep him safe?"

"Work to hurt Cardan," Vivi says with a fierce light in her eyes. She has never been particularly forgiving.

Right now I am glad of it.

"How?" I say, but the strategic part of my brain is grinding slowly back into action. Grimsen is still in play. If he could make a crown for Balekin, what could he do for me?

"I don't know, but don't worry about it yet," Vivi says, getting up. "Revenge is sweet, but ice cream is sweeter." She goes to the freezer and removes a tub of mint chocolate chip. She brings that and two spoons back to the sofa. "For now, accept this delight, unworthy though it is for the Queen of Faerie in exile."

I know she doesn't mean to mock me, but the title stings anyway. I pick up my spoon.

You must be strong enough to strike and strike and strike again without tiring. The first lesson is to make yourself that strong.

We eat bathed in the flickering light of the screen. Vivi's phone is silent on the coffee table. My mind is whirling.

ACKNOWLEDGMENTS

Getting through the second book in this series would have been a lot harder without the support, encouragement, and criticism of Sarah Rees Brennan, Leigh Bardugo, Steve Berman, Cassandra Clare, Maureen Johnson, Kelly Link, and Robin Wasserman. Thank you, my rakish crew!

Thank you to the readers who came out to see me on the road, and those who contacted me to tell me how much they liked *The Cruel Prince*, and for all the character art.

A massive thank-you to everyone at Little, Brown Books for Young Readers, who have supported my weird vision. Thanks especially to my amazing editor, Alvina Ling, and to Kheryn Callender, Siena Koncsol, Victoria Stapleton, Jennifer McClelland-Smith, Emilie Polster, Allegra Green, and Elena Yip, among others. And in the UK, thank you to Hot Key Books, particularly Jane Harris, Emma Matthewson, and Tina Mories.

Thank you to Joanna Volpe, Hilary Pecheone, Pouya Shahbazian, and everyone at New Leaf Literary for making hard things easier.

Thank you to Kathleen Jennings, for her wonderful and evocative illustrations.

Thanks most of all to my husband, Theo, for helping me figure out the stories I want to tell, and to our son, Sebastian, for being a distraction and inspiration, all at once.

THE WICKED KING DISCUSSION QUESTIONS

1. On page 6, Madoc tells Jude, "Power is much easier to acquire than it is to hold on to." Do you agree with him—why or why not? Based on what happens in *The Wicked King*, how is this true for Jude?

2. On page 38, Jude says of Taryn, "She is a mirror, reflecting someone I could have been but am not." In what ways is Taryn a mirror to Jude? How are the choices they've made in the past similar? How are they different?

3. What does Val Moren, the old High King Eldred's human seneschal, represent to Jude (page 93)? What does she think of his presence in Elfhame?

4. At the end of chapter 19, Jude practices her sword-fighting technique while watching herself in the mirror and says, "I battle on until perspiration stains her shirt, until she's shaking with exhaustion. It's still not enough. I can never beat her" (page 188). What does Jude mean by this?

5. How do you think what happens to Heather at Taryn's wedding will affect Heather and Vivi's relationship in the future?

6. Knowing Cardan's childhood in Elfhame, why do you think Cardan becomes a cruel prince (and a wicked king)? Or is Cardan cruel and wicked at all? Why or why not?

7. While being tortured in the Undersea, Jude thinks of the Folk, "They are more like mortals than they believe" (page 235). How are the fey like humans? How are they different?

8. What do you think of the excerpts from the poems "Nymphidia" and "The Fairies" that begin Book One and Book Two of the story? Why did the author choose these lines to introduce these sections?

9. Throughout the book, it becomes more difficult for Jude to deny her attraction to Cardan. Why is she so resistant to her feelings for him? If she expresses her feelings to Cardan, what does she have to gain and to lose?

10. *The Wicked King* begins and ends with Madoc's advice to Jude: "You must be strong enough to strike and strike and strike again without tiring. The first lesson is to make yourself that strong" (page 1). What does this mean to Jude at the beginning of the book versus the end? Why is this piece of advice important to her?

11. Why do you think Cardan betrays Jude at the end of *The Wicked King*? Do you think he was planning on betraying Jude this whole time? What do you think will happen to Jude in the next book, *The Queen of Nothing*?

Turn the page for a preview of

AVAILABLE NOW

PROLOGUE

The Royal Astrologer, Baphen, squinted at the star chart and tried not to flinch when it seemed sure the youngest prince of Elfhame was about to be dropped on his royal head.

A week after Prince Cardan's birth and he was finally being presented to the High King. The previous five heirs had been seen immediately, still squalling in ruddy newness, but Lady Asha had barred the High King from visiting before she felt herself suitably restored from childbed.

The baby was thin and wizened, silent, staring at Eldred with black eyes. He lashed his little whiplike tail with such force that his swaddle threatened to come apart. Lady Asha seemed unsure how to cradle him. Indeed, she held him as though she hoped someone might take the burden from her very soon.

"Tell us of his future," the High King prompted. Only a few Folk were gathered to witness the presentation of the new prince—the mortal Val Moren, who was both Court Poet and Seneschal, and two members of the Living Council: Randalin, the Minister of Keys, and Baphen. In the empty hall, the High King's words echoed.

Baphen hesitated, but he could do nothing save answer. Eldred had been favored with five children before Prince Cardan, shocking fecundity among the Folk, with their thin blood and few births. The stars had spoken of each little prince's and princess's fated accomplishments in poetry and song, in politics, in virtue, and even in vice. But this time what he'd seen in the stars had been entirely different. "Prince Cardan will be your last born child," the Royal Astrologer said. "He will be the destruction of the crown and the ruination of the throne."

Lady Asha sucked in a sharp breath. For the first time, she drew the child protectively closer. He squirmed in her arms. "I wonder who has influenced your interpretation of the signs. Perhaps Princess Elowyn had a hand in it. Or Prince Dain."

Maybe it would be better if she dropped him, Baphen thought unkindly.

High King Eldred ran a hand over his chin. "Can nothing be done to stop this?"

It was a mixed blessing to have the stars supply Baphen with so many riddles and so few answers. He often wished he saw things more clearly, but not this time. He bowed his head so he had an excuse not to meet the High King's gaze. "Only out of his spilled blood can a great ruler rise, but not before what I have told you comes to pass."

Eldred turned to Lady Asha and her child, the harbinger of ill luck. The baby was as silent as a stone, not crying or cooing, tail still lashing.

"Take the boy away," the High King said. "Rear him as you see fit."

Lady Asha did not flinch. "I will rear him as befits his station. He is a prince, after all, and your son."

There was a brittleness in her tone, and Baphen was uncomfortably reminded that some prophecies are fulfilled by the very actions meant to prevent them.

For a moment, everyone stood silent. Then Eldred nodded to Val Moren, who left the dais and returned holding a slim wooden box with a pattern of roots traced over the lid.

"A gift," said the High King, "in recognition of your contribution to the Greenbriar line."

Val Moren opened the box, revealing an exquisite necklace of heavy emeralds. Eldred lifted them and placed them over Lady Asha's head. He touched her cheek with the back of one hand.

"Your generosity is great, my lord," she said, somewhat mollified. The baby clutched a stone in his little fist, staring up at his father with fathomless eyes.

"Go now and rest," said Eldred, his voice softer. This time, she yielded.

Lady Asha departed with her head high, her grip on the child tighter. Baphen felt a shiver of some premonition that had nothing to do with stars.

High King Eldred did not visit Lady Asha again, nor did he call her to him. Perhaps he ought to have put his dissatisfaction aside and cultivated his son. But looking upon Prince Cardan was like looking into an uncertain future, and so he avoided it.

Lady Asha, as the mother of a prince, found herself much in demand with the Court, if not the High King. Given to whimsy and frivolity, she wished to return to the merry life of a courtier. She couldn't attend balls with an infant in tow, so she found a cat whose kittens were stillborn to act as his wet nurse.

That arrangement lasted until Prince Cardan was able to crawl. By then, the cat was heavy with a new litter and he'd begun to pull at her tail. She fled to the stables, abandoning him, too.

And so he grew up in the palace, cherished by no one and checked by no one. Who would dare stop a prince from stealing food from the grand tables and eating beneath them, devouring what he'd taken in savage bites? His sisters and brothers only laughed, playing with him as they would with a puppy.

He wore clothes only occasionally, donning garlands of flowers instead and throwing stones when the guard tried to come near him. None but his mother exerted any hold over him, and she seldom tried to curb his excesses. Just the opposite.

"You're a prince," she told him firmly when he would shy away from a conflict or fail to make a demand. "Everything is yours. You have only to take it." And sometimes: "I want that. Get it for me."

It is said that faerie children are not like mortal children. They need little in the way of love. They need not be tucked in at night, but may sleep just as happily in a cold corner of a ballroom, curled up in a tablecloth. They need not be fed; they are just as happy lapping up dew and skimming bread and cream from the kitchens. They need not be comforted, since they seldom weep.

But if faerie children need little love, faerie princes require some counsel.

Without it, when Cardan's elder brother suggested shooting a walnut off the head of a mortal, Cardan had not the wisdom to demur. His habits were impulsive; his manner, imperious.

"Keen marksmanship so impresses our father," Prince Dain said with a small, teasing smile. "But perhaps it is too difficult. Better not to make the attempt than to fail."

For Cardan, who could not attract his father's good notice and desperately wanted it, the prospect was tempting. He didn't ask himself who the mortal was or how he had come to be at the Court. Cardan certainly never suspected that the man was beloved of Val Moren and that the seneschal would go mad with grief if the man died.

Leaving Dain free to assume a more prominent position at the High King's right hand.

"Too difficult? Better not to make the attempt? Those are the words of a coward," Cardan said, full of childish bravado. In truth, his brother intimidated him, but that only made him more scornful.

Prince Dain smiled. "Let us exchange arrows at least. Then if you miss, you can say that it was *my* arrow that went awry."

Prince Cardan ought to have been suspicious of this kindness, but he'd had little enough of the real thing to tell true from false.

Instead, he notched Dain's arrow and pulled back the bowstring, aiming for the walnut. A sinking feeling came over him. He might not shoot true. He might hurt the man. But on the heels of that, angry glee sparked at the idea of doing something so horrifying that his father could no longer ignore him. If he could not get the High King's attention for something good, then perhaps he could get it for something really, really bad.

Cardan's hand wobbled.

The mortal's liquid eyes watched him in frozen fear. Enchanted, of course. No one would stand like that willingly. That was what decided him.

Cardan forced a laugh as he relaxed the bowstring, letting the arrow fall out of the notch. "I simply will not shoot under these conditions," he said, feeling ridiculous at having backed down. "The wind is coming from the north and mussing my hair. It's getting all in my eyes."

But Prince Dain raised his bow and loosed the arrow Cardan had exchanged with him. It struck the mortal through the throat. He dropped with almost no sound, eyes still open, now staring at nothing.

It happened so fast that Cardan didn't cry out, didn't react. He just stared at his brother, slow, terrible understanding crashing over him.

"Ah," said Prince Dain with a satisfied smile. "A shame. It seems *your* arrow went awry. Perhaps you can complain to our father about that hair in your eyes."

After, though he protested, no one would hear Prince Cardan's side. Dain saw to that. He told the story of the youngest prince's recklessness, his arrogance, his arrow. The High King would not even allow Cardan an audience.

Despite Val Moren's pleas for execution, Cardan was punished for the mortal's death in the way that princes are punished. The High King had Lady Asha locked away in the Tower of Forgetting in Cardan's stead—something Eldred was relieved to have a reason to do, since he found her both tiresome and troublesome. Care of Prince Cardan was given over to Balekin, the eldest of the siblings, the cruelest, and the only one willing to take him.

And so was Prince Cardan's reputation made. He had little to do but further it.

CHAPTER 1

I, Jude Duarte, High Queen of Elfhame in exile, spend most mornings dozing in front of daytime television, watching cooking competitions and cartoons and reruns of a show where people have to complete a gauntlet by stabbing boxes and bottles and cutting through a whole fish. In the afternoons, if he lets me, I train my brother, Oak. Nights, I run errands for the local faeries.

I keep my head down, as I probably should have done in the first place. And if I curse Cardan, then I have to curse myself, too, for being the fool who walked right into the trap he set for me.

As a child, I imagined returning to the mortal world. Taryn and Vivi and I would rehash what it was like there, recalling the scents of fresh-cut grass and gasoline, reminiscing over playing tag through neighborhood backyards and bobbing in the bleachy chlorine of summer pools. I dreamed of iced tea, reconstituted from powder, and orange juice Popsicles. I longed for mundane things: the smell of hot asphalt, the swag of wires between streetlights, the jingles of commercials.

Now, stuck in the mortal world for good, I miss Faerieland with a raw intensity. It's magic I long for, magic I miss. Maybe I even miss being afraid. I feel as though I am dreaming away my days, restless, never fully awake.

I drum my fingers on the painted wood of a picnic table. It's early autumn, already cool in Maine. Late-afternoon sun dapples the grass outside the apartment complex as I watch Oak play with other children in the strip of woods between here and the highway. They are kids from the building, some younger and some older than his eight years, all dropped off by the same yellow school bus. They play a totally disorganized game of war, chasing one another with sticks. They hit as children do, aiming for the weapon instead of the opponent, screaming with laughter when a stick breaks. I can't help noticing they are learning all the wrong lessons about swordsmanship.

Still, I watch. And so I notice when Oak uses glamour.

He does it unconsciously, I think. He's sneaking toward the other kids, but then there's a stretch with no easy cover. He keeps on toward them, and even though he's in plain sight, they don't seem to notice.

Closer and closer, with the kids still not looking his way. And when he jumps at them, stick swinging, they shriek with wholly authentic surprise.

He was invisible. He was using glamour. And I, geased against being deceived by it, didn't notice until it was done. The other children just think he was clever or lucky. Only I know how careless it was.

I wait until the children head to their apartments. They peel off, one by one, until only my brother remains. I don't need magic, even with leaves underfoot, to steal up on him. With a swift motion, I wrap my arm around Oak's neck, pressing it against his throat hard enough to give him a good scare. He bucks back, nearly hitting me in the chin with his horns. Not bad. He attempts to break my hold, but it's half-hearted. He can tell it's me, and I don't frighten him.

I tighten my hold. If I press my arm against his throat long enough, he'll black out.

He tries to speak, and then he must start to feel the effects of not getting enough air. He forgets all his training and goes wild, lashing out, scratching my arms and kicking against my legs. Making me feel awful. I wanted him to be a little afraid, scared enough to fight back, not *terrified.*

I let go, and he stumbles away, panting, eyes wet with tears. "What was that for?" he wants to know. He's glaring at me accusingly.

"To remind you that fighting isn't a game," I say, feeling as though I am speaking with Madoc's voice instead of my own. I don't want Oak to grow up as I did, angry and afraid. But I want him to *survive,* and Madoc did teach me how to do that.

How am I supposed to figure out how to give him the right stuff when all I know is my own messed-up childhood? Maybe the parts of it I value are the wrong parts. "What are you going to do against an opponent who wants to actually hurt you?"

"I don't care," Oak says. "I don't care about that stuff. I don't want to be king. I *never* want to be king."

For a moment, I just stare at him. I want to believe he's lying, but, of course, he can't lie.

"We don't always have a choice in our fate," I say.

"*You* rule if you care so much!" he says. "I won't do it. Never."

I have to grind my teeth together to keep from screaming. "I can't, as you know, because I'm in exile," I remind him.

He stamps a hoofed foot. "So am I! And the only reason I'm in the human world is because Dad wants the stupid crown and you want it and everyone wants it. Well, I don't. It's cursed."

"All power is cursed," I say. "The most terrible among us will do anything to get it, and those who'd wield power best don't want it thrust upon them. But that doesn't mean they can avoid their responsibilities forever."

"You can't make me be High King," he says, and wheeling away from me, breaks into a run in the direction of the apartment building.

I sit down on the cold ground, knowing that I screwed up the conversation completely. Knowing that Madoc trained Taryn and me better than I am training Oak. Knowing that I was arrogant and foolish to think I could control Cardan.

Knowing that in the great game of princes and queens, I have been swept off the board.

Inside the apartment, Oak's door is shut firmly against me. Vivienne, my faerie sister, stands at the kitchen counter, grinning into her phone.

When she notices me, she grabs my hands and spins me around and around until I'm dizzy.

"Heather loves me again," she says, wild laughter in her voice.

Heather was Vivi's human girlfriend. She'd put up with Vivi's evasions about her past. She even put up with Oak's coming to live with them in this apartment. But when she found out that Vivi wasn't human *and* that Vivi had used magic on her, she dumped her and moved out. I hate to say this, because I want my sister to be happy—and Heather did make her happy—but it was a richly deserved dumping.

I pull away to blink at her in confusion. "What?"

Vivi waves her phone at me. "She texted me. She wants to come back. Everything is going to be like it was before."

Leaves don't grow back onto a vine, cracked walnuts don't fit back into their shells, and girlfriends who've been enchanted don't just wake up and decide to let things slide with their terrifying exes.

"Let me see that," I say, reaching for Vivi's phone. She allows me to take it.

I scroll back through the texts, most of them coming from Vivi and full of apologies, ill-considered promises, and increasingly desperate pleas. On Heather's end, there was a lot of silence and a few messages that read "I need more time to think."

Then this:

> I want to forget Faerie. I want to forget that you and Oak aren't human. I don't want to feel like this anymore. If I asked you to make me forget, would you?

I stare at the words for a long moment, drawing in a breath.

I can see why Vivi has read the message the way she has, but I think she's read it wrong. If I'd written that, the last thing I would want was for Vivi to agree. I'd want her to help me see that even if Vivi and Oak weren't human, they still loved me. I would want Vivi to insist that pretending away Faerie wouldn't help. I would want Vivi to tell me that she'd made a mistake and that she'd never ever make that mistake again, no matter what.

If I'd sent that text, it would be a test.

I hand the phone back to Vivi. "What are you going to tell her?"

"That I'll do whatever she wants," my sister says, an extravagant vow for a mortal and a downright terrifying vow from someone who would be bound to that promise.

"Maybe she doesn't know what she wants," I say. I am disloyal no matter what I do. Vivi is my sister, but Heather is human. I owe them both something.

And right now, Vivi isn't interested in supposing anything but that all will be well. She gives me a big, relaxed smile and picks up an apple from the fruit bowl, tossing it in the air. "What's wrong with Oak? He stomped in here and slammed his door. Is he going to be this dramatic when he's a teenager?"

"He doesn't want to be High King," I tell her.

"Oh. That." Vivi glances toward his bedroom. "I thought it was something important."

CHAPTER 2

Tonight, it's a relief to head to work.

Faeries in the mortal world have a different set of needs than those in Elfhame. The solitary fey, surviving at the edges of Faerie, do not concern themselves with revels and courtly machinations.

And it turns out they have plenty of odd jobs for someone like me, a mortal who knows their ways and isn't worried about getting into the occasional fight. I met Bryern a week after I left Elfhame. He turned up outside the apartment complex, a black-furred, goat-headed, and goat-hooved faerie with bowler hat in hand, saying he was an old friend of the Roach.

"I understand you're in a unique position," he said, looking at me with those strange golden goat eyes, their black pupils a horizontal rectangle. "Presumed dead, is that correct? No Social Security number. No mortal schooling."

"And looking for work," I told him, figuring out where this was going. "Off the books."

"You cannot get any further off the books than with me," he assured me, placing one clawed hand over his heart. "Allow me to introduce myself. Bryern. A phooka, if you hadn't already guessed."

He didn't ask for oaths of loyalty or any promises whatsoever. I could work as much as I wanted, and the pay was commensurate with my daring.

Tonight, I meet him by the water. I glide up on the secondhand bike I acquired. The back tire deflates quickly, but I got it cheap. It works pretty well to get me around. Bryern is dressed with typical fussiness: His hat has a band decorated with a few brightly colored duck feathers, and he's paired that with a tweed jacket. As I come closer, he withdraws a watch from one pocket and peers at it with an exaggerated frown.

"Oh, am I late?" I ask. "Sorry. I'm used to telling time by the slant of moonlight."

He gives me an annoyed look. "Just because you've lived in the High Court, you need not put on airs. You're no one special now."

I am the High Queen of Elfhame. The thought comes to me unbidden, and I bite the inside of my cheek to keep myself from saying those ridiculous words. He's right: I am no one special now.

"What's the job?" I ask instead, as blandly as I can.

"One of the Folk in Old Port has been eating locals. I have a contract for someone willing to extract a promise from her to cease."

I find it hard to believe that he cares what happens to humans—or cares enough to pay for me to do something about it. "Local *mortals*?"

He shakes his head. "No. No. Us Folk." Then he seems to remember to whom he's speaking and looks a little flustered. I try not to take his slip as a compliment.

Killing and *eating* the Folk? Nothing about that signals an easy job. "Who's hiring?"

He gives a nervous laugh. "No one who wants their name associated with the deed. But they're willing to remunerate you for making it happen."

One of the reasons Bryern likes hiring me is that I can get close to the Folk. They don't expect a mortal to be the one to pickpocket them or to stick a knife in their side. They don't expect a mortal to be unaffected by glamour or to know their customs or to see through their terrible bargains.

Another reason is, I need the money enough that I'm willing to take jobs like this—ones that I know right from the start are going to suck.

"Address?" I ask, and he slips me a folded paper.

I open it and glance down. "This better pay well."

"Five hundred American dollars," he says, as though this is an extravagant sum.

Our rent is twelve hundred a month, not to mention groceries and utilities. With Heather gone, my half is about eight hundred. And I'd like to get a new tire for my bike. Five hundred isn't nearly enough, not for something like this.

"Fifteen hundred," I counter, raising my eyebrows. "In cash, verifiable by iron. Half up front, and if I don't come back, you pay Vivienne the other half as a gift to my bereaved family."

Bryern presses his lips together, but I know he's got the money. He just doesn't want to pay me enough that I can get choosy about jobs.

"A thousand," he compromises, reaching into a pocket inside his tweed jacket and withdrawing a stack of bills banded by a silver clip. "And look, I have half on me right now. You can take it."

"Fine," I agree. It's a decent paycheck for what could be a single night's work if I'm lucky.

He hands over the cash with a sniff. "Let me know when you've completed the task."

There's an iron fob on my key chain. I run it ostentatiously over the edges of the money to make sure it's real. It never hurts to remind Bryern that I'm careful.

"Plus fifty bucks for expenses," I say on impulse.

He frowns. After a moment, he reaches into a different part of his jacket and hands over the extra cash. "Just take care of this," he says. The lack of quibbling is a bad sign. Maybe I should have asked more questions before I agreed to this job. I definitely should have negotiated harder.

Too late now.

I get back on my bike and, with a farewell wave to Bryern, kick off toward downtown. Once upon a time, I imagined myself as a knight astride a steed, glorying in contests of skill and honor. Too bad my talents turned out to lie in another direction entirely.

I suppose I am a skilled enough murderer of Folk, but what I really excel at is getting under their skin. Hopefully that will serve me well in persuading a cannibal faerie to do what I want.

Before I go to confront her, I decide to ask around.

First, I see a hob named Magpie, who lives in a tree in Deering Oaks Park. He says he's heard she's a redcap, which isn't great news, but at least since I grew up with one, I am well informed about their nature.

Redcaps crave violence and blood and murder—in fact, they get a little twitchy when there's none to be had for stretches of time. And if they're traditionalists, they have a cap they dip in the blood of their vanquished enemies, supposedly to grant them some stolen vitality of the slain.

I ask for a name, but Magpie doesn't know. He sends me to Ladhar, a clurichaun who slinks around the back of bars, sucking froth from the tops of beers when no one is looking and swindling mortals in games of chance.

"You didn't know?" Ladhar says, lowering his voice. *"Grima Mog."*

I almost accuse him of lying, despite knowing better. Then I have a brief, intense fantasy of tracking down Bryern and making him choke on every dollar he gave me. "What the hell is *she* doing *here*?"

Grima Mog is the fearsome general of the Court of Teeth in the North. The same Court that the Roach and the Bomb escaped from. When I was little, Madoc read to me at bedtime from the memoirs of her battle strategies. Just thinking about facing her, I break out in a cold sweat.

I can't fight her. And I don't think I have a good chance of tricking her, either.

"Given the boot, I hear," Ladhar says. "Maybe she ate someone Lady Nore liked."

I don't have to do this job, I remind myself. I am no longer part of Dain's Court of Shadows. I am no longer trying to rule from behind High King Cardan's throne. I don't need to take big risks.

But I am curious.

Combine that with an abundance of wounded pride and you find yourself on the front steps of Grima Mog's warehouse around dawn. I know better than to go empty-handed. I've got raw meat from a butcher shop chilling in a Styrofoam cooler, a few sloppily made honey sandwiches wrapped in foil, and a bottle of decent sour beer.

Inside, I wander down a hall until I come to the door to what appears to be an apartment. I knock three times and hope that if nothing else, maybe the smell of the food will cover up the smell of my fear.

The door opens, and a woman in a housecoat peers out. She's bent over, leaning on a polished cane of black wood. "What do you want, deary?"

Seeing through her glamour as I do, I note the green tint to her skin and her overlarge teeth. Like my foster father: Madoc. The guy who killed my parents. The guy who read me her battle strategies. Madoc, once the Grand General of the High Court. Now enemy of the throne and not real happy with me, either.

Hopefully he and High King Cardan will ruin each other's lives.

"I brought you some gifts," I say, holding up the cooler. "Can I come in? I want to make a bargain."

She frowns a little.

"You can't keep eating random Folk without someone being sent to try to persuade you to stop," I say.

"Perhaps I will eat *you*, pretty child," she counters, brightening. But she steps back to allow me into her lair. I guess she can't make a meal of me in the hall.

The apartment is loft-style, with high ceilings and brick walls. Nice. Floors polished and glossed up. Big windows letting in light and a decent view of the town. It's furnished with old things. The tufting on a few of the pieces is torn, and there are marks that could have come from a stray cut of a knife.

The whole place smells like blood. A coppery, metal smell, overlaid with a slightly cloying sweetness. I put my gifts on a heavy wooden table.

"For you," I say. "In the hopes you'll overlook my rudeness in calling on you uninvited."

She sniffs at the meat, turns a honey sandwich over in her hand, and pops off the cap on the beer with her fist. Taking a long draught, she looks me over.

"Someone instructed you in the niceties. I wonder why they bothered, little goat. You're obviously the sacrifice sent in the hopes my appetite can be sated with mortal flesh." She smiles, showing her teeth. It's possible she dropped her glamour in that moment, although, since I saw through it already, I can't tell.

I blink at her. She blinks back, clearly waiting for a reaction.

By not screaming and running for the door, I have annoyed her. I can tell. I think she was looking forward to chasing me when I ran.

"You're Grima Mog," I say. "Leader of armies. Destroyer of your enemies. Is this really how you want to spend your retirement?"

"Retirement?" She echoes the word as though I have dealt her the deadliest insult. "Though I have been cast down, I will find another army to lead. An army bigger than the first."

Sometimes I tell myself something a lot like that. Hearing it aloud, from someone else's mouth, is jarring. But it gives me an idea. "Well, the local Folk would prefer not to get eaten while you're planning your next move. Obviously, being human, I'd rather you didn't eat mortals—I doubt they'd give you what you're looking for anyway."

She waits for me to go on.

"A challenge," I say, thinking of everything I know about redcaps.

"That's what you crave, right? A good fight. I bet the Folk you killed weren't all that special. A waste of your talents."

"Who sent you?" she asks finally. Reevaluating. Trying to figure out my angle.

"What did you do to piss her off?" I ask. "Your queen? It must have been something big to get kicked out of the Court of Teeth."

"*Who sent you?*" she roars. I guess I hit a nerve. My best skill.

I try not to smile, but I've missed the rush of power that comes with playing a game like this, of strategy and cunning. I hate to admit it, but I've missed risking my neck. There's no room for regrets when you're busy trying to win. Or at least not to die. "I told you. The local Folk who don't want to get eaten."

"Why *you*?" she asks. "Why would they send a slip of a girl to try to convince me of anything?"

Scanning the room, I take note of a round box on top of the refrigerator. An old-fashioned hatbox. My gaze snags on it. "Probably because it would be no loss to them if I failed."

At that, Grima Mog laughs, taking another sip of the sour beer. "A fatalist. So how will you persuade me?"

I walk to the table and pick up the food, looking for an excuse to get close to that hatbox. "First, by putting away your groceries."

Grima Mog looks amused. "I suppose an old lady like myself could use a young thing doing a few errands around the house. But be careful. You might find more than you bargained for in my larder, little goat."

I open the door of the fridge. The remains of the Folk she's killed greet me. She's collected arms and heads, preserved somehow, baked and broiled and put away just like leftovers after a big holiday dinner. My stomach turns.

A wicked smile crawls across her face. "I assume you hoped to challenge me to a duel? Intended to brag about how you'd put up a good fight? Now you see what it means to lose to Grima Mog."

I take a deep breath. Then with a hop, I knock the hatbox off the top of the fridge and into my arms.

"Don't touch that!" she shouts, pushing to her feet as I rip off the lid.

And there it is: the cap. Lacquered with blood, layers and layers of it.

She's halfway across the floor to me, teeth bared. I pull out a lighter from my pocket and flick the flame to life with my thumb. She halts abruptly at the sight of the fire.

"I know you've spent long, long years building the patina of this cap," I say, willing my hand not to shake, willing the flame not to go out. "Probably there's blood on here from your first kill, and your last. Without it, there will be no reminder of your past conquests, no trophies, nothing. Now I need you to make a deal with me. Vow that there will be no more murders. Not the Folk, not humans, for so long as you reside in the mortal world."

"And if I don't, you'll burn my treasure?" Grima Mog finishes for me. "There's no honor in that."

"I guess I *could* offer to fight you," I say. "But I'd probably lose. This way, I win."

Grima Mog points the tip of her black cane toward me. "You're Madoc's human child, aren't you? And our new High King's seneschal in exile. Tossed out like me."

I nod, discomfited at being recognized.

"What did *you* do?" she asks, a satisfied little smile on her face. "It must have been something big."

"I was a fool," I say, because I might as well admit it. "I gave up the bird in my hand for two in the bush."

She gives a big, booming laugh. "Well, aren't we a pair, redcap's daughter? But murder is in my bones and blood. I don't plan on giving up killing. If I am to be stuck in the mortal world, then I intend to have some fun."

I bring the flame closer to the hat. The bottom of it begins to blacken, and a terrible stench fills the air.

"Stop!" she shouts, giving me a look of raw hatred. "Enough. Let me make *you* an offer, little goat. We spar. If you lose, my cap is returned to me, unburnt. I continue to hunt as I have. And you give me your littlest finger."

"To eat?" I ask, taking the flame away from the hat.

"If I like," she returns. "Or to wear like a brooch. What do you care what I do with it? The point is that it will be mine."

"And why would I agree to that?"

"Because if you win, you will have your promise from me. And I will tell you something of significance regarding your High King."

"I don't want to know anything about him," I snap, too fast and too angrily. I hadn't been expecting her to invoke Cardan.

Her laugh this time is low and rumbling. "Little liar."

We stare at each other for a long moment. Grima Mog's gaze is amiable enough. She knows she has me. I am going to agree to her terms. I know it, too, although it's ridiculous. She's a legend. I don't see how I can win.

But Cardan's name pounds in my ears.

Does he have a new seneschal? Does he have a new lover? Is he going to Council meetings himself? Does he talk about me? Do he and Locke mock me together? Does Taryn laugh?

"We spar until first blood," I say, shoving everything else out of my head. It's a pleasure to have someone to focus my anger on. "I'm not giving you my finger," I say. "You win, you get your cap. Period. And I walk out of here. The concession I am making is fighting you at all."

"First blood is dull." Grima Mog leans forward, her body alert. "Let's agree to fight until one of us cries off. Let it end somewhere between bloodshed and crawling away to die on the way home." She sighs, as if thinking a happy thought. "Give me a chance to break every bone in your scrawny body."

"You're betting on my pride." I tuck her cap into one pocket and the lighter into the other.

She doesn't deny it. "Did I bet right?"

First blood *is* dull. It's all dancing around each other, looking for an opening. It's not real fighting. When I answer her, the word rushes out of me. "Yes."

"Good." She lifts the tip of the cane toward the ceiling. "Let's go to the roof."

"Well, this is very civilized," I say.

"You better have brought a weapon, because I'll loan you nothing." She heads toward the door with a heavy sigh, as though she really is the old woman she's glamoured to be.

I follow her out of her apartment, down the dimly lit hall, and into the even darker stairway, my nerves firing. I hope I know what I'm doing. She goes up the steps two at a time, eager now, slamming open a metal door at the top. I hear the clatter of steel as she draws a thin sword out of her cane. A greedy smile pulls her lips too wide, showing off her sharp teeth.

I draw the long knife I have hidden in my boot. It doesn't have the best reach, but I don't have the ability to glamour things; I can't very well ride my bike around with Nightfell on my back.

Still, right now, I really wish I'd figured out a way to do just that.

I step onto the asphalt roof of the building. The sun is starting to rise, tinting the sky pink and gold. A chill breeze blows through the air, bringing with it the scents of concrete and garbage, along with goldenrod from the nearby park.

My heart speeds with some combination of terror and eagerness. When Grima Mog comes at me, I am ready. I parry and move out of the way. I do it again and again, which annoys her.

"You promised me a threat," she growls, but at least I have a sense of how she moves. I know she's hungry for blood, hungry for violence. I know she's used to hunting prey. I just hope she's overconfident. It's possible she will make mistakes facing someone who can fight back.

Unlikely, but possible.

When she comes at me again, I spin and kick the back of her knee hard enough to send her crashing to the ground. She roars, scrambling up and coming at me full speed. For a moment, the fury in her face and those fearsome teeth send a horrible, paralyzing jolt through me.

Monster! my mind screams.

I clench my jaw against the urge to keep dodging. Our blades shine, fish-scale bright in the new light of the day. The metal slams together, ringing like a bell. We battle across the roof, my feet clever as we scuff back and forth. Sweat starts on my brow and under my arms. My breath comes hot, clouding in the chill air.

It feels good to be fighting someone other than myself.

Grima Mog's eyes narrow, watching me, looking for weaknesses. I am conscious of every correction Madoc ever gave me, every bad habit the Ghost tried to train out of me. She begins a series of brutal blows, trying to drive me to the edge of the building. I give ground, attempting to defend myself against the flurry, against the longer reach of her blade. She was holding back before, but she's not holding back now.

Again and again she pushes me toward a drop through the open air. I fight with grim determination. Perspiration slicks my skin, beads between my shoulder blades.

Then my foot smacks into a metal pipe sticking up through the asphalt. I stumble, and she strikes. It's all I can do to avoid getting speared, and it costs me my knife, which goes hurtling off the roof. I hear it hit the street below with a dull thud.

I should never have taken this assignment. I should never have agreed to this fight. I should never have taken up Cardan's offer of marriage and never been exiled to the mortal world.

Anger gives me a burst of energy, and I use it to get out of Grima Mog's way, letting the momentum of her strike carry her blade down past me. Then I elbow her hard in the arm and grab for the hilt of her sword.

It's not a very honorable move, but I haven't been honorable for a long time. Grima Mog is very strong, but she's also surprised. For a moment, she hesitates, but then she slams her forehead into mine. I go reeling, but I almost had her weapon.

I almost had it.

My head is pounding, and I feel a little dizzy.

"That's cheating, girl," she tells me. We're both breathing hard. I feel like my lungs are made of lead.

"I'm no knight." As though to emphasize the point, I pick up the only weapon I can see: a metal pole. It's heavy and has no edge whatsoever, but it's all there is. At least it's longer than the knife.

She laughs. "You ought to concede, but I'm delighted you haven't."

"I'm an optimist," I say. Now when she runs at me, she has all the speed, although I have more reach. We spin around each other, her striking and my parrying with something that swings like a baseball bat. I wish for a lot of things, but mostly to make it off this roof.

My energy is flagging. I am not used to the weight of the pipe, and it's hard to maneuver.

Give up, my whirling brain supplies. *Cry off while you're still standing. Give her the cap, forget the money, and go home. Vivi can magic leaves into extra cash. Just this time, it wouldn't be so bad. You're not fighting for a kingdom. That, you already lost.*

Grima Mog comes toward me as though she can scent my despair. She puts me through my paces, a few fast, aggressive strikes in the hopes of getting under my guard.

Sweat drips down my forehead, stinging my eyes.

Madoc described fighting as a lot of things, as a game of strategy played at speed, as a dance, but right now it feels like an argument. Like an argument where she's keeping me too busy defending myself to score any points.

Despite the strain on my muscles, I switch to holding the pipe in one hand and pull her cap from my pocket with the other.

"What are you doing? You promised—" she begins.

I throw the cap at her face. She grabs for it, distracted. In that moment, I swing the pipe at her side with all the strength in my body.

I catch her in the shoulder, and she falls with a howl of pain. I hit her again, bringing the metal rod down in an arc onto her outstretched arm, sending her sword spinning across the roof.

I raise the pipe to swing again.